SOUTH OF DENVER

C.J. PETIT

TABLE OF CONTENTS

PROLOGUE

Soapy Smith sat behind the enormous oak desk in his large office as he tapped his right index finger on its hard surface. He wasn't pleased with the three men standing before him and having Soapy displeased was never a good thing.

He glared at them and snarled, "You had a simple job to do. Why am I now just getting told by my other sources that they only found the man's body?"

Abe Thompkins, John Berringer, and Gerald Price all stood with their Stetsons held low in both hands and their eyes downcast. They looked like third graders standing before the mean old school principal having been caught playing hooky. This was despite the Colt Peacemakers on their hips and the heavy stubble on their leathery faces.

Abe replied, "I don't know, boss. We just left 'em there. Maybe some coyotes took 'em."

Soapy leaned back knowing it was possible. The report he had been given had said that the man's body had been mutilated by scavengers, so the others could have been carted off and not found. He may not be convinced, but there was a good reason for him to believe their story. He knew he had screwed up by not having someone report the murders right away, so that all three bodies could be reported, and his client satisfied, but it was too late now. If he didn't believe their story, the mistake would be his; and Soapy never admitted to any mistakes.

After thirty seconds of silence, he said, "Alright. You three get outta here."

Each of them quickly nodded and gratefully backed out of the office keeping their eyes on Soapy; much like supplicants leaving the king's chambers.

After they'd gone, Soapy decided he'd just tell the client that coyotes or a mountain lion got there before the woman and the kid's bodies were found. If he complained, too bad. He already had the money, but he didn't like loose ends, and those two were loose ends.

CHAPTER 1

Boulder, Colorado
May 3, 1879

It was all happening too fast. In just five years, the town had grown from a nice, easily controlled town of four hundred to an over-populated burg of almost three thousand. Sam could understand it if they had discovered gold or silver nearby, as they had in many of its Colorado neighbors; but this boom was started by a bunch of damned politicians who decided that Boulder would be a nice place for the state university. They had done that over a decade ago and hadn't done much over the past ten years. But the days of bureaucratic bumbling had passed and since they started building academic halls and other structures four years ago, a lot of newcomers began showing up.

Sam didn't like any of it. He could handle it alright; it was just annoying. The city fathers enjoyed the increase in businesses and paying customers for those businesses but refused to give him even one more part-time deputy. His only deputy; one each Harvey Greenwald, was only his deputy because his daddy was on the town council and he was still only making sixty dollars a month plus room and board. Granted, they did let him use all the ammunition he needed to stay proficient, and he got first pick of any lawbreaker's rigs after he was hanged, but it still didn't make up for the increase in workload.

Sam Brown had been sheriff of Boulder County for more than eight years now. When he had arrived, he was a bit wet behind the ears to be a sheriff, and he would be the first one to admit that. He'd been a deputy in a small, make that tiny, town in western Kansas for a year, until the town pretty much dried up and blew away in the prairie winds.

He'd been in Boulder for two days on his way to the silver mines and was there when the sheriff was plugged by some no-account that saw Sam watching nearby and thought he'd want a piece of the action, too. When he swiveled his pistol Sam's way, he'd made a mistake –a fatal mistake. Sam's Colt Walker cleared leather and both weapons fired at the same time. The sheriff killer had missed, but Sam didn't, and neither did Sam's second shot. He never trusted a pistol to bring down a man on the first shot and always fired a second round automatically.

The county commissioners offered him the job and he took it. At the time, fifty dollars a month including room and board was a mighty sweet deal, but that was almost a decade ago, and he'd only received one raise in that time.

He had spent most of those eight years in town, having to run down miscreants only a few times, and only three of those were prolonged tracks out in the county. He had developed a reputation for keeping the peace, and a nickname: The Shotgun Sheriff.

Early in his tenure as sheriff, he had found that carrying a twelve-gauge shotgun was a much more convincing argument than trying to talk some drunken cowboy from doing something that he shouldn't be doing. He had a Remington twelve-gauge in his office that he had modified with an even shorter barrel length than the eighteen inches it had when it was made. He had three inches cut from the barrels and another three inches removed from the stock. The entire weapon was just a bit over three feet long. He didn't worry about the stock because he never had any intention of putting

5

it against his shoulder, but simply held the shotgun at waist level and pointed it. If it didn't have its intended effect and had to be fired, he'd pull the trigger and let the gun go at the same time. He even had the front half of the trigger guard removed, so the gun wouldn't break his index finger on the way back. If need be, he'd be reaching for his Colt Peacemaker with the same motion.

But it rarely came to that. In the eight years he had been carrying the shotgun, he'd only had to fire it a half-dozen times outside of practice. He had even made a personal scabbard to carry the shotgun on his back. It was a simple thing; little more than a belt with a wide loop. He could pull the shotgun quickly if need be and usually wore the scabbard while on duty and was accustomed to having it on his back. The shotgun only was added to the scabbard when he made his morning, afternoon and evening rounds. He didn't let Harvey make the rounds because he tended to be a bit smarmy in his dealings with the citizens; just like his father. How the man was reelected was a mystery.

Over the years, he had acquired quite a gun collection from those departing this earth due to their failure to abide by the law. In addition to the shotgun and Colt, he had two Smith & Wesson Model 3s, two more Colt Peacemakers, two Winchesters and a Henry, and one of his favorites; a Webley Bull Dog. The Webley he kept in a shoulder holster under his vest; sometimes his brown vest, but usually one of his two black vests. The rifles he kept at the livery under the care of his friend, Henry, and the pistols he kept in his personal gun locker in the sheriff's office. The rifles in the office belonged to the town, but he rarely used them because he was already a very well-armed man.

Today was a brown vest day as he leaned back on his chair on the boardwalk in front of his office. The late spring weather was a tonic after a typically cruel winter. He was working alone and had no idea where Deputy Greenwald was, nor did he particularly care. All he was good for was watching the occasional prisoner, bringing him his meals and running him to the privy. He hadn't managed to screw that job up yet; but give him time.

It was a quiet Tuesday morning and the commissioners had again turned down his request for another deputy at Monday's meeting, and it stuck in his craw. His Stetson, another gift from a wayward soul, was pushed back on his head as he scanned the streets. He could hear the almost constant construction work from the far end of town and wondered if that college would ever be finished. It was already bigger than the town itself.

Sam was thirty-one now and wasn't sure if that was young or old. He guessed it depended on whether the observer was a teenager or a codger. He knew that he didn't want to be sheriff much longer and was anxious to be moving on. He'd been here too long but had no idea where he would go.

One place that he'd be sure to go before he made his final choice was to visit his little sister, Cora, down south of Denver City. He knew they had changed the name to just Denver, but he couldn't stop adding the 'city' to the name.

Cora had married Richard Short, a man closer to his age, a few years ago. Sam liked Richard, which had initially surprised him. Richard had met Cora in Kansas City where she had lived with their parents. Richard had bought a ranch south of Denver City, or Denver, a few years earlier. Fortunately, it was the Circle S, so the brand was a good fit. It was a small ranch, only a quarter section, so they didn't run many cattle, but it had a nice house and plenty of water.

Cora and Richard seemed happy and had a daughter named Catherine. Sam thought she was the cutest person on two legs. She was almost five years old now and he missed seeing his niece almost as much as he missed his sister. He should really go and pay them a visit soon and shouldn't have waited this long. It was only a day's ride if he pushed the pace; about forty miles, and he hadn't visited in eight months. Little Catherine must be a lot bigger now and he wondered if she'd even remember him.

Aside from Cora, he had no other family. His parents had both died in the past two years; his father died first from a stroke, and his mother less than a year later. The doctors said she had died due to pneumonia, but Sam thought it was from a broken heart. He had gone back for both funerals and then had to stay after his mother's funeral to settle the estate. He had sold the family home and most of its belongings, and let Cora keep all the family heirlooms and anything else she wished to take. He gave her half of the money from the house sale, even though she insisted that he take it because she had a home. There was less than two hundred dollars in the bank account when it was closed, which he thought was a bit sad after such a long life of hard work.

Sam had stopped back in Denver on the way back and opened an account there rather than in Boulder where the bank was still too small to be particularly safe. He had six hundred dollars or so in his account here, his savings over the past eight years; to what end, he didn't know.

Sam was thinking of getting some lunch at Sandy's Café, when he noticed three riders trotting down the main street. Normally, horse traffic wouldn't attract his attention, but these three were different. They had purpose in the way they were riding, which is hard to describe to someone not wearing a badge.

The two outside riders were scanning the town while the one in the middle was just staring straight ahead. Most strangers, and they were definitely strangers, would be more inquisitive. These men weren't looking at the buildings; they were looking for threats. The sun was in their eyes, so they obviously hadn't seen him.

Sam dropped his chair to the front legs, stood, then casually walked back into his office, went to the gun rack and picked up his shotgun. He split it open and checked the load. He normally kept it loaded with bird shot to keep the damage down, so he popped those shells out and dropped in two #4 buckshot shells.

He then slid his hammer loop from his Colt, then walked close to the doorway where he stood by the window and watched. The three men had stopped in front of the bank, and Sam was not surprised. He watched as the two outside riders dismounted and handed their reins to the center rider, obviously the lookout, as they went inside the bank.

Sam had a decision to make and make it soon. If he walked out of the office now, the lookout would spot him, then all hell would break loose and anyone in the bank would be in danger from the two robbers inside. If he waited until they came out, he'd have to act before they got on their horses and skedaddled. He quickly decided on the second option and needed to minimize his exposure while he got into a good position.

He turned and quickly walked out the back door of the jail, then turned left down the alley. After a hundred yards, he turned left again into the narrow space between the hardware store and the livery stable then walked slowly forward until he was as close as he could be to the bank yet still remain in the shadows. Then he just waited for the two in the bank to exit.

He didn't have to wait long. The two robbers calmly walked out of the bank as if they were normal customers just thirty seconds after he'd pulled to a stop in the darkened space. He had the shotgun ready as they hopped onto the street and reached for their horses' reins from the lookout's extended hand. It was time.

He took three fast steps out into the street, about twenty feet from the thieves and held the shotgun off to his right side about waist level.

He shouted, "Stand where you are! Drop your weapons!"

The startled men turned to see the twin barrels of Sam's shotgun aimed in their direction and knew that they were going to get hurt or die if they didn't comply. But these were desperate men with few options, so almost as one, they turned and reached for their holstered weapons.

Sam changed his angle slightly to keep the shotgun pellets from going into the bank and hitting any innocent customers or employees, then pulled the trigger of the Remington scattergun. The recoil from the blast threw the gun from Sam's hands as he reached for his Peacemaker, which turned out to be unnecessary.

The spread of the sawed-off shotgun was so wide, at forty feet the #4 pellets covered a wide enough diameter to cause havoc among the thieves. Most of the lead slugs found nothing but dirt or wood, but eight of them found the three bank robbers, who fell from their horses onto the newly cobblestoned street. Unfortunately, the outermost horse took another three itself and went down, writhing in pain.

Sam raced across the street to the scene and quickly disarmed the three men. All three were still alive but had sustained significant injuries from the shotgun blast and then the fall to the hard rocks of the street. The bank façade had taken some damage from the blast, too, but that could be repaired easily enough. Once the three would-be robbers were weaponless, Sam took a few seconds to quickly end the suffering of the wounded horse with his Colt.

Sam then quickly tied the moaning outlaws' wrists behind their backs with some pigging strings he kept in his vest pocket for just such occasions, picked up the bags they were carrying that contained the bank's money, and trotted into the bank.

"Is everyone okay?" he asked loudly.

One of the clerks said, "Mister Simmons was struck by one of those men. He's unconscious, but I think he'll be okay."

"Good. Here's the cash that they tried to steal. How much did they try to get away with?"

"About three hundred dollars."

"That's all? They risked their lives for three hundred dollars?" he asked in astonishment as he shook his head.

Once he was sure that no one had been hurt, he quickly turned and left the bank to clean up the mess out in the street.

A sizeable crowd had gathered by the time Sam walked past the men, picked up their gunbelts and threw them over his shoulder. Then, one by one, he pulled them to their feet and marched them to the doctor's office under his pistol, never getting close enough to give them any opportunity to do anything but walk.

Once inside the office, Doc Wheeler told Sam to have them sit in chairs while he tended to their wounds in turn.

Sam wished he had a deputy to watch them, but with their injuries and bound wrists, he figured they weren't going anywhere, so he left the doctor's office and returned to the scene to continue his cleanup. The dead horse would have to be moved, but after he reached the body, he yanked a nice Winchester from the dead horse's scabbard, then led the two good horses and walked them across the street to the livery.

Once inside, he called, "Henry! Are you in there?"

"That you, Sam?"

"No one, but. Why are you hiding?"

Henry Cobb stepped out from the back stall and said, "When I saw what was happenin', I figured there'd be shootin' once you saw them baddies. I was just waitin' for the shootin' to end."

"Well, two things I can tell you. I had to shoot one of their horses and hated doing it, too. It wasn't to blame for its rider being an idiot. I need to have it removed, so can you arrange that? Charge it to the county. I also have these two horses. They look like good mounts, so go ahead and take care of them until the judge figures out what to do with their owners."

"I'll do that, Sam."

Sam pulled the two rifles from the other horses; one was an old Henry and another well-maintained Winchester. It was a good weapons haul overall, he thought as he carried the three rifles to his rifle cache in Henry's back room and laid them inside.

"Thanks, Henry. See you later."

As Sam re-entered the street, he headed back towards his office, scanning the ground and found his shotgun wedged under the boardwalk near the hardware store. He pulled it out and gave it a quick inspection. Once he was satisfied it was still functional but in dire need of a good cleaning, he slipped it into his back sling and returned to the doctor's office.

"Well, Doc," he asked on entering the examination room, "what's the verdict?"

"They'll survive. They won't be happy cowpokes for a while, though."

"When can I have them back?"

"I'm checking out the last one now. I need to dig out the gifts you gave him, then I'll bring him over myself when he's done."

"Thanks, Doc."

Sam pointed at the other two and said, "Let's go. I have a nice room for you boys."

Both glared at him but said nothing as they stood with their wrists still tightly bound. He marched them across the street to the jail, and when they passed into the office, he wasn't pleased to see Harvey Greenwald sitting in his chair with his feet on the desk.

He looked at Sam and grinned as he said, "I thought you might need some help, Sheriff."

Sam was still escorting the two prisoners to their cell as he said, "I needed your help when these three were robbing the bank, Harvey, not after the shooting was over. I'd have been

13

satisfied if you had at least shown up afterwards to help me manage these two."

Harvey didn't' reply as Sam grabbed the cell key from its hook, walked the two silent men back to one of the two cells, opened the door and gave them a nudge to let them know that they had found their new home. He closed the door behind them and locked it, then had them turn so he could remove the pigging strings from their wrists.

After hanging the keys, Sam went to his personal weapons locker and tossed in the three gunbelts. He'd check them out later.

He turned to Harvey and said, "Keep an eye on them. The doc's bringing over the third one as soon as he's done removing pellets from him."

"I heard you shot up the bank pretty good, too. My pa's not going to be happy about that."

Sam gritted his teeth as he held back what he wanted to say, but the fact that Harvey even said it pushed him closer to his decision to leave.

He just said, "I'll bet," and walked out the door.

He stepped onto the boardwalk, waited for a carriage to pass, then crossed the street to the bank to check on Mister Simmons' condition. As he approached the building, he saw the bank president and Harvey's daddy, Horace Greenwald, surveying the damage.

Horace spotted Sam as he approached, turned, furrowed his brow and said, "Sheriff, you're going to have to answer for all the damage done by firing that damned shotgun at my bank."

"Horace, it wasn't fired at the bank. In fact, I changed my position to minimize the damage. I was firing at the three men who were robbing your bank."

"Nonetheless, I believe that there were better ways of stopping the robbery than by destroying so much private property. I'll file a claim with the county for damages."

"You can do that, but Horace, you weren't here. I had two options. I could wait for them to exit the bank and keep them from taking hostages or hurting any of your customers, or I could have shot the one lookout man they had posted outside; but if I did that, the two inside bank robbers would be alerted and probably have taken hostages. As it worked out, the only casualties were the three thieves and one of their horses. You got off cheap, so if I were you, I'd count my blessings instead of worrying about having to patch a few holes and slap on some whitewash."

Horace's glare didn't diminish in the slightest when he snapped, "Sheriff, I think you're getting too impressed with yourself; and flippant as well, I might add."

"Hardly. I'm honest enough with myself to know that all I am is a two-bit sheriff in a no-account county in the west. If I die, no one will even notice. Your problem is that you think you're important."

"I am important. I am the president of this bank and a member of the county commission, if I need to remind you."

"You don't need to remind me of that tidbit of information. You and those other cheap bastards can't even see that the town is turning into a city overnight. You'll need a sheriff and two full-time deputies that can do the job; not one that's just some kid who can't even find his nose with his finger."

15

Harold exclaimed, "You are talking about my son, Sheriff! I'm going to take up the topic of your continued employment with the mayor and the council immediately."

Mister Greenwald then stormed away of the bank, and Sam assumed he was going to go and visit the mayor and his fellow council commissioners; he'd done it before.

Sam sighed, and said aloud, "Well, I guess he just made my decision for me."

He entered the bank, approached the clerk, and asked, "Al, how much do I have in my account right now?"

Al Harper opened a ledger, found his name, and replied, "$832.65"

"Okay. Close the account and give me a draft for five hundred dollars and the rest in cash."

Al understood the reason for Sam's decision, and suspected it was coming when he heard Greenwald's outburst outside the open door.

"Not a problem, Sam," he said.

Al returned to the cashier window, took the cash from the drawer, filled out the draft, and returned to his desk.

Al counted out the cash, then Sam signed the receipt and stuffed the money into his pocket before he accepted the bank draft for the balance.

"Are you going to stay, Sam?" Al asked.

"No, I don't think so. I'll be moving on."

"I'd just like to say that Greenwald was way out of line in what he said. You did everything right, and we're all grateful what you did, even if he didn't."

"Well, I appreciate the comment, Al," Sam said as he reached across the desk and shook Al's hand.

He then turned, left the bank and headed back across the street to his office.

The doc was just leaving the jail, saw Sam approaching and waited until he was close enough for normal conversation.

When Sam was close, he said, "I just dropped off the last one. Do I send the bill to the county?"

"As usual. Thanks for everything, Doc. You've been a good friend."

The doctor's eyebrows arched as he asked, "What do you mean? Are you leaving?"

"Yup. I just got dressed down by Greenwald for putting some shotgun pellets into his woodwork. He never liked me much even before he saddled me with Harvey. Now he's off to the mayor and county council now to see if he can get me fired, but I'm not waiting around. I figure it's time anyway."

The doctor knew there was no point in trying to talk him out of his decision, so he stepped closer and shook his hand.

"You take care, Sam."

"You, too, Doc."

After the doctor left, he continued to his office, and when he opened the door, he ofund Harvey Greenwald with his feet still on the desk, but this time Sam smiled.

He walked to the gun locker in his small office, picked the heavy crate off the floor and set it on his desk. He knew what was inside: seven gunbelts with cartridge pistols, eight boxes of .44 cartridges and three boxes of shotgun shells. He carried the heavy box out to the front office, set it down on the floor and looked at Harvey, whose feet still adorned the desk, and gave him a big grin.

"Like this job, Harvey?" he asked.

"Sure. The pay is good, and I like the side benefits, too," Harvey replied.

"Well, now you get to earn the pay, Sheriff," Sam said as he tossed his sheriff's badge onto the desk, picked up his crate of guns and carried it out the door, leaving a stunned Harvey in his wake.

He lugged the locker down to the livery, and after entering, went to the back stall where he kept one of his three horses, and set it on the dirt floor.

Henry saw him lower the box to the floor and asked, "What are you doing, Sam?"

"Moving on."

"*Really? You're leaving?*" he asked incredulously.

"It's about time, Henry. Keep an eye on my guns, will you? I've got to collect the rest of my belongings. Could you get my rifles for me?"

"Sure thing, Sam," Henry replied as he turned to go back to his living quarters in the big barn where he stored Sam's repeaters.

Sam left the livery and walked back to the same small room at the Boulder Hotel that he had occupied for almost eight years. Aside from his weapons and horses, he didn't have much in the way of possessions: an extra set of saddlebags, two vests, two pairs of pants, three pairs of socks, one spare union suit, four shirts, a pair of moccasins, and an old, but still useable pair of boots. He stuffed his clothes into the extra set of saddlebags in four minutes and his packing was done.

After he threw the saddlebags over his shoulder, he took one long look at the place he had called home for almost a decade. If this was home, then he really didn't have much at all; but he did have Cora and her precious daughter to brighten his life.

He turned, closed the door for the last time and walked down to the lobby to hand in his key, hoping that the hotel owner, Warren Clark was at the desk and not his wife, Mattie; but he wasn't that lucky when he spotted Mattie's smiling face at the small counter.

He smiled back as he reached the counter and laid his key on the shelf.

"Mattie, I'll be checking out."

"*Sam*," she asked, wide-eyed, "*you're not leaving*?"

"I think it's time, Mattie. The final straw was Horace Greenwald getting all high and mighty about a few shotgun pellets hitting his bank; not caring that the majority went into the three men who were holding up his pride and joy."

"I heard about the holdup. You're not going to give in, are you?"

"It's not just about that, Mattie, I feel that it's time anyway. Boulder is growing up and maybe it'll be as big as Denver in a few years. The mayor and his cronies on the county commission don't seem to believe that they need more deputies. Now, maybe they'll figure that out after I leave them with Harvey."

"It won't be the same without you around, Sam."

"I'll miss you, too, Mattie," Sam said with a heartfelt smile.

Mattie then rushed around the desk and gave Sam a big hug and a kiss on the cheek. She had always had a crush on Sam, even though she'd been married for six years now and Sam was well aware of it, too.

"You take care, Sam," she whispered as tears rolled down her cheeks.

"You too, Mattie," he said as he patted her on the shoulder, then turned, crossed the lobby and exited the hotel.

He'd been fond of Mattie for a long time, but never could bring himself to do anything more than smile at her. When she married after he'd been the sheriff for two years, he just chalked it up to his inexperience with women.

Sam then walked to the Evans General Store across from the hotel.

After entering, he waved at the owner, then walked the well-stocked aisles, picking out things he would need for the trail to whatever his unknown final destination may be: a steel frypan, coffeepot, two plates and two sets of utensils, a grate for cooking over a fire, two extra blankets, a new bedroll, and four heavy leather panniers. As he filled his arms, he'd drop them on the long counter and return to the aisles to refill, finally ending with most of the counter loaded with his purchases.

"Going somewhere, Sam?" asked Josh Evans, the proprietor.

"Yup. Tossed my badge to Sheriff Harvey Greenwald a few minutes ago. I'm clearing out, Josh."

"You're not going to do that to us, Sam; are you? You're not gonna stick us with Harvey, not really. Tell me you aren't doing that to us."

"Not my choice, Josh. His blowhard of a father was going to demand my head on a platter, but I was thinking of leaving anyway, so this was just the nudge that I needed. I'll have to get some food, too. I'll be right back,"

Sam grabbed four cans of beans, five pounds of coffee, a slab of bacon, and just because he felt like it, two tins of peaches. He added a poke of salt and some onions and potatoes for variety and carried them to the counter.

"This should do it, Josh. What's the bill?"

It took Josh a couple of minutes to add the new items to the total.

"$37.22."

Sam paid for the order and told Josh he'd be back in a little while to pick them up, then gave him a short wave and returned to the livery.

When he entered the large barn, Henry had his repeaters all lined up and leaning against the wall right next to the locker that he had just dropped off. He didn't look happy as he stood with his arms folded across his chest.

When he saw Sam, he unfolded his arms and silently began helping Sam as they began preparing his three horses for departure. Sam saddled his primary mount, a five-year-old red chestnut gelding he named Cump because he was an admirer of General William Tecumseh Sherman, who was known as either 'Uncle Billy' by the troops under his command or by 'Cump' among his friends, and the animal had dark red hair like the general. Henry used Sam's second saddle for his second horse, a tall black mare that Sam had named Coal for obvious reasons.

Sam's third horse, also a chestnut gelding, was a bit shorter and seemed to have a bit of mule in him, even though Sam knew that it was biologically impossible. He was called Glass because Sam noticed that when he walked his hooves had a slight hesitant hitch, as if he was walking on something that might break. He put the pack saddle on Glass, then he and Henry fashioned a trail rope to Glass, attached it to Coal, and finally hooked it onto Cump's saddle.

Cump already had a bedroll, but Sam wanted the new one because his first one was getting long in the tooth.

It was time to load up the guns. There was one Winchester '66 rifle and three of the '73s, which were all the shorter carbine versions of the repeater. The '66 Yellowboy with its brass side plates showed its heritage to the Henry rifles. If it wasn't for the loading gate on the right side and the wooden forearm under the barrel to keep from burning your fingers when you fired a few shots in rapid succession, they looked the same. Then there was that huge difference in the way the repeaters were loaded. Henrys were odd compared to the much more popular Winchesters, but when they first showed up on the battlefields during the War Between the States, they were a revelation; not that the army was smart enough to buy them.

Henrys had to be loaded by flipping the rifle upside down, sliding a tab up a slot under the loading tube and compressing the spring inside. Then the end of the loading tube with the compressed spring would be swung to the side and the .44 caliber rimfire cartridges would be inserted into the tube, and always carefully. It was never a good idea to slam them in quickly, no matter how many bullets were flying around. Once the tube was filled, the compressed spring mechanism was swung back in place, the tab released, and the spring would press against the row of bullets keeping them in place for loading into the breech.

The one other difference was that the Winchester '66 added a handy little switch called a safety, which was lacking on the Henry.

So, all in all, it was easy to understand why the Winchester became so universally accepted in favor of the Henry, but those that owned Henrys swore by them, despite having to be careful not to let any dirt get into that loading tube under the barrel which could ruin their day.

Each horse had two scabbards, which worked out well as he slid one repeater into one. He slung his clothing saddlebags over Cump and took the saddlebags that would be going over Coal and walked to the gun box. After flipping open the locker's cover, he examined the three latest rigs in more detail. The guns were in good condition, although only two were cartridge weapons. One was an old Colt Walker like he had used when he first started the job. He left that pistol and belt aside. The other two were both Colt Peacemakers in reasonably good condition, so he rolled the pistols in the belts and put them in the second set of saddlebags. Then he put the other two Colts and the two Smith & Wesson Model 3s from his locker into the saddlebags. He couldn't squeeze in all the ammunition into the saddlebags, so he made room in his clothing saddlebags and managed to find room for them inside. He lifted the heavily weighted bags over Coal's back, then turned to Henry.

"You can have that Colt Walker if you have a mind to, Henry."

Henry replied, "I'll hang onto it, but I don't know if I'll ever have any use for the thing."

Sam and Henry had been good friends over the years and despite the fact that he was wearing his shotgun on his back, and men didn't do such things, he walked up to Henry and gave him a manly hug, then stepped back and shook his hand.

"Thanks for everything, Henry. You're a good man."

Henry looked as if he was going to cry, so he just nodded, and then said, "I put new shoes on Cump yesterday, Sam. Coal and Glass are both good."

Sam smiled and said, "Thanks, Henry."

Then he turned, took Cump's reins and Sam led the three animals out of the livery stable.

He walked down the cobbled streets leading his small parade, and in a short while, arrived back at the mercantile. Josh had everything packed and ready for loading, so he and the proprietor began hanging the heavy panniers on Glass's pack saddle, then Sam tied them all down to prevent them from being jostled free.

He was ready to leave, so he shook Josh's hand, climbed aboard Cump, then took one last look at Boulder and started his cavalcade moving.

Sam exited the eastern end of the town, examining the new buildings of the university as he led his caravan southeast toward Denver. It was roughly thirty-five miles to Denver, and his sister's ranch was just seven miles south of the city, but it was an easy ride, and he normally would make it in less than five hours. But his speed would be much lower this time because of the trailers, so it would take him eight or even nine hours to complete the journey. If he'd been able to get out of town sooner, he could have made it there in one day, so maybe he should have stayed overnight and left in the morning, but he just wanted to go. The perfect weather was a bonus, though, and he was in good spirits as he sat in the saddle.

He did wonder what he'd be doing after he visited Richard, Cora and little Catherine. With his experience, and he hated to admit it, his reputation, he knew he could get a job as a lawman easily but wondered if other towns and counties had similar political problems that he had encountered in Boulder. He'd be surprised if they didn't.

Technically, when he started, he should have been a town marshal, but they had called him a sheriff because that was what the badge read. Usually, counties had sheriffs and towns and cities had marshals, but some town fathers seemed to latch onto having sheriffs. As it turned out, he became a real sheriff when the county commissioners appointed him to the job just a year later.

One thing he was sure about, though, he wasn't going to lay his life on the line for sixty dollars a month anymore.

Three hours later, he stopped at a creek with a small copse of pine trees for a break, watered the horses and let them graze while he had a quick lunch that was really a snack of some jerky and water.

He remounted after half an hour's rest and pressed on, keeping his leisurely pace. He was planning on stopping north of Denver and setting up camp, then he'd go through Denver the next day and reach the Circle S by mid-morning.

He found his campsite about five miles from Denver as the sun dropped low in the sky and set up between two enormous boulders. There was a nearby bowl that still had water from a recent rain, so he led the horses to the bowl and let them drink, and when they were happy, he led them to the campsite and began removing their loads for the night.

After the panniers were on the ground, he unsaddled the animals and hitched them near some grass to let them graze. He built a small fire pit then once the fire was lit, he placed the cooking grate on top and soon had bacon frying and a can of beans waiting to be dumped into the mix. He chopped up some onion and dumped it onto the bacon, and after the bacon and onions were cooked, he dropped in the beans. As the mix simmered, he added coffee to the boiling water in the coffeepot, completing his roadside dining experience.

After eating, he saved half of the bean and bacon mix for his breakfast. He may not miss his job, but he definitely missed the meals at the café, especially, the biscuits and bread. He was never able to figure out how to make either and was well aware of his overall shortcomings in the food preparation arena. He was a terrible cook and had to suffer through his occasional forays into the discipline and eat his own cooking when he had to leave the confines of Boulder, so he kept it simple when the need arose.

He let the fire die down and unraveled his old bedroll, but didn't bother with blankets, expecting it to be cool but not cold.

With everything settled, Sam finally slid into the bedroll and just admired the night sky spread overhead. He was beginning to get excited about seeing Cora, Richard and little Catherine again after eight months. It had been too long. and he had no excuse for the delay, but it would be wonderful to see them all again.

CHAPTER 2

When he awakened in the early light, Sam soon realized that he had been wrong in his offhand weather prediction before he went to sleep. It was cold, but there was nothing he could do about it now. He slid out of the bedroll quickly, grabbed his boots, turned each one upside down, shook any overnight crawly squatters out and pulled them on. Then after walking away a few feet from his campsite and answering nature's call, he returned to the granite bowl and splashed some water on his face and ran his fingers through his too-long, sandy brown hair to straighten it out. He then started a new fire and reheated the beans and coffee from dinner. He knew the coffee would be horrible, but he didn't want to just toss it out. After tasting it, he began to second-guess his decision, but the beans and bacon weren't bad.

After his leftover breakfast, he cleaned his cookware, then saddled and loaded the horses, mounted Cump and set off to Denver.

He picked up the outlines of the growing city shortly after mounting, arriving at the outskirts before midmorning and headed for the bank to deposit most of the money he had withdrawn from his Boulder account.

He was impressed by how much Denver had grown in the past eight months as it was noticeably more populated; more of the streets were paved with stones and the amount of new construction was well ahead of Boulder's too.

He led the horses through the streets until he reached the bank, then tied off Cump, and after leaving his shotgun in one of the panniers walked inside. A man could walk into the bank wearing two pistols at his waist and no one would pay attention but entering a bank with a sawed-off shotgun was a different thing altogether. He did look a bit odd with his empty shotgun strap still over his back, but it wasn't threatening.

He made his deposit and checked his balance, finding it to be a very healthy $3765.34. He still had no idea what he'd do with it, though. He asked for some blank drafts, and after the cashier slid them across the small shelf, Sam folded them and put them in his vest pocket.

He returned to the horses, removed the shotgun from the pannier and replaced it in his back scabbard, then mounted and headed south for Cora's place, anxious to see his sister, her husband, and especially little Catherine. She was growing so fast now, he regretted not visiting for eight months. He still owed her a Christmas gift and a birthday present, too and should have bought her something in Denver, but he was in a rush to get to the ranch and see everyone again.

It was almost eleven o'clock when he spotted the access road of the Circle S and smiled in anticipation of seeing his baby sister and her cute Catherine; He'd like to see Richard again as well; but Cora and Catherine were both extra-special to him.

He crossed a mild rise and saw the ranch buildings in the distance, and could almost hear Catherine's excited shout, "Uncle Sam!" as he approached the access road, leading his two horses.

As he walked his animals closer to the long access road, he noticed something odd. He didn't see any cattle and there was no one outside working either. That in itself wasn't unusual, but added to the lack of cattle, it became so. It had never been a big herd, but the sounds of cattle lowing were omnipresent and the utter silence from the ranch sent a chill down his back.

He turned into the ranch access road under the large Circle S crossbar; the silence surrounding the ranch becoming eerie. There wasn't any smoke coming from the cook stove pipe, either, which was very bizarre. Even hours after breakfast, the smoke from the stove should still be drifting from that pipe and Cora should be preparing lunch already.

Now Sam's lawman instincts kicked in. Something was wrong at the ranch, so he picked up the pace and had the horses trotting faster to the house. No one came to the door, which added to his concern and suspicions. They could hardly miss the sound of twelve hooves pounding the dirt.

He pulled Cump to a stop and leapt down from the saddle, tossed Cump's reins over the hitching rail, and quickly climbed the steps to the porch, walked to the front door in two long strides, knocked loudly and then waited. After fifteen seconds, he opened the screen door, then the front door.

"Cora? Richard? Are you there?" he asked loudly.

There was no response, so he slowly entered, drawing his Peacemaker as he did.

He slowly searched the house room by room, finding the house completely empty. He noticed that the beds were unmade then headed to the kitchen. When he arrived, he found two place settings on the table, and a bowl and spoon on one side with some dried oatmeal still inside the bowl. He walked to the cold stove, discovered a dry, rusty pot on the stove with a frypan and moldy bacon sitting in hardened grease; a bowl with four eggs sat nearby.

His stomach was twisting in knots, and not because of the smell of the old food. All the indications pointed to a sudden and probably violent event. Whatever had happened, had happened quickly and in the morning, but there were no signs of a struggle. There was no blood anywhere. The Short family was simply gone.

He had seen them eight months ago, so whatever had happened to them had occurred since then. He checked the larder, knowing that by examining how the food had aged, he could estimate how long the house had been empty. After a quick evaluation, everything he found pointed to at least three or four months.

He went out the back door and trotted to the barn, finding it empty. There was still hay on the floor, but no sign that any animals had been here at all; no droppings or clumps of hair. There were still some tools and a harness for their wagon, but that was all. He replaced his Colt, but left the hammer loop off.

He walked out to the trough, finding less than two inches of nasty water, scooped some water out, primed the pump, and began to work the handle and was soon rewarded with a gush of water. He filled the trough to overflowing to get the detritus out of the water then walked to the front of the house. He untied Cump and led the animals to the trough, and as they drank, he thought about what he had found; his deep fear for the missing family growing as he mused on the evidence. There couldn't be good explanation for what he had discovered.

After the horses were quenched, he led them to the back of the house and tied off Cump, then began unloading the packs. After the supplies were in the kitchen, he removed the saddlebags and repeaters, moved the horses to the barn, unsaddled them and brushed them down. He put one in each of the three stalls and then filled the small troughs in each stall, spread hay into the stalls for them to eat and returned to the house.

Even while he was unsaddling the horses, he was thinking; but now, as he walked to the back entrance, Sam was able to concentrate solely on the mystery.

He was in the kitchen, removing the supplies from their packing wondering where he might find more information, and suddenly he dropped the can of peaches in his hand and popped to his feet. *The safe!* He wondered if that was the reason for their disappearance.

Richard had cut out a floorboard and made a small safe space in the kitchen corner, then had replaced the board and covered it with a rug. They had showed Sam the location as a precaution that he had thought unnecessary at the time. It loomed of much greater importance now.

Sam walked over to the corner of the kitchen and slid the rug to the center of the room. The removable board was still in place, so maybe it hadn't been opened. Thieves rarely took the time to put things back in order.

He dropped to his heels, took out his knife and pried the board loose and lifted it away, setting it down beside him. The safe area looked untouched, so he reached in and pulled out a leather pouch and took it to the kitchen table.

He sat and opened the flap, finding a few gold double eagles, some paper money, and a few blank bank drafts from the same bank that he used. There was also a letter. He took out the envelope and saw the return address was Amos Short, St. Louis Missouri. It was addressed to Richard, so Amos was most likely Richard's father and felt slightly embarrassed that he didn't know his father's name.

He slid the short letter from the envelope and read:

My Dear Richard,

I hope this letter finds you, Cora, and my granddaughter well. I am writing to tell you that my health is failing. Do not try to return. What is happening to me is the way of all men. I have had a good life. I had a wonderful wife and a good son.

Although you chose to leave us to strike out on your own, I do not condemn you for that. I applaud you. It is what I would have done at your age.

However, now that I see the great change upon me, I just wanted to know that should you decide to return with your family, the shipping firm will still be here for you to skipper.

Enough of business. I know that you love your wife and daughter as I loved my wife and my son. Treasure them always. Soon, I will join her again and will be happy.

But I give you a word of warning. Your cousin, Ferguson, has been trying to pull legal shenanigans to gain control of the firm. He has failed because I have the best attorneys that money can buy. He is an arrogant and ruthless man and will stop at nothing to gain control of the company, but if he does, he will bring about its ruin. He only wants the money it represents and doesn't care a wit about the men who need the jobs to care for their own families.

Take care of your family, my son, and I hope you will return to protect what I have built. You are the only one I can trust.

Affectionately,

Your Loving Father

Sam reread the letter, wondering if somehow Ferguson had been involved with what had happened to the Shorts. He doubted it, though. Sam knew that he had a suspicious mind and tended to think poorly of most people until proven otherwise. A decade running afoul of all levels of miscreants can do that.

He counted out the money. Altogether it amounted to three hundred and seventy dollars. He replaced the money and bank drafts along with the letter into the leather pouch and put it back into its safe under the floor. After reinserting the floorboard, he slid the rug back into position.

So, it wasn't a robbery, so maybe it was about the cattle. They were all gone, but it wasn't a big spread, and if that had been the case, Richard would have notified the county sheriff. He wouldn't have left his wife and daughter alone to chase after rustlers. Sam knew he'd have to get a lot more information to even start his hunt for his sister, niece and brother-in-law.

He decided to cache most of his weapons in the house and barn but would keep his Webley and the Colt with him and only take one of the Winchester '73s when he went to Denver in the morning. He'd leave the other two horses and tack in the barn, leave in the morning and make two stops in Denver to find out what happened.

He left the kitchen and walked to Cora and Richard's bedroom. When he entered, he could see that it had been a long time since the bed had been made, so he ripped off the linens and took the sheets and pillowcase into the kitchen. He pumped some water into the sink and used the dry, cracked bar of white soap nearby to give them a quick scrubbing, then when they were reasonably clean and rinsed, took them outside and hung them over the line to dry. He was about to return to the house when he spotted two riders clearing the horizon to the south.

He still had his shotgun handy, so he pulled it from its scabbard and waited as they continued to approach. The men looked like regular cow hands, and neither had pulled his Winchester or pistol, but their faces registered either anger or distrust when they were close enough for Sam to see them. He wondered what their purpose was in coming to the ranch.

They rode to within fifty feet, pulled to a stop, but made no motion to step down as Sam waited for them to open the conversation.

"What are you doing here, mister?" asked the taller of the two.

"I was about to ask you the same question," Sam replied.

"That's not your concern. We don't take to squatters, so I suggest you move along."

"That's an interesting comment. I'm not the squatter here. I'd say you two are trespassing, not me."

"You ain't got no right bein' here."

"More than you do. What happened to the family that lived here?"

"Ain't nobody lived here for a while."

"That's not what I asked, but I'll find out soon. All you need to know is that there's somebody living here now, so I'd suggest you return to where you started."

"Mister, maybe you're just too dumb to understand, my boss claimed the ranch because it's gone empty."

"It was empty because I didn't get back in time. Now, the Colorado law on delinquency has a one-year limit, and I was here eight months ago visiting my sister and her husband, and the taxes were up to date back then, so it fails to meet that legal requirement. Now I'd appreciate you telling me just what happened to the small herd that they had on the property. That's cattle theft, and that's still a hanging offense in Colorado."

"We didn't steal no cattle. They must've wandered off."

"Cattle don't wander off if they have grass and water and I see plenty of both. Now I aim to visit the county sheriff tomorrow and bring up the subject. I suggest you go and tell your boss to keep his hands off the ranch."

"I'll tell him," he answered before they wheeled their horses back to the south.

Sam wasn't sure if it was his legal argument or the presence of a menacing shotgun that convinced them, but it didn't matter; maybe it was simply a land grab that had caused the problem after all. But the cause didn't matter. His sister and her family mattered.

After he was sure that they were clear of the ranch, he returned to the house and began placing his excess handguns in hidden locations throughout the house but decided to leave the ammunition with the saddlebags.

After returning to the bedroom to store his clothes, he pulled out a drawer and found his sister's clothes, and a deep sense of grief stabbed him in the heart. The thought that something bad probably had happened to Cora filled him with dread.

They had grown up as close as any brother and sister could have. He was her big brother and her protector. She was his ray of sunshine and made him smile whenever he saw her. She was six years younger than he was, so when he was a teenager, undergoing all of those changes that make teenagers the moody and unpredictable humans they are, Cora was there in her precious years to even him out.

Before she married, he gave Richard a thorough examination before giving his approval of her choice. Richard became a good friend, and he was happy for them both. At their wedding, it was the first time he recognized the difference between them and other couples that he knew. He could see it in the way they looked at each other. Their faces almost glowed, and he knew then what sharing true love between and a man and woman could be; something he had never come close to experiencing.

Then they brought little Catherine into the world, and she was almost clone of his beloved sister; except for the hair. Cora's light brown hair was replaced with Catherine's bright blonde curls. Her blue eyes were deeper than Cora's, but they had the same dancing quality.

Sam wasn't the only one smitten by little Catherine. Her parents seemed in awe of her as well and now they were all gone. Where they had gone was the question. He had lost six months or so, and the trail would be cold, but he would find them.

He finally just put his clothes on top of the dresser, then went to examine the closets when he noticed a scrawl on the wall near the door above the bathtub. It was almost illegible.

It read:

For a good time, see Trixie in Hinkley.

He knew Hinkley. It was a small dirt town about thirty miles south of Denver, or twenty-three miles from where he now stood. He guessed that Trixie was a prostitute in Hinkley; *but why take time to write that on the wall?* It must have been done by the ones who invaded the house: *but why leave a clue?* That was either really stupid or it was a trap. He hoped it was stupid, because it was the only lead that he had.

After he had set the weapons where he wanted them, he decided he needed to eat, but didn't feel like cooking, so he just opened a can of beans and ate them cold. After he finished, he went outside, removed the now dry linen from the line, took them inside and made the bed before he spent a few hours doing a basic cleaning to make the house somewhat more livable.

As he cleaned, he tried to make some sense of that cryptic scrawl on the wall in the bedroom. It still bothered him because it made no sense at all.

By the time the sun was down, and he was ready for sleep, he found it difficult to even close his eyes as he laid on the same bed that had been shared by Cora and Richard. He felt useless and thoughtless, too. If only he'd visited more often, then at the very least, he'd have a fresher set of clues to be able to find them.

After three hours of deep thought, Sam finally drifted off to sleep.

CHAPTER 3

Sam half expected someone to break in overnight to try to make him leave but was pleasantly surprised to wake up to the early sunshine flooding the room. He quickly hopped out of bed and walked into the kitchen and out the door to the privy.

When he returned, he pumped some water into the sink, washed his face and shaved, then decided to forgo his own version of breakfast and went outside to the barn and saddled Cump.

Just thirty-five minutes after waking, he trotted his gelding down the access road and turned toward Denver. The ride took forty-five minutes, with his first stop at a nice-looking café where he had a solid breakfast of ham and eggs, biscuits and loads of butter and honey. He almost sighed when he first tasted the biscuit. He thought that he had a curse by being born with no ability to make even simple biscuits or anything else for that matter.

After paying for the breakfast, his next stop was to the land office to ask about the Circle S; particularly the taxes. He didn't want the ranch to go delinquent so the neighbor could take the spread.

After entering, he found three clerks available, and approached the long counter.

"How may I help you, sir?" he asked.

"I just got into town and went to my brother-in-law's ranch and found it empty. I talked to some of the neighbor's

39

cowhands and they said that the taxes had gone delinquent. I can't see Richard doing that, so could you check on the records for the Circle S? I'll pay the taxes if they are in arrears."

"Just a moment," he replied before turning and stepping to a large file cabinet and pulling open a drawer.

The clerk pulled the appropriate binder, returned to the counter and spread it on the surface.

As he began turning pages, Sam said, "The deed should be made out to Richard and Cora Short."

The clerk paused, then flipped the previous page back over, scanned it and said, "Well, yes, but there's a third name on the deed. You say you're Mrs. Short's brother?"

"Yes. Sam Brown. She's my sister, she used to be Cora Brown."

"Well, Mister Brown, your name is on the deed as well."

That surprised Sam as he asked, "Why would they do that?"

"It's not unusual at all. Many families include other members on the deed in case anything happens to them. It's like a cheap way of making a will. It keeps the property from going back to the state for auction."

"That surprised me. Neither Cora nor Richard said a word to me."

"Also, not unusual."

"Are there any taxes due?"

He looked at the last sheet, then said, "Yes, in fact, there are. This year's taxes were due in April but weren't paid."

"What's the amount due?"

"$34.55"

"Can I pay you now?"

"Certainly."

Sam pulled out one of his bank drafts and wrote it out to the county for the taxes. He decided to keep his cash intact as he might need it later. The clerk accepted the draft then wrote a receipt and marked the tax bill as paid. Sam was glad he had checked. Granted, the ranch wouldn't go to auction until they'd been delinquent for the second year, but he was glad to have caught it.

"Can you tell me which ranch is directly south of the Circle S?"

"I don't even have to look. That would be the Diamond M. Chuck Martin's ranch."

"Well, thank you for your help, sir," Sam said as he reached across the counter and shook his hand.

"It's been a pleasure, Mister Brown."

Sam left the land office wondering if what Richard and Cora had done was really a common practice or were they worried about something.

He then walked to the same bank he had his account and the one listed on the drafts in Richard's safe and stepped to the desk of a clerk behind a desk rather than a cashier.

41

"May I help you, sir?"

Sam read the man's name on the plate sitting atop the desk and said, "I hope so, Mister Mortimer. I need to find out something about my brother-in-law and sister's account. I arrived at their ranch yesterday and no one was there. I know they have an account here as well as I do, but I need to know when the last time there was any activity on the account. I don't know if that violates any banking rules, so I'm reticent to ask."

"Normally, it does, but let me access the records. What were the names on the account?

"His name is Richard Short. His wife is my sister, Cora. I'm Sam Brown, her brother."

"Just a moment," he said as he rose and stepped back into an office area.

Sam wondered if he was just getting too touchy, but he thought Mister Mortimer flinched when he said that his brother-in-law's name was Richard Short.

Mister Mortimer returned with a ledger book and took his seat.

"Yes, Mister Brown. I can give you that information. You are actually listed on the account, so all the information is available to you."

Again? They put his name on their bank account? He wondered if Richard was afraid of something or someone; maybe Mister Martin or that Short cousin, Ferguson.

"How could they add me to the account? I never signed anything."

"Normally, that would be the procedure. However, as you already had an account with us, Mrs. Short was able to verify your signature."

"Okay, that's fine. So, has the account been used in the past six months?"

"No, the last time the account was accessed was the 3rd of December, last year. It was for a withdrawal of one hundred dollars, leaving a balance of $8,329.45."

Trying not to appear astonished at the amount, Sam asked, "One other question, Mister Mortimer. Was the account opened with a large draft on a St. Louis bank?"

He looked at the ledger, then replied, "Why, you are quite correct, Mister Brown. The account was opened with a ten-thousand-dollar draft on a St. Louis branch of the First National Bank."

"Thank you, Mister Mortimer. You've been most helpful."

"You're quite welcome, Mister Brown, and if I may, I'd suggest you stop by the sheriff's office pertaining to Mister Short."

Sam didn't even ask why. That had been his final destination, anyway.

"I intended to go there next after obtaining some information. That's why yours was so helpful. Thank you again, sir."

"A pleasure meeting you, Mister Brown."

Sam shook his hand and crossed the lobby to the street. He knew where the sheriff's office was, and even though it was only two blocks away, he decided to take Cump because he wanted the horse nearby.

He mounted, rode the two blocks, halted at the county sheriff's office, stepped down, crossed the boardwalk, opened the door and was greeted immediately by a young deputy. He was tall with a strong face and a full crop of black hair.

"Can I help you, mister?"

"I hope so. I'm looking for the sheriff. My name is Sam Brown. Richard Short was my brother-in-law."

The deputy blanched and said, "Just a moment, Mister Brown."

He left the desk and walked into the hall running to the back of the office and disappeared. A minute later, he returned with a large, weathered man of about fifty with the look of a lawman.

"Sam? Sheriff Dan Grant," he said as he reached his meaty hand to Sam who grasped it. Sam was not a small man; standing six feet and an inch and weighing just under two hundred pounds, but Sheriff Grant's hand almost engulfed Sam's. He must have stood four inches taller and had him by fifty pounds or more.

"Nice to meet you, Sheriff."

"Why don't we go back to my office?"

Sam nodded and followed the giant to his office. Sam noticed that he ducked his head through the doorway even though he had enough clearance. He must have developed the much-needed habit over the years after his noggin had taken its share of punishment.

"Have a seat, Sam," he said as he indicated a chair opposite his desk.

"Thanks, Sheriff."

"So, what can I do for you?"

"Well, I came down from Boulder to see my sister and her family. I got there, and found the ranch completely empty, and it looked like everyone was taken without warning, and without a struggle as far as I could see. If I had to guess, I'd say between six and seven months ago."

"You're the sheriff from Boulder, aren't you?"

"I was. I quit yesterday."

"I know. I got a telegram asking if you came this way to tell you that you could have a second deputy and a raise if you came back. So, why did you leave? I hear you were doing a hell of a good job."

Sam explained why he left in a very quick synopsis.

"Well, Sam, can't say I blame ya. Politicians are always a pain in the ass. Are you staying at the Circle S now?"

"I am, but I've got to find out what happened to my family. Haven't you heard anything about what happened? Surely someone must have reported something over the past six months."

Dan Grant had been dancing around telling Sam, but finally let out a breath and leaned forward.

"Sam, I hate to be the one to tell you, but we know what happened to Richard Short. A neighbor reported seeing a bunch of buzzards over the house, so I sent a deputy down there, and he found Richard in the front yard with a bullet hole in his back. When we got him back, the doc pulled out a .44 and it looked like close range, too. There were powder burns on his jacket."

Even though Sam knew that this might be a possibility, he was shaken by the news.

"But what about Cora and Catherine? Where are they? Did they get hurt?"

"We never found a trace of either of them. We tracked some horses out of the ranch heading south but lost them among all the other traffic on the road. There were too many tracks by the time we found the body. We've been looking, Sam, but haven't turned up any evidence at all."

"Why didn't anyone send me a telegram? Or notify his father?"

"We did send a telegram to his father but didn't get a response."

Sam wasn't angry at the sheriff. He'd done what he could, but he was still annoyed that no one had told him.

"Thanks for the information, Sheriff. I'm going to take it from here. I'll let you know what I'm doing so I don't step on any toes. My primary mission is to find my sister and niece, but I think there are people trying to keep hurting them or keep them hidden, so this could get ugly."

"I know. It's such an unusual case. But I'll tell you what I'll do. You're a good lawman with a distinguished record, so I'll appoint you as a temporary deputy. I can do that as long as you don't cost the county any money. Is that okay?"

"I'm fine for money, Sheriff."

"Call me Dan, by the way. You've earned it."

The sheriff swore Sam in and handed him a badge. Sam pinned it on his shirt under the vest on the opposite side of the Webley.

"Do you need any firepower or ammunition?"

Sam laughed and replied, "No, Dan, I was going to ask you if you needed any."

Dan guffawed and shook his head, then said, "I heard you were the most heavily armed lawman in the state."

"It's probably true. They wouldn't pay me anything, but they let me keep the guns of the ones they hanged. I'm going to head over to the grocery store and stock up on some grub and head back. I'll still give you reports if I find anything. Oh, one more thing, did your deputies go through the house?"

"Just checking for the rest of the family, but not an extensive search. Why?"

"Someone had scrawled on the wall in the main bedroom 'For a good time see Trixie in Hinkley'."

"Must be a whore in Waxman's. It's a cheap saloon that has a few loose women."

"Did you notice that all the cattle and other livestock were gone?"

"No, they were there when we got there. In fact, the deputies turned the horses loose into the pastures so they could graze."

47

"A couple of riders from the Diamond M came over to the house and tried to order me out. I asked them about the missing cattle, and they said the beasts probably wandered off."

"Well, it's been six months, but I'll send Zeke down to Martin's place to check and see if any of his critters have a Circle S brand."

"Thanks, Dan. I'll be heading back."

Dan shook his hand again then Sam left the office and rode back to the ranch, stopping at the grocery to pick up two large bags of food.

When he returned to the Circle S, he stopped by the back door and brought the food into the kitchen, then returned Cump to the barn and pulled off his gear, and after a good brushing, he threw some more hay into the stalls. Tomorrow he may let the other two run around in the corral if he could trust that he'd have no more visitors.

Once back in the house, he set to work to complete the cleaning and repairs necessary in the neglected house. He cleaned out the kitchen of all the decaying food and buried them in a deep hole fifty feet from the house and then cleaned out the ashes from the cook stove and fireplace and dumped the ashes on top of the food before filling the hole with the removed dirt, hoping it would keep out the critters. Then he went through the house more extensively, cleaning and making small repairs when needed, then brought some more firewood from the pile outside and moved it to the inside box near the stove.

He then washed the linen in what must have been Catherine's bed and hung it on the clothesline. He was doing all this, so it would be neat when his Cora and Catherine returned. He would find them. He had to. He knew that there was a good chance that they were already dead, but he refused to give that likelihood any thought.

Once he was satisfied with the condition of the house, he set out to make an inventory of the family's clothing. Most of it was in drawers, so it was in good shape. He found their shoes and boots in closets, and somehow, seeing Cora's boots saddened him more than seeing her other things.

He finished his cleaning chores and set to making himself some dinner; first starting a fire in the stove. Initially, there was a funny smell when the fire began, but it cleared once the heat built up. It must have been from some spilled liquid on the stove that had burned off.

After fixing Catherine's bed, he had his dinner and cleaned the dishes, then went into the main room and started a fire in the fireplace. With the blaze going well, he sat down and thought about what he had in the manner of clues.

Richard and Cora must have perceived some threat because they had added him to their account at the bank and to the deed. Then in one day, probably in December last year, someone shot Richard at close range in his own yard. He must have known the man because he allowed his murderer to get so close. Then. whoever it was that killed him, kidnapped Cora and Catherine. It had to be more than one because Cora would have run with Catherine back into the house if she saw Richard being shot and there would have been signs of a struggle, but there weren't.

Then there was the Trixie in Hinkley scrawl. Trap or no trap, he'd head that way tomorrow, but he had to be ready for the loud snap as the jaws to the trap closed around him.

CHAPTER 4

The next morning, Sam was getting ready to head south for Hinkley, and was considering taking his shotgun, but thought it would mark him as either a lawman or a troublemaker. He could handle the Colt better than most anyway, and the Webley was a great backstop.

He loaded up his saddlebags with food and supplies for two days. He had no intention of staying in Hinkley overnight and would rather camp out than sleep in what was probably a bug-infested bed. He added his bedroll and slicker, and, remembering the last time when he thought it wasn't going to be too cold, he packed two blankets.

He and Cump hit the road before nine, not wanting to get there too early. He needed to see a whore and they didn't usually work in the daylight hours.

The twenty-three-mile ride could have been done in three hours without a problem as the road was fairly straight and level, but Sam stretched it to five, arriving in early afternoon, and rode down what he assumed was the main street. It wasn't as bad as he had expected; he'd seen worse. There was a mercantile, a hardware store, a feed and grain, a church and there, the last building on his left, stood Waxman's saloon.

He noticed that there was no law office, which could be good or bad. It meant he had no backup, but it also meant he had no interference. Lawmen in small towns tended to be less than competent. Most were awarded the job as a favor, maybe from an uncle or brother-in-law. Some were either reformed criminals or just plain criminals. Overall, he was pleased to note the lack of local law enforcement.

He rode to the mercantile to waste some time and get some information.

He dismounted and looped Cump's reins around the hitching rail, then strode through the open door and was greeted with a friendly face.

"Good afternoon, sir. How may I help you?" asked the proprietor.

"Good afternoon. I just need to pick up a few supplies before hitting the road again."

"Well, enjoy perusing our stock."

"I will, thank you."

"Perusing?" thought Sam, "Now that's impressive for such a small town."

So, Sam perused. Needing to buy something, he picked up four cans of beans, a can of corned beef, and some more salt and coffee. Then he added some crackers from the barrel near the counter, which he put into a paper sack from the stack of bags near the crackers.

"Will that be all, sir?"

"That should do it. What's the damage?"

"Your total is $2.76."

Sam counted out three silver dollars and handed them to the proprietor, who took the silver and handed him back his change.

"Thank you for your business, sir."

"You're welcome. Say, what can you tell me about the saloon?"

The proprietor shook his head and replied, "That place is a blight on the town. All sorts of unsavory characters frequent the place and no decent citizen would enter those doors. There are young prostitutes that they bring in, but none seem to last very long. As a rule, we try to ignore the place, because we don't have a town marshal. They let us alone mostly, but just having it there is an embarrassment."

Sam asked, "Would it be safe for me to get a beer; do you think?"

"I suppose. Those girls need customers, so they let gents come and go."

Sam wanted to ask about Trixie, but figured he'd pressed his luck.

"I appreciate it. I'll probably go and get a beer before I shove off."

"Good luck."

Sam smiled, took his purchases to Cump and loaded them into his now stuffed saddlebags, then led him away from the dry goods store and headed down the street to the café. He may as well eat something while he waited, not wanting to get to Waxman's too soon.

The café didn't look like much on the outside, but the food was surprisingly good. When he finished, he tossed a fifty-cent piece on the table. It was only a two-bit meal, but it was worth it.

After leaving the café, he stepped out into the street, took a deep breath, then unhitched Cump and headed for Waxman's. He led Cump to the saloon's hitching rail in case he needed to get out quickly and looped his reins over the dried wood rail, then stepped across the rickety boardwalk, pushed through the batwing doors and was met with the strong smell of saloon.

Most of the drinking establishments in the west smelled like this; a mixture of stale beer, the pungent aroma from the dinners left on the floor by drunk cow hands, and the perfume of painted ladies. For the first time in his life, he would be seeking out a one of the members of the world's oldest profession; one named Trixie.

He stepped up to the bar and tilted his Stetson back on his head. The universal cowboy sign that he was just here for a drink.

The bartender approached, but he wasn't your typical barkeep. Most tended to be jolly sorts and a little on the plump side, but this one was neither. He seemed surly before Sam even stepped up to the bar and looked like someone who could do some damage in a fight, and probably went looking for them to boot.

"Watcha drinkin'?" he asked without even an attempt at civility.

"Give me a beer. Cold, if you got it."

"We ain't. That'll be a nickel."

Sam tossed a nickel on the bar and was rewarded by an almost flat, warm beer. He was glad he had food in his stomach as he took the beer and headed for a table.

There were only two other customers in the bar, both already deep into their whiskey, but no women, painted or otherwise. Well, he'd make his beer last as long as he could.

Twenty minutes later, he had to order a second beer and had just taken a sip when he was rewarded by the appearance of lady of the night, even though it was early afternoon. She seemed to be quite young, and Sam was unable to determine whether she was good-looking or not under all that makeup or if her blond hair was real. She glanced around the room, saw the two whiskey-drinkers already tanked and then noticed Sam. She put on her phony smile and wiggled her hips as she stepped in his direction, then when she arrived, she pulled up a chair across from him and sat down.

"Buy me a drink, mister?"

"Maybe. What's your name?"

"Buy me a drink and maybe I'll tell you," she answered, flashing an all-to-obvious wink at him.

Sam noticed her stunning, deep blue eyes that somehow didn't go with the makeup, the outfit, or the performance. She almost seemed innocent, which was a real stretch.

"Sounds fair," Sam replied before he signaled to the bartender who poured out a glass of what was probably tea.

He brought it over and said, "Two bits."

Sam tossed him a quarter as the woman began sipping her 'whiskey'.

"So, what's your name, darlin'?" Sam asked, using his best cowboy lingo.

"I'm called Trixie. What's yours?"

Sam couldn't believe his luck as he replied, "Sam."

"Well, hello, Sam. I haven't seen you in these parts before."

"Nope. Never been this way. Just travelin' through. Thought I'd have me a beer and maybe a good time before I hit the road again."

"Well, I've been known to give many a cowboy a good time. Do you have any money?"

"Just enough, I think. Got paid off a month ago, and now I'm runnin' low."

"Got two dollars?"

"Yes, ma'am. I can handle that."

"Well, why not just follow me then, Sam. I'll show you a good time, but you need to give the bartender the two dollars before you take one step up those stairs."

"You just hang on, darlin', and I'll pay the man."

Sam reached into his pocket and counted out two silver dollars with his fingers, hoping he didn't grab the double eagle instead. He was lucky and only pulled out silver coins and handed the two coins to the bartender who had sidled up to the table, probably on a signal from Trixie. He then nodded and returned to his place behind the bar.

Trixie stood, took Sam's hand, and led him to the stairs, having to let his hand go when they reached the narrow staircase, so he followed her up the steps, impressed with the view as he walked before him.

When they reached the hallway, she looked back at him with a 'come hither' look, and Sam smiled at her but scanned the hallway for the possible trap. He even took a quick glance behind him to make sure the bartender wasn't going to unload on him. He didn't see any danger, so he stepped toward Trixie, needing her to enter the room so he could take a quick look inside before entering.

Trixie led him to the middle of three rooms on the right side, and as she opened the door, Sam quickly removed his Colt's hammer loop, before she turned and beckoned him in, always wearing that fake smile.

He entered the semi-dark room as she closed the door behind him and quickly scanned the room for any kind of trap but couldn't see anywhere that someone could hide. It would have been very difficult as the room was sparse; having just an old bed and a small chest of drawers with a mirror. There was no window, just a dirty lamp for illumination.

Trixie had already started to undo her dress strings seductively as she kept her blue eyes trained on Sam, and for just a few seconds, Sam found himself mesmerized by those eyes until he snapped his mind back to the task at hand, and then was momentarily seriously distracted when she slid her dress to her waist and revealed her perfect breasts.

Sam quickly regained his senses, then surprised Trixie when he took one long stride, took hold of her wrist, then sat her down on the bed and sat down beside her before he released her wrist.

Trixie wasn't comfortable with the sudden change in her customer's demeanor. Too many of her customers had been rough lately, but his man seemed to be gentle until he entered the room, and the sudden change frightened her more than the gruff ones.

"What's the matter, Sam? Don't you like me anymore?" she asked plaintively, hoping to smooth away his obviously hostile intent as she took his hand and placed it on her right breast.

Sam was fighting to keep his urges from overtaking his purpose for being there and regretfully pulled his hand free.

She was staring at him with genuine fear in her eyes, which surprised him. He couldn't believe that she could be afraid of him. Surely, she must have had much more frightening customers. He didn't want to try and force answers from her, so he let his eyes and face calm.

He exhaled and said softly, "Trixie, I just want to talk to you, alright? I know the game and I have no intention of hurting you. Out of curiosity, what does the bartender give you out of the two dollars?"

"Ten cents," she answered quietly.

Sam shook his head and said, "Well, Trixie, I'll give you twenty dollars right now just to talk to me."

"About what?" she asked; the thought of twenty dollars exciting her.

Sam noticed the effect the offer had on Trixie, then replied, "Cora Short."

Trixie's eyes flew open and her hand went to her mouth before she whispered, "Cora? You know Cora?"

Sam shouldn't have been surprised that she knew Cora, but her reaction did. He had expected her to be angry or at least try to pretend that she didn't. He saw genuine concern in those big blue eyes before he replied, "She's my sister. Where is she, Trixie? Do you know?"

C.J. PETIT

Sam was stunned when Trixie suddenly burst into tears and hung her head. This was no act; she was sobbing like she'd just witnessed her mother's death; assuming she loved her mother.

Sam laid his hand softly on her bare shoulder and said, "Trixie, stop crying and tell me what you know."

Trixie's tears were dripping onto the dry wood floor as she stammered, "She's...she's dead. Cora is dead."

"*Dead? Cora?*" Sam exclaimed shaken by the news even though he had almost expected to hear it. His baby sister was dead.

It was his turn to be upset, but because he'd almost been expecting the news, he was able to steel himself from expressing his grief.

He quickly asked, "What happened Trixie? I need to know."

Trixie began wiping the tears from her face, then looked at Sam and replied, "She came here six months ago. She was brought here by some men, and they sold her to Freddy, the bartender. The last words one of them said to her before they left were 'Be good. Remember we have her.' So, she stayed and behaved."

"Go on," Sam said, his stomach churning, already understanding who 'her' was.

"She worked in the next room, at the end of the hall and I could hear her crying every night. Most of us get used to it after a month or two, but she cried a lot, sometimes even when there was a customer. Freddy would hit her when she did that.

58

"She told me her real name and said that four men came and killed her husband and then grabbed her and her daughter. She told me that one of the men said to the others, 'We're supposed to kill them all', but she thought one decided to make some extra money and brought her here and kept her daughter, so she wouldn't tell the law."

Sam couldn't say anything more, despite his resolve to keep his lawman's facade. He couldn't move, but felt the tears rolling down his cheeks and didn't care if she saw them. His sweet little sister was gone, and her precious daughter was being held by some bastards. Just as suddenly as it had arrived, his sorrow gave way to unfathomable anger.

Sam didn't wipe the moisture from his face as he looked at Trixie and growled, "Did she say who these men were?"

"No, she hadn't seen them before."

"How did she die, Trixie?" he snapped.

"There's this cowboy from one of the ranches that shows up every few weeks, but none of us wants to service him. We call him the whore-puncher, because after he's finished, he likes to give us one big punch in the belly. He thinks it's funny. We know it's coming, so we're ready for it. It still hurts a lot, but we get over it. We asked Freddy to keep him away and he told us it was our job to keep them happy and just get used to it.

"About a month ago, the whore-puncher came in and Cora, her whore-name was Dolly, was assigned to him. No one had told her about him because he hadn't been there in a couple of months. When he left, I could hear her moaning and I went in to check on her and she was hurt bad. I told Freddy, and he got mad at her instead of helping her and told her to get ready for her next customer. She tried, but she started throwing up and Freddy got mad at her for that, too. Then she just passed

59

out on the saloon floor and Freddy had two of us girls carry her to her room and laid her in bed. We all tried to help her, but she was in so much pain. She must have known she was dying, because she looked at me and said, 'When he comes, tell Sam to find Catherine,' and then she just died."

Sam closed his eyes and said softly, "I'll find your little girl, Cora, or die trying."

Then he opened his eyes, looked at Trixie and asked, "Where did they bury her, Trixie?"

"Out behind the saloon."

"Well, Trixie, you've earned your twenty dollars."

He reached into his pocket, pulled out the gold piece and held it out to her, but she just stared at the coin and shook her head.

"I don't want your money. I owe that to Cora. Just tell Freddy you had a good time."

"No, I'm not going to tell Freddy that."

"But he'll hit me!"

Sam stared into those hypnotic eyes and growled, "No, he won't Trixie, because he'll be dead."

Trixie was horrified and said loudly, "But you can't do that! What will we do?"

"You'll be able to do whatever you want to do. I can't let that bastard get away with what he did to my sister."

"We're whores, for God's sake. What can we do about anything?"

"Well, let me go and see Freddy and see what happens."

"Please don't kill him," she begged.

"Trixie, it'll be up to him."

She began to cry again as Sam left the room and went down the stairs to the bar. For some reason, he wanted to punish the man for what he did to Trixie as well as what he did to Cora. Either way, he really wanted to shoot the bastard.

The saloon was still empty except for the two drunks when he reached the floor.

"Was she good to you?" asked Freddy.

"The best," replied Sam, "But I was looking for Dolly. Our drover said she was even better."

"She don't work here no more."

"Too bad. She got some lonesome cowpoke to take her away, huh? Heard that was pretty common."

"Not here, it ain't."

Sam leaned over and said conspiratorially, "Tell me Freddy, where did you get Dolly, anyway?"

Freddy became very suspicious and replied, "None of your damned business."

Suddenly, Freddie realized that it was Sam's business as he stared down the barrel of Sam's Colt Peacemaker with its hammer pulled back.

"Yes, it is my business, you bastard. Dolly's real name was Cora Short, and she was my sister. Now, if you want to live

61

more than five minutes, you're going to answer some questions. And remember, I'm about a hair-trigger mad away from shooting you anyway. I know where you buried her. Now, who brought her in here?"

Freddy was terrified, and his hands were at his shoulders with his palms facing Sam as he replied in a shaking voice, "I don't know. I never seen them before. They just came in and offered me her services."

Sam wasn't sure he was lying or not as he snarled, "You paid for my sister, didn't you, Freddie? Then those bastards told her that they had her daughter as a threat to keep her here and you knew that. But you didn't care that they had kidnapped her and her daughter. You didn't mind one bit that she was an innocent victim.

"If you had one tiny drop of human compassion in you, you would have let her go; but no, you had a pretty, young woman to add to your collection, and now you claim you don't know who they were. Well, Freddie I'm getting a little shaky holding this Colt in your face. It's a heavy gun, you know. Well, how about if you tell me who this whore punching cowboy that killed my sister is?"

"I don't know his name or nothin'. I only know that he works out at the Bar C."

"And where is the Bar C?"

"North of here, about six miles. You must have passed it on your way in. It's on the east side."

Sam suddenly noticed that Freddie was looking over his left shoulder and glanced up at the mirror behind the bar in time to spot a fat man lifting his pistol into position.

Sam dropped to the floor, rolled, then turned to the threat as the man was cocking his hammer, and fired twice before the back shooter pulled his trigger voluntarily. When the fat man did reflexively pull his trigger, he was falling backwards, and his pistol went off, the bullet punching a hole into the ceiling as he dropped.

Sam then continued his roll and popped up on his right knee as Freddie was bringing a shotgun to bear. He quickly dove to his right as the shotgun blew a table and two chairs to pieces.

Freddie was preparing to drop to safety behind his heavy bar, but wasn't fast enough as Sam quickly put three rounds into Freddie, the .44s doing massive damage, all of them placed in a four-inch diameter circle in the middle of his chest. He stumbled back against his cash drawer and slid to the floor. Sam then turned around to ensure that the fat man was down, finding him lying in a large pool of blood.

Sam stood, then walked behind the bar and looked down at Freddie; his eyes stared lifelessly at the keg of beer under the bar. He wasn't going to be running any whores any longer; unless it was in hell.

The smoke still hung in the room as three women in various stages of undress boiled from the upstairs hallway and looked at the scene in horror.

Sam caught sight of them and gestured for them to come downstairs, and after a few moments of hesitation, they began stepping down the stairs as if they were sleep walking.

Sam was surprised that none of the women seemed older than thirty. Usually, in small towns like this, if they had any saloon girls, they'd be over forty and looked older.

"You killed Freddie!" exclaimed Trixie.

"Not my choice, ma'am. That fat man over by the door tried to put one in my back. I saw him in the mirror and took him down. But then Freddie, who could have just let it go, took it upon himself to try to blast me with the shotgun. Look at that table and you can see where his shots went. He wanted me to be that way, but he missed, and I didn't. By the way, who was that fat man, anyway."

"That was Freddie's cousin. He used to show up every few days and ask Freddie to make us give him a free one," answered Trixie.

Sam glanced over at the grossly obese body and said, "I'm sorry that you had to deal with that. It's a hideous thought."

"The law's gonna come down real hard on you, mister," warned one of the other whores.

"I don't think so," Sam answered as he showed her his badge.

"So, what are we gonna do now?" asked the third, as tears began to well in her eyes.

"Trixie mentioned that issue a little while ago. What options to you have? Do any of you have any relatives? Do you have someplace you can go away from here?"

Each shook her head before Trixie answered, "You could take us with you."

"*Excuse me*?" Sam exclaimed.

Now that was an answer he hadn't expected.

"You owe us, Sam. You took away our livelihood. It wasn't much, but it was all we had."

"I realize that killing Freddie put you all in an awkward position."

Trixie exploded as she shouted, "Awkward position! Is that what you call it? We're now stuck in this damned town with no money and no way of making any."

Sam awkwardly suggested, "Well, couldn't you go into business on your own? You know, take over this place and then you wouldn't have to pay Freddie. You'd keep all the money yourselves."

Trixie blew that idea apart, saying, "Sam, you're either naïve or an idiot. Freddie owned this place. Someone else will buy it and we'd be right back where we started, if not worse. And that's only if the new owner decides to keep a bunch of whores around. He may decide to be all prim and proper and get rid of us."

Sam was really in a quandary, so he said, "Okay. How about this? I'll take any of you that want to come with me to my ranch about twenty-three miles north of here. You can relax and take it easy until we come up with a permanent solution. How's that?"

One of the other women asked sharply, "You want to turn your ranch into a whore house?"

Sam was horrified and said, "No! No! Nothing like that. You could just stay there for a while and almost vacation until we figure something out."

The women consulted for almost a minute before Trixie turned to Sam and said, "Okay. We'll try it out and see how it works. How can we get there?"

"Do you have any horses or wagons?"

"No."

"Well, I'll tell you what. I'll go down to the livery and see what I can rustle up. Could I ask a favor, though?"

"Maybe," answered Trixie.

"Could you all go upstairs and wipe off the makeup and look a little less like painted ladies?"

That struck them as hilariously funny for some reason, and Sam didn't understand why, but they all turned around and headed upstairs as they continued to giggle.

Sam wondered what he had gotten himself into, but he knew he couldn't turn them out. He also knew that Trixie and maybe the others knew more about Cora and the men who brought her here and that could prove invaluable. They could point out the whore-puncher, too, and Sam fully intended to visit the bastard and bring justice to his sister and those three other young women one way or the other.

He turned and scanned the still barroom, saw that the two drunks were still passed out, having never even noticed the gunfire. Sam went to the front of the establishment, closed and locked the full doors, then crossed the floor and exited the back door.

He walked down the street to the livery and on entering, shouted, "Anybody home?"

"Over here, mister," came a voice from the loft.

Sam looked up and said, "Howdy, need to see what you have available for sale or rent."

"Well," said the liveryman as he stepped down from the ladder to the loft, "what you lookin' for?"

"I need a wagon, but I'd settle for a horse or a mule."

"I have one horse for sale, and that's it."

"Can I see him?"

"Her. She's a mare. About nine years old. Not too bad."

"That's a pretty weak sales pitch."

"Always try to be honest."

"That's a good way to be. Let's see the lady."

He was led to the front stall and shown a mare that looked a little older than nine, but not too bad. He checked the shoes and the teeth.

"How much are you asking?"

"Twenty-five, but I'll throw in a blanket, saddle and bridle if you make it fifty."

"Make it forty-five dollars and you have a deal."

"That'll work."

Sam paid him and said, "I'll be back in a few minutes and pick her up. I need to go and pick up some things at the store."

"I'll have her ready to go for ya," he replied.

Sam gave a wave and headed to the mercantile.

When he entered, he was greeted by the same jovial voice.

"Back already?"

"Yup. Things got a little dicey over at Waxman's, so I need to get some things."

Sam walked back to the clothing section and bought three small union suits, three pairs of pants and three shirts then headed for the counter.

"Kinda odd purchases for hitting the road."

"I'll be honest with you. I came down from Denver to investigate the disappearance of my sister and her daughter. I found out they had been kidnapped and my sister was brought down here to work in the whore house while they kept her daughter hostage. She was murdered by some cowboy last month. When I was questioning the barkeep, some fat man tried to shoot me in the back. I turned and got him, and then the bartender tried to blast me with his shotgun but missed, so I shot him. I now have two dead bodies and three very upset whores to deal with. I closed the bar doors, but the ladies asked me to get them out of here because they had no other choice. These clothes are for them."

"I heard the gunfire, but it wasn't that unusual in that hole. Are you gonna notify the law?"

Sam flashed his badge, bringing a big smile to the proprietor.

"That's good. Maybe we'll burn the place to the ground. I'll notify the mayor. We'll take care of the bodies, and we appreciate you removing that blight on our town."

"Thanks for your help. The name's Sam Brown, by the way."

"John Arden."

Sam shook his hand as he said, "Well, John, I've got to be heading back. I'll notify Sheriff Grant."

Sam took his purchases and returned to the livery finding the mare saddled and ready to go.

"Thanks. By the way, what's her name?" he asked as he accepted the reins.

"Emma."

"Good name."

Sam led Emma down the alley and stopped behind the bar, tied the mare to a post and entered the bar through the back door.

The women were already cleaned up and sitting in chairs. Their dresses still indicated their profession, though, showing a lot of cleavage, bare arms, and more leg than he'd ever seen. He had a hard time prying his eyes loose, but managed, especially after already seeing Trixie's impressive display.

He looked at the three clean, and very pretty faces, and said, "Ladies, all I could get was a horse, so what we'll have to do is to double up. The next question is when do you want to leave? We can start now, but we may have to camp one night, or we can wait and leave in the morning. It's your choice."

Trixie seemed to be the leader of the group and replied, "We'd rather leave. But how can we ride in these dresses?"

Sam put the pants, union suits and shirts on the table.

"I picked these up at the store. By the way, the store owner said they'd take care of the bodies and the bar after we're gone. Go ahead upstairs and get changed. Are you hungry?"

"Sam, we're always hungry. Freddie never gave us anything to eat so we didn't get fat."

Sam automatically glanced at their nicely formed figures that didn't need any modifications and asked, "Did you want to go to the café after you're changed, or do you want me to go and get something for you?"

Trixie answered, "They won't be too happy to see us there. Can you just bring us something?"

"Sure. You all go ahead and get changed. I should be back in a few minutes."

The three women ran up the stair with their clothes and Sam unlocked the front door and headed to the café.

Once he arrived, he asked if he could get a few plates, some knives and forks, and a pot with a large order of the stew that he had eaten for lunch. The waitress said it would be no problem and asked about the gunfire that she had heard from Waxman's. As Sam explained what had happened, she listened with raised eyebrows and when he finished, she smiled and said she'd be right back with his order.

She brought out the big tray just two minutes later, Sam gave her three dollars, which was more than enough, then walked across the street to the saloon, and entered the back door. The women were back down on the floor, sitting around the table.

Sam was stunned by the change in appearance. Once the paint was removed and the cheap dresses were gone, he was looking at three very attractive young ladies.

He brought the tray to the table and set it down in the center. He gave each woman a bowl, a spoon and a knife, so they could put spread butter on their biscuits. There was a ladle in the pot.

"Go ahead and serve yourselves, ladies. I'll get some water."

As they began dividing up the food, he went behind the bar to get some glasses and was surprised to see some bottles of sarsaparilla, so he took four bottles and walked back.

"If you'd prefer water, I'll go back, but these look pretty good."

Evidently, they didn't know that the sarsaparilla existed either because they all smiled.

"We'll take those, Sam," Trixie said as he set them on the table while one of the other women was ladling out the stew.

Soon, the women were eating like they were starved and maybe they were. He simply sipped his drink and watched them devour the stew and biscuits, with short breaks to drink the sarsaparilla.

When their bowls were empty, they began spooning the remaining stew into the bowls for a second helping. Sam smiled when he noticed that they ensured each had equal servings.

71

When they finished, one of the women belched loudly, and they all began giggling like schoolgirls as Sam just grinned.

They all looked at Sam with contented faces when they calmed down.

"Well, ladies, if you've finished, I'll take these back to the diner. If you have anything you want to bring with you, go ahead and bring it along. Trixie, can you go out the back door and bring the mare around the front? My horse is already tied there."

"I'll do that," she replied as she stood.

Sam dumped the utensils into the pot and picked up the almost clean bowls, walked out the back door and carried them across the street. When he exited the café, he saw the three women standing next to the mare and Cump.

"Have you decided on the seating arrangements?" Sam asked as he approached.

Trixie said, "I'll ride with you and Cleo and Jez will take the mare."

"Fine. Her name is Emma, by the way. Front or back, Trixie?"

"I'll take the front."

"Okay, ladies, let's mount up."

Sam climbed on Cump and put a hand down for Trixie as Cleo mounted Emma first and helped Jez aboard. Sam pulled Trixie onto Cump and she wiggled herself into position in front of him, making Sam more than a bit uncomfortable having her so close.

But they had to go, so Sam turned Cump away from Waxman's and the two double-loaded horses walked out of Hinkley.

As they walked the horses north, Sam asked Trixie, "Trixie, may I ask you a question?"

"As close as we are, I'm surprised you haven't asked before."

Sam had no idea what she was talking about as he asked, "What's your real name?"

It wasn't the question she was obviously expecting, so there was a short delay before she replied, "Grace Felton."

"That's a good name. It suits you much better than Trixie."

"I had it a lot longer."

"What are the other women's names?"

"Cleo is Carol Early, and Jez is Julia Crook."

Sam sighed and said, "That's terrible."

"What's terrible?" Grace asked as she turned to look at Sam, just inches away.

"Taking away your freedom and your lives is bad enough but trying to take away who you are is even worse."

"We're whores, Sam. We don't need real names."

"Grace, you are not whores. You may have been forced by circumstances to have to do that, but all three of you are young and pretty women who still have your lives to live."

"What are you, a preacher or something?"

"No. I was a sheriff for eight years, so I've seen the worst of people. I've also seen some that I thought were doomed to be in trouble for the rest of their lives change. Now, I don't even see the slightest bad in any of you. I watched you eating and was impressed when I noticed that you shared the stew. No one was out for herself. You watched out for each other."

"We have to. But you miss the point. We could dress like princesses, but we were whores. No decent man would go near us now."

"You are wrong about that, Grace. If a man won't have anything to do with you, then he's not a decent man in the first place."

"How about you? Would you marry one of us knowing we had been had by half the men in the county? Men who could see us on the street and know what we look like naked? Could you live with that?"

"I could live with anything if I loved the woman. It's really kind of a strange thing in our society. If a man is a womanizer and beds every female he sees, he's admired and called a woman's man. If a woman has relations with one man not her husband, she's a tart or a whore, or any of dozens of other names you could think of."

"I've never looked at it that way."

"Most people don't, Grace. That's why it stays that way."

They rode on in silence for another hour. Sam estimated they were ten miles from Hinkley.

He had been impressed by Grace's quick mind and forceful demeanor. This was no shrinking violet and wanted to talk to her more but had hesitated because he didn't want to make her uncomfortable. Besides, he needed to talk to them all as a group.

"Ladies, I think we should stop and set up camp. We're still fifteen or so miles out and at our current pace, that would put us in around one o'clock in the morning. We can press on or camp for the night. Which would you prefer?"

Carol, a.k.a. Cleo, replied, "I'm getting kind of sore, to tell the truth and don't think I can handle much more saddle time. I'm not used to riding horses this long."

Grace was going to make some comment about riding cowboys versus riding horses but decided against it for some reason.

"Okay, folks, let head over to that copse of trees over on the right."

He angled Cump in that direction and Emma followed. Sam looked for a place that was hidden from the roadway, even though it was unlikely that anyone would pass this way late at night. They rode toward the trees and Sam was pleased to find a small stream near the stand of aspens.

He let Grace down gently, dismounted, then walked over to Emma and helped each of the other sore women to the ground. They all sat down under the trees while Sam brought the two horses down to the stream to drink.

When they finished, he led them back and hitched them near a heavy growth of grass, then removed his saddlebags and bedrolls and extra blankets. After he unsaddled the horses, he set the saddles on the ground, hung his saddlebags over his shoulders and picked up the bedrolls and blankets.

He walked over to the trees and set his load down.

"Now dinner tonight won't be nearly as good as the stew you had earlier. I am the first to admit that one of my failings is that I am a horrible cook and even worse at baking. I never could make a decent biscuit, but I can build a fire."

The women all just looked up at him and smiled without comment.

He walked around gathering kindling and heavier branches, which were plentiful, and had a fire going in a short time, then put the grate across three heavy rocks and went down to the stream to fill the coffee pot.

When he returned, Grace was going through the saddlebags, taking out cans of food. She handed the cans to Carol and Julia who walked to the fire.

"Can you open these, Sam?" Grace asked.

"I can do that, Grace," he replied with a smile as he took each can and opened each one with the can opener in his pocketknife.

Carol and Julia noticed he called her Grace.

Sam then looked at her and said, "Carol, will you and Julia like some coffee? I'll have to share my one cup, though."

"That's fine. Coffee will be great," replied Carol.

"I'd like some, too," answered Julia.

"I'll have to warn you, though. I didn't pack any sugar for this trip. Can you drink it black?"

"We all drink it black anyway, Sam," replied Grace.

"That's handy," he said as he took the steaming pot and poured the hot liquid into the tin cup and handed it to Julia.

She sipped it and handed it to Carol who did the same before passing it to Grace. After she had a few swallows, she gave it back to Sam who took a sip and started the cup for the second round.

Grace had added beans and corned beef to the mix and crumbled up some crackers and sprinkled in some salt. After a few minutes, she tasted the concoction and added more salt, then a few minutes later, she slid the pan onto the ground.

"The bean whatever-you-call-it is ready," she announced.

They all encircled the fry pan; Sam filled the coffee cup again and then stood, walked to the saddle and removed the canteen. When he returned to his seat, he removed the stopper and noticed that none had begun to eat.

"Go ahead, ladies, enjoy Grace's concoction. I'm sure it's better than I could have done."

"You try it first, Sam," said Grace.

"Okay," he said as he took the spoon and put a bite in his mouth.

It was surprisingly good considering the ingredients she had to work with.

He handed the spoon to Julia and said, "Grace, I have to tell you. That's amazing. Considering what little you had to work with, it's exceptional."

"You must be a seriously bad cook to believe that," she said, but Sam noticed the smile on her face.

"One thing you all will learn about me is that I never lie. If I thought it was terrible, I'd make some ubiquitous remark like 'that's different' or 'not bad'."

"You've never told even a little white lie?" asked Carol.

"It depends on how you define a lie."

"That's simple," said Julia, "a lie is something that isn't true."

"No, that's not how I view a lie. To me, a lie is an untruth spoken to benefit the speaker. For example, say my wife is getting a little plump and asks me if she's getting fat. Now, if I tell her the truth, she'll feel bad. If I tell her that she looks fine, she feels better. Now I don't benefit at all by telling her that, so I don't believe it's a lie. But if I expected to benefit from telling her that, then it is a lie."

"That's confusing, Sam," said Grace.

"Not at all. When you say something you know isn't true, just ask yourself if you hope to gain anything by telling it. If not, then it's not a lie."

"I'll think about it," she said, then asked, "So, do you have a wife? Plump or otherwise? Because if you do, there's going to be hell to pay when you show up with us."

"No, ma'am. No wife, no fiancé, nor girlfriend, either."

She looked at him curiously. Then it was Grace's turn to take a bite and she looked away.

The other women all agreed with Sam's evaluation of the beans.

———

After the dinner, Carol and Julia cleaned up because Grace had done the cooking.

Sam spread out the two bedrolls, then he put his slicker on the ground, covered it with a blanket and then added the second blanket.

"So, how are we handling the sleeping arrangements?" asked Grace, expecting Sam would want to be serviced by one of them despite his gentlemanly demeanor.

"That's up to you. Two get the bedrolls and one will get the blankets."

"What about you?"

"I'm keeping watch."

"Why?"

"We're reasonably close to the road and I like to play it safe."

"Is that one of your non-lies?" Grace asked with a smile.

"Could be," he replied with a grin.

"Won't you get cold?"

"Not really. I'm used to it. Just relax, get a good night's sleep and we'll head out in the morning. We'll get there by noon."

"Alright," she answered, then headed for the dying fire thinking that maybe he didn't like girls at all, and that would be a shame.

Sam watched her go and was glad she didn't push the point. It was going to be chilly tonight, and he hoped it wouldn't be as cold as the night he spent outside on the way from Boulder.

The women tucked into their temporary bedding and were soon sound asleep as Sam walked out to the road and looked both ways, but knew it was silly because he could see the same locations from the camp.

Then he began to think about Cora. *How could anyone be so cruel to someone so good?* For the first time in years, Sam fell to his knees and prayed. He prayed that Cora and Richard were together in heaven and that he would find Catherine, fulfilling Cora's last request. He asked God's help in finding the little girl and finding her safe.

Around two in the morning, Sam simply lay down on the ground with his head on the saddle and fell asleep.

———

He awakened as the predawn sky was brightening and sat up quickly, rubbing his stiff neck. It was definitely chilly, and his teeth were chattering as he began to walk around to get his blood pumping. He found some privacy nearby and breathed a sigh of relief before he returned to the camp.

He stepped past the sleeping women, began to relight the fire, and had it burning brightly in a few minutes, then walked down to the stream to fill the pot. He returned, set it on the grate, then he took out the frypan and laid it alongside the coffee pot, cut some slices of bacon and laid them in the frypan, then opened the last two cans of beans and waited.

The scent of frying bacon woke the women as Sam knew it would. While they were still warm, he walked to each, handed her a strip of bacon, then returned to the campfire and chopped up some more, smaller pieces of bacon and dropped them into the pan. After they had cooked, he dumped the two cans of beans into the greasy pan and stirred the mix.

The coffee was ready, and the women finally slipped out of their assorted sleeping arrangements.

"Sam, may we have some privacy?" Grace asked as she smiled.

"Oh, excuse me. I'll get out of your way."

Sam jogged to the road and checked both routes. Then he concentrated on the mountains to the west and noticed how beautiful they were in the morning sun. He had never really paid attention before because they were always there, but now found it mesmerizing.

He was broken from his reverie by the touch of a gentle hand on his shoulder, then turned and saw a smiling Grace.

"We've been calling you to tell you it was safe to come back and eat."

"Okay. I was just looking at the mountains. You know I lived in Boulder for eight years and never once paid attention to such extravagant beauty."

Grace followed his gaze and said, "Neither have I. But you're right."

"Come, let's eat," he said as she removed her hand.

They completed their circular-sharing breakfast and coffee and then Sam began getting the horses ready for their final fifteen miles. The women were all sore, but anxious to finish the journey.

After they had mounted and started back, Grace, her face still facing forward said, "It was cold last night, Sam."

"A bit, but not too bad."

"You could have shared with me or one of the other women."

"No. That wouldn't be right. Besides, I wouldn't have gotten any sleep at all."

Grace laughed and realized that he liked girls after all, then she asked, "How come you haven't asked about Cora?"

"Last night I believe that you were all too tired and sore to talk about it, and I want to ask all three of you at the same time, so you can share information and build on it. For example, maybe one of you will remember that one of them had red hair and that will trigger another to confirm it and add that he had a receding hairline. That, and I want to talk about Cora's death as little as possible."

"I understand. Now, can I talk about something else?"

"Anything."

"I'm getting really sore already. How long do we have to go?"

"About ten miles, or two hours."

"That's going to be hard."

"Hold onto my neck."

"What?"

"Just hold onto my neck and hold tight."

She did, and as soon as her grip was firm, Sam slid his hand under her thighs and lifted her off the saddle and swung her sideways before lowering her to Cump's neck.

"You can let go now. Just hold onto the saddle horn with your left hand."

"Thank you! This is so much better."

"Hold up, Julia," he said as he held up his hand.

Julia reined Emma to a halt as Sam pulled Cump to a stop and dismounted.

He stepped over to the mare and plucked Carol from the horse and set her down. Then he lifted Julia from the saddle and turned her sidesaddle. Because all the women were petite, Julia's behind fit the western saddle reasonably well. He then lifted Carol and placed her sidesaddle just in front of the saddle horn, as he had Grace. Then he handed the reins back to Julia.

"Better?"

"Much," said Julia. Carol just sighed as she wriggled into the seat.

"Let's head to the barn," he said as he returned to his horse.

Sam mounted Cump behind Grace and both horses resumed their journey.

————

It was around eleven o'clock when they topped the small rise before the Circle S and Sam noticed that the pastures held a small herd of around two hundred head of cattle.

"Looks like Dan Grant's deputy paid the Diamond M a visit," he thought.

"Sam, that's a pretty ranch," said Grace.

"I'll explain everything when we get in."

The two horses entered the access road and soon reached the front yard of the ranch house. Sam lowered Grace to the ground where she stretched and rubbed her abused bottom.

Sam stepped down and helped Carol and Julia down from Emma and both mimicked Grace's actions and Sam remembered the first time that he had ridden a horse for longer than an hour and empathized.

"You can go into the house and relax while I take care of the horses."

"Can I see the barn?" asked Grace.

"Sure. Come along."

"We'll come, too," said Carol, "We'd rather walk than sit for a while."

Sam laughed and replied, "I can understand that."

He walked Cump and Emma to the barn and saw a crowded corral out back. In addition to Glass and Coal, there were four more horses and two mules, and when they entered the barn, they found a wagon and a collection of tack in the wagon bed.

"Well, I'll be," he said as he tilted his Stetson back.

"What?" asked Grace as she stood beside him.

"When I left to go to Hinkley a couple of days ago, the only animals on the place were my three horses. There were no cattle, no horses and no mules or wagon. I had mentioned to Sheriff Grant that some Star M riders stopped by and told me to move on, so I guess they were told to put everything back that they borrowed."

"Maybe this explains it, "said Carol as she held up a note, "It was in the wagon."

She handed it to Sam, and he read:

Sorry about the mix-up. I had been told that the ranch had been abandoned. The deputy explained that it belonged to you. I had my men return all the stock and gear that had been removed.

Sorry about Richard. He was a good man.

Chuck Martin

85

"Yup. It sure does," he said as he gave it to Grace so she could read it.

She read the note and handed it to Carol who scanned it and gave it to Julia.

He unsaddled Cump and Emma and brushed both horses, assisted by the three women. When it was done, he walked Cump and Emma to the neighboring corral and set them loose among the crowd. Sam carried out a bundle of hay, cut the binding wire and then pumped the trough full again before they headed to the house.

Once in the ranch house, Sam gave them a quick tour before they took seats in the kitchen.

"Now, did you want to eat, or did you want me to start explaining what's going on?"

"I could eat," answered Carol as the other women nodded.

"Can I assume that none of you want to eat my cooking again in your lifetimes?"

"That would be a good guess," answered Julia with a smile.

They snickered and set about cooking lunch.

Sam took the time inspecting the house to ensure his weapons were still there and was pleased to find everything where he had left it. Nothing in the house was disturbed, which meant that the Diamond M hands had kept their borrowing to the outside.

He also checked that the three beds were still made and ready for the women to use. While doing his inspection, he thought about how he would go about finding Catherine. As much as he'd like to go racing off to begin the search, he knew that it would be bad idea. Whoever had her was keeping her safe. They may not be aware that Cora was dead yet and he would have to come up with a plan to bring her home. The three women were at least safe and could stay as long as necessary. He was just not sure where they could go in the long term.

He returned to the kitchen and took a seat before lunch was served.

As they ate, Grace's cooking skills continued to impress him, and Sam wondered about their past lives. Maybe the same group that took Cora and Catherine had taken them as well, but for now, the links to the murderers and kidnappers was tenuous at best.

After lunch, they were all gathered in the main room at the front of the house.

"Ladies, I'd like to give you some background on what happened and why I had to find my sister and my niece. After that, I'll need to ask you about how you wound up there and what you could tell me about the men that brought Cora to Waxman's."

The women nodded, so Sam continued.

"A few days ago, I was the sheriff in Boulder, and I'd been there for almost eight years. There was an attempted robbery at the bank that I ended by shooting the three robbers with my shotgun. All three survived and the money they had stolen was returned, but the bank president, a member of the county commission, was upset because some shotgun pellets struck his building. He and I had words and I tossed my badge and left.

"I had planned on visiting my sister and her husband on the way out, but found the house deserted. No one had lived here for over six months, and I had no idea what had happened to them. I went to Denver to get some information, and when I went to the land office, I found that they had not paid the taxes due earlier this year. I went to the bank and found their account had not been accessed since early December.

"At the sheriff's office, Sheriff Grant told me that they had found my brother-in-law, Richard Short, dead in the front yard with a single .44 caliber bullet in his back fired at close range that same month, but no one knew where Cora or Catherine were. They had searched but couldn't find anything. I told the sheriff about going to Hinkley and he made me a temporary deputy. He'd heard about me in Boulder, so he knew I'd follow the law."

"How did you know to come to find me?" asked Grace.

"That's probably the oddest thing about my search of the house. On the wall in their bedroom, just by the door, someone had scrawled, 'For a good time, see Trixie in Hinkley'. It made no sense then and it makes no sense now. I knew it was either a trap or someone was just being stupid, so I gambled because it was all I had, and went to Hinkley.

"But thinking about that message, now I think that there may be another reason for it being there. I think it's possible that one of the men who had been assigned to kill everyone, felt remorse about taking a young woman and her child away. He left that as a clue to send someone down to find her. If I had been here two months ago, I could have rescued Cora."

Sam paused to keep his emotions in check. It ate at his soul whenever he thought of his living, vibrant sister and his failure to save her from being killed.

He opened his mouth to continue the story, then said, "Hold on. I'll be right back," before he quickly rose and trotted into the kitchen.

He reached the sink, started the pump gushing and took a double handful of water and splashed it over his face. The cold water helped him to regain his composure and hide the tears that were beginning to well up in his eyes. He sighed, took a towel. dried his face and returned.

Once he reached his chair, he sat down and took a deep breath.

"Sorry. Anyway, after reading the message, I knew I had to go to Hinkley, so I stashed most of my weapons in the house and then set out. You know what happened in Hinkley. But there is another problem with this whole situation. I need to know who wanted to have the family killed and who they hired to do it. If I can't find that, then Catherine will never be safe, I need to know the motive behind the murder and kidnapping.

"At first, I thought it might be a simple land grab by a neighboring rancher, but I'm pretty sure that's out. I know that it wasn't robbery, because I found their small stash of money. But when I found the stash, I also found a letter to Richard from his father.

"It seems that his family owned a shipping company in St. Louis. In the letter, his father warned Richard of a greedy, ruthless cousin who was trying to gain control of the company. I'm reasonably convinced that he is the man behind all this. I'd like nothing more than to go to St. Louis, find him and blow a hole through him, but that wouldn't help me find Catherine. And it wouldn't it help her if her only relative isn't around to protect her until she is old enough to claim her inheritance. So, that's where I am right now. If you don't mind, and I know it may be painful, and for that I apologize, but I need to know

89

how each of you wound up in Waxman's and then we'll talk about how Cora got there."

Sam then walked to the desk where he picked up a paper pad and pencil, then set them on the table with the pencil in his hand ready to take down pertinent facts.

Once Sam was ready, Carol began, saying, "I've been there the longest, almost two years. I was living in Denver, if you can call it living. My husband, Alfred, was working in a local timber mill and was killed in an accident, but they didn't tell me how. I couldn't afford the rent for our small place, so I looked for a job, and I answered an ad for a housekeeper in the Rocky Mountain News.

"When I arrived, there were dozens of women waiting to fill the position, and many were in similar circumstances to mine. To be honest, I wasn't as well dressed as some, but I was prettier than most. There was a man doing interviews, and what was unusual was that he wasn't asking about our housekeeping skills at all. He only wanted to know if we were married or had children, and I had neither. I was surprised when I was told at the end of the interviews that I had the job and was to report the next morning.

"I was excited and thought my worries were over, but when I got there the next morning, two men met me in the parlor and took me to the back and put me in a carriage that was almost as big as a stagecoach. They stayed with me and threatened to cut my throat if I made any noise and looked like they meant it, too.

"It was early in the morning when we left and for the entire duration of the ride, they fondled me, grabbed me and told me to get used to it. It was terrifying. We were in the carriage for five hours until we stopped at Hinkley. Then they pulled to a stop in front of Waxman's and walked me inside. Freddie saw them coming, looked me over, then paid them. I think it was three hundred dollars. They left and the first thing he said to me was, 'You're gonna have to work that off, girlie.' And I did. It was horrible at first and then you just get numb to it, but you have to do what Freddie said or you'd pay the price."

Sam asked quietly, "Can you describe the two men that took you there, Carol?"

"I can see them today as clearly as I did then. The first one was average sized, maybe a little shorter than average, around five feet and seven inches. He was only a couple of inches taller than me. He was about thirty and had a thin face that reminded me of a rat. He had a thin mustache and long sideburns that weren't bushy. He had dark eyes and a thin nose, and he talked funny, too. He sounded like he came from back east.

"The second man was taller, almost six feet. He was average in build and was older, too, about forty. His hair was already graying and thin on top. His face was boring with nothing that made him noticeable. He did have a small scar above his right eyebrow. When he was grabbing me, I noticed that he was wearing a wedding ring."

"Thanks, Carol. You should have been a Pinkerton agent," said Sam as Carol smiled.

It was Julia's turn, so she said, "My story is a lot like Carol's. I arrived there about six months after she did and had answered an ad for a domestic. I had been orphaned when I was eleven and was put in an orphanage in Denver and stayed there for seven years. When I turned eighteen, I was turned out and for two years, I worked at a clothing factory making worker's pants. It was numbing work.

"When I saw the ad, just like Carol, I hoped for a way out. I answered the ad and the interview process was exactly as she described it."

Sam interrupted, and asked, "Julia, was it the same house?"

"No. But it was on the same street that Carol had been taken from. When I was told that I had been hired, I was more than relieved, I was euphoric. I almost bounced to the house for my first day. Then things happened almost the exactly as they had to Carol. I believe it was the same two men. It was almost the same process, even to the words spoken by Freddie when I arrived."

"Thank you, Julia. You're helping a lot."

Finally, Grace's turn arrived, and she said, "My story is different. It's a lot like what happened to Cora. I was living on my father's ranch, and it wasn't doing well. Our last cowhand had quit because we couldn't afford to pay him. Our herd was down to seventy-three skinny cattle and it looked like we were going to lose our ranch when three men rode in one morning. They asked to speak to my father about selling the ranch, and he was pleased because he knew he was going to lose it anyway, so he invited them in. I was in the kitchen, putting on some coffee for our guests when I looked back down the hallway and saw one of them simply pull his pistol out and shoot my father in the head without saying a word.

"I screamed and ran into the room, even though I knew that my father was dead. It was a foolish thing to do. I should have run out of the back door and tried to get a horse. Anyway, the two that didn't have guns out grabbed me. Then I don't remember anything for a while. I think one of them hit me in the head. I woke up in the carriage with the same two men whom Carol and Julia had described. One of them, the smaller of the two, reached over and said, 'Well, girlie, now that your head's better we can get to know each other better.' Then they began groping me and laughing for the rest of the ride. We got to Waxman's after dark. After that it was the same story as theirs."

"Grace, the three men that killed your father. Were they different men than the two that took you to Waxman's?"

"Yes. I had never seen them before."

Sam looked at all three women and asked, "The four that brought Cora in. Were they familiar?"

Grace answered, "The smaller man with the eastern accent was one of the two that brought all three of us to that place. Two of the others I hadn't seen before, but one of them was with the three that shot my father."

"Can you describe the three men and let me know which one shot your father and which one you saw again in Waxman's with Cora?"

"Vividly. The man that shot my father was younger, no older than twenty-five. He was very short, about my height, five feet and four inches. He wore very unusual boots. They looked like they were made from snakeskin, and he had a band of snakeskin around his black hat. He had light hair, almost white, and dressed in mostly black and had a regular mustache. He had almost girlish hands.

"The second of the men that came to our house looked like just a regular cowhand with medium height and build. He had no scars or anything, but he had a white streak in his black hair running from the top of his head to his left ear. The one that I saw in both places was easy to recall. He was about thirty, tall, about your height, but a lot heavier. He had a noticeable belly and wore two guns. The guns had bright white handles. His face was round, almost pig-like, and had an unusual way of laughing, too. He snorted and it made his face look even more like a pig. He had brown hair that he wore long in the back, almost to his shoulders. That's about it."

"Thank you, Grace. That is an outstanding description. By the way, did you ever find out what happened to your ranch?"

"No. I haven't been out of Waxman's in over a year. He never let any of us out. The ranch was the Slash F. It's nearby, but probably owned by someone else after the taxes weren't paid."

"Can any of you recall anything that was said by any of them that might help?"

Grace replied, "Not that I recall, but Cora said something that was interesting to me. She said that when the four men took her, one said 'Soapy isn't going to be happy with this.' Then another said, 'Well, Soapy doesn't have to know, does he. It's quick money and it's all for us.' She said that they had been ordered to kill the whole family, but I guess that one saw money to be made and another probably got weak kneed about killing a woman and her child."

"That's very good, Grace. Do you know if Cora was brought down in the carriage like the rest of you were?"

"No, she wasn't. She told me that they rode down to Hinkley with one carrying her and the other carrying Catherine. They threatened to drop Catherine on her head if she made any trouble."

"It sounds like you three were abducted by some sort of system that Soapy Smith uses to supply whore houses in the region. By taking single women with no connections, there would be no one to complain. But the crew that were sent to eliminate Richard and his family included one member of his girl supply crew who saw an opportunity to make some money. He had to head south so Soapy didn't get wind. That would mean Catherine is somewhere south of here. I'm beginning to see the connections, now."

"Who's Soapy Smith?" asked Carol.

"I'm surprised that you wouldn't be familiar with the name. He's a gangster; a thug who operates in Denver, running cathouses, saloons and strong-arm crews that engage in all sorts of crime. I'll bet that my brother-in-law's cousin, Ferguson Short, hired him to eliminate Richard and any of his children."

"He'd do that to his own family?" asked a stunned Julia.

"I've seen people do bad things to family members for a lot less than a big company."

Sam sat back and stared at his words. He could see the tendrils but was unsure of how to untangle them.

"What are we going to do now, Sam?" asked Grace.

He looked up from the pad and replied, "Good question. I have enough time to go to Denver and tell the sheriff what happened in Hinkley. I'd rather that he heard it from me than someone else. Now, tomorrow, ladies, we'll need to take the wagon to Denver and go on a spending expedition. I was thinking of buying a wagon and a team, but that situation has resolved itself. Now, who will be coming along?"

"We can't go into Denver. Especially dressed like this," said Julia.

95

"I think you all look quite nice, by the way. But I understand your concern. My sister's clothes are in the big bedroom. Go ahead and check out what will fit while I'm in Denver. I should be back in three hours. Okay?"

"Okay," replied Grace.

"When I get back, I'll tell you what we'll be doing tomorrow and the day after."

"Alright," answered Carol.

Sam smiled at them all and commented, "I just want to know how grateful I am for the help you've provided that will aid in the recovery of my niece."

He stood, then waved and exited through the front door, headed for the corral and found Coal. He thought Cump could use the break. He led him into the barn, saddled the black horse then headed down the access road and took a right toward Denver.

———

In the house, the women stayed in the big room, talking.

"Well, Grace," began Carol, "you've been closer to him than we were. What do you think is going to happen?"

"I'm not sure. I know he is determined to get his niece back and is heartbroken about his sister. Did you see how he reacted just talking about her? Neither of you noticed, but last night, while you were sleeping, I wasn't. I laid there like I was asleep because it bothered me that he was going to sleep outside in the cold. I watched him, and he walked toward the road and then fell to his knees and prayed for a while. Now, he doesn't strike me as a particularly religious man, which makes sense if he was a sheriff for ten years. I'm sure was praying for his sister. But I think the first thing he'll do is go to the Bar C and find the whore-puncher. I think he's going to kill him."

"Good," said Julia.

"No, Julia, that's bad," said Grace, "If he kills him, then he'd go to jail and not find his niece, but we probably can't stop him. We'll see if we can do anything to keep him from doing it. I just don't know what he'll do with us, either. No one wants a bunch of whores around that aren't acting as whores."

"You don't believe what he says about us being women and not whores?"

Grace sighed and replied, "I think he means well. I think he's about the most honest and considerate man I've ever met. But saying something and doing it are two different things. As soon as he figures out that he'd be an outcast by keeping us here, we'll be on the road."

"What about the shopping trip?" asked Carol.

"I have no idea what his plans are. We'll have to see. But, just like before, we don't have any control over anything. We just need to wait. But at least we have a good man around instead of Freddie."

Carol grinned and said, "It sounds like you're falling for Mister Brown, Grace."

"What good would it do for any of us to fall for any man? We are what they made us, Carol."

"Maybe, but I'm a little more optimistic than you are. I have to be. I must have hope that the rest of my life won't be worthless. I want a life, Grace. I had mine taken from me, and I want it back."

"Don't we all. Now, let's go see if there are any clothes that fit, and we can wear to Denver."

———

Sam made good time on the ride to Denver. Coal wanted to run, and he let big mare have her head. He stepped down at the sheriff's office at in the early afternoon and walked into the office.

"Afternoon, Sam," shouted Dan Grant from the back of the main office.

He was obviously just leaving his own office to add some coffee to his empty cup.

"Howdy, Dan. Got a few minutes?"

"Sure. Just let me fill my cup. This coffee's been sitting here all day, so it's probably thicker than molasses by now. Go ahead into my office."

Sam passed the sheriff and sat down in the same chair he had occupied just two days earlier.

Less than a minute later, Dan Grant passed him and sat down, taking a sip of his coffee followed by a grimace.

"Lord! This is terrible," he said before taking a second sip.

"What do you have, Sam?"

"Well, I went down to Hinkley yesterday to see what I could find, and I found plenty."

The sheriff leaned back in his chair and said, "Go ahead."

"I got there and after a wait, I went into Waxman's. I had to drink two flat, warm beers before Trixie showed up at my table; the one girl I needed to see. She invited me upstairs and I had to cough up two dollars to Freddie Waxman for the privilege. By the way, he was giving them all of ten cents of the fee for their services.

"Anyway, I went with her into her room and sat her down and asked about Cora. She began crying and told me that Cora was dead. She had been brought there six months earlier by four men and had been killed by some cowpoke working at the Bar C. The women called him the whore-puncher because when he was finished with them, he would haul off and punch them in the stomach for some reason."

The sheriff growled, "Bastard."

"He struck Cora so hard that he must have busted something inside of her. She was always a small woman and Freddie didn't even bother to get a doctor. He told her to get back to work and she died an hour later. They buried her behind the saloon. That reminds me, I need to have Richard's body returned to the ranch. I'm going to create a family plot for him and Cora when I get her body returned."

"I'll take care of it. Just let me know when you're ready."

"Thanks, Dan. After she told me what had happened, I said I was going to go down and see Freddie and she panicked, Dan. She was scared to death. Even though that bastard had treated her and the other girls worse than we would treat a dog, they were so desperately afraid of being thrown out in the street that she begged me not to kill him. I told her I was just going to talk to him and went downstairs.

"I pulled out my Colt persuader to make him give me information about the men that dropped Cora off, but he didn't know where they came from, or at least that was what he told me. I knew he was lying, but before I could go any further, I saw him glance over my shoulder. I looked in the mirror and saw a fat man drawing on me. I dropped and put two rounds into him, then Freddie unloaded his shotgun at me. I had already moved, so I put three rounds into Freddie. The women came downstairs and were all scared about their situation, so I got them some food, and the proprietor of the store across the street seemed genuinely happy that Freddie was gone. He said the town would take care of it. I told him I'd tell you what happened. So, here I am."

"What happened to the whores?"

"They're at my ranch."

Dan grinned and said, "That must be an interesting place."

"It's not like what you think, Dan. I brought them along initially because they had no other place to go. I had no idea what to do with them when we left Hinkley, but as I began talking to them and heard their stories, I realized that I had to help them. These are three young women, Dan, that were taken from their homes and sold into prostitution by Soapy Smith."

At the mention of Smith's name, the sheriff's ears perked up and his eyebrows followed suit.

"Did you just say Soapy Smith?"

"Cora had told Trixie, her real name is Grace Felton, by the way, that when she had been taken, one of the men reminded the leader that they were supposed to kill the whole family. The leader then said that there was money to be made by

100

bringing Cora to Waxman's and the other man replied that Soapy wouldn't be pleased and the response was 'what Soapy doesn't know won't hurt him.'."

"Too bad that's just hearsay. We could move on that son of a bitch otherwise."

"Well, I have an idea that may help you to get him. I'll talk to you about it later, but first, I intend on heading down to the Bar C and arrest our whore-puncher. Can you get me a John Doe warrant?"

"Do you want some help?"

"That depends. What's Orville Crandall like?"

"Kind of a cranky oldster, but honest."

"That's fine. When I tell him what happened, I think he'll be more than happy to give him up, unless he's kin."

"No. He hasn't got any kids; just cattle."

"Okay. I'm probably going to go down there in a couple of days."

Dan reached into his drawer and pulled out a folded sheet of paper and two sets of handcuffs.

"Here's your warrant, and you may need these. Be careful."

"You don't have to tell me. Too many times we walk into situations we think will be downright easy and they turn into nightmares. You know, the husband and wife having a loud disagreement and we show up to calm things down and the wife takes a swing at you with a butcher knife for interfering."

"Been there a few times myself."

"I'll keep you informed, Dan," Sam said as he rose.

They shook hands and Sam returned to Coal for the ride back to the ranch. Coal took a slower pace on the return trip as she had expended a lot of her energy on the way to Denver and Sam didn't want to tire her out.

As he rode, Sam realized he had told the sheriff about what had happened to Cora and it hadn't bothered him at all. He guessed it was because he was just giving a report to a fellow lawman and not a brother talking about his sister. Maybe he should try to stay in that frame of mind when he met the whore-puncher to keep from shooting the bastard.

Sam led Coal into the barn around just before dinnertime, and fifteen minutes later, he headed for the house. As he cleared the barn and saw the back porch, he was greeted by the sight of three very pretty young women in nice dresses.

He smiled as he drew closer and said, "Well, ladies, you are a sight for sore eyes. You are all quite stunning."

"This from a man who likes horses," joked Grace with a smile.

"Maybe. But only good-looking horses."

They were all laughing as they entered the house.

"So, how did your visit with the sheriff go?" Grace asked after they'd all taken seats in the front room.

"I have a John Doe warrant in my pocket for that cowpoke down on the Bar C. I'm planning on going down there the day after tomorrow and arresting him."

Grace was surprised, and asked, "You're going to arrest him?"

"Of course, I'm going to arrest him. If I shoved my shotgun into his gut and pulled the trigger, which is what I'd like to do, that would be murder. I'd go to jail, as I would deserve, maybe hanged, and then Catherine would have no one. None of you have met my niece, but she's so much like Cora, and has the same personality, too.

"I'm sure when Cora was with you, you never got to see my Cora; the one I spent every day of my life with until she went off with Richard. She was pure, unfiltered sunshine. She was so full of life that she sparkled and no matter how bad my mood was, when Cora came to see me, I'd feel happy again. I never knew how she did it, either, but I was always so grateful to have her as my sister. She was somber when our parents died, but the vitality, the spirit was still alive in her eyes."

Sam hung his head. He had to stop those memories. He took a deep breath and reminded himself to put his head into lawman mode.

He exhaled sharply, then looked up again before he said, "Anyway. I must save Catherine. I have to be here to tell her about her mother when she's old enough to understand. That's why I'll only arrest that bastard. I may not arrest him gently, but I'll bring him in to stand trial. Being hanged isn't enough for what he did to my Cora, or to you Grace, Julia, and Carol, but I'll give him a chance first. I want to hurt him like he hurt you, but I won't do it when he's in cuffs. I'll stand up toe-to-toe with him and beat him to a pulp."

"He's a big man, Sam. Even bigger than you," whispered Grace.

"It doesn't matter. I need to do this. Let him think he's going to get a chance to walk away. It doesn't matter how big he is. He can hit me all he wants, but it won't matter. When I bring him back to Denver, he'll be in pain, and it still won't be enough pain for what he did to innocent women. And I think of you all as just that; innocent women being put into that horrible situation."

None of the women commented. They wanted the whore-puncher to feel as much pain as possible just as Sam did. They were only concerned that Sam may be hurt worse than he believed he will be; and none of them considered themselves innocent, either.

"Sam?" asked Grace quietly, "What is going to happen to us? You know after you find Catherine?"

"Well," Sam answered softly, "I guess one of you will need to share a room with her until I can add on a couple of more bedrooms."

Sam could not have uttered a more surprising response.

"Sam, that's silly. Why would you have three whores around the house with a young girl?"

Sam exploded as he exclaimed, "Stop it! Stop it, all of you! Right now! I won't have it anymore! You aren't whores. You are young and very beautiful women. Catherine can learn from all of you, as I already have. I've been thinking about how to manage the living arrangements, but not for one second did I think about you going anywhere unless you chose to.

"This will be your home as long as you want it to be. You can help around the house. You can work with the animals. You can do anything you want to, but I never want to hear that word again. I've never met three finer women, outside of my sister, in my life. You are all very special. Don't make me angry again by thinking of yourselves that way."

"But Sam," said Carol, "this isn't even your ranch."

"Yes, it is. I found out when I arrived that Richard and Cora put my name on the deed. The clerk at the land office said people do that like a cheap last will. I think they did it because they were afraid that Richard's cousin would do something, and they wanted to protect Catherine. They also put my name on their account at the bank."

"So, you're serious about letting us stay here?" asked Julia.

"As serious as I can be. You'll be like aunts to Catherine, and a little girl needs the presence of women more than some clumsy man. I may love her, but it's not enough. Besides, I like having you around. As long as you realize that it's your future that makes you, not your past. So, promise me, from now on no more references to being whores or prostitutes or any other colorful synonym you can dream up. From here on, you are Grace Felton, Julia Crook, and Carol Early. You are my friends and you are staying with me to help me recover and care for my niece. Understood?"

"Yes, sir," they replied in unison.

"So? Who's cooking dinner?" he asked before three hands went up and they all laughed, including Sam.

With Sam in tow, the three women walked to the kitchen. The meal preparation was a pleasant time with the women taking turns needling Sam about his lack of culinary skills in even the rudimentary steps. He wasn't sure if they'd taken to heart what he'd just told them and knew it would take time, but he hoped that they'd spend that time at the ranch before they ventured back into Denver. He really did enjoy having them with him as they reminded him of the pleasure he had being with Cora. They were almost the same age as his sister would be and once removed from that hellhole, seemed to be happy. He didn't want to admit to himself that he was especially attracted to Grace, and not just because he'd seen more of her than the others. There was something special about her; something deep in her character that spoke to him.

Sam was eagerly awaiting the biscuits that Grace had just popped into the oven and wasn't disappointed an hour later when they were eating dinner.

"Sam, you can eat food other than biscuits, you know," teased Carol.

His mouth still full of biscuit, so he held up a finger until he swallowed.

"I know, but I always dreamed of biscuits like this. I must have tried making my own twice a month for ten years and barely wound up with dark brown crackers; and those were the good ones."

They laughed thinking he was making a joke, but he wasn't.

———

After dinner, Sam built a fire in the fireplace and everyone settled in the big room.

"Sam, you know this is going to be difficult for you," said Carol.

"I know. I think Catherine is being held in a ranch near Hinkley. How to get in and get her out of there will be the problem. I think I may have an idea, though."

"No, that's not what I meant," she clarified, "I mean you're still a young man, and, as you keep telling us, we are young women. We sometimes may not be fully clothed, like when we are bathing, for instance. There are times when you may be challenged, shall we say."

"I already have been, challenged, as you say. As you've obviously noted, you are all attractive women. It's not difficult to understand what effect all those bumps and curves have on a man. And, yes, despite all my flowery talk, I am still a man. I was just born that way, I guess. So, when I begin to notice a bit too much, I go to the kitchen, start the water flowing out of the pump and stick my head under the water. It gives me something else to think about. Why do you think my hair is wet all the time?"

That brought the women to a rocking level of hilarity.

Sam watched them as they laughed and was pleased to see them so comfortable already.

When they almost stopped, he said, "So, when you females are finished laughing at my pain, let's talk about tomorrow."

They finally were reduced to a few titters as they looked at him.

"Okay. Here's my basic plan. We leave in the morning around seven o'clock. Whoever wants to go can go. If you feel uncomfortable, I'll understand and that's fine. But when we get to Denver, I plan on taking the wagon to the grocery store to load up on things we might need. You will be a better judge of that. Once that's done, we head over to the clothing store, and I will go with you, but will have no idea what you'll need, except for heavy jackets, some good boots, some ladies' riding clothes and shirts, some gloves and a wide brimmed hat for each of you. Oh, and don't forget you'll need purses as well. After that, just head over to the female clothing section and go crazy. Buy whatever you want. I'm going to walk over to the hardware store to buy some manly items, so I don't turn too red. Take your time. Don't worry about money. I'll be back in an hour or so, and I doubt if you'll be done. Just make sure that the clerk understands the order will need to be crated up and loaded onto our wagon."

"Sam, why do we need so much?" asked Julia.

"Because there is a limited supply of clothing here and you'll need more for cooler weather when you're outside."

"But why dresses?"

"For when you may want to go to dances or the theater or just shopping in the future."

"Dances?" asked Carol.

"Well, I admit I'm not the greatest dancer in the county; I'm probably near the bottom, but if anyone would like to go, I'll take you and I'd be honored. But when we get back from shopping tomorrow, I'll show you my purchases. They'll be for you, too; just not as feminine."

Sam then asked, "Okay, who gets which bedroom?"

They looked at each other but didn't reply so Sam continued.

"The biggest bedroom was Richard's and Cora's. Catherine's room was the bedroom opposite. The last bedroom was the one I used when I came to visit."

Grace looked at him and asked, "Which one are you going to use?"

"None of them. I'm going to use the couch out here."

She furrowed her eyebrows as she asked, "We're not going through this again like we did on the ride, are we?"

"It's not really an issue, Grace. This way, each of you gets your privacy, and I get to stay out here and ogle all of you," he replied with a grin.

That may have elicited a giggle or two, but Grace wasn't buying it as she quickly said, "Sam, it's your house."

"No, Grace, it's our house. Besides, I'll be in and out for a while. Then, there's the clothing issue. I don't have much, and soon you'll each need room for the clothing you'll be buying tomorrow. I may have been flippant about the ogling comment, but it really doesn't matter to me. I really am just as comfortable out here on the couch."

The clothing argument had weight, so they eventually gave in and agreed.

After they'd all turned in for the night, Sam had to shift cushions and only managed to create a reasonably comfortable sleeping arrangement.

As he lay on the couch with his feet dangling off the edge, he stared into the dark ceiling and prayed silently for Cora and Richard.

When he finished, he whispered, "I'll find Catherine, Cora. Then I'll find those bastards who did this to you; every last one of them, including that cousin of yours, Richard. After the last bit of justice has been done, I'll do all I can to raise Catherine as I know you both would."

He closed his eyes, and as he thought about how he'd go about finding his precious niece, he finally succumbed to a deep sleep.

———

Early the next morning, as the women were preparing breakfast, Sam went out and brought the mules to the wagon and put them in harness. The wagon was in good shape; the grease was good, and the axles looked strong. He had them pull the wagon into the front yard, left it there, then he went back into the barn and saddled Glass. He hadn't been ridden in three days and was more twitchy than usual.

He only had his Colt and Winchester with him; and the Webley, of course. He walked back into the house and joined the women for breakfast. They ate quickly and cleaned the plates and cups. Sam enjoyed some of Grace's exquisite biscuits again, but had some bacon and eggs, too.

When the women followed Sam to the wagon, the question came up about who was going to drive. None had handled a team before, so Sam asked for a volunteer, and Carol was 'volunteered' by Grace and Julia.

Sam gave her a rudimentary class on handling the mules, and she proved to be an adept student, so the three women boarded the seat. It was a tight fit, even though all three women were small.

———

The trip to Denver was uneventful and they made good time considering they were limited to the speed of a mule-drawn wagon and Carol grew more comfortable handling the wagon as the miles passed. When they entered the city, Sam guided them to the grocery first where Sam had to strong-arm the mules to get the wagon to the loading area before the women stepped down, and they went inside.

The ladies wandered the well-stocked aisles and began piling up cans, canisters and boxes in a whirlwind of shopping. They added flour, sugar, coffee, a large ham, three slabs of bacon, four dozen eggs, and bags of onions and potatoes and also included many spices that Sam had never heard of, as well as baking ingredients that he had never used; which was probably a good thing.

When the order was complete, Sam paid for the order with a bank draft on his account and their items were packed into crates and loaded onto the wagon. It still wasn't noon when they left the greengrocer.

When the women were getting into the wagon, Sam approached and asked, "Where to next, ladies? Did you want to go shopping at the clothing store or get something to eat at the restaurant?"

"It's a little early to eat, Sam. Let's get the shopping done," suggested Julia.

"Okay. Let's go."

Sam climbed aboard Glass and led them three streets over to an enormous clothing store, where they parked in an area designated for customers of the store.

"Well, here's where I leave you, fair ladies. I'll find you in about an hour. Okay?"

They all were smiling as they waved him off and Sam turned Glass back into the street where he found the shop he had been searching for. It was closer than he hoped.

Sam walked into the gun shop and saw the proprietor talking to another customer. While he was talking to the man, Sam walked over to the knife section, looking for something not as large as his blade. He examined several types until he found a nicely balanced knife with a five-inch blade with a leather-bound handle that provided a nice grip and came with a leather sheath that could be fitted for a belt.

He found belts of all lengths that would fit the knife sheath, selected three of the shorter belts, then he picked up three of the boxed knife and sheath sets and walked to the front. The other customer had left the store as he laid his purchases on the counter.

"Will that be all, sir?" the shop owner asked.

"No. Do you have any Remington double derringers in the .41 caliber?"

"Of course, sir. They're a big seller."

He turned behind his counter, reached up to a shelf, pulled down a box and handed it to Sam.

"It comes with a cleaning kit, as well."

"Nice touch," Sam replied as he took the diminutive gun from the box.

He opened the gun and looked down the twin rifled barrels. They were still covered in the manufacturer's grease, which is what he expected.

"Let me have three, please, and two boxes of the ammunition."

The owner smiled and took down two more derringers and then the two boxes of the small cartridges.

Sam inspected the other two and was satisfied. Unlike revolvers, the derringers had fewer moving parts and the trigger pulls were usually consistent. He replaced the guns in the boxes.

"Will that be all today, sir."

"As sad as it is to say, yes. I feel like a little boy standing in front of the penny candy display. I may turn out to be one of your best customers. I just moved here from Boulder and every time Colt, Smith & Wesson, Remington or Winchester comes out with a new model, I'll be here."

"Well, sir, don't forget some of our more exotic makers."

Sam opened his vest and revealed the Webley and while not exotic by any means, it showed the gunsmith that Sam loved his weapons.

Obviously impressed with Sam's penchant for firepower, the proprietor beamed.

"Your total today is $58.44."

Sam wrote out another draft and handed it to him, asking if he had a nice container for the items.

The owner put up a finger and scurried back to his office behind the shop. He emerged carrying a leather pouch emblazoned with his store's name, believing it to be a wise investment. Sam thanked him as he loaded the knives, little guns, and ammunition into the bag. He shook the man's hand and returned to Glass, put the pouch into a saddlebag and swung Glass back in the direction of the clothing store.

When he reached the store, he tied Glass to the wagon and threw the weighty saddlebags over his shoulder. While not as stylish as the other customers would be, Sam didn't really mind his appearance.

He strode through the store and searched for his women, realizing how strange it was that he should think of them that way already, but he did; not in a possessive way, but more in a protective way. They were in his care and to keep safe, but he sure did admire each of them, too.

Eventually he found them with a salesgirl in the dress section. Carol was talking to the salesgirl and Grace saw him striding toward her and headed his way.

"Sam, come on over," she said as she took his hand and walked him to Julia and Carol.

Carol looked at him and said quietly, "I was talking to the salesgirl and she gave me the price on this dress I really liked. It was fifteen dollars. Sam, I can't spend that much money."

"You aren't spending fifteen dollars, Carol," he paused watching the light dim in her eyes, "I am. You go right ahead. I gave you all the rules yesterday. Tell that to Grace and Julia as well."

To say that Carol perked up would be an understatement. She leaned forward, gave Sam a big kiss on his cheek before she turned to the sales girl and nodded with a big smile on her face. It made Sam happy to see the joy on her face. It was well worth the money.

He turned to Grace and Julia and asked, "Did you get everything you want or need?"

They both said, "Yes," but Sam could see in their eyes that they weren't being quite honest.

"Liars," he said, "I told you get what you'd like. You may never get this chance again."

Their faces lit up and they walked back to the salesgirl, who was obviously pleased when she heard Sam's statement.

Sam waited until they had finished all their woman talk, obviously having already mentioned what they had hoped to buy before he arrived but were hesitant to place the order. When they finished, his three ladies walked over to him with their faces looking like angels.

"Well, ladies, did you get everything now? Including all of those female fripperies you need to go with the dresses?"

"Yes, sir," Grace answered solemnly, "We will cause no more damage to your bank account."

"Ah! But I will. Come with me, my angels."

They were surprised but pleased by the title, and Grace and Carol took his arms and Julia walked down the aisle to the waiting salesgirl. She gave him his bill and he was surprised a bit to find it at $103.22 but wrote out a draft and asked them to crate up the purchases and they would return in an hour to the loading dock. The clerk smiled at him and said it would be ready.

He continued to hold their arms as they made their way out of the store and crossed out into the daylight. Once on the boardwalk, they turned left, and Sam led them to a nice restaurant.

They were seated, as Sam lowered his saddlebags carefully to the floor, concerned about the loud thump they would make if he wasn't careful.

They placed their orders, and when their meals arrived, Sam noticed that they each added a little sugar to their coffee, despite their earlier claim that they always drank it black. He'd have to remember that and bring some sugar if they ever to go on the trail together again, although he doubted if that was likely to happen.

After they had finished, Sam asked if they would like any dessert. They all demurred, saying they couldn't eat another bite, so Sam paid for the lunch, picked up his heavy saddlebags then escorted the ladies back across the street.

They boarded the wagon and Sam led the mules back to the loading dock and was surprised to see four large crates with his name on them. The dock workers seemed anxious to be rid of the large order and lifted them onto the wagon and Sam gave them each a silver dollar and an apology. At least now he could understand the large bill.

Carol took the reins and drove the wagon back toward the ranch as Sam rode Glass alongside.

They pulled back into the yard late in the afternoon. The day had gone well, and Sam was pleased that the women were happy, which was one of the main goals of the trip; to let them know that they belonged at the ranch now.

Carol stopped the wagon near the house and the women stepped down as Sam rode Glass to the hitching rail nearby, dismounted and looped his reins, leaving his saddle bags on the horse.

He walked to the wagon and stepped to the back with the large crates. He wasn't sure how much they weighed, so he lifted an edge and gave a heave. They weren't too bad, but they were bulky.

The ladies were all standing behind the tailgate as he said, "Here's how we're going to handle the crates. They're not too heavy, but they'd be annoying to try to carry them inside. So, I'll just slide them off the back, open the tops and you can empty the contents out here and bring them inside. Okay?"

"Okay," replied Grace for the trio.

"I'll start unloading the crates, but I'll need to open them after they're off. Can someone go into the barn and get a hammer and a screwdriver?"

"I'll get them," replied Julia, who then trotted off toward the barn.

Sam pulled on the first crate and as it teetered on the edge of the wagon, he lifted it and lowered it to the ground. After he slid it out of the way, he repeated the exercise for each of the other crates from the clothing store. By then, Julia had returned with the tools and handed them to Sam.

He slid the screwdriver under the first crate's top and created a gap. Then it was just a case of popping it up and releasing the nails. The women peered into the first box as Sam began opening the second. The ladies had begun removing boxes of items from the first box and taking them inside as Sam was moving onto the third crate and was opening the fourth crate as the women were unloading the second.

Once the clothing cases were removed, Sam jumped back onto the wagon's bed. He knew that the food crates were a lot heavier than those containing clothes, so he didn't move them at all and began opening the three cases. Once they were all opened, he began emptying their contents and placing them on the back of the wagon. It took nearly an hour to get the wagon emptied, and Sam wondered what use he could make of the lumber from the crates. Never waste boards, even if they were emblazoned with a store's name and logo.

The women began taking the food into the house, and Sam lugged in the heavy sacks of flour, sugar, and coffee.

With all the food and clothes in the house, Sam put the empty crates on the bed of the wagon with the others and led the mules and wagon into the barn. Once inside, he unharnessed the mules and brushed them down, then led them into stalls with water and hay, before returning to Glass, bringing him to the barn, unsaddling him before he led him back to the corral, then took the saddlebags and returned to the house.

He was not surprised to find his ladies opening the multitude of boxes when he entered.

"Okay, ladies, let's see what you bought. Except for those things that I have no idea what they are anyway."

For an hour, the women showed him dresses, shoes, and even some frilly things that, although he was impressed, he didn't understand their purpose, at least not what they were really used for other than to impress the males of the species.

He was surprised by their choice of hats that they had chosen; no flowery, feathered bonnets. Each woman had bought a nice Stetson, and each was a different shade.

"Those are very nice. Can I see how you look in them?"

They smiled and sat the hats on their heads, and he was genuinely pleased with the effect and told them so.

They each had bought two pairs of women's pants and skirts for riding, a pair of Texas-style boots, and some shirts that may have looked like men's shirts but seemed to be tapered differently.

"I am overwhelmed, ladies. You made excellent choices. Before you put them away, I'll show you what I bought for each of you today. Don't be disappointed that they don't accentuate your wardrobe. I really did buy them for a reason."

He pulled his saddlebags onto his lap, almost rendering himself impotent on the spot when the heavy bag landed in a strategic location. He blew out his breath at the close call, then he opened the first bag and took out the three knives and belts.

"These are some very good blades. They have leather-wrapped handle for a good grip, even if they get wet. I bought these small belts so you could wear them anywhere and even conceal them under your skirts. Besides being very good to have for self-defense, they are so useful that I couldn't imagine being without mine."

He looked at their faces, not knowing what to expect as he slid the boxes and belts toward their side of the table.

Then he pulled out the three derringers and the boxes of ammunition then placed the small guns on the table.

"These are Remington .41 caliber derringers. They are ideal for self-defense. You can carry them in your purse or in a coat pocket. They fire two rounds, and the cartridge is powerful enough to stop any man who gets within twenty feet."

It was Julia who brought up the obvious when she asked, "Sam, why did you buy them. Do you think we're in danger?"

"Not now. But until I get things settled with Catherine and whomever was trying to hurt her, I want you to be able to protect yourselves. I won't be here all the time over the next few weeks. These will make me feel better when I'm not here. If I'm out chasing bad guys, I don't want to be worrying about you."

"Thank you for the weapons, Sam," said Grace, "but thank you even more for your concern."

"You're welcome. When I come back from the Bar C tomorrow, we can set up some classes to learn how to use them."

Julia asked, "You told us that you have more guns. How many?"

"A lot. I'll tell you what, before you put away all your clothes, go ahead and start dinner. I'll start collecting my cache of firearms. I need to clean and oil them all, anyway."

"Why do you have so many?" asked Carol.

"Well, for one thing, I like guns; they're like works of art to me. When I was the sheriff in Boulder, the politicians didn't like to raise my pay, so they told me that whenever I caught a bad guy, I had first choice of his guns. If he was going to be hanged, I could get his horses, too. That's why I have three very nice horses. Outlaws may not have much money, but they always have great horses."

Carol's eyebrows rose as she asked, "Outlaws never have any money? That's silly. They rob banks and stagecoaches."

"I've never arrested an outlaw that had more than ten dollars on him. They get drawn into the dark side of the law because they're lazy and think it'll be a quick way to get money, but it isn't. It's dangerous and they quickly discover that it's not so simple. They're easily detected, like those three morons that tried to rob the bank in Boulder the last day I was there. I saw them coming as soon as they entered town. The nice horses give them away, too."

"I never thought of that."

"That's because you're all honest people, and you're not lazy. Now, if someone will prepare dinner, I'll get my armory assembled."

After the ladies left, it took Sam close to thirty minutes to transfer the guns and ammunition to the main room. When he finished, he walked into the kitchen.

Julia was just putting down plates when he entered and said, "It smells really good in here."

"Don't forget, we have a lot more things to work with now. Dinner will be ready in about twenty minutes," answered Grace as she smiled.

"Need any help?" he asked seriously.

The three women looked at him and started laughing.

"I guess not. I'm going back to my guns. At least they understand me," he said, hanging his head as he left.

The laughing amplified as he walked down the hallway.

Sam smiled as he sat by his arms cache. He hadn't spent a lot of time with his latest acquisitions, so he examined the two

Winchesters, the Henry, and the two Colts. As with most outlaws' weapons, they were in superb condition. When you're on the wrong side of the law, you can't afford a jam or misfire; neither can lawmen, for that matter. He removed the cartridges from the weapons and felt the action of each and was pleased with the results as they were smooth and almost effortless. It may have been his last day on the job in Boulder, but at least it was worthwhile. He had just laid down the Henry when Grace entered to tell him that dinner was ready.

She stared at the large expanse of firearms and exclaimed, "My God, Sam! You weren't kidding! You could outfit an army."

"Not a whole army; just a company, maybe."

"Well, come out and have some dinner and then you can introduce us to your friends."

Sam popped up from the chair and followed Grace to the kitchen watching her as she stepped smoothly down the hall in front of him and felt another dousing under the pump may be necessary.

But when he got into the kitchen, he decided it was unnecessary when his stomach took control and the food sitting on the table bordered on exotic.

"Where on earth did you ladies learn to cook like this?"

"Where most women learn to cook; from our mothers," answered Carol.

"Well, you learned well. This looks and smells amazing."

"But it's for eating, not looking. Have a seat, Sam," directed Julia.

Sam enjoyed one of the best meals he had ever eaten, including in the nice restaurant in earlier that day, and told them so. They accepted the compliment knowing it was genuine.

After dinner had been consumed, the table cleared, and dishes cleaned, Sam led the ladies to the family room. Only Grace wasn't shocked by the number of weapons displayed, because she had already had her moment of surprise.

"How many guns do you have?" asked Julia with wide eyes.

"Let's see. Three Colt Peacemakers, two Smith & Wesson Model 3s, four Winchester Model 1873s, one Model '66, and two Henry repeaters. Now that doesn't include the Winchester I keep in the scabbard in the barn."

"Does it include the gun you're wearing?" asked Carol.

"No, it doesn't include either one."

"You have more than one? Where is the other one?" asked Grace.

He opened his vest, revealing the Webley in his shoulder holster.

"Sam, this is a bit frightening," said Carol.

"It shouldn't be. Guns are just tools. It's the person behind the gun that determines whether it's good tool or a bad tool."

"Is that all of them?" asked Grace.

"All of them except the one that was my favorite weapon when I was a sheriff," Sam replied as he reached onto the floor and picked up his modified shotgun.

"That looks different," commented Julia.

"I've heavily modified it for the way I used it. I'll show you."

Before he stood, Sam cracked it open to make sure that there were no shells in the barrels, then he snapped it closed. He picked up his back scabbard and put it on, then he slid the shotgun into place and rose from his seat.

"When I was a sheriff, I found that to calm a bad situation, nothing impresses as much as a shotgun. The problem is that when I needed one, sometimes it would be sitting back in my office. So, I modified this one by cutting the barrels down to fifteen inches and then took three inches off the stock. It made the shotgun very easy to handle, but it also meant that when I fired it, I couldn't put it against my shoulder. So, I took off most of the trigger guard and made this scabbard. I wore it most of the time I was on duty, which for all practical purposes, was all the time. I had a useless deputy, so I handled everything.

"Anyway, I've only had to fire it a few times. The last time was stopping those three bank robbers. Usually, I'd enter a bad situation and show the business end of the shotgun and things would quiet down fast. They all knew that with a barrel this short the pellets would scatter shot in a wide field. I normally loaded it with bird shot so no one would be anything more than wounded unless they were really close, but in the case of the bank robbers, I changed to a heavier load because I knew I had to stop them.

"But when I fire the gun, I immediately have to let it go. The thing blows out of my hands and flies back about twenty feet. But I expect it and can get my Colt out of holster as the gun is moving. Against those bank robbers, it wasn't even needed."

"You're the Shotgun Sheriff?" asked Carol with wide eyes.

"I hear that's what some people called me, but I never paid attention."

"We heard all sorts of stories about you."

"Well, I was there, Carol, and I can tell you, if they were accurate stories, they weren't worth telling. So, is there anything else that you'd like to know besides wondering if I'm some sort of loner who is going to go crazy."

"Are you a loner?" asked Grace quietly.

Sam had to think about it for a few moments before he replied, "I don't really know. I've lived alone since I left home and always worked alone, but I always had my sister, niece and Richard. Now, I guess I am alone. But I've always gotten along with people and like people as a rule, but I just wind up being by myself. I never knew why, but just didn't notice."

The women sat quietly for a minute, then Carol pointed at the pistols and asked, "Can you show us how to use one of those?"

"If you'd like to learn, I can. I've known other women to use them."

"Can I try one on?" she asked.

"Come over here and we'll try."

Carol stood, walked to Sam, then he took one of the Colts out of its holster.

"Go ahead and lift your arms out of the way."

When she did, Sam held the holster against her right hip and flipped the belt around her back, catching the other end.

He tightened it around her waist until he could pull it down onto her hips, then he put the Colt back in the holster. He was surprised that the holes in the belt still allowed the gunbelt to tighten enough to keep it from sliding to the floor. He guessed that despite their small waists, their hips were big enough to keep the gunbelt in place. Men had bigger waists but smaller hips, so it all worked out.

"What do you think, Carol?"

"It's heavy, but not as bad as I thought it would be."

"Once you get used to its being there, you don't notice the weight at all. Now if you want to wear one, you need to be wearing pants. Dresses could cause issues with the holster and the skirt. Not to mention any wind that may come up."

Carol turned to Grace and Julia and smiled as he asked, "What do you both think?"

"I think it might be a good idea," answered Grace.

"Me, too," added Julia.

"Did you want to try one on?" Sam asked.

"Yes. I'll try," replied Grace as stood and stepped forward.

Sam took the second Colt out of the holster and turned to find Grace standing two feet in front of him. His face was a foot away from her chest and his imagination exploded knowing what was behind the cloth. As she lifted her arms, Sam knew that a serious pump dousing was in his near future.

He wrapped her belt around her waist and tightened it, tugging it down to her hips. She lowered her arms and Sam put the Colt in the empty holster. She smiled at him before she turned back to Julia and Carol.

Sam tried to hide his discomfort but didn't know if he was successful or not.

Julia was last. She followed Grace's lead and popped in front of Sam with her arms in the air.

Lord, this was a lot more difficult than he had expected, he thought.

He managed to get her gunbelt tightened and snugged down successfully, then he placed Julia's Colt in her holster.

"Well, ladies, what do you think?"

Grace smiled and replied, "I think we're ready for lessons when you return because I do believe the kitchen pump is calling."

"You are quite correct," he replied as he stood, then quickly walked awkwardly into the kitchen and pumped as if he was trying to fill Lake Michigan.

Even after several dunkings, he didn't feel much relief. He wondered if they had done that on purpose. He didn't think so, *but why were they all giggling in there?*

Eventually he felt restored enough to reenter the family room.

When he stepped out of the hallway, Julia snickered and said, "You do have clean hair, Sam."

"Well, I hope you're all pleased with yourselves. I'll get even, but I have no idea how to do it. But revenge aside, I'd

127

like you to keep the guns you have with you now. Keep the chambers empty but get used to handling them, so when you practice, the weight isn't as noticeable."

"We'll do that, Sam. We're sorry for making you uncomfortable, it just happened that way when we saw you put Carol's gunbelt on. We could have put them on ourselves, you know," said Grace.

"I know, it was partly my own fault. I didn't know how they'd fit on your hips because they're different than men's, just in case you haven't noticed. I had to make sure that the gunbelt didn't just slide off. Once I was sure that it would stay put, I was going to offer to let you each put on your own, but when you came over, Grace, I thought I may as well keep going. I'll be honest with each of you and tell you that I did enjoy the fitting, but it wasn't unpleasant until it was finished, and I paid the price."

Grace laughed lightly, then said, "Well, if you'll forgive us, we'll forgive you."

He smiled back at Grace and said, "That sounds fair. Okay, tomorrow I'm going to be getting up early. You can all sleep as late as you'd like. I'll just grab some coffee and head out. After I arrest the bastard, I'll have to take him into Denver, so I should be back around six o'clock or so.

"There's something else we need to talk about, too. Now that we have a lot of horses, I'll keep Cump and Glass. Glass can be ornery if he is in the mood and I don't want any of you to be thrown. One of you can take Coal. She's a wonderful horse; very gentle and can still run all day. Don't bother with Emma. She's old and probably not durable. She can be used for riding around the ranch, but not much else. I've checked the others and they're all geldings and are reasonably young. I've talked to them and rubbed them down, and neither seems skittish. The good news is that whoever gets them gets to name them. You decide who gets which one. They'll be yours to ride and care for. After a while they'll become your friends and will recognize your voices and your feel when you're on their backs. They'll respond to simple nudges or taps."

"We'll have to learn how to saddle them and everything," said Carol, "except for Grace. She grew up on a ranch."

Grace said, "I did, but I didn't have to saddle my own horse. My father did that because he thought I was too small and, well, I was a girl. So, I could use some help in that area."

"That's not a problem. After I come back, we should have a few days to do that and get some shooting practice in. I still have a lot of thinking about my plans to get Catherine back, and I'll ask for your input when I come up with one, too. I need to do this right and not risk her safety."

"We will," said Grace.

"I'll also be placing a Winchester in each scabbard, and when we get time, I'll show you how to shoot them as well. They are actually easier to shoot, but you have to get used to cycling the lever. The good news is that except for the shotgun and the derringers, all of the guns use the same ammunition."

"No wonder you have so much of it," commented Julia.

"That. and if you want to be any good, you need to practice."

"Are you any good?"

"Better than most, not as good as some," was his standard non-committal answer.

He didn't want to sound like a braggart, but he knew that he had yet to find anyone as good with a Colt as he was; or the Winchester either, for that matter.

"Okay, ladies. Take all your weapons into your rooms and I'm going to clean up my mess, then I'm going to get some sleep. I have a big day, tomorrow."

"Sam," said Grace quietly, "be careful."

"I will," he said, smiling at her.

———

It was another difficult night for Sam as he kept picturing Grace standing before him and tried to push those thoughts from his mind to concentrate on more serious issues, but she kept returning. Maybe if she was just another pretty young woman, he would have been able to do it, but Grace was already worming her way into his heart.

CHAPTER 5

It was very early, even for Sam, but even before his eyes opened, he began going through in his mind what he planned to do that day; going through various possible situations and outcomes. Once he'd finally succeeded in getting past Grace thoughts, it had kept him awake most of the night and after three hours of restless sleep, he pulled off his blanket, stood, stretched to work out the kinks from sleeping on the couch, then walked to the kitchen in stocking feet.

After a quick visit outside, not necessarily to the privy because of his stockinged feet, he returned to the kitchen, quietly added some wood to the stove and started the fire, pumped water into the coffee pot and set it on the stove. He wasn't going to bother with cooking breakfast as there were still some of Grace's magnificent biscuits wrapped in a paper bag near the table, and some would be going with him on the ride, too. He went to the shelves and took some beef jerky and began chewing as he padded back to the main room.

He pulled on his denim pants and a clean plaid shirt, slipped on the shoulder holster, pinned on his badge and put on a black vest. He pulled the warrant from his old shirt pocket and transferred it to the new one, then picked up his Stetson and boots and slipped back into the kitchen.

The water was beginning to boil, so he added coffee and pulled it off the hot stove, quietly opened the bag containing the biscuits, took two out, put them on the table, then poured a cup of coffee, and took a seat before finally taking one of the two biscuits in his hand. He closed his eyes as he took a bite, finding it just as tasty as it was yesterday, even though it was

131

cold. *Boy, could that woman cook!* He savored every bite as he finished the biscuits and coffee.

When he was finished, he took the bag of biscuits and jerky, opened the back door and stepped out onto the rear porch, closing the door as quietly as he could behind him. He pulled on his hat, tugged his boots onto his feet and stepped out into the yard, pleased he hadn't awakened the women.

But inside the house, in three separate bedrooms Grace, Julia and Carol were all wide awake. They knew he was leaving, and they silently prayed he would come back to them safely. Each of them already considered him much more than just their savior, or even their ticket to a new life.

———

Sam entered the corral and had to wake Cump and made sure the chestnut gelding ate and drank as he checked his gear. He wouldn't need his regular rig for this trip but took his spare set of saddlebags that contained some extra ammunition and his slicker, then put the bag of biscuits in the saddlebag, threw the blanket over Cump and then his saddle. After he had cinched the saddle, he put the saddlebags on his back and led him as quietly as he could into the brightening morning sky. When he had gone about a hundred feet, he mounted Cump and headed down the road.

———

The sun was well up as he neared the entrance to the Bar C, turned into the access road and headed toward the distant ranch house.

As he approached the house, the front door opened, and an older man stepped out.

"Good morning, sir. I assume you're Mister Crandall?" Sam asked loudly.

"I am. And who might you be?"

"Deputy Sheriff Sam Brown. May I speak to you, please?"

"Step down and come on in."

Sam dismounted, tied off Cump, stepped up onto the porch, and followed Mister Crandall into his house.

"I don't recall seeing you before, Deputy. You been with Dan Grant long?"

"Actually, I'm a temporary deputy appointed by Dan to investigate the death of Richard Sharp and the disappearance of his wife and daughter."

"Why'd he hire you instead of having one of his regular deputies do it?"

"I just left my job as the sheriff of Boulder and came down to Denver to visit my sister. She was married to Richard Sharp. I asked him to investigate, but he knew my history as a lawman, and asked me to do it. He knew I'd follow the law, and not just seek revenge."

"That's commendable. Most men I know would go and gun the bastard down."

"I follow the rule of law, Mister Crandall. I fully expect the guilty to hang."

"So, what brings you here today, Deputy? I heard of the killing but didn't know his wife and child had been taken."

"I know that, sir. I'm here to serve a John Doe warrant on one of your hands for murder."

The elderly rancher's eyes split wide as he exclaimed, *"Murder! Are you being straight with me? I've got a murderer working on my ranch? One of my men murdered Richard Short?"*

"No, sir, not my brother-in-law. We're talking about a different killing, and yes, sir, I'm certain it was one of your men. I have several witnesses. They describe the murderer as a tall man, bigger than me, who worked on the Bar C."

"I only have one hand that big, Steve Rawls. Are you sure? He doesn't seem the murdering kind and doesn't even carry a gun."

"Does he frequent Waxman's down in Hinkley?"

"That's his one weakness. He doesn't even drink too much, but he does love the ladies."

"No, Mister Crandall, he does not love the ladies. They told me that Mister Rawls, whose name they never knew, would come to their establishment and pay for their services. Then, when he finished, he would reach back and punch them hard in the stomach; every time. The women called him the whore-puncher and hated to see him arrive."

"He killed one of those girls?" he asked quietly.

"He killed my sister, Mister Crandall. They had kidnapped her six months ago after killing her husband and brought her to Waxman's. They told her if she didn't stay there and keep her mouth shut, they'd kill her daughter. Mister Crandall, my sister was the sweetest, most loving person I've ever known. I would have found her and saved her if Steve Rawls hadn't

134

smashed his huge fist into her small body and destroyed something inside her. He left, and she died an hour later."

Crandall sat down in the closest chair with a horrified look on his weathered face and tears began to slide down his cheeks tracking along the wrinkles.

When he finally spoke, it was in a low monotone as he said, "That bastard. That low-life, crawling bastard. I should have known. He would make comments about showing them whores a thing or two, but I thought he was just bragging about his prowess in bed. My God! That man should be hanged."

"He will be, sir. Where can I find him?"

"I'm not sure at the moment, but I want all the hands to come in and hear this."

He stood on shaky legs and walked to the front of the ranch house as Sam rose and followed.

Sam hadn't noticed it, but there was a large bell that looked like it belonged in a church steeple or a schoolhouse hung from the rafters of the porch.

"Can you give that a few good tugs, Deputy?" he asked.

"Yes, sir."

Sam reached for the rope and started pulling, needing a few silent pulls before the bell's clapper struck metal, and then it pealed loud, resonant notes across the ranch. After six rings, he returned to the center of the porch where Mister Crandall had taken a seat in a rocking chair.

"That will bring the whole crew within ten minutes, Deputy."

"Call me Sam, Mister Crandall."

"Okay, Sam. Thank you."

It was less than five minutes before the last of the eight hands arrived in the front yard and Sam could spot Rawls easily. He was about two inches taller than Sam and probably outweighed him by thirty pounds, but it didn't matter. That bastard killed his sister and had hurt his ladies.

"What's up, boss?" asked one of the hands.

"I want you all to stand down and come forward."

They seemed curious but all of them dismounted and approached the porch as Mister Crandall rose from the rocking chair and stood beside Sam.

"This is a special deputy appointed by Dan Grant to investigate the murder of Richard Short," he said before he turned and added, "Sam, go ahead."

"Thanks, Mister Crandall," Sam said as he reached into his pocket and produced the warrant, then said, "I have a warrant for the arrest of Steve Rawls for murder."

The cowboys, in unison, jerked their heads to look at Rawls.

Rawls snarled, "I didn't have nothing to do with that. I never even been on that spread."

Sam looked at him and said, "I never said you did, Mister Rawls. I'm arresting you for the murder of his wife, Cora Short. My sister."

Rawls got a wild look in his eyes; he never knew that he'd murdered anyone, but even though he guessed that one of those whores might have died, he still didn't make the connection.

He finally squawked, "I never knew your sister, neither"

"Oh, yes you did. Six months ago, four men rode onto my brother-in-law's ranch. They shot and killed Richard and kidnapped my young, wonderful sister; the sweetest person I've ever known. They took her precious four-year-old daughter, Catherine hostage to ensure her silence and obedience; my precious, beautiful niece.

"They then took my sister to Hinkley, sold her to Waxman and threatened to kill her daughter if she didn't stay there and service the likes of you, Rawls. I have three witnesses who will testify that you routinely punched the women you had just bedded. You used that big fist of yours and slammed it into their stomachs; every damned time. They called you the whore-puncher."

Sam glared at the big ranch hand as he continued in a firm, level voice.

"Well, you did that to my priceless sister. You reared back with that fist and with all your size and weight, crashed it into her small body, and then you just walked away not caring about the terrible pain you inflicted on her. She died an hour later from the incredible damage you did to her insides, and that's why I'm here to arrest you, Rawls."

"She was just another whore. Who cares if she was your sister," he said, either because he thought his size would protect him, or he was just plain stupid.

After he finished his incredible confession, Sam slowly stepped down from the porch and wanted badly to pull his Colt and empty it into his stomach, but he didn't. He simply let this rage swell until it filled him.

The other hands were walking away from Rawls in disgust as Sam and Rawls stared at each other.

Sam looked at the nearest cowhand, and through gritted teeth, asked, "Come here, will you?"

The man approached Sam and stood in front of him. First, Sam handed him his Stetson, then removed his gunbelt and handed it to him. He removed his vest, his shoulder holster, then finally removed his badge from his shirt and handed it and his handcuffs to a second man who had stepped forward to help when the first man's hands were full. His eyes never left Rawls' face.

Rawls was smiling as Sam removed his weapons, knowing that he wanted to fight and assumed that he would pummel the smaller lawman.

"Okay, Rawls," Sam said as he stepped forward, "You beat innocent women and you killed my sister, but I won't kill you. I'm going to let the state do that. I am going to beat you to a pulp, so you can feel the pain that you caused those women."

Rawls barely let him finish when he leapt at Sam, who knew it was coming. He let Rawls almost reach him before turning quickly aside, and as the man passed, Sam unleashed a wicked roundhouse shot into his right ribs and could feel the ribs crack as his fist slammed into the flesh.

Sam thought, "That was for Julia."

Rawls hit the ground; the pain from his cracked ribs intense in his side. Now he was enraged, so he scrambled to his feet and raised his fists, took two long strides toward Sam then suddenly lashed out with his right, but Sam ducked under the blow and as Rawls' fist flew over his head, he unloaded a massive undercut into Rawls' exposed stomach, lifting him from the ground. Rawls lost all his air as he fell to the ground on all fours.

"That was for Carol," Sam said to himself.

Sam stepped back. He didn't want it to end this quickly. He wanted Rawls to regain his footing because he needed at least one more shot for Grace. It took thirty seconds, but the big ranch hand finally stood, wavering, his feet spread wide apart to try to maintain his balance as he swayed toward Sam.

"You, yellow bastard!" he screamed, "Come here and fight fair!"

Sam had no idea what he was talking about but didn't care one bit. He wanted him to feel pain but stepped forward again to give him his chance. When he got close, Rawls tried an uppercut to his chin, but Rawls was slower now and it was easily avoided.

Sam leaned back and as Rawls was fully extended, Sam dropped down to his right knee and brought his right arm to full extension, and exerting every bit of force he could, swung his right fist and crushed it into Rawls' crotch.

He screamed and crumpled to the ground, grabbing at his lower regions and squirming in the dirt like a worm exposed to the sun. He wouldn't be getting up very soon, and when he did, he'd be in agony for hours.

Sam glared at the whore-puncher and thought, "That, you bastard, was for Grace."

Sam was satisfied for now. He knew that Cora's revenge would come when Rawls felt the noose tighten around his neck.

No cowhand said a word as Sam walked up to the two men holding his gear. The two men looked at Sam and one handed him his hat. Sam put it on his head and noticed he hadn't even worked up a sweat. Then, one by one, he and the second man handed Sam his gear. When he was done, Sam walked up to the now moaning Steve Rawls and tossed the warrant on his writhing form.

"You are under arrest, Steve Rawls, for the murder of Cora Short, and the assaults of Carol Early, Julia Crook, and Grace Felton."

Sam looked at the faces of the other cowboys. They looked at him and simply nodded, then returned to their horses. One, as he walked past Rawls, spit on him.

Sam then turned to the ranch owner and said, "Mister Crandall, if you want to send someone along, they can bring back Rawls' horse."

"Put his ass on that horse and I never want to see him or the horse again. Sam, I can't tell you how bad I feel about this. That monster worked for me for five years, and I never knew."

"Don't blame yourself, sir. There are monsters everywhere in plain sight. We'll never catch them all. The best we can hope for is that we hang them when we find them, so they don't hurt anyone else. I'll make sure that this monster hangs."

Crandall stepped down from the porch and Sam was expecting a handshake, but instead Crandall walked up to him and embraced him, and he could feel the old man trembling. Sam simply patted him on the shoulder. Crandall finally sighed and returned to his house.

Sam walked over to the groaning form of Steve Rawls and yanked him to his feet. He was too weak to protest as Sam walked him to his horse and lifted his left foot up into the stirrup, then with great difficulty got him into the saddle. He whimpered as tears flooded from his eyes as he sat in the saddle with his painful privates. Sam snapped on the handcuffs and tied them to the horn with pigging strings, then he tied his feet to the stirrups with more pigging strings.

Once he was aboard, Sam took the reins and walked the horse to where Cump awaited. He already had a short lead rope, so he tied it to Rawls' horse and was going to wave to Mister Crandall, but he'd already reentered his house, so he started back to Denver seventeen miles north.

————

Rawls groaned and whimpered the entire trip as the horse bounced along. Sam could have reduced the speed to a smoother walk, but he didn't. Sam was glad to see him in such pain.

As he passed the Circle S, he briefly contemplated bringing his prisoner to the women for true justice but realized that a manacled prisoner was different than the free man he had beaten.

It was mid-afternoon when he tied Cump to the sheriff's office post, walked in the door and saw a deputy he recognized behind the front desk, but couldn't recall his name.

141

"Sam! How are you doing?" he asked as he stood.

"Can you help me get a prisoner down from his horse?"

"Sure. Can't walk too well. Huh?"

"You could say that."

The deputy grinned, then Sam and the deputy went outside, removed the pigging strings and the handcuffs, and lowered Rawls from the horse, walking him inside. He walked funny, but at least he had stopped crying.

By the time they entered, Dan Grant had come out of his office.

"This the whore-puncher?" he asked as the deputy put him in a cell.

"Yup. His name is Steve Rawls. After I notified him of the reason for his arrest, the murder of my sister, his response was that she was just another whore, so I removed all my weapons and let him have a go, but he didn't do so well. I have several witnesses who can testify to that. Now he's yours. Did you want me to write a report?"

"If you can spare the time."

"Sure. But first, I'll go grab some biscuits out of my saddlebag."

"Would you rather go and get something to eat?"

"No, I'll eat the biscuits while I'm writing."

After retrieving his bag, Sam sat down at the desk and wrote out the facts of the arrest, leaving out the fight, if you could call it that. He ate the biscuits, drinking some of Dan's abominable coffee to wash them down, ruining the normally lovely aftertaste.

He finished the report and handed it to Dan and said, "I'd recommend only charging him with the murder. I don't want to put the women though too much more interrogation by the public defender during the trial."

"We'll do that, Sam. You did a great job. If you need anything else, let us know. I know that you'll find your niece."

"I know I will, and when I do, I'll bring you more prisoners to hang. Oh, by the way. Mister Crandall doesn't want the horse back. He seems like a nice animal, so you should take it."

Dan replied, "No, we'll let the county dispose of it at auction."

Sam nodded, then turned and left the office.

He mounted Cump and headed south; still not feeling full satisfaction over what had happened to Steve Rawls. He didn't believe that there was any punishment that he could dream of that was enough.

Fifty minutes later, he was turning onto the entrance road and was emotionally exhausted; and that, combined with his lack of sleep made him as weary as he'd felt in years.

He walked Cump directly to the barn and let him munch on some hay while he removed his saddle and gear. When he was bare of leather, Sam brushed the gelding down. After he was finished, he tossed his saddlebags over his shoulder and walked to the ranch house.

As he stepped onto the porch, he heard a shout from inside, "Sam's back!"

143

He had barely opened the door when he was bowled over by the three females. He felt them pulling him in but was barely aware of it. He reached the couch and dropped onto the cushions, pulled off his hat and then dropped his saddlebags to the floor.

"Sam? Are you all right?" asked Grace.

"I'm fine. Just a bit tired."

"What happened?" asked Carol.

"I'll tell you if you can bring me something to drink and munch on."

Julia raced off to the kitchen and returned minutes late with a glass of water and a biscuit with two slices of bacon inside.

"Thank you, Julia," he said as he smiled up at her.

Sam took a big bite of the bacon laden biscuit and closed his eyes.

"Boy! Does that taste good," he said, then took a sip of water and set it on the table.

"Okay. Here's the short version. I got to the Bar C in late morning and rode up to the ranch house and met the ranch owner, Mister Crandall. I explained that I had an arrest warrant for a John Doe for murder and assault and asked him if he had any hand bigger than me, and he said it was a ranch hand named Steve Rawls. He admitted that he frequented Waxman's and I explained what he had done.

"He was very upset, so we went out to the porch, I rang this big bell and all eight of his hands showed up and I picked out Rawls right away. They all got off their horses, and I announced that I was arresting Steve Rawls for murder and assault. When he asked who he was supposed to have murdered and how, I told him that it was my sister and I told all of them the circumstances of her kidnapping.

"The cowboys looked at him like he was the monster that he was. I called one of them over and gave him all my guns. Rawls stood there smiling as he realized I wanted to fight. He was a lot bigger than I was, and he thought it was going to be easy, but he had no idea of the level of anger inside of me for what he did to my sister and to my girls."

Sam paused, took the last bite of biscuit and took a long drink, then blew out his breath and continued.

"I let him have the first shot, but he was overconfident and clumsy, missed with his first punch and as he went by, I unloaded a punch into his side feeling his ribs break, thinking to myself that that one was for Julia. He went to the ground, and when he got back up, he tried another roundhouse and I ducked under it and buried my uppercut about two inches into his stomach. That, I thought, was for Carol.

"He went down a second time but stayed down longer. I stepped back and wanted him to get up because I owed him one more for Grace. He finally stood and had to spread his legs apart for balance. He tried an uppercut, but I leaned back and dropped to my right knee and with everything I had, I hit him in the groin. And that, Mister Rawls, I thought, is for Grace.

"He dropped to the ground and moaned and cried for a while as the other ranch hands all nodded at me as a way of saying that they approved of the beating I had given him. Then I stood over him and tossed the warrant on him and told him he was under arrest for the murder of Cora Short, and the assaults of Julia Crook, Carol Early, and Grace Felton. The boys went back to their horses, one of them even spit on him as he passed. Mister Crandall said to put him on his horse and he never wanted to see Rawls or the horse ever again.

"Then I took him all the way to Denver. He was moaning in pain and whining the entire three hours, and I didn't care one bit. When I got to Denver, I filled out my report and told Dan to charge him with the murder only, so my ladies didn't have to endure any more verbal abuse from the defense attorney than necessary. Then I came home and here I am."

The women were almost as emotionally drained as he was, hearing the administration of justice that they never thought they would hear and each of them noticed that he referred to them as his girls and his ladies.

"Sam, do you want something more to eat?" asked Carol.

"No. I'm good. The biscuits were perfect. They always are. If it's okay, I'll just stretch out here and take a brief nap."

Without waiting for a reply, he lay down on the couch and was asleep just seconds later.

The women looked at each other.

"We have to help him find Catherine. He needs our help," said Carol.

"I agree. We need to learn to use the weapons and ride horses," added Julia.

"We have to protect him. We're his ladies," Grace said with finality.

They covered Sam with a blanket and as they left to go to their rooms, they filed by and each woman gently kissed him on his forehead.

CHAPTER 6

Sam's eyelids moved – barely. For a few seconds, he wondered where he was, but then recognized the fireplace and chairs, and remembered he had fallen asleep talking to his ladies. He opened his eyes wider, felt the blanket over his shoulders, then smiled.

He swung his feet to the floor and stood. It was early and could see a weak light outside the windows. It must be just before five o'clock, so he wandered out to the kitchen and started a fire in the stove. *How many days had it been since he left Boulder? Six? Eight?* Whichever it was, the change in his life was dramatic. So was the change in the three women still sleeping in the house, but now, he must find Catherine.

After a brief, necessary stroll outside, he returned, put the coffee on, thinking of the little girl and wondering if she would still remember him. It had been almost nine months since he had seen her last and it bothered him that it had been so long.

Where would they be hiding her? It had to be near Hinkley. Most likely it wasn't in the town, but a ranch nearby. It would have to have a woman there to care for the girl; probably an older woman. That would cut down the number of possibilities to a half dozen or so, but even if he knew which one, he'd need to devise a plan to get into the ranch house and retrieve Catherine before anything happened to her.

He had poured his second cup of coffee and was still ruminating on how to approach the problem when he heard footsteps behind him, turned and was happy to see Grace.

"Good morning, Sam," she said as she touched his shoulder.

"Good morning to you, Grace," he replied as he smiled at her.

"We never did get a chance to thank you for what you did yesterday."

"It was a very selfish thing to do, in a way. I sought retribution for what he did to Cora and you. It was satisfying to watch him suffer some of the pain he had inflicted on you, Julia, Carol and Cora. The good news is that he'll be in pain a while. Between the Julia shot that broke some ribs and your blow that may have crippled him for the rest of his short life, he won't know a moment without pain. But it wasn't enough, Grace. Hanging won't be enough. In such a short time, I've grown to love you and Julia and Carol just as much as I cared for my Cora. Anyone who hurts any of you deserves much worse."

"We're all rather fond of you, too, Sam, but we all regretted one thing about what you did yesterday."

"And what was that?"

"That we didn't get to see you beat him."

"Did you know that as I passed by the entrance to the Circle S with Rawls in tow, I came very close to bringing him to the ranch house? I finally decided against it because he was manacled and in no condition to defend himself. When I beat him, he had an equal chance to win. If I let you get in some licks, he could have filed a complaint against all of us, and I didn't want to give him the slightest chance of not being hanged. Grace, have a seat, would you, please? I want your opinion on something."

149

Grace sat down and looked at him.

"Grace, I'll be getting notice sometime today or tomorrow with the date of Rawls' trial. It'll be soon. We'll all be subpoenaed to testify, and I need to know if you want to do it. I can have Dan Grant drop the charges and let him go if it will keep from having to have my ladies sit before a jury of leering men telling about their past."

"Sam, we can handle it. We talked about it yesterday while you were gone. We knew we would have to testify in court, and we knew what the defense attorney would try to do. We're ready. We want to see him hanged."

Sam smiled and laid his fingers on her hand before he said, "Thank you, Grace. I just hope I can control my temper watching it happen. When you're on the stand, look into my eyes and I'll be looking into yours. Tell that to Carol and Julia, too."

"We know, Sam. Now, I'll make you some breakfast."

Sam smiled at her, then stood and walked back to the family room to clean up the mess he had left the evening before.

Carol and Julia were up and out of their rooms by the time Grace had breakfast ready. After hurried trips to the privy, they returned and washed in the kitchen sink. When Sam arrived to eat, he was greeted by two broad smiles.

"Good morning, Sam," they echoed.

"Good morning, Carol and Julia. Are you both ready for shooting and riding lessons?"

"We're looking forward to it," answered Julia.

"Great. I'm looking forward to demolishing about a dozen biscuits and some bacon and eggs."

By the time he finished eating, he may not have gone through a dozen, but it was close.

Breakfast was done, they were all in the family room and the women were dressed in their new riding pants. When Sam watched them walk into the room, he was struck by their abundant femininity.

As they sat, Sam stood and said, "If you'll pardon me for a minute, ladies, I have a date with the kitchen pump."

He was not exaggerating, either, even as he heard laughter behind him. He put his head under the pump letting the cold water flow over his hair and neck for a good minute. Then he dried his hair and face and ran his fingers through his hair as a comb. When he finished, he returned to the family room.

"Ladies, I have to ask if it would be alright to keep wearing the men's pants that I bought the first time until you could get some riding skirts. I'll never be able to function until you do. Besides it would be dangerous if any other man saw you in those."

They laughed and Grace asked, "We're sorry, Sam. But why would it be dangerous for some other man?"

"Because I'd kill him out of jealousy. I know that you are all very special women. You are smart and have good souls, but you've all been blessed with the highest level of feminine equipment that God put on the planet."

"Why, Sam, that's a very nice compliment," cooed Carol.

"Just telling the truth, ma'am. I told you that I never lie."

151

"Can you survive the day if we keep these on? They are rather comfortable."

"I'll survive. Maybe. I just hope there's enough water underground."

He sat among the laughter, then said, "Before we begin training, do you have any questions about yesterday? I know I was a little short when I returned."

Julia asked, "When you told us the story, you said that as you hit him, one was for each of us. But you didn't hit him for Cora. I was just curious why?"

Sam looked at her and replied, "He hit each of you, probably more than once. I wanted him to suffer for that as much as it was in my power to do, but he killed my sister, and for that, he'll die. I just wish I had been able to do it myself. It would have been a more personal justice, but I had to follow the law."

Julia nodded as Sam asked, "If you have no more questions, let's get started on the day. Who has which horse?"

"We forgot to do that. We were all caught up in the day and getting everything organized when you came home," answered Carol.

"Well, you can go and take care of that. I'm going to go outside and look around."

They smiled as he left the room, going out the front door before they left through the back door and went to the barn.

Sam had an idea where he wanted to go to find a place for the cemetery. There was a grove of aspens growing about four hundred yards north of the house. To get there he had to walk up a slight rise. When he was about hundred feet from the trees, the ground leveled, and he turned to look at the ranch house.

After he turned back to face the trees, he looked left and could see the mountains in the distance. To his right was where the sun would rise. This was perfect. He looked around, found an aspen branch lying closer to the trees, then picked it up and broke it over his knee. Then he snapped each half leaving him with four aspen stakes.

He then paced off about fifty feet and made small hole with his knife blade and rammed one stake into the ground. He counted off the same number of steps toward the trees and placed another stake.

When he had finished, he had staked out a nice plot for a family gravesite when he brought Richard and Cora's bodies home. He would go to Denver and engage a construction firm to build a wrought iron fence around the small cemetery and would also have them give him an estimate for adding two bedrooms and an office library to the house.

While Sam was locating the burial site, the women were in the barn looking at the three horses.

"Who gets Coal?" asked Grace.

"That's not a question, Grace, you do," said Julia.

"Why isn't it a question?" Grace asked.

"Because you're his favorite," answered Carol.

"That's not true. He likes us all the same," she replied, but hoping Carol was right.

153

"Trust me, it's true," said Carol.

"We've noticed the little things, Grace," added Julia.

"Well, then, I guess I get Coal," Grace said as she happily acquiesced, pleased she had gotten the pretty black mare.

"I'll take the dark brown one if that's okay, Julia," said Carol.

"That's fine with me. I liked the light brown gelding better anyway."

Once their choices were made, they approached their animals and began to get acquainted.

Sam was striding down toward the horse when he saw a rider coming down the entrance road, and even at this distance, he could spot the shining star on his chest, so he waved at the rider who spotted him and turned his horse toward him.

He reined up, dropped to the ground and stepped toward Sam.

"Morning, Sam!"

"Morning," Sam said, still unable to remember the deputy's name, "What news from Denver? Got a court date?"

"Nope. Rawls is dead."

"Dead? What happened?" asked Sam in astonishment.

"Dan sent along a note," he replied as handed Sam a folded sheet of paper.

Sam read:

Sam:

Rawls died about four hours after you left. He was turning yellow, so we called the doc. He was going to do an autopsy, then I told him the story. He asked if it was a fair fight and I told him it was and that there were eight witnesses. He wrote it up as a burst appendix, so, there will be no trial. Tell Deputy Smith to get his ass back here and not lollygag over your ladies.

Dan

Smith! Zeke Smith! Now he remembered.

"Thanks, Zeke. Dan says to get your ass back to Denver."

"I know. He told me to drop this off and not to lollygag."

He shook Sam's hand and said, "We're mighty pleased to know you, Sam."

Then he mounted his horse and turned back toward the access road as Sam watched him leave. So, Rawls was dead, probably from Carol's shot to his gut.

"How poetic," he thought.

He died as Cora had died, but the difference was that he deserved it, and now his ladies wouldn't have to be harassed in court, and Sam was very happy about that.

He walked down to the house, note in hand.

The women had heard Deputy Smith's horse departing and watched Sam walking toward the house, so they left the barn, wondering how soon they'd be appearing in court.

Sam saw them approach and waved them over.

When they were close, Julia asked, "So, when's the court date?"

"There won't be a trial, so none of you have to worry about that torture."

"*They let him go?*" cried Carol.

"No. I freed him, myself, in a manner of speaking. Rawls died a few hours after I dropped him off."

"*He's dead?*" exclaimed Julia.

"Yes. I have a note from Dan. It seems that Rawls began turning yellow and died. They called the doctor in and he was going to do an autopsy, but Dan explained what he had done and about the fight. He asked if it was a fair fight and Dan told him it was and there were eight witnesses. Now, we know Dan didn't interview those witnesses, but he knows I told the truth. So, the doctor just said he died from a burst appendix, and that is the end of the whore-puncher, once and for all."

Each woman felt an enormous relief from the dread of having to testify because they knew what it would be like. They had told Sam that it wasn't that important because they knew he needed Cora's murderer hanged, but it was important. No matter how pretty they were, nor how well-dressed, the defender would portray them as wanton women whose word could not be trusted. But that was gone, and they could go back to just being women.

"In a way, it was poetic justice," Sam said, "He died as Cora died. It was Carol's punch that did him in. I knew I had hit him hard because I was so enraged. But he's gone and I need to let that go and return to the work at hand. We need to get all of you prepared and then I need to find and rescue Catherine. I think I have an idea where she would be, too. We'll talk later, because I think you can give me some valuable input, especially on this. So, did you choose horses?"

"Yes," answered Julia, "Grace has Coal. I have the light brown gelding. I'm going to call him Suede. Carol has the dark brown one, and she named him Coffee. She said she was going to name him Sam, but then she realized he wasn't a stud stallion, so she settled on Coffee."

That caused a round of giggles, and Sam was glad that Grace had Coal. As much as he hated to admit it, because he loved all his ladies, he knew that it was always Grace and recalled her question the first ride they'd shared where she had asked if he would marry any of them. He already had her answer even when she'd asked and was sure of it now. He just didn't know how she thought of him.

He looked at her and asked, "So, Grace, did you want to keep Coal's name, or did you want to give her a new name? She's yours now."

"Oh, no. I love the name. It suits her."

"Good. Let's go back to the barn and start learning to ride, and if you don't mind, I'll walk in front. My hair is getting tired of being soaked."

They were all laughing as they walked to the barn, Sam taking the lead as they ogled his behind for a change, not that he knew it.

Sam brought the three horses out of the barn into the yard, then returned with the tack for each animal.

As he dropped the saddles and the rest of the tack near each horse, he began his class.

"Now for you, the hardest part will be getting the saddle on the horse. These saddles weigh over thirty pounds, and because you're all short, you'll need to use your hips and a swinging motion to get it on the horses back. First, the easy part, the blanket."

Sam tossed a blanket across Coal's back, then showed them how to swing the saddle onto the horses back, letting the saddle's weight take it over the top. It took a few attempts before Grace succeeded, but when she did, she grinned and bowed to each of them.

Next, he showed her how to get the girth tightened and the rest of the tack in place, then he asked her to mount Coal, and had her hang her legs down so he could adjust the stirrups.

"Once I've adjusted the stirrups, Grace, it would be difficult for any man to ride Coal with this saddle because it fits you. So, if you have to use another horse, use your saddle. That goes for each of you, but because your heights are so similar, you could just use one of the other lady's saddles. Obviously, I'd look like a jockey if I tried it, with my knees bunched up. I could ride it okay if I didn't use the stirrups, though.

"By the way, did you know that the Romans didn't have stirrups at all? Their cavalry would go riding into battle with their legs hanging down. I wonder how a group of people that could engineer an aqueduct that traveled hundreds of miles with a perfect slope of about a foot per thousand feet, couldn't figure out something as simple as a stirrup."

"You are a river of knowledge, Sam," said Julia with a big grin.

"More like a dried-up creek, really," he replied with a smile but knew he was just showing off.

Then he helped Julia and Carol with their horses and adjusted their stirrups for them. They all agreed sitting on the horse was much better with the stirrups adjusted for their heights.

Just getting ready to ride took all morning, so they broke for lunch.

While they were at the kitchen table eating, Carol asked, "Sam, didn't you notice that the stirrups on Emma were too long."

"Sure. I just didn't have the time to adjust them."

"I think you just didn't notice."

"Of course, I did. I'm very observant."

Carol said, "Alright, Mister Observant, close your eyes."

Sam asked, "Why?"

"Just do it."

"Okay," he said, closing his eyes.

"What color are my hair and eyes?" Carol asked.

With his eyes tightly closed, Sam replied, "Your hair is a light brown, but with slight shades of a darker brown. They look like autumn leaves that have already fallen. Hold those leaves against the sunlight and you'll see your hair. Both are miracle of nature. Your eyes are a hazel green with flecks of gray. It's how I imagine the angry ocean would look as the waves meet the shore. You have daring eyes that challenge anyone to understand you but accepting those that do."

Before he could open his eyes, Julia quickly asked, "What about mine?"

Sam smiled before answering, "Julia, your hair is almost black, but not quite. It has lighter highlights that reflect the light and suggest a dark, moonless night with the band of the Milky Way crossing the sky, creating an awe in even the hardest of hearts. Your eyes are a dark indigo with streaks of black. Royalty is in your eyes. They are sparkling eyes that express vitality and life and a generous nature so seldom seen."

Grace quietly asked, "And mine?"

Sam's smile softened as he replied, "Your hair, Grace, is gold, but not the cheap gold you see in jewelry. It's a deep gold imbued with a darker red that we can see on those rare sunsets in the Rockies to the west; the sunsets that bring tears as you recognize the magnificence of God's creation. Your eyes are a dark blue with sky blue highlights that mimic the Alpine Forget-me-nots, reminding those that see them to never forget you. They are smiling eyes that reveal a caring and thoughtful soul that is willing to give so much and expect so little in return."

He paused, waiting for permission to open his eyes but didn't hear a word.

Finally, he asked, "Can I open my eyes now?"

Sam still didn't get a response, so he opened them anyway and saw each woman looking at him through misty eyes.

Finally, Carol spoke, sniffling as she said, "I was expecting brown and green, if you even noticed that."

"How could anyone who knows each of you could be so shallow as to only see color? You are all very special people. So, ladies, should we go for a ride?"

They nodded, still finding speech a bit difficult.

By the time they reached the barn, they could converse normally again, but each of them was deeply touched by his poetic description that gave them weak knees and goosebumps.

Sam saddled Cump and each woman mounted her animal in turn. They were wearing their Stetsons and, except for the obvious, resembled diminutive cowboys. At first, they were tentative in the saddle, except for Grace who had ridden before.

"Ladies, talk to your horses as you ride. Pat them on the neck so they get to know you," Sam said loudly as he rode among them.

Sam picked up the pace and headed away from the access road into the pastures to the east. The cattle were all bunched in the southeastern corner near the creek, so they posed no problems.

Soon, the women were enjoying being in control of the large animals. They talked to them constantly and the horses responded.

Sam halted Cump and just watched as they trotted their animals across the pasture, turning them in almost a choreographed motion; it was an impressive sight for many reasons.

Sam was caught up in the sight of Grace, her long golden hair contrasting with Coal's deep black coat. It was enough to make him breathless. But each of these women, just weeks away from that hideous existence, were now free to be themselves; to show the world that they were not powerless any longer. They controlled their destinies as they controlled the horses beneath them. He was extraordinarily proud of them and if they weren't such attractive young women, he would have felt like a father.

After almost thirty minutes of riding at different paces, even an occasional gallop, the three women rode up to Sam.

"Sam, this is incredible," said Grace, "I've ridden horses before but none of them were as smooth as Coal."

"It's wonderful!" echoed Carol.

Julia, as she patted Suede on the neck said, "Suede is a great horse."

"I'm happy that you all took to the saddle so well. It's important. Now, let's head back to the barn and you can learn how to take care of them."

Sam led them back to the barn, and once inside, showed them how to remove the tack and groom the horses. He cautioned them about letting a thirsty horse drink too much at first but letting them drink enough to satisfy their immediate needs before letting them drink more later.

When they returned to the house, Sam led them into the family room to discuss more horse issues.

After they'd all taken a seat, he said, "One thing that is critical is to understand is, that just like us, horses burn fuel. They tire when they are pushed. I can't tell you how often criminals, after committing some crime, will gallop their horses away from the scene. I'd catch them a couple of miles away;

their horses exhausted. Most of our horses are young and strong, and they can keep up a moderate pace for hours, but then they must be rested, fed and watered. Never leave the saddle on too long, either. So, any questions about horses or saddles?"

"Just when can we ride again?" asked Julia.

"They're your horses and your tack. When you want to ride, go for a ride. I'd advise against going too far, though. I'd like to know where you are, so if you need help, I can find you."

Each had a smile on her face as they nodded in unison.

"Now, onto the second thing that I want to talk about – Catherine. I've been thinking about this and I'm reasonably sure she's on a ranch near Hinkley. It'll have to have at least an older woman, maybe with her husband. I wouldn't think there would be any other children there either. So, that should narrow down the search. Does anybody have any ideas about how we could narrow it further?"

In less than thirty seconds, Carol said, "If a woman is minding Catherine and it's been nine months, I think that the woman would have to go and buy some more clothes or maybe some canned milk."

Sam stood, then stepped to the front of her chair, put both hands on the sides of Julia's head and kissed her on her forehead.

"Thank you, Julia! That's great! I never would have thought of that. Of course, they'll need to get some things to keep her going. If it had been a few weeks, it wouldn't have mattered, but in nine months they'd have to get some things. As it turns out, I've met the store owner and I think if I explained the situation, he'd let me know if someone had done that. Okay, good."

After Sam returned to his chair, Carol asked, "Once you find the right ranch, then what?"

"It depends. I don't think they'd have a bunch of watchers in the place; not after nine months. That would be too expensive. Besides, the four that took her were working for Soapy Smith and he didn't even know what they did, so they'd have to return to work.

"My guess is that she's with a couple that one of the four knew and told them to keep her there. The problem will be getting to the house without causing suspicion and being able to find out if she's there without setting off warning bells. I could go there after dark and look around, but there's a risk of being seen and Catherine may be in a bedroom without windows."

"Why don't you go there in the middle of the day in plain sight and pretend to be someone that knows some relative of theirs and are stopping by to visit?" asked Grace.

Sam smiled, quickly stood and repeated his kiss on the forehead with Grace, causing a slight reddening of her ears before he returned to his chair.

"Perfect. I could get right up to the front door and say something loud enough for Catherine to hear. I don't think she'd be bound or locked in a room after all this time and if she heard my voice, hopefully she'd come running. But I think going in alone on a horse would be a problem. I think I need a wife."

That minor comment startled the women, who simply stared at him.

Sam didn't notice but said, "I was going to buy a carriage and horses anyway, so I could escort you all to the theater or opera, so if I buy it now, I can show up in a nice carriage with my wife by my side and step out pretending to be friends of some brother or something. With a woman next to me, I won't be perceived as a threat. I won't be wearing my Colt, either. I want to be as innocent as possible. I'll have my Webley, of course, but nothing showing. So, I'll need someone to volunteer to be my wife for the day."

"You sure you don't want to make that wife for the night as well?" Julia asked and then giggled.

"As much as the idea appeals to me, I think we'll stick to the day for the sake of the plan. So, who'll be my wife?"

Julia and Carol pointed at Grace, who slipped into a full blush.

"I guess that'll be me," she said, astonished that after what she'd been doing at Waxman's, she could still blush at all.

"Okay, Mrs. Brown, I'll go into Denver tomorrow and get the carriage and team. Do we need anything else while I'm there?"

"I suppose you need to get us some riding skirts."

"I was going to buy you each two pair. I was going to get them as close to the color of the horse you ride as possible. How's that for compromising to my prudish behavior?"

"That's fine, Sam," replied Grace, whose face still hadn't returned to its normal shade.

"Now, the details. Depending on where the ranch is, the ride could be as long as six hours. The carriage will be a lot quicker than the wagon, and it'll be more comfortable too. I want Carol and Julia along as well. Because I don't think any of your muscles are ready for a ride of that length yet, we can all ride in the carriage and tie Coffee and Suede as trailers.

"When we near the ranch, Carol and Julia can mount and stay in a suitable location. We'll figure out where to do it when we get to the town. You'll have your Winchesters with you, so you'll be there as backup in case something goes wrong. There will be an extra Winchester in the floor of the carriage along with my shotgun. After we get Catherine, we take the carriage as far as Hinkley. It'll be too late to drive back, but I don't want to stay in Hinkley, either. Suggestions?"

Carol said, "We need to pack the carriage's boot with enough blankets and supplies to camp out for a night. Catherine will be able to sleep on the cushions in the carriage. We can sleep around the carriage, so she'll be protected. Now, where's my kiss?"

Sam laughed as he stepped across the room, took her face in his hands and kissed her forehead.

"And well-earned, Carol. This is a well-thought out plan. Any other ideas on how to approach this?"

No one added anything to the concept, so Sam said, "If you come up with anything, let me know. We have a couple of hours before dinner, so do you want to learn how to use the Colts?"

They unanimously agreed to the idea and went to their rooms to get their weapons and returned just seconds later with their gunbelts.

"Okay, go ahead and put them on."

"By ourselves? Really, Sam?" Julia asked with a grin.

"It was bad enough with those dresses on. With those pants on, you'd have to shoot me."

"Well, we can't have that, can we?" continued Julia, her eyes sparkling.

Sam waited as they strapped the weapons across their hips.

"Okay, let's head out to the back yard and learn the basics."

They all rose, and he made the mistake of letting them precede him down the hallway. The heavy pistols only exaggerated the sway of their walk and he tried to look away but couldn't. He was hypnotized.

Once outside, he tried to concentrate on the guns. He had already marked a location with a small, ten-foot-high ridge that would make a good backstop. Before they had even reached the spot where he wanted them to stand, roughly fifty feet from the ridge, he was talking the fundamentals of safety; keeping only five rounds in the chambers, never pointing a pistol, even empty, at someone you weren't aiming to kill, and always keeping the weapon clean and oiled to prevent it from exploding in your hand or jamming when you most needed it.

He hadn't brought any real targets, but after telling the women to stop at the shooting distance, he walked to the ridge and using a small stick he found nearby, traced three, foot-wide circles about six feet apart into the soft sand of the ridge, then returned to his well-armed ladies.

"Now the Colts you are wearing are .44 caliber, single-action revolvers. That means you need to pull the hammer back before pulling the trigger. So, I want you to take out your guns and make sure the cylinders are empty. Just rotate the cylinder until you've seen six empty chambers."

They each began rotating the cylinders, even though Sam was sure the guns were empty because he wanted them to get used to checking.

"Now that you know you can't accidentally, or purposefully, for that matter, shoot your instructor, I want you to just aim at the circles I've drawn in that bank, bring your guns to bear, cock the hammer and squeeze the trigger until the hammer snaps, which would normally fire a round. Now, don't aim the guns using the sight. It'll slow you down and not improve the accuracy. Just make believe it's your finger and point it at the target. You can also use your left hand as a support for the pistol's handle."

Each woman brought out her Colt, aimed it at the target, cocked the hammer, then Sam was gratified to hear three heavy snaps as the hammers fell.

"How did that feel?" he asked.

"Not as hard as I thought it would be," said Grace.

"Same here," agreed Julia.

Carol nodded without replying.

"Good. Now, we're going to load the guns, so come over here where I have a box of ammunition. Don't take bullets from your belt unless you need to. Those are your emergency cache. If you have a box of cartridges available, use those. Now, I'm only going to let you shoot one at a time, so I can evaluate you individually."

Julia was first, so Sam loaded her Colt with three rounds, spinning the cylinder so the first round would rotate to firing position when she cocked the hammer, then handed her the gun and followed her to the firing location.

"Alright, Julia. If you're ready, take a smooth breath and let it out softly, then raise the gun and aim at the far-left target."

Sam stepped back, and Julia did exactly as she had been instructed; brought the gun to bear and held her breath. The gun bucked in her hands, and Sam looked at the puff of dust. It was just above and to the left of the target.

He walked up to Julia, noting with satisfaction that she kept the gun pointed downrange.

"Well done, Julia! That was very close for your first shot with that Colt. How bad was the kickback?"

"It was noticeable, but not too bad."

"Good. Now you can take the next two at the same target. Don't rush the second shot."

She nodded and looked at the target. Up came the Colt and just three seconds later the next shot left the barrel, hitting the target at the ten o'clock position. Her second shot was only three seconds after the first, a very fast recycle for a first time and it also hit the target.

"Julia, you're a natural. Go ahead and eject your brass."

As a smiling Julia removed the spent cartridges, Grace stepped close and didn't need to be told anything as she'd listened to what Sam had told Julia. Sam didn't even have to comment on her first shot as it hit high on the target, then it was soon followed with the next two; one closer to the center and the other lower, but still within the circle.

She lowered her smoking pistol, turned to Sam, smiled and said, "You're a very good instructor, Mister Brown."

"You're a better student, Miss Felton," he replied with his own smile.

They both stepped back to let Carol fire, and all of her three shots were within the circle, which earned her smiles and congratulations from her sisters and Sam.

Sam looked at his three charges and said, "Ladies, I have to admit, I'd hate to face any one of you in the streets of Dodge City."

They all laughed as they gathered their gear and returned to the house and more domestic chores like cooking dinner.

———

After dinner, they adjourned to the main room.

"Tomorrow, I'll head to Denver and get the carriage and your riding skirts. I'll need to get a suit as well if I'm going to be the domesticated husband of Miss Grace," he said as smiled at her, noting the mild red tinge in her cheeks.

"I should be back by three o'clock, so feel free to ride, shoot or do anything else you want to do. When I get back, I'll show you how to use the Winchesters."

"Can we watch you shoot the shotgun?" asked Julia.

"Let me think about it. Okay?"

"Alright. We can wait."

They talked about the upcoming journey to Hinkley to find Catherine, but no changes were made to the plan, and everyone turned in for the night.

CHAPTER 7

After having breakfast, Sam waved good-bye to the ladies and headed for the barn to saddle Cump. He was running through the plan in his mind, and he couldn't find any major flaws, although it was all dependent on them being right about the location.

He had Cump trotting toward Denver by eight o'clock.

After he'd gone, the women decided to ride in the morning and shoot in the afternoon after Sam returned when they'd get to try the Winchesters.

———

Sam arrived in Denver before nine o'clock and had to hunt around a bit to find the carriage maker because of the size of the growing city. He rode into the large yard, seeing a variety of models outside, but no horses, and he wondered about that.

He walked Cump to the front of the shop, dismounted, and after looping his reins around the hitch rail, he walked into the main shop as a small bell tinkled as he entered, announcing his arrival. The strong smell of varnish permeated the establishment.

A man dressed in stained overalls stepped out from the back room and had the appearance of being the owner. Obviously, the maker didn't bother keeping salespeople on the payroll.

"Can I help you, sir?"

171

"I'm looking for a carriage."

"Glad to help. Anything in particular in mind?"

"Can you show me what you have available?"

"Sure, come on in back."

He led Sam into the assembly area where four workers were working on carriages in various stages of completion. The owner walked past the workers and showed Sam to an interior storage area with completed carriages, and he liked what he saw. They looked like solid construction with a minimum of ostentatiousness.

"These look perfect. Some carriages look like they were built for the Queen of England but probably wouldn't survive a ride on a country road."

"That's very true. All of our carriages use hardwoods for the chassis and lighter woods on top to keep the weight low over the wheels. The springs provide a good ride, but not overly soft. That would ruin the handling. The top is made of heavy, treated canvas and can be locked in place easily. Are you looking for a two or four horse harness?

"Two. Speaking of horses, I'll need a team as well. Do you know where I can buy one?"

"If you need one today, I have several teams out back in our small pasture. If you'd rather have a wider selection, we have a horse ranch out of town."

"No, I'll look in back after making my selection. Do you have any recommendations for the carriage? You know much more about them than I do, and I'll defer to your judgment."

That pleased the builder. He hated when customers pretended to know more than he did. Sam knew that as well and by deferring to the builder, he knew he'd get the best carriage available.

"Well, my personal favorite is the coach in the middle of the row. It's a two-horse rig that has great balance. The seats are cushioned, and it has a large boot in the back. It's not fancy, but it is a solid carriage."

"How much is it?"

"With the horses, it will cost you three hundred and sixty dollars."

"That's a fair price for a well-build carriage and team. Does that include the harness?"

"Yes, it does."

They shook hands on the deal, then they went to the back pasture to look at the horses which turned out to be an easy choice for Sam. He saw a pair of matched gray mares and noticed that most of the horses were in pairs.

He told the shop owner of his selection, which he approved, and Sam told him that he'd be back in an hour or so to pick up the carriage.

He returned to the front of the building, stepped up on Cump, then wheeled him around and headed for the clothing store that he had visited just a few days before.

Once he'd arrived, before heading to the ladies' section, he went to the more comfortable men's area, found a salesclerk and told him he needed an everyday suit, and it didn't take him long to find a nice gray suit that wasn't expensive. The clerk found one in his size and he paid for the suit with cash.

Then he made the long trek to the women's department and quickly found a salesgirl.

"Excuse me, ma'am. I need to pick up some riding skirts."

"Yes, sir. Follow me."

She led him to an aisle filled with a row of riding skirts.

"Now, what size is your wife?"

"Actually, it's for my three sisters. I don't know their sizes, but they're all slim. The tallest, Carol, is about five feet six inches. The shortest, Julia, is about five feet and three inches and Grace is in the middle."

"That makes it easy then. With riding skirts, the biggest concern is the waist size. So, what colors do you need?"

"If possible, I'd like two black, two dark brown, and two light brown or tan. Is that possible?"

"Yes. I think we can handle that. Let me get your order together."

She had his order assembled and ready to go in ten minutes. Sam was able to add the box with his new suit into the large bag that the salesgirl provided for the riding skirts.

He carried his purchases out of the store and returned to the carriage maker where he found the carriage harnessed and waiting.

He stepped down and tied his trail rope to Cump and then to the carriage.

He went inside and met with the builder and wrote him his last draft, which meant that he'd need to pick up some more at the bank. So, after completing the purchase, he exited the office, climbed into the carriage, released the handbrake, and snapped the reins. The team moved the vehicle out into the street smoothly and he was impressed with the nice ride. The seats were comfortable, and he was sure the ladies would appreciate the roof above as well.

He drove to the bank, picked up the blank drafts, then returned to the carriage. He was just getting ready to board the carriage when he noticed the shop next to the bank, returned to the boardwalk and entered.

He noticed several display cases that appealed to him as a salesperson approached him and voiced the eternal, "May I help you, sir?"

"I'm interested in three of the turquois necklaces."

"Very well, sir. Perhaps this design?"

"A little larger, I think."

He reached into the case and showed him a larger pendant.

"That's fine. Do you have three in that type?"

"Yes, sir, we do."

"Very good. Go ahead and put them in nice display boxes, if you could."

"Of course, sir. Will that be all?"

"Yes, thank you."

The clerk and presented Sam with a nice bag containing the three boxes, Sam wrote a draft for the jewelry and returned to the carriage. He moved the clothing bag to the carriage but slid the necklace bag into his saddlebags.

Then he climbed back into the carriage and turned it south to return to the Circle S. It was a very pleasant ride, as the two grays pulled the carriage effortlessly. Sam was thinking he could get used to this, and silently apologized to Cump for thinking such things.

When he returned to the ranch house, he heard gunfire from behind the house and could tell by the rhythm that the ladies were shooting. It made him smile knowing that they actually enjoyed the target practice.

He parked the wagon in the front yard and stepped down from the carriage, then walked in back to Cump and removed the small bag from his saddlebags. He then jogged inside the house and went to each of the three bedrooms, leaving a box on each bed, almost giggling as he envisioned their faces when they found them.

He then returned just as quickly to the carriage without being seen, and after climbing back to the front seat and releasing the handbrake, he drove the carriage to the barn and untied Cump from the carriage. He led him into the barn, unsaddled him quickly, gave him a quick brush-down and let him have some hay and water.

After leaving Cump in his stall, he trotted back to the carriage again and soon had it rocking and rolling as it made its way over the rough ground of the pasture where the women were still shooting.

Carol was the first to see the beautiful conveyance rolling toward them being pulled by two matched gray horses.

Julia was preparing to shoot when she heard Carol call, "Sam's back, and look what he's driving!"

Grace, who was watching Julia, turned and saw what Carol had already seen.

Julia put her Colt down and automatically removed the one empty casing and the four cartridges from the gun.

Sam stopped within fifty feet of the ladies, stepped down from the carriage, then patted the left gray on the neck as the pistol-packing women approached the carriage.

"Sam, that's magnificent!" exclaimed Carol.

"It's really nice to drive, too. If everything is clean out here, why don't you all climb aboard, and I'll give you a ride to the house."

They quickly policed the area and as they climbed into the cabin, and Julia noticed the boxes on the back seat.

"These will be our riding skirts, I assume?" she asked.

"You are quite accurate in your assumption, Julia," Sam replied with a grin as he sat in the front seat beside Grace and took the reins.

Once he turned the carriage back to the house and had it rolling, Carol said, "This is really comfortable, Sam."

While keeping his eyes forward, he replied, "I have to admit, the ride down from Denver was the easiest one I've made and even had to apologize to Cump for thinking it."

The ladies laughed as Sam guided it toward the house and soon stopped at the back porch and let them enter to clean

177

their guns and put away their new riding skirts while he unharnessed the grays and led them into the barn.

Once inside, he took his time as he brushed them and led them into their stalls. There was barely enough room for the carriage in front of the wagon, so he'd probably add a carriage house extension to the barn when the added bedrooms were built. He'd need the room for all of the horses, too.

———

Inside the house, the women had placed their boxes on the floor and had just finished cleaning their revolvers at the kitchen table. They knew that Sam would be pleased with their prioritization of tasks.

"Do you think Sam got our sizes right?" asked Julia.

"As much as he watches us, I think he'd have a good idea," Carol replied before she laughed.

"Well, let's see whose box belongs to whom," said Grace.

They slid their clean and reloaded pistols into their holsters, then lifted the three boxes to the tabletop. Each opened one box and slid them around until Grace wound up with the black skirts, Carol the dark brown and Julia had the tan.

"I have to admit, they're of very good quality," said Carol.

"Let's put them away and get Sam to show us how to shoot the Winchesters," suggested Julia.

They agreed and walked into the bedrooms, chatting as they walked.

After entering their rooms, the house fell silent as each found a small box sitting on her quilt. The silence continued as each opened her box and stared at the beautiful necklace inside. None knew if the other had received one, so no one commented as each woman hid her necklace in the same top drawer of her chest of drawers.

———

Sam entered the front door carrying the box with his new suit and was a bit surprised not to hear any reaction from the ladies, who were still in their bedrooms. They must have found the gifts as they weren't exactly hidden.

He shrugged it off, knowing he would never understand women. Never.

He walked to the corner of the main room where he left three of the Winchesters, picked them up, returned to the seating area, then leaned two of them on the next chair, sat down and cycled the first one, ensuring the chamber was empty.

The Winchester's loud and easily recognized lever action brought the women scurrying from their rooms. Sam glanced up and noticed none of them were wearing the necklaces, which surprised him; maybe they just didn't want to wear them while shooting.

"Did you get lunch in Denver, Sam?" asked Grace uncomfortably as she took a seat.

"No, now that you mention it. I got distracted. I had to go to the carriage maker, the bank, the clothing store and made one more stop before I left."

"And what was that store?" queried Julia.

"You don't know?"

"Why don't you enlighten us," Carol said.

Sam looked at their faces, unable to make out their mood, before he replied, "Well, it was a spur of the moment thing, to be honest. I was leaving the bank and saw this jewelry store and I knew that none of you had any at all.

"I said to myself, 'How can the three prettiest women in the state have no jewelry?'. So, I went in and picked out three necklaces. I didn't want anything splashy or ornate, because that's not who I think you are. You are all naturally beautiful women, so I picked out what I thought was appropriate. Don't you like them?"

"Of course, we like them, you, big idiot!" exclaimed Carol, "They're absolutely perfect. I just didn't know why it was there and I wasn't sure if you bought one for each of us. They're so expensive."

Sam suddenly saw the problem. They thought he might be picking a favorite and that was something he'd been trying to avoid; even though he had.

"I am so sorry! I did this all wrong. I just wanted it to be a surprise. I wanted to know how much I love each of you and just thought I'd let you know."

"We knew that long before we found the necklaces, Sam," Grace said softly.

"Well, thank you for that, but you really do deserve something nice every once and a while."

Grace said, "Sam, you've done nothing but give us nice things since we've known you and not just the material kind either. In fact, those are the least of the gifts you've given us."

"Thank you, Grace, Carol and Julia. So, where do we go next?"

"We can go shoot the Winchesters for an hour or so before we start dinner," answered the pragmatic Carol.

"Okay. I have the rifles ready. When you pick them up, note the serial number on the one you take. Each gun has a different last digit, so just remember that number. That'll be your rifle, although these are technically carbines, and because I messed up the jewelry presentation, I'll demonstrate my shotgun as well."

Julia was pleased with his announcement as each woman picked a Winchester, then looked at the serial number to memorize that last digit.

Sam pocketed a box of ammunition, then rose and went to the kitchen where he kept his shotgun. He put on his scabbard, put two #4 shells into the chambers and slid the shotgun home. He still wore his Colt and figured he may as well put on a full display. The last thing he took with him was an empty bean tin.

He returned to the sitting room where all of his ladies were standing with their repeaters in their hands and their pistols at their hips.

"You are a scary gang of females," Sam said as he smiled at them.

Julia giggled before they walked back down the hallway and left the house though the back door.

When they arrived at the usual firing location, the women began cycling their empty Winchesters to get a feel of the weapons.

Sam was still smiling as he said, "Ladies, I have some bad news. You're way too close for rifle shooting. We need to back up another fifty yards."

They all looked at him and then realized that Winchesters were longer range weapons, so, of course, the targets would have to be further away.

They all stepped back until they reached a new mark that Sam had designated. He had noticed that his old targets had been totally obliterated and wondered just how much shooting they had done while he was gone. They had drawn new circles in the bluff in preparation for today's practice, though.

He had plenty of ammunition, but worried about the fatigue on their smaller wrists. He'd mention it later when they finished their orientation with their Winchesters.

"Are you comfortable with the repeaters?" he asked.

They all nodded before he said, "Okay. Who will be first this time?"

"I'll try," answered Grace as she stepped to the firing line.

Sam handed her three cartridges and told her to load the rifle. He had given them the loading lesson two days ago when they dry-fired the guns.

Grace inserted the three cartridges and cycled the lever bringing one into the chamber, brought the rifle to her shoulder and aimed deliberately. She squeezed off a shot and was gratified to see a dust cloud in the center of one of their new targets. She then recycled the lever, fired, and keeping the sights in place, fired again. All three were inside the target at seventy-five yards.

Sam slowly turned to look at her, then exclaimed, "Wow! Grace, that was superb shooting! Are you really sure that you've never fired a rifle before? I'm not being a smart aleck, either. I've never seen anyone do that well with a Winchester before."

She smiled and replied, "No, Sam, I really haven't fired one before."

He turned to the second shooter and said, "That's going to be a tough act to follow, Carol."

Carol stepped in front and took her three cartridges. Her shots were a bit wider, but very acceptable for a new shooter.

Julia did better than Carol, but neither was close to Grace's performance.

"Once again, ladies, you astonish me."

"Can we see the shotgun now?" Julia asked.

"Sure. I may as well give you the full show. There's a reason I modified the shotgun the way it is, and it's why we'll move back to the pistol range. The shotgun is a close-in weapon, and this one is even more so. It's usually even closer than the pistol when I've had to use it, but I'll use that distance."

He walked downrange to the ridge with the ladies walking behind him, when they reached the firing spot, he said, "Wait here. I'll be right back."

Then he picked up the empty tin, walked fifty feet to left of the target where he found a melon-sized rock and placed the can on its top before he returned to where the women waited with curious looks on their faces.

"Okay. Now don't stand behind me at all; stay to the right about twenty feet away. Now this distance is a little further back than the Boulder bank robbers were and assume that the can over to the left is another bad guy who's acting as their lookout."

They had been wondering what the purpose of the can was, but still didn't quite believe that the shotgun's spread was that wide to be able to hit the tin.

He watched them move to his right and when he was satisfied that they were far enough away, he said, "Ready? This won't take long, so you have to keep your eyes open."

"We're ready, sir," Grace replied.

He nodded, then turned and faced the ridge. Suddenly, he yanked the shotgun from the scabbard, then his left hand ran across the barrels and pulled back both hammers as he slid the gun to his right side. He immediately pulled the trigger sending the gun flying backwards across the pasture, and as soon as it had discharged, he was reaching for his Colt. He turned the pistol toward the can and fired. The can leapt into the air and Sam fired again, making it leap higher, then followed it with four more shots each sending the can higher until it fell to the ground.

The smoke still hung over the range and the ridge was still enveloped in a cloud of dust from the shotgun pellets.

As he holstered his Colt, he turned to find his shotgun and noticed the women were either in a state of shock or just in awe of the amount of firepower that Sam had just unleashed.

He walked the twenty feet to retrieve his shotgun and noticed that it had dug a straight furrow some ten feet long. He thought that it must be a record.

He snatched up his scattergun, then walked back to the shooting area.

"Sam," asked Carol quietly, "can you do that every time?"

"Pretty much. Why?"

"If you can shoot the Colt that well, why use the shotgun at all?"

"Because a pistol shoots one bullet. Bad guys think they have a chance against one bullet; especially if they think they're a stud with a Colt themselves. It was never my intention to develop any kind of reputation as a gun hand because that causes more trouble than it solves. The shotgun, on the other hand, can be wielded by someone who barely knows which direction the bullets leave the gun. Troublemakers see those two big barrels pointed at them, and even the biggest, meanest gunfighter in the West isn't going to draw. That's why while I was sheriff, I never had to kill anyone. The added advantage was that I have never been hit."

"Have you been shot at?" asked Grace.

"A few times, but I could see the shooter, so it wasn't that big of a problem. The drygulchers now, those are the hombres you need to watch out for. You never see them. You're just riding along, minding your own business and suddenly you're hit with a bullet. The sound reaches you second later and if you're lucky, you get to hear it."

"Did anyone ever try to drygulch you?" Grace asked softly.

"Once. I was riding out of town looking for a horse thief that had taken one from a livery. I tracked him about a half mile out of town, but noticed he was really flying right after he began his escape, but the horse had been slowing down after that. So, I thought he'd most likely pull over and wait to see if anyone followed while the horse rested.

"I gambled that he had, so I pulled over and tied Cump to a tree. The only location he could use was a small hill to the left. The road curved around it, so I figured he'd be on the other side of the hill if at all. I walked around the hill to the back side and as I cleared the other side of the hill, I found him lying there with a Henry rifle pointing down the road. I snuck up behind him and pointed the scattergun his way and suggested he may want to join me for a trip back to Boulder. He dropped his gun and we returned. His Henry is in the house, by the way."

"Sam, one of these days, you're going to have to tell us some more stories," said Julia.

"It'll break up the monotony, I suppose. Let's head back. Tomorrow should be a momentous day."

They walked back to the house, chatting about the Winchesters and Sam's incredible display.

"I'll give you ladies a break tonight and I'll clean the guns while you make dinner. Unless you'd prefer that I cook dinner while you clean the guns."

They all laughed and didn't bother providing the obvious answer.

So, when they entered the house, Sam walked back to the main room and laid the rifles on the floor and began to clean his Colt first. He didn't know that he was the topic of conversation in the kitchen.

———

In a lowered voice, Carol asked, "What are we going to do with Sam?"

Julia asked, "What do you mean?"

Carol replied, "In case you haven't noticed, Sam is the most remarkable man we've ever met. He's treated us like we were queens instead of what we were. He buys us things; he tells us how wonderful we are and never asks for anything, and it's not an act. I honestly believe that he expects nothing."

Grace said, "I know what you mean, Carol. I feel guilty about it sometimes. He tells us not to feel bad, but it's hard. He's fun to be around and more considerate than anyone I've ever met; male or female. And don't tell me you didn't feel what I felt when he described each of us. He was a lawman for all those years, and we all expected a lawman's concise description, but what he gave us was poetry. What made them even more special was that they came from his heart. He wasn't trying to woo us or make us crawl into his bed. He was telling us how he felt about us."

Leave it to Julia to say, "I, for one, wouldn't mind crawling into his bed. Even if it was the couch."

Grace didn't snap at her, but instead quietly asked, "I think you'd scare him to death. Do you know why?"

187

"No."

"Because he doesn't want us to think he has a favorite."

"But he does, and it's obvious," said Carol.

Grace hoped she was right, but didn't want to admit it as she replied, "Even if he does, Carol, he'll never say or do anything to show it because he doesn't want to hurt any of our feelings. That's why you were right to ask the question about what to do about him. I know we joke with him about his having to use the pump to cool himself down, but it really must be tough on him with us being here. I'm sure in a normal world, he'd have one of us in his bed just to keep himself sane, but he doesn't want us to think that we're still whores. He's going to keep his hands off. Period. It's a real dilemma for him."

"One thing we can do is try to dress less seductively," suggested Julia.

"Maybe, but I'm not sure that will help much," replied Grace.

She then continued, saying, "All we can do is keep on going. We're going to try to rescue Catherine tomorrow and maybe that will create some major changes. I feel so bad for him. His sister was taken from him and his niece is being held. He had to get that bastard whore-puncher, and even with all that, he has taken time to tell us how much he cares for us. He makes us feel like the focus of his life."

Carol nodded then said, "Well, Grace, we are. Think about it, for years, his focus has always been on just keeping his town safe. No one really cared much what happened to him. If he was gunned down trying to stop bank robbers, they'd just shrug their shoulders and hire a new sheriff. All he had to care about was Cora and Catherine and now they have been taken.

"The best thing we can do is help him get Catherine back, and then when she's here, we take care of her. It'll be kind of nice really; being a substitute mother to a little girl. I've always wanted a little girl of my own to pamper. When I was down in Hinkley, I thought that could never happen, but now I think it could."

Grace replied, "Let's just finish cooking and we can talk about this later."

Julia and Carol nodded, then they resumed their cooking chores and Grace even added a touch of honey to the biscuits.

———

Twenty-six miles south, Catherine sat in her bed. She was so lonely. She missed her mama and papa. *Why did they leave her?* Aunt Clara was nice to her, but it wasn't the same. Her mama would make her laugh and sometimes her papa would tickle her tummy. It just wasn't the same.

CHAPTER 8

It was time for Catherine to come home and Sam couldn't sleep. Just as he had before, he had laid in his couch/bed until the early hours of the day before even falling into a light sleep. Now he was awake again and he had to be ready for any contingency, which was impossible. All he knew was that he had to rescue his niece.

After he thought it was close enough to dawn to get ready for the day, he threw off his blanket and swung his legs to the floor. Ten minutes after rising, he had the cookstove heating, the coffee pot on its hotplate and was dressed except for his Stetson, Colt and boots. He had remembered to put on his new suit's pants, and the fresh wool itched something fierce.

He knew better than to start breakfast but noticed some of Grace's biscuits nearby and knew she had added a little honey to her recipe. He didn't think anything could make them better, but as soon as he took a bite, he discovered that he was wrong. Why he enjoyed the biscuits more than anything else, he'd never guess. It just was, but he knew it was better than developing a taste for whiskey.

He finished the one biscuit, returned to the family room and was slipping on his boots when he heard a door open behind him and knew who it was before he turned around. It was Grace. He could tell by the way she walked as each of his ladies had a different step, and he knew hers best, maybe because he anticipated it so often.

Without turning, he said quietly, "Good morning, Grace."

She asked, "How did you know it was me?"

"The sound of your footsteps. You each have different steps."

"I should remember that," she said as she walked closer behind him.

Sam could almost hear her smile before she asked, "Why so early, Sam?"

"I couldn't sleep much because I spent too much time thinking. I want this to go perfectly."

Grace took a seat across from him and said, "It will, Sam. We'll have Catherine back in the house tomorrow and we'll get to meet her today."

Sam smiled at her as he said, "Wait till you get to know her, Grace. She's everything that any parent could hope for in a child. I don't know how to tell her about her parents, though. I picked out a plot north of the house, near that aspen grove for their resting place. I plan on having Cora and Richard brought home. This is their home, Grace. It's where they should be; together.

"I haven't talked much about Richard, and that wasn't fair of me. He was a good man, Grace. When Cora first brought him home to introduce him to me and our parents, I tried hard to hate him for taking my sister from me, but I couldn't. He was a warm and generous man, and I knew he would always be there for her. They were so much in love that it made me feel small for every doubting him.

"We became good friends, and whenever I came to visit, they'd both welcome me like some long-lost friend. In a way, I guess that I was. I should have visited more often because they were much more precious to me than that town I was protecting. I should have been protecting them. Did you know Richard didn't even own a gun? He trusted everyone. That's probably why those murderers got so close to him. Well, Grace, today we go and find their little girl."

"Yes, we will, Sam."

He stared into her bright blue eyes as he said, "Thank you for everything you've done for me, Grace. Without you, and Carol and Julia, I probably would have gone off on some aimless war of revenge that I couldn't win. You've all given me so much that you could never begin to realize."

Grace wanted so much to wrap him in her arms, but knew it wasn't the right time. They had a job to do.

"I'm going to get breakfast started, Sam," she said as she rose, then touched his shoulder.

"Oh, and Grace?" he said as he looked up at her.

"Yes?"

"The honey was a nice touch in those biscuits."

She laughed and said, "I was wondering if you'd notice," then left the front room and walked to the kitchen to start breakfast.

Carol and Julia joined her shortly and after visiting the privy, they returned to help with breakfast. It was going to be a big breakfast as they didn't know how the rest of the day would go. They also sliced some ham and wrapped a loaf of bread in some waxed paper and packed some canned beans and other tins into a bag, along with some salt and onions and even included some hard-boiled eggs. If anyone had watched, they might have thought they were preparing for a picnic rather than a rescue mission.

————

After they had eaten, Sam went out to the barn with Carol and Julia. They saddled their horses while Sam harnessed the grays to the carriage.

Sam looked over at the ladies and said, "Carol and Julia, you know we need to name the grays. Seeing that you did such a good job on your horses, did you want to give it a shot? We'll have a long ride in the carriage."

"It'll give us something to do, Sam," answered Julia.

"Good. Let's get this show on the road."

The Sam led the grays and the carriage to the front yard where Carol and Julia tied Coffee and Suede to the tie bars in back of the carriage.

They all entered the house, Carol and Julia took their Winchesters out to their horses and put them in the scabbards, then returned to help load the food and blankets into the boot before adding two more bedrolls to those already on their horses' saddles.

Sam was wearing his suit with the Webley in its familiar location then grabbed the last Winchester that would be making the trip. He had given Carol and Julia each an extra box of ammunition to add to their saddlebags, which also contained their Colts.

"Have we forgotten anything, ladies?" he asked as they stood by the carriage.

"Just a few canteens of water. I don't think the two on Coffee and Suede would be enough," said Carol.

"Good, I'll grab a couple more."

After the two additional canteens were added to the trailing horses, they all stepped into the carriage. Grace looked very wifely in her conservative dress as Sam placed the Winchester on the floor and they started south.

The grays kept up a steady pace; even faster than Sam had expected and they didn't seem stressed at all.

———

They arrived in Hinkley three hours later, so it was mid-morning when they drove the carriage to the mercantile, but only Sam entered. The women were all staring at Waxman's across the way as he walked into the store. *Was it only a few weeks ago that they were almost imprisoned in there?*

Sam strode inside and spotted the pleasant proprietor, who met his eyes and smiled.

"Welcome back! The folks were mighty pleased with what you did to that sin haven across the street. The town is a much happier place now."

"I'm glad to hear that. Good people should be able to live in peace."

"What can I get for you today?"

"John, I hope you can help me with some information, but first, let me tell you why I was here last time. I was the sheriff of Boulder and came down to visit my sister, her husband and their four-year-old daughter. When I arrived, their ranch was deserted. I found out from Dan Grant that my brother-in-law had been murdered in his front yard, and my sister and niece had been taken. Then I discovered that my sister had been taken down to Waxman's and sold into prostitution. They threatened to kill her precious little girl if she made any trouble. Then a month ago, some cow puncher from the Bar C named Steve Rawls killed her. I arrested him and turned him over to Sheriff Grant, but now I need to find my niece. I think she's being held nearby, but I don't know where. Do you remember if anyone, probably an older woman, has purchased any clothes for a young girl? You know, a dress or something."

John Arden was a mixture of being choked up and furious upon hearing the story, but after taking a deep breath, he said, "About two months ago, Clara Ashley, out at the Lazy A came in and bought three little girl's dresses. I thought that was odd because she doesn't have any children at all. Never did. She and her husband own that run-down ranch about six miles due east. They don't have a sign or anything, but the access road is easily spotted. There's a big pine tree right across from the access road."

"Thanks for the information. Have any hard types been spending any time around the ranch?"

"Not that I know of, but I never go out that way."

"Well, I'm going to go and check. I'll bring my niece by so you can meet her when we get her back."

"I'd really like that."

"Thanks again," Sam said as he headed back to the carriage.

As he stepped out, he saw that the women quickly turned their heads from staring at Waxman's to look at him with anxious eyes and was more than happy that he'd taken them from that place.

"I think we have a winner, ladies," he said as he climbed aboard.

He snapped the reins and the grays started moving as he continued, saying, "The proprietor told me that two months ago, a woman named Clara Ashley, who lives with her husband on a poor ranch about six miles down the road, bought some little girl dresses even though she had never had any children."

"Sam, that has to be it!" said Julia excitedly.

"I also asked if any hard cases were around town or the ranch, and he didn't think so."

"I'm so excited, I can hardly breathe," said Grace.

"Same here. I can't wait to see her," echoed Carol.

"I only hope she remembers my voice. It's been almost nine months and she's almost five."

Carol said, "Sam, you're a hard person to forget."

"In this case, I hope you're right."

They rolled on and when Sam spotted a lone pine standing by the side of the road, he stopped.

"There's the pine that marks the entrance to the ranch on the other side. Does anyone see any good hiding places?"

"There!" pointed Carol.

Sam looked where she was indicating and saw a stand of cottonwoods a few hundred yards behind them. How he had missed it, he'll never know.

"Okay, ladies. Get mounted and get armed."

"We're a regular whore army," cracked Julia.

Sam quickly said, "No, Julia. You are my Avenging Angels."

Properly chastised, and receiving death glares from Carol and Grace, she said, "You're right, Sam. That's much better."

Carol and Julia exited the carriage and released their horses. They reached into their saddlebags, removed and strapped on their Colts, then mounted and waved as they trotted to the trees.

Sam and Grace both waved back then Sam looked at Grace and said, "Well, Mrs. Brown, we're almost ready. I think our story is going to be that we recently arrived in Denver and were looking to buy a small ranch. We stopped at the land office and they suggested to try theirs. Now, I'm going to be talking loudly, so act like it's not important. Ready?"

"Yes, dear husband," said Grace with a big smile.

She was surprised and pleased when Sam said, "I like the sound of that."

Then he flicked the reins and the carriage rolled ahead. When they reached the pine, Sam looked on the other side of the road and saw an access road, but it barely qualified as it was just some ruts in the ground. He turned the carriage and drove toward a distant ranch house. In its day, it might have been a nice place, but a long time without maintenance had left its mark.

As they approached the house, Sam saw an older man exit the front door and stare at them. This may be more difficult than he anticipated.

"Howdy!" Sam shouted as he kept the carriage rolling.

The old man said nothing as he continued to glare at him.

Sam stopped the carriage and stepped out, then turned to Grace and said in a loud voice, "I'll be just a minute, sweetheart. You just stay right there and relax."

Sam turned and took a few long strides toward the house, reached the steps at the bottom of the porch and stopped before the old man spoke.

He growled, "I didn't give you permission to step down."

Sam all but shouted, "Oh, excuse me. Is that a requirement out here in the West? We just arrived here from Indiana a few days ago. We arrived by train and bought this carriage."

In her bedroom, Catherine stopped rocking on her bed after hearing the loud, familiar voice. It sounded like her Uncle Sam. She rose from the bed, walked slowly out of her room toward the front of the house and saw Aunt Clara standing behind Uncle Fred who was talking to a man. She couldn't see his face because her aunt and uncle were in the way, but she took a few quiet steps toward the door.

"I ain't deaf, mister, and I don't care where you come from either. You just turn that fancy rig around head back to Denver."

"We stopped at the land office to see if any ranches were available and they suggested we look at yours. We'd offer you a good price. What does land sell for around here? I know what a good farm goes for back in Indiana, but my wife Cora there needed to be closer to her dear niece, Catherine, so we moved."

Catherine heard her name and her mama's name. *It was her Uncle Sam! He's come to take her home!*

Suddenly, she didn't care about being quiet. She screamed, "Uncle Sam!" and ran for the door.

Sam didn't need any more incentive and bounded up the steps and threw both old people out of the way as he charged into the main room. If they broke a bone, too bad. He saw the bright eyes of his niece and dropped to his heels to let her jump into his arms. She was crying, and Sam wasn't too far behind as he clutched onto her.

The old couple behind him recovered from Sam's surprise entrance then entered their house quickly as Clara screamed at him, "You leave my daughter alone, mister! You get out of my house or my husband will fill you full of holes!"

Sam lifted Catherine and turned to see the old man holding an old Colt Baby Dragoon that looked as if it would explode if he pulled the trigger.

He lowered Catherine and pushed her behind him.

He stared at the couple and said, "Do you two know how much trouble you're in? This is my niece, Catherine Short. She and her mother were kidnapped eight months ago and that makes you both accessories to kidnapping."

Sam then flipped open his jacket displaying his badge.

"I told Sheriff Dan Grant that I was coming down here today, so he knows where you are. You drop that gun or you'll both hang."

Fred snarled, "Not if we kill you and take the little girl away."

"With what? You don't have two nickels to rub together."

Sam continued to speak in a loud voice, hoping Grace would hear and do what was necessary.

Then Clara surprised Sam when she said, "Our nephew will take care of us. He works for Soapy Smith, and if you knew who he was, you'd run all the way back to Indiana."

The Ashleys were paying too much attention to Sam, and at least one should have been watching his cute little blonde wife.

Just about that time, the petite lady was quietly stepping behind Fred Ashley with the Winchester pointed at his back.

Sam saw her and smiled as he said, "Mister Ashley, I suggest you drop your antique firearm, or my sweet wife will punch a hole through you with her nice new Winchester."

As he finished his sentence, the Ashleys were rewarded with that distinctive sound of a Winchester levering a round into the chamber and the metallic sound of the expelled cartridge hitting the floor.

"Drop it!" yelled Grace, in case they hadn't heard the Winchester's threat.

Fred complied, opening his hand and letting the ancient Colt clatter to the floor.

Sam kicked the old pistol out of the way and grabbed his Webley from its holster.

He kept the pistol pointed at the couple, but glanced at Grace, smiled and said, "Come in, wonderful, well-armed wife, and meet Catherine."

Grace released the hammer, so the Winchester wouldn't go off, and lowered it.

Catherine looked around from behind her Uncle Sam's legs and saw a pretty lady who reminded of her of her mama looking at her and smiling.

Sam gestured with the Webley and waved the Ashleys back away from the door.

"Grace, why don't you pick up Catherine and take her to the carriage. I want to have a chat with our elderly friends."

Then without looking down, he said, "Catherine, this is your Aunt Grace. We're going to take you home now, okay? You can go with her. She's been waiting to meet you for a long time."

Catherine was drawn to Grace by her smile then quickly ran to her and hugged her legs. Grace reached down with her free hand and rubbed her head.

"Let's go home, Catherine," Grace said in a soft voice.

Catherine looked up at her face and smiled as Grace took her hand and led her out of the house.

Sam watched them leave, then returned his focus to the Ashleys and said, "Now, Fred and Clara Ashley, I should take you both in and have you charged with kidnapping. That carries a death sentence, by the way. Now I'd be willing to let that go if you tell me a few things. First, I want to know who brought Catherine here."

They mulled it over; their bluster about having an in with Soapy Smith had been a bit of an exaggeration. Their nephew said he worked for him, but never showed any evidence of it. But the big man with the badge sitting in front of them was very real, as was his threat of hanging.

Finally, Clara said, "We didn't know about no kidnapping. Our nephew, Gerald Price, told us he found the little girl wandering around, that's all."

"Now, I know, and you know that story is nothing but horse manure. Your nephew, Gerald Price, and that had better be his real name, was involved in a kidnapping and murder. They shot and killed my brother-in-law, that little girl's father, and they kidnapped my sister and sold her into prostitution down at Waxman's. I killed the owner, his cousin, and then the cow hand who beat my sister to death. I beat him to death with three punches, so you do not want to make me angry. Trust me."

He paused to let the threat sink in, then said, "Now, I want to know the name of the three men he was with, and their descriptions. You would do well to start talking"

Clara spoke first when she said, "One was very short. He wore snakeskin boots and had white hair. His name was Ted Robinson. The second man was medium height and build with a white streak in his hair. That's Abe Thompkins. The last one was about your height, but fat. He had long, greasy hair. His name is John Berringer."

"Can I guess they're one of Soapy's crews?"

"I think so."

"All right. I appreciate that you didn't abuse my niece, and for that, I'll forget I was here, but I wouldn't let your nephew know about my visit. If he or any of them come down here and ask, just tell him the little girl ran away."

Sam walked out the door, hoping that Fred would try to retrieve his pistol, but he didn't.

When he reached the carriage, Grace and Catherine were chatting away and Sam smiled as he stepped into the carriage, snapped the reins, then turned the carriage back down the access road.

Catherine was very happy. She had her Uncle Sam and her new friend, Grace, with her.

"Are my mama and papa waiting at home Uncle Sam?"

This was happening faster than he planned, but he thought that he'd better tell her now rather than later.

He stopped the carriage, turned to Catherine, then plucked her from the seat and sat her on his lap.

"Catherine, sweetie, remember when those bad men took you away?"

"Yes. They hurt my papa and made my mama cry."

"Well, they hurt your papa so bad that he died, sweetie. He's in heaven now."

"He's in heaven with God and the angels?"

"Yes, sweetie. And after they took you from your mama, they hurt her badly, too, and she died. But she found your papa in heaven, so they're together again, and they're happy. They're with God and all the angels. They look down on you all the time and they are very happy that I found you. Your mama and papa told me to come and find you and then take care of you. Your Aunt Grace was with your mama when she died and the last thing that she told Aunt Grace was to tell me to find you, and we have. Do you understand, sweetheart?"

Catherine didn't cry. She would miss her mama and papa, but if they were in heaven with God and happy, then she could be happy, too. She still had her Uncle Sam to watch over her and her Aunt Grace now.

"I understand, Uncle Sam. Is Aunt Grace going to stay with us?"

Grace, tears dripping onto her dress, said, "Yes, honey, I'll stay."

"That's good, Aunt Grace. I like you a lot."

"I like you, too, Catherine."

Sam then said, "You know, Catherine, I have a surprise for you. You have two more aunts waiting just down the street. Want to go meet them?"

"More aunts? Do you collect them, Uncle Sam?"

Grace was wiping her face as she laughed and Sam replied, "It sure seems that way, sweetheart."

He got the carriage rolling down the access road and turned west toward Hinkley.

He stopped at the trees and waited while Carol and Julia rode out to greet them.

Catherine watched them ride close and asked, "Are those my new aunts? They sure have a lot of guns."

"Just like us, they are here to protect you, Catherine," answered Sam.

Grace waved her hand quickly, indicating that the mission was successful. Both horse-mounted women smiled as they dismounted, tied off their horses, removed their gunbelts, stuffed them into their saddlebags, then trotted to the carriage and hopped in.

"Carol, Julia, I'd like you to meet my niece, Catherine. Catherine, this is your Aunt Carol, the one with the brown hair, and your Aunt Julia, who has black hair."

Carol and Julia were as enchanted with Catherine as Grace had been as Catherine stood on the front seat smiling at her new aunts with her big blue eyes.

"Hello, Aunt Carol and Aunt Julia."

"Hello, Catherine," they both said as they smiled.

Catherine then turned and plopped down on the seat as her Uncle Sam started the carriage forward and had them trotting toward Hinkley as his ladies and his niece became acquainted. Catherine was pleased to be the center of attention of so many pretty ladies.

Sam stopped the carriage in Hinkley outside of the mercantile, scooped Catherine into his arms and said to his ladies, "I'm fulfilling my promise to John Arden, who gave us the information that led us to find Catherine."

They nodded and waved at Catherine as she looked at them with her bright, blue eyes. She smiled and waved back.

Sam entered the store and saw John standing in his customary location, and when he saw Catherine, his face brightened.

"John, I'd like you to meet my niece, Catherine. We would never have found her without your help, so we thank you."

"Well, I'm just tickled to meet you, Catherine. You look like a very sweet, little girl."

"I try to be nice," she answered.

"Wait a minute," John said.

He went to the penny candy display near the register, took out a paper bag and filled it with treats, then stepped back and handed the bag to Sam, who opened it and let Catherine choose her favorite. She reached in and picked out a peppermint.

"Thank you, sir," she said with a giant smile as the candy rattled around against her teeth.

It was one of those smiles that could melt even the grouchiest old man's heart, and John was far from grouchy, so his melted a bit more.

"Thank you for your help, John. It meant more to me than you'll ever know. Right now, Catherine's mama is in heaven looking at you and telling us to thank you from her as well."

John sniffed as he took Sam's offered hand and gave him strong shake.

"We need to get back now, so we'll be off. If you ever need anything, John, you can find me at the Circle S, seven miles south of Denver."

John nodded, and Sam left the store as Catherine waved at him over her uncle's shoulder.

When they reached the carriage, Sam handed Catherine to Carol in the back as she held onto the bag of candy.

"Catherine, why don't you spend some time getting to know Aunt Carol and Aunt Julia. Okay? And you can share your candy with your aunts because they're just big little girls."

Catherine giggled, then said, "Okay, Uncle Sam," and offered each of her new aunts a treat from her bag of candy.

The backseat ladies were enormously pleased to have Catherine as a traveling companion as they each took a piece before Catherine stood, leaned over the front seat and held the bag open for her Aunt Grace, who smiled and took a peppermint before Catherine returned to her seat between her Aunt Julia and Aunt Carol.

Sam climbed back into the carriage and looked over at Grace. He didn't want her to think that he wanted her to spend less time with Catherine but was trying to be fair, so he looked over at her and winked.

Then he said, "Well, Mrs. Brown, shall we go home now?"

"That's a wonderful idea, Mister Brown," she replied as she winked back.

The two women in back were too engrossed with Catherine to notice.

———

The grays were showing signs of fatigue when they were five miles north of Hinkley, but even though the sun was still up, Sam estimated they had less than an hour of sunlight left.

"We need to stop and rest the horses. It will probably be best to camp here. I see a nice area up ahead on the right. That stream we used last time should still be near the road. Let's check it out."

Sam turned the carriage, pulled well off the road and stopped near some trees. There was plenty of grass and the creek was nearby, as he had hoped.

He stepped down from the carriage and began unharnessing the grays. They could smell the water and were getting anxious. As he was handling the team, Carol and Julia were unsaddling their horses. To Grace's delight, that meant she had Catherine to herself, and she took full advantage of it, too. She held the little girl as she chatted excitedly about seeing her Uncle Sam again and finding out she had so many aunts.

She was taken aback when Catherine said," Uncle Sam likes you best."

"Why do you say that, sweetie?"

"When he looks at you, it's different. It's like how my papa looked at my mama. He likes my other aunts, but he likes you best."

"You love your Uncle Sam, don't you, Catherine."

"Oh, yes. My mama said he was special. I think so, too. Don't you think so?"

"Yes, I do, Catherine."

"That's good. Because you look at my Uncle Sam like my mama looked at my papa."

Grace couldn't respond to her innocent perception. Children could see through adult's facades sometimes, and Catherine was obviously more attuned to it than most youngsters.

The horses were all quietly munching grass as Sam walked up to Catherine and asked," Would you like to have a picnic, Catherine?"

Her eyes lit up, as she excitedly replied, "A picnic? Really? That will be fun! Are we going to have a fire, too?"

"Of course, sweetie. And then we're going to camp here because the horses need to rest from all the walking they had to do."

"That sounds like fun, too."

Carol and Julia approached, and Catherine smiled at them as she said, "We're going to camp because the horses need to sleep. What are your horses' names?"

Carol replied, "My horse is the dark brown one. His name is Coffee."

Julia then said, "Mine is the light brown horse. I named him Suede. It's like a soft, brown leather."

"Those are good names. What are the gray horses' names?"

They all looked at each other. They had forgotten to take care of that minor task.

"We forgot to name them," said Julia. "Do you have an idea?"

"That's easy," she replied, pointing at the left animal, "That one's Humpty and the other one's Dumpty."

The adults all laughed, and Sam said, "Why not? Okay, Catherine, you just named the horses. Good job!"

Catherine beamed. This was turning into a wonderful day.

Julia looked at their rumps and said, "Well, from behind, they do look like eggs."

Unlike their last camping expedition, they were better prepared this time. Sam started a large fire as the ladies set out the food they had brought and with all the blankets and bedrolls, everyone would stay warm later.

Catherine was the center of attention and enjoying every minute. She missed her mama and papa, but because she knew they were happy together and watching her, she enjoyed being with her Uncle Sam and all her aunts.

For Carol, it was her dream come true. The adorable little girl that she always had dreamed of, even in that hellhole in Hinkley, was with her now. She may have to share, but she cherished every second she could hold her and talk to her.

The sun was long gone, and the food and plates were all put away. It was a balmy night, but even then, at this altitude, it would get chilly later, so set out their four bedrolls near the carriage as Sam put the carriage's roof up.

Once everything was ready, Sam plucked Catherine from the middle of her conversation with her aunts.

"Catherine, I think you need to get some sleep. Tomorrow, we'll be home and if I know your aunts, they'd be keeping you awake all night. Or am I wrong, ladies?"

They all laughed in agreement.

"Say good-night to your aunts, sweetie."

Sam handed her to Carol, who hugged her, gave her a kiss on the forehead and said sweet nothings to her, then regretfully passed the smiling bundle to Julia. After Catherine had told her good-night, Julia enjoyed her goodnight time with Catherine, then sighed, and gave her to Grace. Grace hugged and kissed her, told her how much she loved her, and after Catherine wished her a goodnight, she suddenly leaned over and pecked Grace on the cheek, then she reached out for Sam, who carried her to the carriage.

Sam laid her on a blanket that had been spread across the wide back seat and after she had laid down, Sam removed her worn shoes and saw the need for another shopping trip soon.

Catherine asked, "Uncle Sam, are you sleeping in the carriage, too?"

"No, sweetie. Your aunts and I will be sleeping outside in our sleeping bags so we can keep any bears from bothering you."

"Are there really bears?"

"Sometimes, but not too many. But you're too precious to us, so we need to be really careful."

"Okay. But you're going to be close?"

"Right next to the carriage."

"I like my aunts, Uncle Sam. Did you marry them all?"

Sam laughed, then replied, "No, sweetheart, I saved them from the same dangerous place where they were hurting your mama. Your aunts had been stolen just like your mama was. They were all hurt a lot, and I got really mad and took them away and brought them home to make them happy. They are all wonderful ladies, and nobody will ever hurt them again."

"Did you hurt the bad men who were hurting them?"

"Yes, I did, Catherine. I shot one bad man after he tried to shoot me. He owned the place that was holding your mama and your aunts. He's dead now and the place that was being used to hurt ladies like your mama and your aunts has been closed. I hoped they would burn it to the ground, too. I found the man that killed your mama too. But instead of shooting him I fought him with my fists, so I could hurt him like he hurt your mama. He died, too."

"I'm glad you killed those men, Uncle Sam. They were bad men and hurt my mama and my aunts."

"Catherine, now that your mama and papa are in heaven, I'm going to ask a judge to make me your papa. Would you like that?"

"Oh, yes! That would be wonderful! I could call you papa, too. It's much easier than Uncle Sam."

Sam smiled and said, "Yes, it is. Now you get some sleep, sweetheart."

He leaned over to give her a kiss on her forehead, when she grabbed his neck and hung on tightly saying, "Thank you for taking me home, Papa."

He hugged her back and whispered to her, "I wish I had come home sooner, sweetie, but I'm very happy we found you."

She gave him a kiss on the cheek and settled down onto the leather seat. He covered her with two more blankets and exited the carriage.

The women had been listening to the exchange. It was a silent night, but would have paid attention if fireworks were going off in the night sky.

After Sam closed the door, he stood and took a deep breath, then walked over to where the ladies were congregating.

"She's a remarkable little girl," said Grace, "For her to be so sweet and responsive after all she'd endured and the news that she had to absorb is amazing. When you were telling her about her parents, I didn't know how she'd take the news, but the way you explained it to her made the news understandable and acceptable."

"I had hoped to postpone telling her, but she asked so quickly, so I had to tell her. What made it easier was that I believed what I told her. To not believe it would destroy the whole purpose of life."

Julia asked, "Could you tell us what you told her, Sam? Carol and I weren't there. We didn't know if she had been told."

Sam answered, "I simply told her that bad men had killed her father and that he was in heaven with God and the angels. Then I explained how the same bad men had taken her mother to a bad place where she had been beaten and killed. The same place where her aunts had been taken to, and

213

where they had been hurt and beaten. Then I said that her mama had died after a man beat her, and that she was in heaven with her papa, that they were happy to be together. They were watching her all the time and her mama was glad that we had found her."

"You're a good man, Papa," said Carol.

"So, you all heard that?"

"It was hard not too, Sam. I'm glad that you told her about our pasts in a way, but how do you think she'll see us when she eventually finds out the rest of it?" asked Julia.

"She'll see you just as I do. The sad thing is that none of you really do. You sometimes lapse into thinking of yourselves as lesser than other women because of what happened to you. But you need to see you as I do. You were victims of a crime, no less than some fancy gentleman who is waylaid by a thief who then beats him for his wallet. You were all taken from your lives and forced into a way of life that continued to hurt you. The gent who lost his wallet and was beaten could get more money and continue with his life. You three, on the other hand, had no such option. You were victimized every day for years. We don't even do that to the thugs we catch and throw in prison. They get fed, housed and if they get victimized, it's by their fellow thugs.

"Catherine will grow up knowing you as the loving women that you are. Someday, she'll learn about men and women and how babies are made, and I will sit down with her and explain the full details of what happened to you. And do you know what her reaction will be? She'll be angry that those men hurt her beloved aunts.

"If you heard the conversation a few minutes ago, did you hear what this precious, sweet little girl said when I told her I had killed the two men that hurt her mama and her aunts? She said she was glad I had killed them, so they couldn't hurt anyone else. So, I'd like you to put that concern out of your minds right now. That little girl in the carriage will love each of you, just as I do. Now, ladies, let's just enjoy the beautiful night and anticipate how much fun it will be having that little person around our house. One of the first things you'll have to do, unless you missed it, will be to give her a nice, warm bath."

Carol laughed, and said, "Oh, we noticed. It looks like she hasn't had a bath in months."

"At least they fed her. What they fed her, I wouldn't know, but I have a feeling that she's going to be fed a lot better now. Tomorrow, I have a lot of things I need to do in Denver. Catherine will be in your care, so you will be free to turn our little girl back into the princess she was before she was taken. Do you need anything while I'm there?"

Grace answered, "She'll need some new dresses and shoes and socks. You may want to get her a hairbrush set of her own, too. We each bought one the last time we were in Denver, but she'd want one her own size and maybe you could pick up some ribbons for her hair, too."

"I can handle that."

After a few more suggestions, they removed their shoes or boots and crawled into the bedrolls.

———

It stayed warm all night for a change and Sam was up at dawn, making a smaller fire for coffee and bacon.

The women crawled out of their sleeping bags and found some privacy to take care of personal matters and were all dressed when Catherine opened the door to the carriage and announced that she had to pee.

A giggling Julia led her to the hidden spot that they had found for that purpose.

They ate a quick breakfast and the horses were saddled just to have a place to keep the saddles. Humpty and Dumpty were put in harness and everyone climbed aboard the carriage. Catherine wanted to stay up front, so she could see better, much to the chagrin of Carol and Julia.

As the grays trotted along at their customary fast pace, Catherine bubbled away with questions as she pointed at different sights along the drive and would occasionally stand in the seat facing Carol and Julia and get them to answer her questions, too, and once she even crawled over the seat to join them.

———

By mid-morning, they were pulling into the Circle S, and Catherine was bouncing in the front seat at the sight of her home.

"Well, Catherine, we're home," said Sam, as if she hadn't noticed.

She didn't answer, but her eyes were gleaming. Her new papa was taking her home.

The carriage stopped in the front yard and everyone disembarked.

Sam turned to Carol and Julia, and said, "Carol, Julia, I'm going to make you a special deal. Why don't you join Grace and Catherine and I'll take care of your horses? Go."

They smiled at him and gave a chorused "Thank you, Sam!" and followed Catherine and Grace into the house.

Sam smiled at their obvious desire to be with Catherine and turned the carriage toward the barn. It took him thirty minutes to get the carriage and horses put away and cared for. When he returned to the house, the women were already preparing a bath for Catherine, who seemed as eager as her new aunts were to get her into the tub.

They had already set some of her older, but cleaner clothes out for her.

He motioned Grace over as Carol and Julia fussed over Catherine.

"I'm going to go to Denver in a few minutes. I need to tell Dan Grant what happened down there and take care of some other issues. I'll pick up the items that you asked me to buy, so I should be back by four or so. One of you needs to keep an eye on the entrance road while I'm gone. I'm not sure that the Ashleys didn't decide to let their nephew know that we took Catherine. Keep a pair of Winchesters by the door, too."

"Sam, do you think they'll come back for her?"

"Catherine is the heir to her grandfather's shipping business, and I believe that Ferguson Short paid Soapy Smith to kill the family so he could inherit. If he finds out that Catherine is still alive, either Soapy will try to fulfill his contract, or Ferguson will send someone else. I'll deal with Ferguson as soon as I take care of Soapy and his crew. Come with me to the kitchen for a moment."

They walked to the kitchen and sat down at the table. Sam pulled the short pencil and a small notepad from his vest pocket that he used as a sheriff.

He wrote:

Ted Robinson - short, snakeskin boots, white hair.

Abe Thompkins - medium height and build, white streak in his hair.

John Berringer – tall, fat, long, greasy hair.

Gerald Price – Ashley's nephew

When he finished, he looked at Grace and said, "These are the crew of Soapy Smith's that were involved in the kidnapping of Cora and Catherine and Richard's murder. I think two of them were part of the team that took you. I'm going to make a copy of this list and take it with me to see Dan Grant. I want to leave this with you. Make sure Carol and Julia see it as well. Try to memorize the names. In addition to stopping any attempts to hurt Catherine, I intend to see that the woman-snatching ring that Soapy has set up is brought down, and I think I know how to do it, too. I can get it done without violence or even using the law."

"You can? How would you manage that?"

"The newspaper. I'll go to the *Rocky Mountain News* and get them interested. It should be a great story for them. Innocent Denver women lured into captivity and sold into prostitution by using ads in their own paper. The possible liability issue alone would compel them to write the story. If we can get a banner headline and story, that operation would be shut down. It's a question of whether or not they have the guts to face down Soapy Smith. I'll even see if they have a woman reporter. That should make it easier to sell the story."

"As long as you don't adopt her," Grace said with a smile.

"I think I've adopted my last female," replied Sam, smiling at her, before he said, "I've got to go."

"Take care, Sam," she said softly.

"I will, Grace. I'll be back soon."

He waved and walked back down the hallway, then entered the doorway of the big bedroom where the women were pouring some cold water into the tub while the warming water sat on the stove.

"Catherine, I need to go to Denver to get some important things done now that you're here. Do you want anything while I'm there?"

"Can I get some nicer soap?"

Sam laughed. He hadn't thought of that, and said, "Of course, you can. I'll bring some with me in a few hours."

He bent over and kissed her forehead then said, "I'll be back as soon as I can, sweetheart."

"Good-bye, Papa," she said, as he stood up to leave.

"Good-bye, Catherine. Good-bye, ladies," he said as he waved and then left the house.

He saddled Cump and was on the road to Denver in fifteen minutes.

———

His first stop when he arrived an hour later was the sheriff's office.

219

"Good morning, Zeke," he said as he entered to the deputy that always seemed to be at the desk.

He had yet to see any of Dan's other deputies, figuring he must have a half dozen. He'd have to ask him about that.

"Mornin', Sam. Go on in, the sheriff has been expecting you for a few days."

Sam waved at Zeke as he passed and when he turned into the sheriff's personal office, he found Dan at his desk, writing on some form. When he heard Sam enter, he put down his pencil and grinned.

"Sam! Welcome back. Any news?"

Sam sat down without invitation and replied, "The best, Dan. Catherine is back at the ranch. She was healthy, but it took a bit of persuasion to get the Ashleys to see the error of their ways and let her come home with us. She's very happy and pleased to meet all of her aunts."

"She has aunts there as well?"

"The ladies I rescued from Waxman's. The Ashleys own a run-down ranch about six miles east of Hinkley. They're an older couple, and none too friendly, either. It turned out their nephew, Gerald Price, is on one of Soapy Smith's crews. The crew had been ordered to kill the entire Short family, probably under a contract Soapy had with a Short cousin named Ferguson. He wants to get control of the family shipping company in St. Louis. They killed Richard, but one of them got greedy. He'd been on the crew that had been kidnapping women and supplying whore houses all through the area.

"I think one or two of the crew were uneasy killing a young woman and a little girl, so the greedy one decided to make a sale of his own, bypassing Soapy altogether. He'd get rid of the woman, make some money, and who'd be the wiser? He used Catherine as a threat to Cora to keep her at Waxman's. It was probably Price who suggested Waxman's in the first place because he had his aunt and uncle so close and probably gave them twenty dollars to keep Catherine there. They didn't hurt her, but they surely didn't provide for her very well."

"That's great, Sam."

"My next concern is to stop Ferguson Short from trying to kill Catherine after he finds out that she's alive. But first I'm going to either adopt her or get appointed her legal guardian, so I can act on her behalf when I go to St. Louis to confront Ferguson."

"I can help you with that. I'm good friends with Judge McNeal. With you being her only relative and your solid background, I don't see any problems with his signing adoption papers. I'll talk to him about it later this morning. Do you have the specifics about Catherine? You know, date of birth, birth parents name, et cetera?"

"Sure, I'll write them all down. I also plan on shutting down Soapy's woman grab scam."

"We don't have a lot of evidence to go on, Sam, but I'd love to be able to do that."

"I won't need the law for this one, Dan. I'm going to go to the offices of the *Rocky Mountain News* and see if they'd be interested in the story. With the potential liability for running the ads that led to the abductions, I think they'd try to clear their name."

"You know, that's a great idea. Shine the light of day on those cock roaches and they'll run like crazy."

"Now today, I intend to visit the undertaker, the land office and I need to get some things for Catherine. I'll stop by when I'm done. I appreciate all the help you've given me. By the way, the only deputy I've ever seen is Zeke. I figure you've got at least six. Where are the rest?"

"You forget, I'm the county sheriff, so I only have two deputies. One has been back east visiting his parents for the past month. He's due back any day. The city marshal, on the other hand, has a dozen deputies."

"That explains that. Let me write down Catherine's information. Oh, and here's the list of the four that were involved in Richard's murder and the kidnapping of Cora and Catherine. I got them from the Ashleys, who didn't want to be hanged for their part in the kidnapping," Sam said as he handed Dan the list.

Dan's eyes opened wide as he looked at the small sheet, then said, "I'll be damned. I know every one of these bastards. This should be fun."

Sam then wrote down all the information Dan should need for Judge McNeal, and as he handed him the slip of paper, he asked, "Dan, can you get me a copy of Catherine's birth certificate while you're in the courthouse? I may need it when I go to St. Louis."

"Not a problem, Sam."

Sam shook his hand and walked out to the street, waving at Zeke as he passed. *Two deputies!*

"And I thought I had it bad," he thought.

He mounted Cump and headed to the land office, and when he walked in, he met the same clerk he had look up the Circle S information.

"Good morning," Sam greeted.

"Hello. What can I do for you today?"

"The Slash F. What can you tell me of its status? The daughter of the owner is staying at my ranch temporarily."

"Let's see," he said before going to his files and pulling out some paperwork.

"It's still in the name of Horace and Grace Felton, but the taxes are overdue. If they aren't paid in the next two months, it will fall delinquent and go to auction."

"Fine. I'll pay the taxes. How much is due?"

"It's for two tax cycles, so the total is $85.76. That includes the penalty for overdue payment."

"That's okay. I understand."

Sam wrote a draft and watched as the clerk stamped 'paid' onto the form then gave Sam a receipt. They shook hands and Sam left the office.

His next stop was a construction firm which he found just ten minutes later, then parked Cump and walked into the company offices. It was a large, well-appointed office and he mentally compared it to the carriage shop.

"May I help you, sir?" asked a cute young lady at the front desk.

Sam guessed she was barely twenty.

"I'd like to speak to someone about some jobs I need done on my ranch."

"Just have a seat, sir, and I'll get one of the job managers."

Sam sat down, but not long before a tall, thin man appeared from an office behind the counter and approached Sam.

"I hear you'd like to engage us to handle some construction work?" he asked.

Sam rose, then replied, "Yes, I may, depending on the timing of the construction. They shouldn't be difficult jobs."

"Step into my office and explain what you need, then we'll see if we can do what you wish."

Sam followed the man into his office, and after he took a seat, he began explaining what he'd like done. He started with the wrought iron fence for the cemetery. When he explained what he wanted, the engineer told him that they could do it, but he'd be wasting his money for that much fencing. Family plots are usually much smaller, he explained. He convinced Sam that a thirty by sixty-foot family cemetery would be more than adequate, then Sam described the addition of two bedrooms to the existing structure.

They discussed design plans, which included a new whitewash on the entire job when done to blend the new with the old. Then, Sam delved into his ideas for the carriage house. He needed six additional stalls for horses and large front and back doors to allow the carriage to drive through. The engineer told him that it was a simple job as well. After they were finished with the details, the engineer worked out a timetable and the cost. The work would be completed in only two and a half weeks, because they would use three separate crews. The fence would be done first, followed by the carriage house and then the bedrooms. Sam had stipulated that one of the new bedrooms have built-in bookcases. The total cost was eight hundred and seventy dollars, so Sam wrote a draft for the order, they shook hands, and Sam left the offices almost two hours later.

His next stop was the one he dreaded as he rode Cump to a well-build brick building and wondered why undertakers always had such nice establishments. No worry about business falling off, he guessed.

He walked into the front office and was met by a surprisingly un-undertaker looking young man with sandy hair and freckles.

"Good afternoon, sir, how may we help you today?"

"I have a rather unusual request."

"Nothing that we probably haven't heard before, sir. Please follow me."

Sam followed him into his office and they each sat on opposite sides of the desk.

"So, explain to me what you need."

"In December, my brother-in-law, Richard Short, was murdered at his ranch. He was buried here in Denver, but I don't know where yet. His wife, my sister Cora, was kidnapped along with her four-year-old daughter, Catherine. I was a sheriff in Boulder and didn't know about it until I came for a visit about a month ago. Since then, I found that my sister had also been murdered two months ago in Hinkley. She had been sold into prostitution and was killed by a cowboy. They buried her behind the establishment, and I'd like to arrange to have them both disinterred, placed in suitable caskets and returned to their ranch to be buried in a new family cemetery. Can that be done?"

The young man leaned back and thought for a minute or so before replying, "We'd need to locate Mister Short's current burial location and notify the county that we were moving his remains. That should take about a week or so. We can send a hearse to Hinkley to disinter your sister's remains but won't need any paperwork for that as she was buried without notice. However, we would need someone to point out the location."

"I'll find it. Can we coordinate the two, so I can have a service for them both?"

"Of course, we can do that. We'll send two men to Hinkley to disinter and place the body in the new casket. You needn't be present at the time. It would be something you'd rather not see."

"You're right. I couldn't bear to see my precious sister in that way."

The young undertaker looked at Sam and said, "I hope those that perpetrated such a heinous act have been punished."

"Just the one that was responsible for my sister's murder. I'm still hunting Richard's killer."

"Are you a lawman?"

"I have been for ten years. Right now, I'm working with Dan Grant."

"Good luck in your search. Today is the twelfth. We'll plan on sending the hearse to Hinkley on the nineteenth. If you could meet them at the entrance to your ranch in the morning and escort them to Hinkley, then we can have a second hearse transport your brother-in-law's remains to your ranch on the twentieth. Which ranch is it, by the way?"

"It's the Circle S. It's about seven miles south on the road to Hinkley."

"Very good."

"If you'll give me the bill, I'll pay it now."

"Very well, sir. Just a minute."

He began writing out services and casket costs on a billing sheet."

"The total will be two hundred and thirty dollars, if that's acceptable."

"That'll be fine. Oh, and I almost forgot, I'll need two headstones made as well."

"I've already included that in the price. Many people forget to think of it. Do you have the information for the headstones? I can give them to our stonemason."

Sam wrote out the information on two sheets of paper and handed them to the undertaker.

He read them and said, "Very good, sir."

Sam shook his hand and returned to Cump and breathed a sigh of relief. It wasn't as bad as he expected. He just had to remember the dates for the exhumations and the burial. Luckily, the receipt the undertaker had given him included the details.

He thought his next stop should be the *Rocky Mountain News*. He should eat something but wanted to do this first.

The offices were easy to find as they had a large sign on top of a three-story brick building. After entering the lobby area, he had to scan the large room to find the receptionist. When he did, he stepped quickly to the small desk and asked her if he could talk to a reporter or an editor. She asked his purpose and when Sam told her he had a story involving kidnapping and murder, she told him to wait and scurried to a back office then returned shortly with a balding man with sharp eyes.

"Beth tells me you have a sensational story for us."

"That's not how I'd describe it. I see it as much more tragic, as it involved my sister, her four-year-old daughter and my brother-in-law."

Sam could almost see the man salivating.

"Well, I understand. Different perspectives," he said as he ushered Sam into his office.

Sam noticed that the door was embellished with *David Belkin - Editor in Chief.*

Once inside, he sat down and after the editor took his seat, he asked for Sam to tell his story.

"I'd rather wait to tell it to a reporter who can write the pertinent facts down. I don't want to do this twice. Also, you may want to realize up front that your paper may have a problem because it was innocently involved in a kidnapping ring run by Soapy Smith."

That got his attention and he said, "Well, that is bad. We've butted heads with that thug in the past, but I'm concerned about the liability factor."

"You weren't aware of the issue because they were innocent sounding ads being placed in your newspaper looking for domestic help. I doubt if anyone would blame the paper, but at the same time, by admitting that you had been duped as badly as those women who answered the ads, and by championing their cause, I should think that the goodwill created by the story would win many to your side."

The editor was calculating the benefits versus the risks. Sam's argument held a lot of merit, so he decided to run with the story.

Sam asked if he had any woman reporters, and he said he did, so Sam asked that she be the one to write the story and the editor acquiesced, even though he would have preferred one of his male reporters.

He sent for the reporter, then they sat and waited for her to arrive. When she did, Sam noticed she had a large pad and several pencils in her hands. She was around thirty, and quite tall, around five feet and eight inches, wore glasses and had her brown hair in a bun. She looked more like a schoolmarm than a tough reporter, but as it turned out, she was a very tough reporter.

Sam stipulated that the names of all involved remain anonymous. He didn't want the family ranch or those residing turned into a circus, and the editor agreed to the terms and even gave him a signed agreement to that fact.

Sam began his story with his arrival and discovery of his dead brother-in-law and the kidnapping of his sister and niece. He described his discovery of the methods used by Smith to kidnap women and sell them into prostitution and gave them the location of the houses that were used and how the interviewers would only select young, pretty women who had no families, and that they would even go and murder male members of a family to kidnap the women. He outlined that Smith was selling these women to brothels throughout the region, and told the tragic story of his sister's death, and his retribution against those who had caused it.

When he had finished his story, even the tough editor was wet-eyed. The grim schoolmarm reporter was reduced to a blubbering mess, but she had kept writing.

When they had recovered, they assured him that the story would be run in the next few days and that no one would know who was involved and would even change the dates and locations so no one could dig up the information. Sam was satisfied, then shook their hands and left to return to Cump.

All that was left now was to head back to Dan Grant's office, see how his efforts worked out, and then stop at the clothing store for Catherine's new clothes; and he'd need to buy some nice soap. He smiled at the thought.

He entered the sheriff's office and was simply pointed to Dan's office by Zeke. Sam soon turned the corner and Dan was behind his desk, smiling.

"What's up, Dan."

Dan slid two sheets of paper across his desk; one was a signed adoption form and the other a copy of Catherine's birth certificate.

"Congratulations, Dad. You are now the legal father of Catherine Brown."

"Really, Dan? That fast? I thought I'd have to appear in court and do all sort of background stuff."

"Usually. But when I told Judge McNeal your story, he couldn't sign the adoption papers fast enough. He thinks you're a saint among men."

"Well, Dan, I've been called many things, but 'saint' isn't one of them."

"How did the rest of your day go?"

"Well. The undertakers will arrange to disinter both Richard and Cora. They'll be placed in matching nice coffins and we'll coordinate the burial on the twentieth at a new family cemetery that I'm having built on the ranch. The *Rocky Mountain News* was really excited about the kidnapping ring story and will be running it on the front page. That should put the brakes on that industry. Now I just need to get some clothes and other things for Catherine, and then I'll just head back."

"You're going to have to bring her by sometime, so I can meet this special little lady."

"I had every intention of doing so, Dan. You won't be disappointed."

He thanked Dan again, slipped the two critical pieces of paper into his vest pocket, then returned to the ever patient Cump.

He decided to skip lunch and wanted to get back to his new daughter and his ladies.

Sam stopped at the mercantile they had used before and found some nice lilac-scented soap, bought a dozen bars, and found a nice child-sized hairbrush set and some hair ribbpons for Catherine. He left the store and slid his purchases into his saddlebags.

He thought his last stop was going to be the clothing store but changed his mind and walked into the jewelry store again. He met with a different salesclerk this time and bought another, but smaller turquoise necklace, and was very pleased he'd thought of it as he slid the small box into his pocket.

He bought everything he needed at the clothing store, including two pairs of little girl's shoes. After paying his bill, he hooked the bags with the clothes around his saddle horn and headed south to his ranch, anxious to see his ladies and daughter.

———

Soapy was livid. One of his many tendrils of information had just passed him a particularly bad bit of news. Ted Robinson, Abe Thompkins, John Berringer and Gerald Price had all lied to him. More than that, they had profited from that lie. They hadn't killed all three of those Shorts last year but had sold the woman to Waxman and had just let the kid live. Now, the woman was finally dead, but the kid was still alive.

He tried to contain his temper. He wanted all four of those cheating bastards dead but that would have severe consequences on his other crews. Replacing four men wasn't as simple as some would think. What was worse was that he hadn't fulfilled the contract, and that wasn't something he could let anyone know because it would hurt business.

He understood the law and it had been so long now that client would be able to inherit soon when the woman and kid were declared legally dead. But if that cowboy, Brown, let it out that he had the kid, then he would have a problem. The client would find out and there would be hell to pay.

As much as he would like to extract revenge on the four more directly, he'd use them to clean up their own mess, but he'd probably have to use more of his crew too. This was getting to be the biggest screw-up he'd ever had, but he had to fix it, and that would be costly.

He then called in the four idiots who put him into this bind.

———

Sam turned onto the access road in the late afternoon. It had been the most productive day he'd had in a long time, if ever.

He rode Cump right into the barn and waved at Grace, who had been waiting on the porch for his return and was pleasantly surprised that she followed him into the barn.

He had just stepped down when Grace entered the wide doors.

"Welcome back, Sam. Your female harem was anxious for you to return."

"And I'm glad to be back, Grace. It was a very good trip."

"Did you talk to the newspaper?"

"Yes, ma'am. I left them crying, including the tough old editor. The story they're going to run will concentrate on the abduction of young women by Soapy Smith but will include our story as well. They won't be using any names and will be shifting dates and locations so no one can track down the specifics. I have that in writing, by the way. I had the editor sign it, so if they deviate even slightly, I can sue them for breach of contract."

"It sounds like you made sure we were safe, as usual."

"I need to protect my angels."

"How did everything else go?"

Sam took a deep breath, then said, "I picked up all of Catherine's things, including a dozen bars of lilac soap, so you all could use them. I talked to Dan, and he made this happen."

He then reached into his vest, pulled out the two sheets, then handed her the copy of the adoption papers. She read them and looked up with a face-splitting smile.

"Sam! You really are her father now!"

"Yes. I am."

She launched herself at Sam gripping him in a big hug, surprising him, but he quickly hugged her back. Then the inevitable happened.

When she looked up at him, he kissed her; not a little peck, either, but a deep, hungry kiss. One that did not go unreturned.

When they finally came up for air, Sam looked down into her deep blue eyes.

Grace asked quietly, "What now, Sam? I know you love all of us and that you can't choose one over the other."

"Grace, come here and sit by me."

Sam sat on the tailgate of the wagon and Grace hopped up next to him.

"Grace, loving someone doesn't mean you can't love someone else. It's the kind of love that's different. I loved my sister more than anyone else I ever knew, but she was my sister. I loved her as only an older brother could, and now I love all my ladies. Each of you is loved just as much as the other.

"But it's only you that I have loved as a man loves a woman. It's been that way since that first night and I found you crying over Cora. I knew then I was meeting someone with true depth and compassion. Even wearing all that makeup, I could see Grace underneath when I first saw those incredibly expressive blue eyes. You've been working your way deeper into my heart every day we've been together, Grace. I've wanted to marry you early on, but we've always had circumstances in the way, haven't we?"

"You want to marry me?" she asked in surprise.

"Naturally, if you'll have me. I love you too much to let you go, Grace. I want to raise Catherine with you and want you to be her mama."

Grace was overwhelmed. *This couldn't be real. When was this dream going to end? When would she suddenly wake up in her small room in Waxman's?*

"Sam, I can't believe this is happening. I mean, this was so out of reach. It was an impossible dream."

"No, it's not only possible, it's going to happen. It's just a question of time."

"But what about Carol and Julia. It would hurt them, Sam."

"I don't think it will hurt Julia all that much."

235

"Sam, Julia jokes more about getting you into her bed than you could imagine."

"Grace, Julia is young and thinks like a teenager sometimes. If some young man were to show an interest in her, she'd be willing to move on."

"Sam, she's two years older than I am."

"I know, but you've always been older, more mature inside. It's Carol I worry about. She's so deep that I can't read her very well. You, I read very quickly; maybe because I wanted to. I spend more time studying you than Julia and Carol combined."

Grace laughed, and said, "They always kept telling me that I was your favorite."

"I guess I didn't do as good a job of hiding it as I thought."

"Sam, can I ask you a question that may sound peculiar coming from someone with my history?"

"Grace, you can ask me anything."

"Have you had a lot of girlfriends?"

"None."

Grace was astounded. *How could this man have never had any girlfriends?*

"How is that possible?"

"I have no idea. I never really got around to it. I became a lawman very early, and the job just never lent itself to many opportunities."

"So, are you telling me that you've never been with a woman?"

"No. Once, when I was eighteen, I met a girl who I was infatuated with that must have been a bit promiscuous. I had no idea at the time that girls could be that way. So, after she had her way with me, she moved on to other boys. It was crushing at the time and I vowed never to do that to a girl or a woman as I aged."

"Once."

"Sorry. I'd like to say I was a regular Romeo, but no; just once."

"That's amazing."

"Just the truth, ma'am," he said as he smiled at her.

"Did you want to change that?" she asked softly.

"More than you can possibly imagine. Remember our first meeting when you held my hand to your breast? That's been driving me to distraction ever since, but until we iron out the other issues, we'll have to wait. It would be too easy for them to notice."

"What would?"

"If we were to be intimate, they'd know in a heartbeat."

"I doubt it. We had to be totally back to normal after a job. It wasn't hard at all."

"That, my dear Grace, is because you were just being used as a seat cushion. There was no emotional value. Now, if I were to make love to you, my love, it would be just that. I wouldn't be caring about me as much as I would about you. When two people love each other, making love is just the apex of that feeling.

"I could tell when Richard and Cora had spent personal time together. They glowed, Grace. It was the same look I saw on them when they were at the altar being married. It was just their incredible love for each other that made them glow. Honestly. You'll know the feeling when I finally get to take you to bed. All the love I feel for you will be there, Grace. Then you'll understand why we have to wait."

Grace sighed and said, "I'll wait, but I won't like it."

"Neither will I. But that glow isn't limited to just that, either. When two people love each other that much, the glow is apparent to those who have seen it before. Making love is just the ultimate expression of that love and it becomes more pronounced. I'm surprised that no one has noticed it when I look at you."

"I hate to disappoint you, but did you know that Catherine has already noticed? When we were in the carriage while you and Carol and Julia were attending the horses, she told me that you liked me the best and that you looked at me the way her papa looked at her mama. Then she said that I looked at you like her mama looked at her papa, and that was just minutes after meeting me."

"That's a very perceptive little girl we have there, Mrs. Brown."

Grace glanced back to the front of the barn, then, seeing no one, turned back to Sam and kissed him again.

When they separated, Sam said, "Well, Grace, we need to be getting back before anything else happens. We'd hate to be glowing even more brightly on our return."

Grace stifled a laugh as she took Sam's hand.

He squeezed her hand and said, "Oh. There's one more thing I need to give you before we go."

Sam reached into his pocket and handed her the receipt for the Slash F taxes.

"Does this mean that the ranch is still mine?" she asked after reading it.

"That's exactly what it means. In another two months, it would have been put up for auction for non-payment of two years' taxes. Now it's yours to do with as you wish."

"I'd kiss you again if I wasn't worried about getting carried away. Thank you so much for this, Sam. It means a lot to me. I thought the ranch was long gone."

"I never even checked to see where it was."

"You don't know?"

"Nope."

"It's right over there," Grace replied as she pointed to the east.

"Really? Your ranch and mine share a border?"

"Along the entire eastern edge of the Circle S."

"Now, that's handy."

"Getting this news will give me an excuse for arriving with a glow."

"I'll have to explain mine as too much sun or something."

They both laughed as Grace began to help Sam take care of Cump and the other horses. Like teenagers, they kept exchanging glances and Sam realized how difficult this would be to hide from Carol and Julia.

After they were done, Sam grabbed his saddlebags and the bag of clothing for Catherine then left the barn with Grace walking alongside.

As they strolled to the house, Sam hoped that Julia and Carol wouldn't notice that he and Grace had spent almost half an hour together in the barn but was relieved to discover that they hadn't because they were busy showing Catherine how to bake cookies.

Sam put the saddlebags and clothing bag down in the main room and stopped, glanced at Grace, who smiled, then quickly trotted down the hallway to the kitchen.

Once she was there, he began to step down the hallway, and when Catherine saw him coming, she bounced his way and squealed," Papa!"

She covered the twelve feet separating them in an instant and with arms outstretched jumped into his waiting arms.

After hugs and kisses, Sam looked at her and said, "Ladies, all, I have an official announcement to make."

Grace alone knew what that announcement would be, and it showed on her almost glowing face.

"Effective today, the 12th of June 1879, Miss Catherine Brown is now officially my daughter."

The ladies all clapped and smiled as Catherine looked into his face and said, "You're really my papa now?"

"The judge said so and gave me papers to prove it. So, now when you're a bad little girl I can paddle your behind."

Catherine giggled and said, "You're never going to do it, Papa. Mama and papa used to say that too, but never did."

"You win this time, sweetie, but I win the next one."

He put her back on the floor, and asked, "If you can spare a few minutes, I'll let you all know what else happened today. It was quite a lot."

There was nothing that couldn't wait, so Sam, now with his four ladies, walked back into the family room.

When they sat, down, Catherine on Grace's lap, Sam began by saying, "First, I have this bag of things for a newly cleaned little girl."

Catherine hopped down, ran over to the bags and asked, "For me?"

Sam reached into the bags and handed her a box containing a dress, then handed the other boxes to the other ladies to present to Catherine.

As she opened each box her squeals of joy got higher. Finally, she found the box with ribbons of many colors – a lot of ribbons.

"Why so many, Sam," asked Carol.

"So, they could be shared between all of my ladies. You know I like your hair down, anyway. This way you can add a nice touch to your wardrobe. Speaking of which; adult ladies, if you would, could you all momentarily adjourn and don your jewelry?"

They were wondering where this was going but went to their rooms and for the first time, put on their turquoise necklaces. They spend a few seconds, or longer, admiring the look, and then returned to the main room.

Catherine noticed the change immediately and exclaimed, "Those are really pretty!"

"I bought them because all of your aunts were so pretty, that they needed something almost as pretty to make them look even nicer. Don't you think that was a good idea?"

"Yes, Papa. That was the best idea."

"Don't you think it makes them look even prettier."

"Oh, yes! They do."

"I think all pretty ladies should wear them. Don't you?"

"Yes."

"Well, so do I, sweetie."

Sam reached into his pocket and pulled out a small blue case. The ladies had caught on pretty quickly that this was going to be his surprise goal.

Sam opened the case and showed it to Catherine as he said, "For my pretty daughter."

Catherine's eyes were almost cartoonish as she stared at the box and whispered, *"For me? Really?"*

"Come here, princess."

Catherine walked toward Sam, her eyes on the box.

Sam pulled the necklace from the box, opened the clasp, then hung it around her neck and closed the clasp. He then pulled out her mirror from her new hairbrush and mirror set and let her see herself wearing the necklace.

"Oh, Papa! It's so beautiful!"

"And so are you, Catherine. Are you going to show your aunts, so you can compare?"

The small girl showed all the adult girls her necklace and was rewarded with the appropriate 'oohs' and 'ahhs'.

"Okay, ladies, and I mean all ladies, have a seat and I'll fill you in on the rest of today's news."

After the women had returned to their appropriate seats, with Catherine parked on Carol's lap this time, Sam resumed his revelations.

"The first thing that will impact you is that the construction crews will be arriving in a day or two to begin their work. They'll be doing all three jobs at the same time. The first one to be done will be the fencing around a new family cemetery near the aspen grove north of the house. They will be building a carriage house near the barn that will include six new stalls, and the one that will be most intrusive will be the addition of two new bedrooms.

"I worked with the engineer and he assured me that the only work needed on the house will be adding a hallway from the main room to the right of the fireplace. There will be a sixteen-foot-long hallway that will lead to the two new rooms. After the new bedrooms are built, the whole house will be repainted so it will look right. The whole job should take less than three weeks. Now, ladies, I'm sure no one has ever told you that you are all quite attractive. It's a well-kept secret and I dared never to say such things, myself, so please, do not try to drive the workers to distraction."

That elicited the expected laughs before he continued.

"I talked to the editor and a reporter at the *Rocky Mountain News* today and they are going to write a story about the kidnapping of women by Soapy Smith. No names will be used, and they are going to change dates and locations to avoid anyone finding out anything.

"The other major thing I had to do today was to arrange for the return of Richard and Cora to the new family cemetery. I'll be leaving here on the nineteenth and returning to Hinkley to bring my sister home. On the twentieth, we'll have a small ceremony."

The somber news affected the adult ladies, but Catherine didn't understand why they seemed so suddenly sad.

"Finally, I didn't want anyone to think that I had forgotten Catherine's parting request."

He opened his saddlebag and produced the twelve bars of lilac soap. That caused smiles all around, until Sam smelled his saddlebag.

"Good grief! This is never going to go away. My saddlebag is going to smell like lilacs for the rest of my life."

Even Catherine thought that was funny.

When the laughing subsided, all the adult females left for the kitchen to start dinner and Catherine remained with Sam, sitting on his lap.

"Papa, what did you mean when you said papa and mama were going to be brought here?"

"Catherine, when we die, and everyone dies, most people are put in a box and buried under the ground so their family knows where they are, and they can leave flowers and talk to them."

"But aren't they in heaven?"

"Yes, sweetie. Their souls are in heaven. Did your mama tell you about souls?"

"Yes, but it was hard to understand."

"A soul is where our love is. When you really love someone, like I love you, that comes from my soul, not my head. When people say that they have won their hearts, they don't mean that thing in your chest that goes thump, thump, thump. They mean they have won the love in their souls. And do you know what the real miracle of a soul is?"

"No, Papa."

"A soul has as much love in it as you need, so you can always give more. It keeps making more love, so when you meet someone new that you want to love, you can give them as much as you want and still give the same love to the people you already love."

"Oh. So, when I loved papa and mama, I could still love you and keep loving my mama and papa the same."

"Exactly. When I met your aunts in that terrible place, I loved them all the same. But when I found you, I loved you, too. But it didn't mean I loved them less."

"But I think you love Grace more than the others."

Sam grimaced inside, but said, "That's not true, Catherine. There are different kinds of love. For example, you love your mama and papa very much, but you love me, too. It's different, though; isn't it? It's the same with your aunts. They are all very special to me. I love your Aunt Carol and Aunt Julia like I loved your mama. I love your Aunt Grace like your papa loved your mama."

"Ohhh! I see."

Sam had to stop the next obvious question that was on the verge of crossing Catherine's mouth and quickly said, "But you can never tell them about this, sweetie. You need to trust me. If you say anything about this, you could hurt Aunt Julia's or Aunt Carol's feelings. We wouldn't want to do that. Would we?"

"No, Papa. I won't say anything."

"Thank you, Catherine. You are a wonderful daughter."

Catherine hopped down, ran into the kitchen and Sam hoped she wasn't going the way of many young children when promising not to tell, then can't wait to blurt out what they had heard. He thought he'd follow just to be sure.

He arrived in the kitchen as Catherine climbed into a chair to watch the food being prepared.

"Say, ladies, have you given much thought to sleeping arrangements for Catherine?"

Julia quickly said, "Well, the biggest bed is in the main bedroom, so it's most logical that she share with Grace."

Sam knew that she was offering but was hoping for a different solution, so he turned to his secret weapon – Catherine.

"Catherine, how would you like to sleep with a different aunt every night? Now, Aunt Grace has the biggest bed, so it has more room, but that means you could snuggle with Aunt Julia and Aunt Carol. Would you like that?"

"That wouldn't be very fair, Papa," she replied, and Sam was stymied. He had hoped Catherine would bail him out on this one, but she seemed to be making it worse.

"Why wouldn't it be fair?"

"Well, only if Aunt Grace lets me snuggle with her, too," she answered as her aunts all laughed.

Sam breathed a sigh of relief. She had come through after all and each aunt seemed pleased with her Solomon-like solution.

———

After dinner, it was bath night for the adult ladies, and everyone pitched in and brought cold and hot water into the bath as Sam served as their pail bearer.

After the tub was filled, Grace was first to get the bath tonight. She winked at Sam when no one was looking, and Sam got the message. They had the water boiling for the second bath, which was for Carol. They had set it up to alternate the order for future bathing. When it was Sam's night, he got the benefit of a longer bath because no one followed him. For some reason, he always had to clean the tub after he finished. He always left a ring and he vowed never to use lilac soap. He would stick with the white soap he always used, having no desire to have the same smell as the offending saddlebags.

After Julia had finished and the water drained, all the ladies scrambled to bed. Catherine joined Grace for the first night, and all was quiet when Sam curled up on his couch. At least he'd have a bed in a few weeks, and that meant he had to go to the furniture store soon, as well.

He lay awake thinking about Soapy Smith and Ferguson Short. He didn't have arresting-type evidence on either of them, but he had to deflect any potential attack on Catherine. Luckily, the construction crews would be here for three weeks, which meant it was safe during the day. *How could he protect the ladies at night?* There hadn't been any nighttime attacks that he was aware of, but that didn't preclude the possibility. He finally came up with what he thought would be a good solution.

CHAPTER 9

It was shortly after breakfast that the construction crews arrived. They showed up driving six freight wagons stacked with lumber and equipment and Sam was impressed already when they pulled down the access road.

He walked out to meet them as they approached the house. One man, Sam assumed the foreman, stepped down from the lead wagon as they drew to a halt.

"Morning!" shouted Sam.

"Howdy," he replied.

Sam stepped up to the man and offered his hand. The heavily built man, around forty years old, shook his hand and Sam couldn't help but feel the hard, calloused skin.

"My name's Joe Schmidt. You must be Sam Brown."

"I am. What do you need me to do?"

"First off, I just need to know where the cemetery site will be. The house addition is drawn up well, so that's not a problem. The carriage house site is shown to be near the existing barn on the west side. Is that right?"

"That's it, unless you can think of a better location."

"No. That's pretty good. We'll leave an alley between the two to allow us to paint them but having it close like that will serve as a windbreak. The only other thing we need to know is where the outside pump is. The crews go through a lot of water in the heat of the summer."

"I'll show you the cemetery site first. The pump is right near the corral. You can see it from here."

"Yup. No problem. Let's go see the location for the fencing. That job will only take a couple of days, if that. Then that crew will join the other two to get the serious building done. We should be out of your hair in two weeks."

"That's pretty fast work."

"Not really. We have three full crews available right now. We have three really big jobs coming up in eighteen days and the boss wants this done by then."

"Great. Let's head over there."

Sam showed him the location for the fencing and Joe thought the location was perfect. He waved down to the crew and one of the wagons pulled out of the convoy and headed his way.

"Well, Joe, I'll try to stay out of your way. I'm sure you don't like owners kibitzing. If you need anything, I'll be in the house. I'll probably be heading off to Denver sometime in the next few days. Just one word of caution, Joe. I have three very pretty ladies in the house. My wife has her two sisters visiting my five-year-old daughter and they can be distracting without realizing it. I'd hate to have your workers hurt by not paying attention. If they are aware that they are there, you should be okay."

"Thanks for the heads' up, Sam. Ladies have that effect on men. I'm sure you realize that."

"More than you know, Joe," Sam smiled, then waved before heading back to the house.

He walked into the main room and found all the women chatting with Catherine.

He stood near the ladies, and said, "The foreman says they should be done in two weeks because he has three full crews working to get the job done. I told him that I had three pretty ladies in the house that could be distracting. To avoid any problems, I told him that my wife had her two sisters visiting Catherine. So, Grace, are you up to being Mrs. Brown for two weeks this time?"

"Shouldn't it be Carol or Julia's turn?" Grace asked.

"I didn't know there was any benefit to the imaginary position but let me know who's going to be Mrs. Brown for a couple of weeks. We also need to get some furniture for the new bedrooms and curtains and linen and all that stuff. When it looks like it's almost done, we can go shopping again, or we can gamble a bit that they'll be done in two weeks and get it picked out and set up for delivery on the twenty-eighth. What do you think?"

"I say we gamble," Julia replied.

"Me, too," agreed Carol.

"Might as well," added Grace.

"Okay. That's settled. Now that we have the carriage, we can make a day of it and all go to Denver and pick out the furniture and other things."

"Sam, with the construction crews here, are we supposed to stay inside?" asked Carol.

251

"No. Just do what you normally do and be yourselves. The only problem is that you can be distracting to the workers and if they are looking at you while working with saws and hammers, there can be injuries. It's not anyone's fault, it's just nature. If you were all old gray-haired ladies, it wouldn't be a problem, but you aren't, so it is. I'm going to go out to the pasture and check out the cattle. I haven't done that in a while."

Grace asked, "Sam, can I go and check out my ranch? It's been so long that I need to see how much work it needs."

"Grace, you have a ranch?" asked Julia.

"I mentioned it to Sam a while ago, and when he was in Denver, he went to the land office and paid the taxes. They were going to auction it off in two months if he hadn't thought of it."

"Where is it?"

"Directly east of here. It borders the Circle S."

"Wow! You're neighbors with yourself," joked Julia.

"Sam, is it okay?" Grace asked again.

"Absolutely. I'm headed that way anyway. Pack your Colt, though. I'll wait until you're ready to go."

"Can we all come along?" asked Carol.

Sam was silently crushed, but said, "That's Grace's decision. It's her ranch."

"Of course, you can. Julia, are you coming?" Grace answered with a distinct lack of enthusiasm.

"I'd rather stay here and mind Catherine."

Grace nodded, then said, "Okay, Carol. You and I can go get changed. We'll be out in a few minutes, Sam."

"I'll be in the barn getting the horses ready. See you and Carol shortly."

Sam strode to the barn and saw that the work crews were already preparing the carriage site and wondered what impact seeing two young females wearing Stetsons and packing Colts would have on the crew. He'd find out soon enough.

He had saddled Cump and Coal and was starting on Coffee when the women entered the barn. They were carrying canteens and two bags and Sam correctly assumed they had packed some sandwiches. In addition to his usual two pistols, Sam decided to bring his shotgun in its scabbard simply because he was a bit nervous about what either Richard's uncle or Soapy Smith might try.

"Well, ladies, I see that you were smart enough to bring water and food along, so we can do a proper investigation of the ranch. I hope you're planning on sharing."

"We'll see, Mister Brown," answered Grace.

"So, who's going to be Mrs. Brown?"

"I am," answered Carol.

"Well, welcome to our barn, Mrs. Brown," Sam said as he smiled.

Grace found herself jealous and was surprised. It was only a temporary, imaginary situation, but she still felt the twinge of jealousy hearing that title being used by someone else, and she was disappointed in herself.

Sam finished saddling Coffee, and they all mounted.

They left the barn and headed east, and as they neared the eastern boundary, Sam saw his cattle still crowded around the stream. The grass was still good, so he guessed that they ate elsewhere and watered in the same spot.

"Do the cattle look okay?" asked Grace.

"They're fine. They water in the same spot, but they wander when it's grazing time; which for cattle is most of the time."

"I forgot about the fence," Grace said as the noticed the barbed wire fence.

"I didn't," replied Sam as he drew out his fence tool.

He walked Cump to the fence and stepped down, clipped the two top wires, leaving the bottom wire to keep some support for the posts. He climbed back aboard Cump and stepped him over the surviving wire.

"Be careful ladies, just walk your horses over."

As they did, Carol asked, "Won't your cattle wander through the fence?"

"It's possible, but if they do, I'll just send them back."

Sam and the ladies trotted their horses over a rise and could see the ranch house in the distance and Sam immediately spotted two horses in the corral and smoke coming from the chimney.

"Looks like you have squatters, Grace. I want you both to stay right here. I'll go take care of the problem."

"Sam, we can shoot," said Grace.

"I know you both can, but this is the kind of thing I'm used to doing. It's not a question of shooting. It's a matter of scaring the pants off of them."

They nodded and pulled up while Sam kept Cump at a walk. He unslung his shotgun and closed the distance to the house; glad he had decided to bring the sawed-off scattergun. The corral was close to the house, and it was possible that if the horses whinnied the squatters would be alerted to his presence, but decided the risk was acceptable and rode on.

When near the corral, the horses nickered but that was all. He stepped down and loose-tied Cump's reins to the corral, then walked toward the front of the ranch house. It was in a poor state of cleanliness, but the construction seemed solid. Sam reached the edge of the house and peered in the front yard finding it empty, which meant that, more than likely, there were just two squatters in the house.

He stepped quietly onto the porch, took two long strides, then when he reached the already open front door, slowly opened the screen door seeing no one in the main room.

He walked in and yelled, "This is Deputy Sheriff Brown! Whoever is in here is trespassing! I want you to show yourselves!"

There was no reply, but then he heard the back door open and heard hurried footsteps crossing the back porch.

He turned and ran back through the front door, crossed the porch and leapt to the ground to get to the corral. The only saddled horse in back was Cump, and he knew that Cump didn't like other people riding him, so he turned to his right and kept running toward the back of the house, where he spotted one man trying to mount Cump, and having a hard time.

He pulled back the hammers on the shotgun and kept running until he was close enough to see the man's face. He hadn't seen him before, but something struck home, then he saw the second man trying to mount his bareback mare in the corral.

Sam rounded a few feet in front of them, pointed the shotgun and shouted, "Step down, both of you, unless you want this scattergun to blow you both to hell and back!"

The man trying to mount Cump said, "You ain't gonna fire that gun, mister. You'd kill your horse."

"It's the county's horse. They'll just give me another one. Now, I mean to tell you boys that this gun isn't loaded with birdshot. I've got some nice #4 buckshot in there. Do you want to see what a mess it makes of the pair of you? I'm not warning you again."

They glanced at each other, mutually deciding that the risk wasn't worth it. It was only trespassing, and they knew that they wouldn't even do any jail time, so they stepped down.

Sam said, "Wise choice. Now you two boys drop those gunbelts on the ground. If I see either hand go near those hoglegs, this thing goes off and you both say hello to the afterlife."

They unbuckled their gunbelts with their left hands and let them drop.

"Now step over here toward me. When you get right here where the grass starts, lay flat on your bellies."

They did as he directed, smiling inside at the show this idiot deputy was putting on for just a simple case of trespassing.

To the west, Grace and Carol could see the drama being played out in the distance and wondered why Sam had to act so carefully if they were just squatters.

Once they were on their stomachs, Sam released the hammers and replaced the shotgun in his back scabbard but unhooked his Colt's hammer loop. He reached in his pocket, pulled out his ever-present pigging strings then quickly tied one squatter's wrists and then the second. Sam knew they weren't squatters. He remembered the white streak on one man and the light hair and snakeskin boots on the other. He wanted these men, and he wanted them both to hang.

He quickly saddled their two horses, then he told the two to get in the saddles, which required his assistance. When they were up, he tied their legs to the stirrups. Then he tied the horses to the corral and picked up their gun rigs, hung them over Cump's saddle horn and climbed aboard.

"Now you boys stay right there for a second while I go talk to my partners up there. I'll be back soon."

"What are you going to do, deputy? Hang us for trespassing?" asked the one with the white streak.

"You never know, do you?" Sam replied as he set Cump to a canter toward Grace and Carol.

After Sam was out of hearing range the snakeskin man said to the other, "He's only got us for trespassin', but what if he looks in the bedroom?"

"Ain't nothin' illegal, besides we can always say they ain't ours."

———

Carol and Grace saw him coming rapidly, yet the two trespassers were tied to their horses in the corral. *What is Sam doing? Why did he leave them back there?*

Sam quickly brought Cump to a halt. He stepped down, approached Grace and looked up at her.

"Grace, give me your Colt."

Grace was startled by his request and hurt as she asked, "Sam, what's the matter?"

"Grace, just give me the Colt and your Winchester, too."

"Sam, why do you want my guns?"

"Please, Grace. You know I wouldn't ask if it wasn't for the best. Trust me, please."

Grace was suddenly afraid. *Why does Sam want her disarmed? Why wasn't he taking Carol's guns?*

"Okay, Sam," she said as she handed him the Colt, then pulled the Winchester out of the scabbard and handed that to him.

Then, even more curiously, he handed the Winchester to Carol and said, "Hold this for a while, will you, Carol?"

He put her Colt into his saddlebags, then looked up at Grace and asked, "Grace, can you step down, please?"

This was so unlike the Sam she loved. He was treating her like a criminal. *Was he going to tie her hands, too?* But she still trusted him. She had to, so she stepped down.

He put his arms around her shoulders and whispered to her, "Grace, my love, I took your guns because I didn't want you to do anything that would hurt you for the rest of your life. I didn't want to ruin our future."

"Sam," she whispered back, "you're scaring me. What's going on?"

"You need to be the strong Grace that I know is there inside you. Okay?"

She nodded as she looked into his eyes searching for an answer to his behavior.

As he stared back into her curious and worried blue eyes, he said, "Those two men aren't just squatters. One is the man who shot your father and the other is one of those that kidnapped you."

Grace jerked her head back and said loudly, "No!"

Sam spoke in a normal speaking voice, saying, "I'm pretty sure, Grace. That accurate description you gave me matched them perfectly. Now those two clowns are going to hang, Grace. Right now, they think some idiot deputy arrested them for trespassing and they are going to walk. But when I bring you down there, if they don't recognize you, just nod to me that they are the two.

"If they do recognize you, that will be the proof that I need. What you can't let happen is to let them get to you. They'll try to rattle you or make me mad enough to do something stupid. That's why I took your guns. I didn't want to risk that you might shoot them and then go to prison for doing it. Even if I lied to protect you, and you know I would, you'd feel guilty for the rest of your life. So, I need to know; can you do as I asked?"

Grace took a deep breath and said, "Yes, Sam. I can do this. And thank you for thinking of me before anything else."

Sam smiled at her and said, "Good. Now let's get mounted and we'll give those two yahoos the shock of their lives."

As she climbed back into the saddle, Sam stepped to Carol's horse and looked up at her curious face and said, "Those two kidnapped Grace and one shot her father."

Carol understood why he had disarmed Grace, and deeply appreciated Sam's lawmaking skills, as well as his concern for his ladies.

After he remounted, the three trotted through the pasture toward the corral, and as they got closer, Sam could see a noticeable tightening of Grace's normally smooth features. She was battling the anger, and he knew how she felt, having been there himself a few days ago.

When they got within twenty feet, the white-haired outlaw shouted, "So, those are your partners, deputy? I reckon we can guess how you partner up with 'em."

He then started laughing. He hadn't remembered Grace, but the second one sure looked as if he did as he stared at Grace while they drew closer.

Then he shouted, "Ted, shut up!"

Ted couldn't help himself and shouted back, "Why? This deputy ain't got nothin' on us but trespassin'. What's he gonna do; send us to the gallows for unauthorized cookin'?"

He began laughing again, but Abe Thompkins had enough and almost yelled, "Will you open your eyes, you idiot, and look at the blondie there?"

Suddenly it hit Ted, and he blurted out, "What the hell! She's supposed to be at Waxman's!"

Sam had his proof, and said, "Abe Thompkins and Ted Robinson, I am arresting you for the murder of Horace Felton and the abduction of Grace Felton."

He turned to Grace and Carol, then said, "Would you two ladies accompany me to the sheriff's office in Denver?"

"We'd be honored, Sam," replied Grace calmly.

Sam hooked a trail rope to both horses, lashed it to Cump and they began walking the horses back across the fields. After they passed the downed fence, Sam stepped down and spent ten minutes repairing the damage, before he remounted and they pressed on.

When they reached the house, Sam asked Carol to notify Julia what was going on and that they'd be back in three or four hours.

Carol stepped down, then she looked at Sam and glanced at Grace. Sam nodded, understanding her question. *Do you want me to give Grace her rifle back?*

Carol handed Grace the Winchester as Sam reached in his saddlebag and took out Grace's Colt.

Grace slid her carbine back into its scabbard and Sam handed her the pistol as she smiled at him, wordlessly telling him that she appreciated why he had taken them and why he was returning them to her.

Carol was remounted just a few minutes later.

As they passed through the front yard, the workers stopped and looked at the caravan passing. It must have been a sight; two armed young women with the property owner trailing two disarmed, bound men. Sam was just impressed how much work they had done in a single day.

They hit the main road and turned north toward Denver.

———

The ride took a little over an hour, then as their small parade made its way through the streets, they created a line of rubberneckers. A man leading two tied up outlaws wasn't that surprising, but the escort was.

Sam stopped at the sheriff's office, dismounted, and wrapped Cump's leash around the rail, then looked back at Carol and Grace.

"Keep an eye on these two, will you? If they try to run, which would be difficult, shoot them both."

Sam faced the office again with a smile on his face, wondering how nervous those two bad guys were.

He walked into the office, noting a different deputy at the desk; the only member of the county's sheriff's office he hadn't met.

"Afternoon, is Dan in?" Sam asked.

"That depends. Who are you?" was his almost snotty reply.

"Sam Brown."

"Is that supposed to impress me?"

Sam had enough of his attitude and yelled, "Dan, will you get your lazy ass out here?"

He heard laughing from the back office followed by Dan bellowing, "Why, do you have a murderer for me or something?"

Sam yelled back, "Strangely enough, I do. And he and his partner can also be hanged for kidnapping."

The laughter stopped, and Dan Grant came double-timing around the corner.

"Are you pulling my chain, Sam?"

"No, Dan. We found them at Grace's ranch house when she wanted to check out its condition. I recognized the men from the description she had given me of her father's murderer and her kidnappers. I drew down on them with my shotgun and they were so convinced that I was some idiot deputy that was showing off that they didn't put up too much of a squawk. That is until they saw Grace and then realized that they were in trouble. She identified them right off."

"I wish she were here to write a statement."

"She's outside, guarding the prisoners with her Colt."

"*She's what?*"

"Dan, after I had them hogtied, I went to where she and Carol were waiting three hundred yards away and disarmed her until I was sure she had calmed down and understood the consequences of doing what she wanted to do. I trust her, Dan."

"Okay, Sam. But this is a sight I have to see."

263

He wasn't the only one. There must have been fifty people congregating across the street watching the scene by the time they exited the office.

Dan and Sam walked to the two trussed-up prisoners and began untying or cutting the pigging strings that bound them to the horses.

When they had them dismounted, Sam turned to Carol and Grace and asked, "Ladies, can you grab their gunbelts from Cump, and then join us inside?"

"Okay, Sam," replied Grace as she and Carol stepped down.

Sam and Dan escorted the two men into a cell and closed the door, then they had them extend their wrists through the bars, so they could cut the pigging strings.

Meanwhile, the two Colt-armed women had entered the office wearing their Stetsons. The deputy stared at them, and Sam wasn't sure if it was because they were so pretty or because they were wearing guns.

"Deputy, quit staring at my ladies. It's impolite!" Sam said sharply.

The deputy shook his head and murmured, "Sorry."

"Ladies, can you come back and talk to the sheriff, please?" asked Sam.

They walked past the embarrassed deputy into Dan's office, removing their hats as they stepped past, and sat down in the only two free chairs in the office.

Sam began the story by saying, "Dan, this is Grace Felton, whose father was murdered by Ted Robinson, the white-haired man. She had been abducted by both those men. Next to Grace is our friend, Carol Early."

Dan had risen from his seat when the women had entered, and said, "It's a pleasure to meet you both. Miss Felton, would you be able to write out a statement with the facts of the event that cost your father his life and you your freedom?"

"Of course, Sheriff. Do you have paper and a pencil?"

Dan produced some paper and a pencil and slid them across the desk.

As Grace started writing, Carol caught Sam's eye and nodded toward the two outlaws' pistols on the floor. Sam nodded and motioned to Dan to follow him. He had just taken a seat and then stood again as Sam reached down and picked up the guns before the two men filed out of the office and walked to an adjoining office.

Sam handed him the two pistols and said, "These belong to those miscreants. Do you want me to write a report on their capture? It was no big deal. We came over the hill, saw smoke coming from the stove chimney and two horses in the corral. I told the ladies to wait and I went down with the shotgun. When I came in the front, they ran out the back. I suggested they lie own on their tummies. They complied, so I tied them up and here we are."

Dan eyed him up and said, "Why do I think there's more to it than that?"

"Not much, really. The stupid thing was for these two younkers to use the ranch house like it was theirs. I guess because they knew it was abandoned, they could stop off there and enjoy themselves out of town away from Soapy. Like most of them, they don't dazzle you with their intelligence."

"That's the truth. I'll tell you what, why don't you crank me out a quick report. I'll include it with Miss Felton's statement."

"Can do. I'll need paper and pencil, too."

"Sure. I'll get them for you, and I apologize for my deputy. He wasn't my choice. Politics, you know. I really appreciate having you around, Sam. I'd pay you if I could."

"Dan, I don't need the money, and now that I'm a full-time father, I'd need too much time off, anyway."

"I don't think that's the only reason you need too much time, either."

"Maybe not. Just get the paper and pencil, will you?"

Dan chuckled and left the office, returning with the paper and pencil in less than a minute. Sam's report took ten minutes to write, and when he finished it, he walked across to Dan's office, and found the sheriff reading Grace's recently completed statement.

"Miss Felton, I have been in law enforcement for over twenty years, and this is the most detailed and descriptive statement I have ever read. I wish they were all this good because it'd make my job a lot easier."

"Sheriff, that day has been burned in my memory for more than a year. I could tell you how many stitches Ted Robinson had on a repaired tear in the left side of his shirt just below the pocket."

"I don't doubt that for a minute."

"Dan, did you want to get their horses?" Sam asked.

"I forgot about them nags," he replied, then shouted, "Ned! Go out there and move those two outlaw horses to the holding pen in back."

The deputy barely acknowledged the order and left sullenly.

"He's a keeper, Dan," Sam said as he laughed, "he reminds me of the son-of-a-banker that I was saddled with in Boulder."

"Don't remind me."

Sam abruptly stopped laughing and said, "You know what's odd, Dan? They didn't have any long guns in their scabbards."

"That is odd. I wonder why."

"When we go back, I think I'll swing over to Grace's place and have a look around. This doesn't seem right."

"Good idea."

"Well, Dan, we've got to be heading back."

They shook hands and Sam escorted Grace and Carol to their horses. The crowd had mainly dispersed, and only a few hung back to see the two Colt-armed women.

They climbed aboard their horses and headed south out of town; Sam still troubled by the lack of rifles. Nobody in their line of work didn't have a rifle in his possession. Even if they had them in the house when they bolted, the first thing they would have grabbed would have been their Winchesters so the lawman wouldn't have an advantage.

267

As they trotted along, Grace could sense his disquiet.

"Those missing rifles are bothering you. Aren't they, Sam?" she asked.

"A lot. I've been looking at this wrong. What if those two weren't using your ranch house as a hideout or a free lodging place. What if they were using it as a starting point for an assault. Think about it. They'd be close and come from a direction we wouldn't expect. I don't think they'll try anything with the construction crews there, though. It's only around three o'clock, and we'll get back before four, so there'll be plenty of light. Did you want to go and check out the house again? You could tell if they modified it."

"That's a good idea."

"I'd like to come along, too. If that's okay," said Carol.

"The more guns, the better," answered Grace.

"But let's stop in the house and tell Julia what's happening," added Sam.

———

They pulled up to the house just about a half an hour later, and quick-tied their horses to the rail. Again, Sam was surprised at the speed of the construction. After the crews were gone for the day, he'd check the quality of the work.

As they walked through the door, Catherine flew across the room jumping into Sam's arms.

"Hello, sweetie," he said as she leaned back and looked at him.

"Aunt Julia said you caught some more bad men."

"Yes, I did. They were two of the men that stole your Aunt Grace from her home. One of them killed her papa."

Catherine turned to Grace and said, "I'm sorry Aunt Grace that those bad men hurt you."

"Thank you, sweetheart."

"Did you kill them, Papa?"

"No, Catherine. I arrested them and they're in jail now. They will have a trial and then they probably will be killed by the law."

"Why didn't you kill them?"

"Because, sweetie, they had put up their hands and surrendered. If I had shot them, I'd go to prison."

"But you killed those other bad men."

"That's because the first two tried to kill me, so I defended myself. I took off my guns and fought the last man fair with fists. He was bigger than me, too, so he thought he could beat me. But I was so mad for what he did to your mama and your aunts, I hit him hard. Do you understand the difference? I can't hurt people that can't defend themselves. It's against the law, even for sheriffs; especially for sheriffs."

"I think I understand, Papa, but you should tell me again when I get older, though."

"I will, Catherine."

He put her back down as Julia arrived.

269

"I hear you three had an exciting day," she said as she smiled.

"Not as exciting as it was for the two morons who were using Grace's ranch house," Sam said.

"Why were they even there?" she asked.

"That's what has me bothered. We're going back over there in a few minutes to see if we can find any clues in the house."

"That's fine. Catherine and I are having a good time."

"Little girls are like that, aren't they?"

"Especially this one," Julia replied.

"Thanks for watching over her, Julia. We'll be back in about an hour or so."

Sam waved goodbye to Julia and Catherine, who was planted on Julia's left hip.

Carol and Grace lined up and each gave Catherine a kiss on the forehead as they followed him back to the horses.

———

Five minutes later, they had reached the fence line again and Sam stepped down, undoing his earlier repairs.

"You know, Grace, I think I'll talk to Joe Schmidt, the foreman, and ask if he can put a gate in here."

"That's a good idea, Sam."

They walked through the downed fence, rode to the ranch house and wrapped their reins around the front hitchrail.

"How does it look, Sam?" asked Grace.

"Not too bad. The basic construction was very solid, and the placement was excellent. Any water runoff would avoid the house completely. Let's go inside."

Sam led the way into the house and had slipped his hammer loop off, just in case.

The house still had its furniture, and Sam noted the lack of dust, which meant it had been used.

"Did you notice the furniture, Grace?"

"There's no dust. Somebody's been staying here longer than just a day or two."

He nodded then said, "Let's keep going."

They began in the first bedroom, finding that the bed had been used recently and left unmade.

"I'm going to burn all that bedding," growled Grace.

"I don't blame you. I noticed the tub hasn't been used in a while, Grace. There's dust in there. They probably didn't even know what it's used for."

"They did smell bad when we took them in," Carol said as she scrunched her nose.

They didn't find anything of significance until they reached the last bedroom before the kitchen.

Sam walked in first, then froze and whistled. There weren't two rifles, there were six; including two Sharps.

"Look at this arsenal!" he exclaimed as he stared at the weapons and slowly walked into the room.

In addition to the rifles, there were boxes of cartridges stacked nearby, as well as two sets of field glasses.

"What are those big ones?" Carol asked as she pointed.

"Those are Sharps breechloaders, and will you look at this?" Sam asked as he stepped to the cartridges, picked up one and opened it.

"These are .50 caliber, 110 grain cartridges. This is very serious weaponry."

He examined the other four rifles. They were almost brand-new 1976 model Winchesters. Sam hadn't seen one before and levered a cartridge out of the rifle and caught it as it popped out.

He whistled again and said, "I can't believe what I'm my eyes are telling me. This is a .50-95 Express cartridge."

Grace asked, "What's that?"

Sam held the heavy cartridge in his fingers, examining it as a jeweler would study a large diamond, and replied, "Winchester wanted to cash in on the big game hunters going west to kill buffalo, elk and bears, so they developed the Winchester '76, like those four over there. This is the biggest cartridge that Winchester has ever put in a repeater. It doesn't have the range of the Sharps, but it has a longer range than the '73 and a lot more power."

He slid the cartridge into the rifle's loading gate and set the Winchester '76 back against the wall with its siblings.

"These are almost new. They'd have to be, really. Winchester has only been making them for three years and they're not nearly as popular as the '73. They're also the musket version with the longer barrel for increased range and accuracy. So, between them and those Sharps, it really make me wonder what they were planning."

"Why, Sam?" asked Grace.

"They were really built to kill large animals like the buffalo at long range. I could probably put a shot through a window at over a half a mile with the Sharps. See the rear sight with those really big numbers? It's called a ladder sight because you can adjust it for those longer ranges, and both the Sharps and the Winchesters have them. Why would they have them here?"

"We're not going to leave them here; are we?"

"I'm debating that question right now. We'll leave them here for the time being and complete our inspection."

The rest of the house showed use, but no damage at all. Sam figured that with some minor external repairs and a good cleaning, the house would be in good shape. They went outside and looked at the barn and found that it was in better shape than the house. All the normal ranch tools were still there, too.

They returned to the house and sat in the kitchen.

"What are you thinking, Sam?" asked Grace.

"The good news is that we can fix your house up pretty quickly. The bad news is that it looks like the bad guys were planning on using the house as a setup for an attack on the Circle S. I'm not sure if it was to kill Catherine or all of us. This is too much firepower for just one little girl, so I believe that when he was looking for Catherine. Soapy's spotter must have recognized one of you and told him about it. That's when he decided to mount a major expedition."

"But that white-haired one didn't know who I was at all," said Grace.

"Soapy doesn't impress me as being someone who gives information to his toadies. He just tells them what he wants done and keeps the planning to himself, as well as the reasons. I was thinking about just disabling the rifles, so they would think they had useful weapons until they tried to shoot, but then I realized that with the capture of Robinson and Thompkins, that plan is gone anyway. So, we may as well take all the guns and ammo. I'll jury rig a sling to hang them around Cump, and we can each carry one of the Winchesters. We'll divide the ammunition and put them into our saddlebags."

"Okay, Sam," replied Grace.

———

An hour later, Sam had one Winchester and Sharps hanging on each side at an odd angle from Cump. He had to arrange it so that they didn't interfere with the horse's normal motion, yet still allowed Sam to mount. Each of them was holding a Winchester '76 as they rode back to the ranch in the early evening.

After the fence un-repair/repair delay, they made it back to the barn around six. The horses were put away and brushed down, and Sam lugged the rifles to the house and Carol and Grace struggled with the heavy saddlebags. As they stepped onto the porch, Julia opened the door wide and her eyes grew wider.

"Good God! Sam, were those all in Grace's house?"

"Yes, and with enough ammunition to supply a long siege," Sam replied as he laid the rifles down in the main room and went back to relieve the women of their loads, as they were having trouble getting them up the steps.

When all the ammunition was stacked, Sam counted eight boxes of .50-95 Express ammunition for the new Winchesters and four boxes of the massive .50-110 caliber rounds for the Sharps. He knew that he had to try out both of the large bore weapons, having never fired either one before and was almost giddy at the thought; and to think he had actually considered rendering these magnificent weapons unusable.

"I'll check out the rifles later, but they all seem in very good condition; almost new. If you ladies are going to make dinner, I'm going to go and check out today's construction."

"Sounds like a plan, Sam," said Julia.

Sam smiled at the rhyme and waved as the ladies left.

Catherine trotted over and asked, "Can I come with you, Papa?"

He smiled at her and answered, "Of course, you can, sweetheart."

He took her hand, then led her outside and walked to the new carriage house first. The framing for the walls and roof were already up, and he examined the wood and how it was put together. He was very pleased with the quality of the work and the lumber they were using. When he inspected the framework and floor joists for the new bedrooms, he was satisfied there as well. Then he and Catherine walked hand in hand to the cemetery.

Catherine was skipping when they arrived at the gate of the completed cemetery fencing; Sam opened the gate and new father and daughter passed through.

"Papa what is this for?" she asked.

"This is the new family cemetery. When we bring your papa and mama home, we'll bury them here. I picked a very peaceful and beautiful place. I know that your mama would love it very much."

"Mama and papa used to take me here sometimes. They would bring food and we'd sit on the ground for supper."

"See? They already knew this would be a special place. I just didn't think it was right for your mama to be buried so far away and your papa in Denver. They belong here together, so we can visit them."

"I think so, too."

"Let's go back and have some dinner. I'm sure your aunts will be making something tasty," he said as they walked back through the gateway and he closed the gate behind them.

"They make good things to eat, don't they?"

"They sure do," Sam said as he scooped her up, put her on his shoulders and then walked down the rise to the ranch house.

———

After dinner, they were all in the main room as Sam examined each of the newly acquired weapons, finding each of them clean and well-oiled, if not unused. When he had finished his examination, he leaned the guns against a wall, then sat down in the only open chair. Catherine was sitting on Julia's lap.

"Sam, do you think that we're in danger?" asked Carol.

"Not during the day with the construction crews here. I think having those two arrested threw off any plans they may have had, so I think things will be fine for a few weeks. After that, we need to think of something. I have some thoughts running around in my head, but nothing solid.

"What I want is to leave two of these new Winchesters by the front and rear doors. They'll be loaded, but the chamber will be empty. Just understand that the new Winchesters are a newer model and use a larger cartridge. You can tell the difference by looking at the brass plate on the rifle's stock. I'll be doing some target practice with one of the Sharps and one of the Winchesters tomorrow, and I want to make a quick run into Denver to find something that may help with our situation. I'll probably leave around eight to go to Denver and should be back by eleven. Does anyone need anything while I'm there?"

The ladies all shook their heads, even Catherine.

"When I return, hopefully, I'll be able to cheer everyone up."

"Why? What are you planning on doing?" asked Carol.

"It'll be a surprise; provided I can do it. I may not be able to, though."

They began guessing what he was going to do, but none even came close.

"Grace, I'll stop by and see Dan Grant and ask about the trial. I'll need to talk to you about that tomorrow when I get back. Okay?"

Sam could see the distress on her face knowing what was going to happen during the trial and wished there could be another way, but they both knew it had to be done.

Grace simply nodded.

Sam changed the subject to lighter topics including the new bedrooms and carriage house, and he hoped it would be enough to help Grace but didn't think it would.

———

Catherine was with Carol tonight, so his daughter gave him a goodnight kiss before she padded off to join her aunt.

Julia headed off as well, leaving Grace and Sam alone.

"It's going to be hard, isn't it? The trial," she asked quietly.

"Yes. It's going to be a difficult few minutes for you. I imagine that Soapy will spring for a good attorney who will try to discredit you. He'll probably attack me as well when I get on the stand. I'm used to it, though, but you aren't.

"Grace, remember that I'll be right there with you. Search me out and keep looking at me. You're a strong woman, Grace. Just remember what those bastards did to you and your father, and you'll get through it fine. But understand, the defense attorney is taking a big risk.

"You are a young and pretty woman who has been victimized. If the jury of men think he is going too hard on you, they'll turn against him and his clients and I'm sure that if they don't know it their attorney will. He'll have to dance on the line without crossing it."

She looked at Sam and smiled weakly as she said, "Okay."

Then Sam looked at her and mouthed silently, "I love you, Grace."

Her smile lost its weakness and her deep blue eyes shimmered as she mouthed back, "I love you, Sam."

Sam then said in a normal voice, "I guess that will have to do for a while."

Grace grinned back, and said, "Well, we can do better later. I'll be heading off to sleep now. Good night, Sam."

"Good night, Grace."

He watched as she left, then turned into her bedroom and closed the door. He exhaled sharply, hoping that it would be as simple as he'd just explained, but suspected it wouldn't be. Trials always seemed to have at least one surprise, and his concern was that Soapy Smith would go all out to destroy Grace. He really wished he could just walk into his place and blow him away with his shotgun, but he'd settle for taking his gang away; piece by piece.

CHAPTER 10

It was just an hour after sunrise when Sam said his goodbyes to his ladies and stepped out into a bright, cloudless day. The crews were already hard at work.

He walked to the barn and saddled Cump, then led him out of the barn and was getting ready to mount when he saw Joe Schmidt working with the bedroom crew. He walked Cump to the group; Joe saw him heading his way and correctly assumed that he wanted to talk to him. He laid down a board he was carrying and stepped towards him.

"Morning, Sam."

"Howdy, Joe. I've got a couple of questions for you."

"Sure. Go ahead."

"Before I ask, I just want to tell you how impressed I am with the speed and quality of work you and your crews are doing. Anyway, I need to go into Denver for a little while, but this afternoon, I was wondering if you could take a short ride with me to the back of the ranch? I want to see about having a gate added to the back fence. Plus, I need to have you get me an estimate on some needed repairs on a house and barn on the next ranch."

"Not a problem, Sam. About what time do you figure?"

"I'm planning on doing some target practice this afternoon with a Sharps and a Winchester '76 chambered for the .50-95 Express cartridge around three, so how about one o'clock?"

"That's fine. What kind of Sharps are you talking about?"

"One of the Big Fifties, and I've got six boxes of the .50-110 cartridges."

Joe's eyebrows shot up as he asked, "Really? I'd like to try a round or two with that monster myself, if you'd let me."

Sam smiled. Joe was a man after his own heart.

"I'd be honored, Joe. Do you like weapons?"

"Love 'em. Ever since I was a tadpole."

"We'll have to chat sometime. Probably later when we're trying out the Sharps and I'll let you try that Winchester, too."

"I'd like that. We're running ahead of schedule, so I can afford to slack off for an hour or two."

"Don't forget, you'll be getting a new job added to the company coffers as well."

"That should keep them happy," he said as he grinned.

"Well, Joe. I gotta run."

They shook hands and Sam wheeled Cump to the west, then after trotting down the access road, turned north and headed for Denver.

———

An hour later, he was walking into the sheriff's office, and was glad to see Zeke at the desk rather than the sub-par deputy.

"Howdy, Zeke. Is the boss in?"

"Mornin', Sam. Go on in."

Sam walked into Dan's office and found him sitting reading a newspaper and drinking coffee.

"Morning, Dan."

Dan looked up and smiled as he said, "Looks like your story stirred up quite a fuss. There are groups of women demanding that we shut Soapy down. I think he's locked himself away in one of those houses he's been using."

"Life's tough sometimes. Do we have any word on the trial yet?"

"I was gonna send Zeke your way in a bit. Trial's set for Thursday at ten o'clock. You and Miss Felton have both been subpoenaed as witnesses. The prosecutor wants to meet with you both in his office tomorrow afternoon at one-thirty."

"Okay. I have something else for you. Yesterday, remember I said I was concerned about the lack of long guns in their scabbards?"

"Yup. I recall you saying that. It was peculiar."

"Well, when we got back to the ranch, we decided to inspect the house. It looked like folks had been staying there for a while; just men, I'm sure. Well, in the bedroom closest to the kitchen, we found the long guns. Four new Winchester '76 models chambered for the .50-95 Express and two Sharps Big Fifties. Next to the guns, we found a dozen boxes of Winchester cartridges and four boxes of the .50-110s."

Dan whistled then exclaimed, "Talk about being loaded for bear!"

"I was just going to disable them, but figured they already figured out we found them when Robinson and Thompkins got pinched, so we moved them all to my ranch."

"You think Soapy is going to try something? You gotta figure he knows that you're behind that news story."

"I know, but I'm pretty sure he found out before that hit the paper. I think the Ashleys probably sent word to their nephew that Catherine was gone, and he had to let Soapy know. It must've been hard on him, too, but it was all he could do. But I don't believe that he'll try anything yet; not for a while. Between the construction crews at my place and the trial, he'll have to come up with something new."

"Probably, but don't let your guard down."

"I won't. Can I get another John Doe warrant?"

Dan opened his drawer and slid the paper to Sam, then asked, "Anyone I know?"

"I'm sure you do, but this is just a backup. Say, Dan, do you know where I can get a dog?"

"A nice dog and not a mutt?"

"Yup."

"About a mile east of the city, there's a farm that raises herding dogs; mostly collies. It's not a ranch, but they have a big sign in front that reads 'Jerome's Canines'."

"Thanks, Dan. I'll keep you informed of any goings on."

"Having you around has been a real adventure, Sam."

Sam smiled, then replied, "If that's what you call it, Dan," then he shook the sheriff's hand and left the office, waving to Zeke as he passed.

————

Soapy was getting exasperated by the constant failure to simply get rid of one damned kid. Once that idiot Gerald confessed what they did, he gave those morons a simple plan to eliminate everyone on that ranch, including that trouble-making Brown. *And what do those two nitwits do? They managed to be captured at the ranch house by that cowboy and two women, for God's sake! They even had a fire going! Didn't they think that would be noticed? And why had they wanted so many damned rifles for such a simple job?*

All he had told them was to use the ranch house, make sure the kid was there, and then do the job. He was beginning to think that they were worried about that ex-sheriff that had the kid and didn't want to get too close.

Soapy snickered. *The Shotgun Sheriff – what a joke!*

He shook his head wondering why everyone else was so stupid. He'd have to take care of the issue once and for all after the trial of those two dunderheads. They'd failed him for the last time and he'd just let them hang.

————

Sam climbed up on Cump, turned east to find the dog farm and less than twenty minutes later, he found the place. As Sam rode down the long access road, he could hear the yapping of lots of canines as he approached.

The main building appeared to be part office and part home, so he brought Cump to a stop, dismounted, and after tying him off, stepped up to the front door and knocked. This was a business, not a residence, so he wasn't breaking any courtesies.

A white-haired gentleman opened the door and asked, "Looking for a dog, sir?"

"Kind of looks that way, doesn't it?" Sam replied with a smile.

"C'mon in, then. The name's Cecil Jerome."

"Sam Brown. Nice to meet you, Cecil."

"So, what kind of dog are you looking for?"

"I need two, actually. I'd like them young, so they can adapt to my family. I need them primarily to keep a watch out for strangers."

"Well, most dogs that are attached to a family will protect those that care for them, but I have some older border collie puppies that would serve that purpose and are good herding dogs as well. Make nice family dogs, too. They're well-tempered and smart as whips."

"Sounds good."

"Come with me."

Sam followed Cecil out of the back of the house to what looked like a long, low barn, and, as it turned out, that was exactly what it was, but there wasn't a horse or a cow in the building. When they entered, Sam saw dozens of screened in miniature stalls, and each had hay on the ground as well as dogs of various sizes. The smell wasn't pleasant.

Cecil led him deeper into the barn until he stopped at a stall about halfway, then turned, opened the screened gate and gestured for Sam to follow him in. Once Sam was inside, Cecil closed the gate as Sam smiled at the eight bouncing puppies. They were, as most young animals were, amazingly cute.

"These are the border collies I was talking about. They don't grow as big as the regular collies. They're twelve weeks old now. See any that you like?"

"They are all health, young dogs. Can you pick me out two females?"

"Smart move, Sam. Females are less aggressive and usually smarter. Just like humans, I guess."

Sam laughed and said, "Yes, sir. I'd have to agree with you there."

"How are you going to get them back to your ranch?"

"Good question. I hoped you'd have a solution."

Cecil grinned at him and said, "As it turns out, most of my customers live on ranches, so I have these special crates made up. The fact that you're getting two makes it easier. We have a rig that rides behind your saddle and supports two of our crates."

"Great! Let's get this all wrapped up."

Sam and Cecil each took a puppy and left the barn. Just before leaving the barn, Sam noticed a stack of what he had thought were just boxes. Cecil took one from the stack, set it on the floor, and opened a latched door, putting the puppy inside, then he took a second one and pushed the second puppy inside. He lifted what appeared to be a small leather harness, hung it over his shoulder, then each of them took a puppy-filled box and returned to the front of the house where Cump stared at the boxes containing the two noisy furballs.

Cecil hooked the contraption to each box, then, after putting a small blanket over Cump's back end, he and Sam lifted the box holder over Cump's hind quarters and laid it behind the saddle, then tied it in place with long leather strings.

"I'm thoroughly impressed, Cecil. That is a brilliant design. You should patent it."

"No need. Let's go inside and handle the paperwork."

The puppies and contraption cost sixteen dollars, which was a bit pricey, but Sam thought it was worth it.

Twenty minutes later, Sam was through Denver and on his way home. The puppies yapped most of the time, and Sam thought it was a pleasant sound, so he smiled most of the way back but didn't think Cump was happy about it. As he saw the ranch house in the distance, he began to grin, anticipating Catherine's reaction to the newest additions to the family.

————

Grace was sitting on the porch steps, waiting for his return with the news about the trial, and popped to her feet when she saw him. Despite her anxiety about the trial, she was warmed at the sight, smiled, and when he saw her and waved, she waved back and then wrapped her arms around herself, thinking that this is how it should be.

She stepped down to the front yard as he walked Cump towards her and could hear the yapping before she could see inside the two caged crates.

When he was close, she asked loudly, "Sam, is that what I think it is?"

He grinned and replied, "It's kind of hard to hide, isn't it?

Sam pulled Cump to a halt, stepped down and after tying off Cump's reins, opened one of the latched boxes, removed its contents and handed the puppy to Grace. She began licking her face and she started laughing.

As Sam was opening the second box, he heard the screen door open and a screech from Catherine.

"Puppies! Papa has puppies!"

She almost missed the stairs as she shot toward her papa; her papa who had puppies.

Sam handed her the second puppy, and she began a tongue attack on Catherine's face as she giggled, loving every lick.

"Okay, you two puppy-laden ladies, let's go inside," he said as he put his hand on Grace's back and gave her a slight nudge, but let his hand linger as long as he dared.

Some of the construction workers stopped and saw Catherine with her young canine and smiled. If there's anything cuter than a puppy, it's a puppy being held by a young child.

Sam followed the two inside, finding Carol and Julia with huge grins on their faces just inside the door.

Once inside, the two puppies were let loose, and as they raced through the house, Catherine ran right behind them, still giggling. The adults were all laughing and/or giggling at the sight and kept their eyes fixed until the chase disappeared into the kitchen.

"So, why puppies, Sam?" asked Carol.

"They'll make great watch dogs. If anyone comes near the house, they'll start barking. I wanted them young, so they could become part of the family. They'll become more protective as they grow older. Right now, they'll just pick up strangers before we will, plus, they're a lot of fun to have around."

"They are that," Julia said as she glanced back to the noisy kitchen.

Catherine had finally caught one and the other followed her as she returned to the main room.

"Papa, can I have this one?" she asked with a grin.

Sam looked down at her and replied sternly, "No, Catherine, I'm sorry, but you can't have a puppy."

"Oh," she said, her head dropping in sudden and unexpected disappointment.

The women all glared at Sam, surprised at his callousness.

Then Sam smiled and replied, "You can't have a puppy, Catherine, you have two puppies. They're both your puppies, sweetie, and they'll be your good friends."

"*Both of them? They're both my puppies?*" she exclaimed, not believing her good luck. Two puppies!

"Well, we do have to name them, you know," he said, smiling at his overwhelmed daughter, who had crumpled to the floor to be with her new friends.

She was laughing wildly as the two little dogs bounced over her and licked her face.

The ladies had all forgiven Sam, and then chastised themselves for even thinking for a heartbeat that he would do such a thing.

"Well, ladies. I'm going to leave you now to deal with the whole puppy issue while I go and get some practice shots with the Sharps and the Winchester. I need to see what I can do with them. The added reach could be important. Then Joe and I are going out to the east pasture, so I can show him where I want the gate."

"Can we shoot the Sharps?" asked Carol.

"No, I don't think that would be a good idea. As it is, I'll have a bruise on my right shoulder from firing that cannon. You could be really hurt by the kickback, and I'll let you know about the bigger-bore Winchesters after I try it."

"Thanks for the warning."

"I'm going to go and get Joe," he said before he turned, then walked out of the main room.

Once he was on the porch, he looked at the different crews and found Joe easily. He was barking at one of the workers, and it wasn't a puppy's bark.

Sam was tickled at the foreman-like behavior of the normally affable man, then strode toward Joe, who saw him coming and waved. Sam gestured for him to come with him and Joe grinned, hopped down, then trotted over to Sam, anxious to shoot the big gun.

"Are we going to do some shooting, Sam?"

"Yes, sir."

"Great. I can't wait."

Joe and Sam went back into the house where the ladies were still with Catherine as she played with the puppies.

"Ladies, this is Joe Schmidt, the foreman of the construction crews. He's going to join me in some target practice."

"Nice to meet you, ladies." Joe said.

Sam reached down and grabbed one of the Sharps and handed it to Joe, then picked up a Winchester '76 and a box of cartridges for each weapon, handing the heavier box of Sharps cartridges to Joe.

"You have two?" Joe asked as he noticed the second Sharps, astounded that anyone could have two of the beasts. He didn't even comment on all the other weapons.

"Yes, sir."

As Sam turned to get ready to leave, Carol walked up to him, put her arms around his neck, slid against him and gave him a big kiss on the cheek. She kept her body tied to Sam and turned her head to Joe and said, "Now, you take good care of my husband, Joe. I may have plans for him later."

Then, she giggled, startling the other two women, and it wasn't just because Carol actually giggled.

Grace was seething inside, and Julia wasn't too pleased either.

"Not a problem, Mrs. Brown," Joe replied with a tinge of red in his ears.

Even Joe was a bit embarrassed by the display.

Sam waited until Carol released him, then looked at the foreman and said, "Well, let's go Joe. We'll go through the kitchen. I need to pick something else up."

Joe and Sam walked through the house and Sam plucked his shotgun and put it in his scabbard before they left the house and went toward the shooting ridge.

Back in the main room, Julia turned to Carol and asked, not kindly, "What was that all about?"

Carol, knowing full well that she had surpassed the unwritten limits, said, "I did get carried away, didn't I? I was going to be the pretend wife and sort of took advantage of the situation. I'm sorry. I'll behave better now."

Grace said nothing and accepted the apology but couldn't dispel the jealousy.

———

Out in the pasture, Sam walked up to the ridge and carved a deep circle into the ridged; the uncovered earth noticeably darker than the surrounding dry dirt.

"Okay, Joe, let's mark off about four hundred yards. Does that sound about right?"

"These beasts are good for longer than that, but four hundred will do."

"I've read of shots being made with this model from a mile out."

"Could be. But it would be as much luck as it was good shooting."

"There's always a measure of luck in long-range shooting, Joe."

"True. Let's do four hundred."

Sam paced off approximately four hundred yards, then they stopped, turned then he handed Joe three cartridges.

As he stood with the Winchester '76 in his hand, Sam said, "Go ahead, Joe. I'll watch for your three."

Joe nodded and loaded his first cartridge, adjusted the ladder sight and released the first trigger. He sighted the target, then held his breath as he slowly squeezed the second trigger. The big rifle pushed a massive cloud of gunsmoke out of its muzzle that followed the massive slug of lead and the thunderous sound of the weapon rolled across the pasture.

Sam was looking downrange and watched as the dirt flew.

"Just a might high, Joe. Maybe I didn't mark it off quite right."

"I'll blame you then, Sam," Joe said as he grinned.

Sam laughed and said, "Any excuse, Joe."

Joe readied his second shot and just seconds later, the Sharps slammed against his shoulder and the big round hit the target almost dead center.

"Great shot, Joe. How's the recoil on that thing?"

"Not as bad as you might think."

Joe took his third shot, again hitting the target but in the upper right corner.

Joe traded Sam the Sharps for the Winchester, then Sam took three of the .50-110 cartridges, dropping two into his vest pocket, pulled out the empty brass, inserted a fresh cartridge and closed the breech. He aimed downrange, checked the ladder sight and released the first trigger, sighted the target, held his breath and squeezed the trigger. He felt the kick and heard the powerful blast then quickly lowered the rifle, trying to find the target through the gunsmoke haze.

Joe said, "You must be lucky or good, Sam. That was square on."

"Hell of a gun; isn't it?" Sam asked.

"It's something to write home about."

Sam's last two shots were either dead center or close enough not to matter.

"Lord, Sam! Now you're making me look bad!" Joe exclaimed as he turned and grinned at Sam.

"You just tweaked all the conditions for me, Joe. Now do we see if the Winchester can reach that far?"

"You think that '76 can hit four hundred yards?"

"Beats me. It's got a lot of power, so I say let's give it a shot."

"Does that ladder sight go up to four hundred?"

"Yup. It goes up to five hundred yards."

"Then let's give it a try."

Joe grinned as he flipped up the rear ladder sight set it to four hundred yards and cocked the hammer.

Neither he nor Sam had heard the new Winchester's report before, but that changed when Joe squeezed the trigger and the repeater bucked. The sound wasn't like the Sharps at all, but it surely wasn't the familiar crack of the '73's .44 caliber round, either.

Sam was watching the target and was surprised when the bullet struck the target, but low.

He kept his eyes downrange and said, "It's about a foot low."

"That's still pretty impressive, Sam," Joe said.

Joe then faced the target again and fired two more quick rounds, and Sam saw two eruptions of dirt in the target.

After Sam told him of the hits, Joe was all grins as he and Sam exchanged rifles again.

Again, all of Sam's shots were in the target, and while not as centered as his Sharps rounds, they were better than Joe's.

"That's a mighty impressive repeater, Sam. I wonder why they aren't selling as many as the '73s."

"Two reasons, I think. Everyone wants a rifle that uses the same cartridge as their pistols, and the '76s all use Winchester center fire cartridges, so there's no competition. It makes them a bit pricey and harder to get. At least, that's what I think."

"It sounds good to me, Sam."

"Let's head over to the ridge, I want to show you something."

The two men, each carrying a large bore rifle, walked until they reached Sam's designated pistol spot.

"Joe, hang here for a second." Sam said.

Sam walked to the ridge and drew six circles in random locations on the left side of the ridge; each one about eight inches in diameter, then he returned to Joe. As he walked, he chambered a sixth round into his Colt, then replaced it in its holster.

"Last year, when I was the sheriff up in Boulder, I carried this shotgun with me most of the times to control bad situations. Some hard cases gave me grief because they figured after I unloaded the shotgun, they'd be able to plug me with their hog leg."

Before Joe could comment, Sam looked downrange, snatched the shotgun from his back scabbard, flipped the hammers and pulled the trigger. As the shotgun flew back, he pulled his Colt and fired six rapid shots at the ridge and holstered the Peacemaker. The entire display had lasted less than fifteen seconds.

"Jesus, Sam! Surely you didn't…," Joe said as he walked slowly to the circles on the ridge and saw that each had been hit by a .44 bullet. They weren't all dead center but would have been in the bull's eye ring in a normal target.

Sam had retrieved his shotgun by the time Joe came back.

"It's you! You're that sheriff in the Rocky Mountain News story."

"I told them that story to get Soapy Smith to stop kidnapping women and selling them to prostitution, Joe."

"So, your three ladies were the ones you rescued."

"They are. They're three amazing women that are trying to get their lives back together."

"When did you marry one?"

Sam grinned and replied, "I didn't. That's a cover we use from time to time to keep gossip down. I figure any man who's anxious to shoot a Sharps isn't the kind of man who spreads that kind of gossip."

"Nah. Nobody wants to talk to me anyway."

Sam then said, "I think Carol, she's the one pretending to be my wife at the moment, took advantage of the assignment."

Joe laughed and replied, "I'm sure it broke your heart, too."

Sam didn't tell him that it did annoy him somewhat, but said, "Let's go get the horses and I'll show you where I need the gate."

"Sounds good, Sam."

They walked the few hundred yards to the house, and when they reached the porch, Joe held the Sharps to Sam.

Sam looked at him, and asked, "What are you doing, Joe?"

"Giving you back your gun."

"I've got one. That's yours."

Joe was flabbergasted as he asked, "Are you serious?"

"Keep the box of ammunition, too. I'll give you another box if you want one. That'll leave me with two boxes and I can special order some more in Denver if I need them. Let's face it, there are times to use the Sharps and times to use something a bit smaller."

Joe laughed. He couldn't believe it. Sam just gave him a Sharps Big Fifty!

They stepped onto the porch and walked into the kitchen. Sam leaned his shotgun and the Winchester against the wall for cleaning later, then went back out the kitchen door and into the barn.

Joe carried his precious weapon and the half-box of ammunition out to the first freight wagon, laid them in the boot then returned to the barn where Sam was saddling Cump. When he spotted Joe entering the barn, he told him to saddle Emma. She hadn't been ridden in a while and this was a short ride.

Twenty minutes later, they arrived at the location for the new gate.

Joe looked at it and said, "Sam, this is nothing. We can use some spare lumber and get this done in an hour."

"Great. I'm going to have to open up our temporary gate to show you the other job."

Fifteen minutes later they had tied their horses to the corral behind Grace's ranch house and entered the unlocked back door.

"What I need, Joe, is to have this house and barn returned to good condition. I didn't find any structural issues and it seems to have been well built. It'll need a fresh coat of paint, too."

Joe grinned and said, "This was well built. I helped build it about twenty years ago. It was one of my first jobs. We were right proud of the build, too. We'd be really pleased to get it back in shape, Sam."

"Great, let me know how much they want for the job and I'll stop by when I get into Denver."

"This isn't a difficult job, Sam. I'll just swing the boys over here after we build that gate. This'll only take a day or two."

"Thanks, Joe. Let's head back."

After they returned, Sam took care of the horses as Joe returned to his foreman duties. As he unsaddled the animals, he hoped that Grace hadn't been too upset by Carol's display but didn't know any way he could make it up to her, even though it wasn't his fault.

Sam arrived back in the house as the ladies were cooking dinner, and Sam could detect a cool air in the room, despite the heat generated by the stove, and he had no doubt what the cause of the chill was and had finally come up with a possible solution when he saw his ladies; and it would be a very enjoyable solution at that.

"How is it going, ladies?" he asked.

"Fine," was the best response he could get and that was from Julia.

He quickly walked up to Julia, picked her up, hugged her close and gave her a big kiss on the cheek. After setting her down, he walked up to Grace, winking at her with his left eye so only she could see, and plucked her from the floor and holding her tightly, gave her a good kiss on the cheek as well.

"Now, all my wives are the same again," he said as he set Grace back to the floor.

That got them all smiling again, even Carol, who had been feeling guilty about causing the stress.

"I think I'll check on Catherine. Has she worn out the puppies or have they worn her out?"

"Go look," said Grace, still smiling and not about the puppies.

Sam walked back to the main room and found Catherine asleep on the couch with both puppies snuggled against her. None moved as he entered, and as he looked at the peaceful sight, he was pleased with his decision to bring the little collies into the home.

Sam turned and quietly returned to the kitchen.

He looked at Grace and said, "Grace, the trial is set for Thursday morning at ten o'clock and the prosecuting attorney wants to meet with us tomorrow afternoon at one-thirty. We'll be taking the carriage for both trips, so we can have time to talk about what to expect. The prosecutor will be able to tell you about the process and what his plans are. I've attended dozens of trials, so I have a good idea what's going to happen."

Grace looked a little pale, but said, "I'll be ready, Sam."

"I know you will. Now what's for dinner? Are there any biscuits?"

Even Grace laughed at the expected question and Julia tossed him one of the warm biscuits. Sam snatched it out of mid-air, took a bite, rolled his eyes and walked back to the main room.

He sat across from the Catherine and puppy laden couch and just enjoyed the scene. He'd have to figure out where the small dogs would stay. Puppies couldn't be left in the house.

"I guess I'll have to build a nice doghouse," he thought.

Carol walked in and glanced at the sleeping trio and sat next to Sam.

"I'm sorry, Sam. I got carried away a bit."

"That's alright, Carol. It's really my fault that I've put you all in this situation. I tend to be a bit selfish. I should make a point of letting you all go Denver and have a good time at the theater or a dance or something. I think that you're all getting as frustrated as I am."

"We are getting frustrated, that's for sure. But I know that I don't need a lot more socializing. I'm happy here, Sam, and so is Grace. I think Julia might enjoy going to Denver, though."

"There's something that I've known for a while. I'll see what I can do. And don't worry about the hug and kiss thing. I did what I did in the kitchen to smooth the rough waters. Besides, it was quite enjoyable."

Carol smiled, and said, "You are a remarkable man, Sam."

"Just lucky, Carol. Let's go wake up our sleeping cutie and get her some dinner."

Just minutes later, a yawning Catherine sat at the table as dinner was transferred from the stove to the kitchen table above two bouncing border collie puppies following each plate eagerly with their eyes.

Sam said, "Catherine, I have to take Aunt Grace to Denver tomorrow. You have an important job to do while we're gone. I need you to think carefully about this, because it's very important."

Catherine, the thought of an important job in front of her, sat up straight and said, "I can do it, Papa."

"I know you can, sweetheart. This decision will be with you for a long time and you'll have to live with it if you make a bad one. Do you understand?"

"Yes, Papa," she replied seriously.

"Okay. Now, tomorrow when I'm gone, you have to come up with two names for your puppies. Unlike Humpty and Dumpty, you'll be seeing the puppies every day for years. You want to give them good names that you'll be happy to call them when they're big dogs. Like when you were a baby, what if your mama and papa had named you Piggy, because you were nice and pink. That would have been cute for a few days, but how horrible would it be when you went to school? Or when you were married? Can you imagine the minister saying, "Do you, Piggy, take this man….?"

Catherine looked horrified. *Who would name their baby Piggy?*

The ladies were stifling their laughter in the background; holding back their merriment as best they could.

"Okay, Papa. I'll do a good job. Are they girl dogs or boy dogs?"

"They're both girl puppies."

"Good. That will make it easier."

"And don't name them after any ladies you know. Some ladies wouldn't like having a girl dog named after them because they don't want to be known as, well, girl dogs."

None of the women could hold it back after that crack, and they began to giggle.

Catherine turned and looked at her aunts and wondered what was so funny. Her aunts were crying, but they were laughing, too. She had a hard time figuring out grownups sometimes.

———

After dinner when things returned to normal after the tension of the 'kissing incident' had been defused, Sam announced his plan to build a doghouse. Catherine objected until she discovered the practical reason for letting the dogs sleep outside, and her aunts had to clean up the mess.

CHAPTER 11

After breakfast, Sam went out to the barn to do a little construction of his own; only not quite as pricey as the carriage house and bedroom addition. He decided to use the crates that had been left from their shopping trip to build a home for the puppies. He had some nice lumber available, but having the heavy boxes would cut the build time to less than half the time if he used just flat boards.

Two hours after he started, the puppy palace was complete. He carried it out to the front yard and placed it on the ground to the right side of the porch, away from the new bedrooms. He believed that from that location, the puppies would be able to spot any intruders before they would.

Once the small doggie dwelling was in place, he returned to the main room where he found Catherine giggling as her young furballs chased each other's tails in a tight circle while the three grinning adult women watched Catherine.

"Okay, young lady," he said as he entered, "bring your four-legged friends with you out to the yard. I have something to show you."

Catherine turned, her big smile still on her face, then walked to Sam, causing her puppy pals to stop their game and trot behind their small human friend, wagging their tails.

Sam smiled as Catherine took his hand then waved to her aunts as she, Sam, and the puppies left the house.

Once outside, Sam pointed to the small house and said, "That's their new home, sweetie. They can come and go as they please and they won't do their business in our house anymore."

"Can they still come in the house, Papa?" she asked as she looked at the doghouse.

"Of course, they can. They're your friends, and when they get older, they'll probably be spending all their time in the house with you because the doghouse isn't big enough for two full-sized dogs, even though they aren't going to grow to be that big."

"That's good. Let's see if they like it."

Catherine seemed to be able to get the little border collies to do what she wanted just by simple hand gestures, because all she did was point to the house and they both bounded inside. They seemed pleased with their new home and piddled in it to show how happy they were and to claim ownership.

"They like it, Papa!" Catherine exclaimed.

"That's because you told them it was their house, so they think you gave it to them."

"But you made it, Papa."

"That's all right, Catherine. It's more important that they think you gave it to them. I've got to go back inside and get cleaned up to get ready to go to Denver with Aunt Grace."

"Can I stay and watch the puppies?"

"You can, but don't forget you still have to give them their names."

"I'm thinking about it, Papa. I want them to be good names."

"I know you'll pick the ones that fit them the best, sweetie," Sam said before patting her on her blonde head and returning to the house.

Sam only needed a quick cleanup to remove the sawdust, so he walked to the kitchen, pulled his shirt off and two minutes later had a hair full of suds and was getting ready to rinse it off when he heard footsteps.

"How are you, Julia?" he asked, his closed eyes still covered in soap.

"How did you know it was me?"

"As I explained to Grace, I can tell each of you by your footsteps. They're unique."

"Well, I'm impressed."

Sam began to rinse as he asked, "So, what can I do for you?"

"Can I come to Denver with you and Grace?"

"We're just going to the courthouse to meet with the prosecuting attorney."

"I know, but I need to get out for a while."

"I understand that. I've known it for a while, so I'll tell you what we'll do. Friday, why don't you ride into Denver on your own and do some exploring? I'll give you some money, so you can do what you'd like."

"I'm not sure that I'd like to go alone."

"Then I can take you in the carriage. How's that?"

That brightened her face considerably.

"That would be wonderful," she replied, then smiled, turned and practically danced away.

Sam wasn't quite sure where this was going, but he was vaguely uncomfortable.

Sam dried his hair and dressed in his suit with a black vest, leaving off his Colt but kept his Webley, so he had the look of an unarmed merchant – a very large, well-constructed unarmed merchant.

Grace was finished dressing and when they met in the main room, Sam thought she looked perfect in a very demure dress that made her look as innocent as she really was.

He smiled at her and said, "I'll go and get the carriage ready and we'll go."

"Okay, Sam," she replied with her own smile; anticipating the long private drive much more than the meeting with the prosecutor.

It took him only fifteen minutes to hook up the grays, then he pulled the carriage out of the barn and into the front yard and stopped six feet before the front porch steps.

Grace was waiting on the porch and stepped down and into the carriage, then they both waved at the assembled females at the door and drove on.

When they were about a mile out, Sam turned to an obviously nervous Grace and said, "Grace, I think I may have created a problem."

She turned to him and asked, "How did you do that?"

"This morning, Julia asked me if she could come along with us today. She said she was getting bored, so I told her that she could ride into Denver on Friday. But she said that she didn't want to go alone, so I told her I'd drive her in the carriage. She went from disappointed to bouncy and practically danced out of the kitchen."

Grace sighed and said, "First Carol and now Julia. By the way, I thought the way you handled that whole incident was brilliant. So, Mister Woman Magician, how will you handle this potential bomb?"

"I was thinking of inviting you or Carol to come along, but Carol has me worried at the other extreme."

"Another problem?"

"Yup. She came and apologized for kissing me. I told her it was okay, and that it was my fault for not letting you get out more to social event. She said that she didn't want to go to any, and that she was perfectly happy staying at the ranch. That's not healthy, Grace."

"Why not? I'm more than happy staying at the ranch."

"I've given you a reason to be that way. You know that I love you and want to marry you, Grace, but I need to defuse both situations. I know that if Julia met some young man that smiled at her, she'd leave. Carol is a much more difficult problem. If I told her that I loved you as a man loves a woman and I thought of her as a sister, I think it would hurt her badly. I think I've screwed this up from the start. Maybe if I'd been more standoffish it would have been better."

"No, Sam, that would have been far worse. To get us back to feeling like normal women again took a lot of love and understanding. And what made it critical, it had to come from a man. Having it come from a handsome, masculine man was even better. You made us feel important again; wanted again, and not just lusted after. Now that we're just ourselves again, it's hard to sever that bond. I'm lucky because I don't need to, but like you said, Julia will be relatively simple. I'm worried about Carol, too."

Sam stopped the carriage, twisted on the leather seat, then slid Grace closer to him and kissed her; a lover's kiss.

When their lips parted, Sam said quietly, "I love you, Grace. You are everything I could ever hope to find in a wife."

Grace was smiling as she whispered, "And you, Mister Brown, are my perfect husband."

Sam sighed, then turned back to the front, flicked the reins and the grays resumed their trot to Denver. Sam and Grace finished the ride to the courthouse in a much better mood and sitting much closer.

Arriving at the courthouse around one o'clock, Sam pulled the carriage into a reserved lot and hitched it to a provided post, then escorted Grace to the large brick building, entered the courthouse and found a directory, then walked upstairs to room 211; the office of County Prosecutor Henry Madsen.

Sam opened the door for Grace, and they entered his outer office. Once inside, Sam told his clerk that they had an appointment with Mister Madsen at one-thirty. The prosecutor must have already finished with his previous appointment because they were ushered right in.

Henry Madsen was impeccably dressed; perhaps overdressed. He was about thirty-five years old, with dark hair showing early streaks of gray. He sported a large handlebar mustache and equally large set of mutton chop whiskers that ran down the sides of his face.

"Good afternoon, Miss Felton, Mister Brown. I'm Henry Madsen. I'll be prosecuting Ted Robinson and Abe Thompkins for murder and kidnapping tomorrow. Won't you both have a seat?"

———

For the next hour, Madsen went over Grace's testimony; and just like Sam and the sheriff, was impressed with her recall accuracy, and was very pleased with her as a witness. He was equally happy with Sam's testimony of the capture before he spent thirty minutes going over what the defense attorney, Louis Dailey, would probably do, and warned Grace that Dailey would attack her because of her background, but that he would try to disarm him by accenting her victimhood. He was very grateful that Sam had already prepared her for what was to come.

They reviewed the written statements and Sam's report, then he asked, "You say there was another witness to hearing Robinson say that she was supposed to be at Waxman's?"

Sam replied, "Yes, there is. Carol Early was sitting on her horse next to Miss Felton as he practically yelled the words."

He was scribbling furiously as he said, "Wonderful. Can she be in the courtroom tomorrow?"

"We can do that."

"Great. She'll only be called if the defense attorney claims that his two clients deny hearing it and only two witnesses say that they did."

"Okay."

That question wrapped up the meeting, and Madsen expressed his confidence in obtaining a conviction. After shaking hands, Sam and Grace left the office and the county courthouse.

They returned to the carriage, and after Sam unnecessarily helped Grace onto the front seat, were soon headed back to the Circle S.

As they left the outskirts of Denver, Sam scooted closer to Grace and smiled at her. She smiled back and slid even closer to him. He made the final scoot until they were wedged tightly together, which may have made driving difficult, but he didn't mind. He put his arm around her, and she leaned her head against his shoulder. Neither said a word for thirty minutes.

A mile from the ranch, Sam said, "I suppose we need to go back to old couple sitting locations."

"If you think it's necessary."

"Necessary, but not preferable," he answered as he and Grace slid back to where they had begun the drive.

Grace then said, "I think I have a solution to the lesser issue of Julia."

"And it is?" Sam asked as he looked at her.

"We all go to Denver Friday to pick out the new furniture. If anyone wants to explore on her own, she can do that, and we'll meet at the restaurant on 16th Street at five o'clock."

"That should work."

"I hope so," Grace replied, but wasn't convinced herself.

They pulled into the yard, and as he scanned the construction, Sam noted that the bedrooms and the carriage house looked complete, but they still needed the interior work and the paint. They also had to apply shingles to the roof of the new bedrooms.

Sam dropped Grace off at the house, then brought the carriage into the barn, unhitched the grays and led them into their stalls as he brushed them down. After the horses were taken care of, Sam returned to the house, wondering if Grace broke the new travel arrangements to Julia or she'd left it to him.

Once he entered, the first thing he did was to hunt down Carol and found her in the kitchen with Julia. Grace was still getting changed, which answered his question, and Catherine was in her room talking to her while her ever-present puppies played at her feet.

Carol and Julia both turned to look at him as he said, "Carol, the prosecuting attorney wants you in the audience tomorrow as a possible witness."

Carol quickly asked, "Witness for what?"

"Just for the conversation we had with Robinson and Thompkins at the corral. The one where Robinson said he thought Grace was at Waxman's."

Carol visibly relaxed as she replied, "Oh, that. Okay. That's no problem."

"Good. The trial begins at ten o'clock, so we need to be on the road by eight."

Ten minutes later, everyone, including the canines, were in the main room at Sam's request.

Once the humans were all seated in chairs with Catherine on Grace's lap, he said, "Earlier this morning, Julia expressed an interest in going to Denver on Friday. It's a great idea, so I thought we'd turn it into a family trip. We need to order furniture and other things like bedding, curtains and other incidentals. Now, you know that having me select all that is a bad idea, so those who wish to go to the furniture store or wherever else you may wish to go, can come along. If anyone wants to explore downtown Denver, you can do that, too. We can set up a rendezvous at the restaurant on 16th Street at five o'clock and have dinner there so no one has to cook. How's that work?"

There was universal agreement on everyone's part, but Sam could see the disappointment in Julia's eyes and felt bad about it, but the consequences of being alone with Julia for a few hours would be much worse.

For the rest of the day, Julia was sulky, and everyone, even Catherine noticed, so Sam had to revisit his plan and see if a revision could help; but first, there was the trial to worry about.

———

The next morning, Sam, Grace and Carol were in the carriage and heading toward Denver. It was a gray day and rain threatened, but Sam had put up the top, so at least they would stay dry in the carriage if the clouds let loose.

Sam parked the carriage in the lot and escorted his two ladies into the courthouse and found the courtroom. They entered and found seats in the front row reserved for witnesses, and Sam noticed that there were no defense witnesses yet, which he disregarded because they were early.

Sam slid his hand over to Grace and gave her hand a gentle squeeze for support and was rewarded with a warm smile but had to pull his hand back lest Carol notice.

The rest of the gallery was filling up, and when he arrived, Henry Madsen smiled at Grace as he sat in his chair at the prosecution table.

The defense attorney, Louis Dailey, also arrived and sat at the defense table then glanced at Grace.

Five minutes later, Dan Grant and Zeke walked the manacled prisoners to the chairs next to the defense attorney, then Dan removed the manacles before he and Zeke sat directly behind the prisoners. There were two armed bailiffs near the doors.

Sam noticed that the defense witness bench was still empty, and there should have been someone there by now. This was already tickling his lawman bone; something was amiss. He had never asked Henry Madsen if Mister Dailey had given him a list of witnesses.

Judge McNeal entered, and everyone stood, beginning the trial.

Madsen soon approached the jury and described in detail the crimes attributed to the defendants. His opening statement was brief and factual, as it should be.

Dailey's opening statement was neither, as he described his clients as innocent men who were nowhere near the victim's home at the time of the crime.

Sam wondered why he would make that claim, yet still have no witnesses to provide their alibi. Surely, Soapy Smith could use some of his boys to perjure themselves to provide the lie of their presence elsewhere. This was getting beyond strange; there was something going on that he didn't understand, and he didn't like it.

As Madsen had briefed them earlier, Grace was called to the stand first, and Sam watched as she nervously took her seat.

After being sworn in and giving her name, Madsen asked her to provide the details of the crime and what had happened to her as a result.

Grace's testimony was perfect. She showed just enough emotion to demonstrate the horror she had witnessed without becoming a weeping mess that would cause many of the male jurors to dismiss her as another hysterical female. Her descriptions were also extraordinarily accurate, leaving none to doubt the accuracy of her testimony.

Madsen asked her to identify the perpetrators and she pointed to the accused.

"No more questions, your honor," the prosecutor said and smiled at Grace before turning back to take his seat.

Dailey strode to Grace, but without any malicious intent, and asked, "Miss Madsen, you were under a lot of stress that day. Could you have been mistaken in your identification of these men?"

Sam thought it was a really stupid question as their hair alone marked them as highly unusual.

"I had a long time to see them closely on that day. Those images are burned into my mind."

"How do we know that you didn't shoot your father to gain control of the ranch yourself, Miss Felton?"

Sam was now convinced the defense attorney was either an idiot, which he doubted, or Soapy was setting his boys up to hang as traitors.

"I was already on the deed, Mister Dailey. As it was, we were about to lose the ranch. We had already missed one tax payment and our only ranch hand had left months before. The three men who rode up that day, including those two, arrived and told my father they wanted to buy the ranch. That's how they were able to get so close."

"Isn't it possible, Miss Felton, that you shot your father to get away from your wasted life and pursue a more exciting life in Hinkley?"

Sam rolled his eyes at the question. It was almost proof that he'd been paid to be just as much a prosecutor as Mister Madsen.

"Mister Dailey, are you suggesting that I gave up living a still comfortable, happy life with my wonderful father to willingly sell myself into prostitution?"

The defense attorney was shooting himself over and over again and Sam could see that the jury was getting angry with him as well. *Had they understood the reason for this charade?*

"Let's talk of that, Miss Felton, as you have brought it up. Why did you not escape your condition? Were you not pleased to be there?"

"Mister Dailey, it was not possible to escape. The owner, Mister Waxman, left only one exit from the upstairs rooms. We had to pass through his saloon to get outside. Either he or his cousin were always there and were armed. Pleased to be there, Mister Dailey? Pleased to be beaten almost daily; to be forced to engage in prostitution against your will? Mister Dailey, your definition of being pleased must be far different than mine."

Sam was proud of Grace, but still wondered how far Dailey was prepared to go. He was asking leading questions, but they were all leading to the hanging of his clients. *How much worse could he get?*

"Then tell me of your experience after you were rescued by Mister Brown."

Madsen popped up from his chair and said, "Objection, Your Honor. This trial is about the events of the murder and kidnapping, not what happened afterwards."

Dailey quickly argued, saying, "Your Honor, it goes to the character of the witness."

Judge McLean hesitated for a moment and stated, "I'll let it go for the time being. But Mister Dailey, you are on dangerous ground here. Stay within the boundaries of decorum."

"Thank you, Your Honor," Dailey intoned as Madsen returned to his seat.

"Miss Felton, since your rescue, where have you been living?"

317

"I've been staying at the Circle S ranch."

"And who owns this ranch?"

"Mister Sam Brown."

"The same Sam Brown that brought you and two other prostitutes from Waxman's back to his ranch?"

"Yes."

"And what have you and the other two prostitutes done since moving into Mister Brown's ranch?"

"Cook, sleep, shoot, ride horses, and other daily activities."

"And have you always slept alone?"

"No."

"How many times has Mister Brown slept with you, Miss Felton?"

Sam thought that Dailey had finally begun to sound like a defense lawyer with the question but had violated the first rule of being a trial lawyer; never to ask a question when you don't already know the answer.

Grace quickly replied, "None."

Dailey looked genuinely surprised but continued his questioning.

"But you said that you had not always slept alone. Were you sleeping with one of the other prostitutes, then?"

"No, Mister Dailey, I was not. And I would ask that you refer to me and my friends as women. When we were in Waxman's, we were forced to be prostitutes. We are no longer being forced to do anything."

Sam could see the fire in Grace's eyes, and he pitied Dailey; whether he was a real defense attorney or anyone else. He took a glance at the jury and could easily see their disgust with the defense attorney as well.

"Very well, for the sake of decorum, I will no longer use that term. If you say you hadn't slept alone, and you were not sleeping with other women, then with whom were you sleeping?"

"Mister Brown's five-year-old daughter, Catherine."

Sam glanced at the jurors and saw slight smiles on most of their faces.

"Are you saying that Mister Brown has not taken you or any of the other women to his bed?"

"Yes, I am. In fact, Mister Brown, since we have been there, is the only person on the ranch who has never slept in a bed. He sleeps on the couch in the main room."

Dailey decided to change his approach slightly.

"Miss Felton, have you ever used the name Mrs. Brown?"

Sam figured he must have gotten that bit of information from the Ashleys but wondered just how much more he'd learned. Surely, he already knew the answer to his question this time if he knew enough to ask it.

"Yes."

"So, you acted as his wife then. Were you married, or just acting as his wife?"

"Acting."

"To access a hotel, perhaps?"

"No. To access a ranch house that was holding Mister Brown's daughter captive. We rode up to the house in a carriage, pretending to be a couple from Indiana looking to buy a ranch. Mister Brown's brilliant idea gave us the ability to approach the ranch and let his daughter, who was being held in the house, to hear his voice and come running to him. So, yes, Mister Dailey I was his wife for a day."

Finally, in an apparent act of desperation, Dailey asked, "Would you like to marry Mister Brown?"

"Oh, yes. So, would half the women in the state if they knew him, including your wife, Mister Dailey."

As most in the audience laughed, including all of the men in the jury, he simply said, "No more questions."

Sam smiled at Grace who held his eyes as she returned to her seat. But, aside from the questioning about her behavior at the ranch, the defense attorney's less-than-stellar performance confirmed his suspicion that his clients were being sent to the gallows by Soapy to send a message to his other men. He began to suspect that Mister Dailey may have been given misinformation rather than instructions to throw the case. If Soapy had been the one to give him a disastrous background of information, that would account for the incredibly poor performance and yet still give it a minimal appearance of a proper defense. He still wondered if the prosecutor or the judge had noticed it.

Sam didn't have too much time to think about it before he was called to the stand. After being sworn in, he was asked to tell the story of the arrest of the two accused at the ranch. He told it succinctly as he'd done many times in Boulder. When he was questioned by the prosecutor, Sam, accustomed to trial testimony, kept his answers short and accurate, so it was only after five minutes of testimony before Madsen gave way to the defense.

Dailey approached with a sneer, which again, surprised Sam. Courtroom attorneys usually maintained an almost aloof, businesslike demeanor. Maybe he had saved it all because he couldn't use it on Grace.

"Mister Brown, you stated that you approached Miss Felton's ranch house to determine its condition. Why was that?"

"When I first met Miss Felton, she told me the manner of her capture, and told me that she and her father owned the Slash F. She was under the assumption that it had been lost to her, so when I was in Denver, I found that it was just delinquent in taxes. I paid the tax bill, so she would not lose her ranch. She requested that we go inspect the ranch to see if there had been any vandalism."

"Did you go alone with Miss Felton?"

"No, I went with Miss Felton and our friend, Miss Early."

"Why did you suspect the defendants? Were they engaging in violent acts?"

"No. They were trespassing and living in a house where they had no right to be. I entered the house, announced myself, and asked them to come out. Instead, they ran out the back. At that point, because of their hurried escape though the back door that I considered it was possible they were wanted for some other criminal activity."

"So, you took away their weapons at gunpoint, threw them to the ground and trussed them up like pigs, just because they were trespassing?"

"No, Mister Dailey, I did those things because they matched the description given to me two months earlier by Miss Felton. I knew I was dealing with a possible murderer and kidnappers."

"So, when you went to fetch Miss Felton and Miss Early, did you go and tell her that you had captured her father's murderer?"

"No. What I did was to remove her weapons and then told her that I would take her down to the corral and see if she could identify the men as her father's murderer and her kidnapper."

"And how did you make the identification?"

"I didn't. Neither did Miss Felton. Mister Robinson did that himself. Robinson was making remarks that indicated that he didn't recognize Miss Felton. It had been over a year, after all. Finally, Mister Thompkins told him to shut up and look at the blondie. That's when Robinson yelled, 'She's supposed to be at Waxman's'. I arrested him at that point."

"Under what authority?"

"As an unpaid deputy sheriff for the county."

"Unpaid? Why is that Mister Brown, are you unqualified?"

Sam was astounded at the question. *Didn't the man do any research at all on his own?* He was sure that Soapy Smith knew who he was by now, but obviously hadn't told him. Maybe he had told Dailey that he was to only use the information he provided.

"No. I was the sheriff of Boulder for ten years. The county doesn't have enough money to hire another deputy."

"Then, why do it?"

"I was going to investigate the murder of my brother-in-law and the kidnapping of my sister and niece, who is now my daughter. Sheriff Grant didn't have the resources, but knew of my reputation, so he deputized me to give me the authority to make arrests."

"And was it using this authority that you strong-armed yourself into Waxman's, shot and killed the owner and another citizen, then rescued three prostitutes that you subsequently transported to your ranch for immoral purposes?"

Sam knew Dailey was trying to get under his skin, but still, it was an incredibly stupid question and even phrased poorly. He began to suspect that Mister Dailey was in fact being paid to send his clients to the gallows after all.

"No."

"Oh. You just happened to be walking past the establishment and thought you'd play the brave knight and rescue three damsels; is that it?"

"No. I had information that my sister had been kidnapped and brought to Waxman's. I went to the establishment to seek information as to her whereabouts. To do that, I arranged to go upstairs with one of the ladies working there. I asked about

323

my sister, Cora, and she told me that she had been murdered the month earlier.

"I went downstairs to ask Mister Waxman who had killed her and who had brought her to his place. I had my Colt in his face as a persuader, before you ask. He told me where the cowboy who had killed her worked but I saw him look behind me, then looked in the mirror and saw his cousin reaching for his gun. I dropped to the floor and shot him as his pistol was coming up. Mister Waxman then decided to pull a shotgun and kill me with it. As he fired, I rolled to the right and shot him three times."

"I'm sure that's an accurate description," he said with a heavily sarcastic overtone, "no one who wins a gunfight is ever guilty. So, then you decided to go upstairs and rescue the women."

"No. It was just the opposite. I was getting ready to leave when they asked me to take them with me. I hadn't realized that they had no resources to live on with Waxman dead. They had no money and no place to go. I offered them money to go where they wished, but they told me that women who had been placed in their position had no place that would ever accept them, and I realized then that they were right. Their lives had been ruined by ruthless men who took them from their homes and sold them into this life; if you can call it a life at all. Now, despite still being young, their lives were effectively over. What man who truly believes in almighty God could turn them away, Mister Dailey? Would you?"

Dailey shrugged off the accusatory question and asked, "So, Mister Brown, you, a virile young man invited three young women who had just been prostitutes into your home to save them?"

"Not to save them, Mister Dailey; to help them realize that their lives were not over. To get them to stop thinking of themselves as whores or prostitutes or whatever else righteous men like you call them to make yourselves think that you're good men. I wanted them to start believing themselves to be what they still are; bright, capable and yes, pretty women.

"I wanted them to be able to walk up to self-righteous men like you and tell you to stick your self-serving judgment up your…nose. I am proud of my ladies. And they are ladies, Mister Dailey, because inside their souls they are honest, considerate, and compassionate, which is much more than I can say for many others."

Grace was bursting with love and pride in her man and noticed that Judge McNeal was suppressing a grin.

Dailey seemed to believe that he'd done the job he'd been paid to do and simply said, "No more questions, Your Honor. Defense rests."

Madsen was beaming when Sam stepped down and returned to his seat next to Grace. Both Grace and Carol took his hands, as he smiled at each of them.

Sam no longer had any doubt about the defense attorney's performance. Even the attacks he'd made on him and Grace were self-defeating. He had to know he'd lose the arguments, even if he'd just read the story in *The Rocky Mountain News.* His whole defense and lack of witnesses was nothing less than an admission of defeat and he was convinced that Soapy Smith was sending a clear message to his employees not to turn on him. It was also a surefire way to keep them from testifying.

The closing arguments were relatively brief, and Mister Dailey appeared to follow his earlier path by regurgitating his weak accusations of both Grace and Sam. The jury was given its charge and filed out of the box to make their deliberations; although there wasn't anyone in the courtroom, maybe even the defendants, who believed that it would take very long.

After the judge left the courtroom, Sam and the ladies left and followed the crowd into the hallway. The women received bows and tipped hats as they walked by and both seemed happy, but not because the trial was over. They each had an arm through Sam's and were pleased to be known as his ladies.

Sam looked for Madsen and waved him over; when he arrived, Madsen began to thank him and Grace for exceptional testimony when Sam interrupted him.

"Mister Madsen, why did the defense attorney want his clients hanged?"

"What do you mean?" he asked, in apparent surprise, which Sam hadn't expected.

"You've been in the courtroom a lot more often than I have. Can you ever recall having no defense witnesses called? I mean I figured Soapy would at least have some of his boys come in and perjure themselves to provide an alibi. And those questions he asked me, and Grace were more than just unprofessional, they were more incriminating that the ones that you asked us. It was as if he wanted his clients to walk up those gallows' steps. I think Mister Dailey was being paid by Soapy Smith to not mount a real defense. It's possible that he just told him to use the information that he provided, too."

"I noticed it as well. I've known Louis Dailey for a long time, and I've never seen him so poorly prepared and ask so many loaded questions. I was curious about the lack of witness list, too, and was prepared to use it to deny their testimony if he called any surprise witnesses but was stunned to see that he had none."

"Soapy wants them both hanged, so I think a good chat with those two after the verdict might prove useful."

"Let's see what the verdict is. With juries, nothing is certain, although this one is as close as I can imagine that I'll ever get."

Sam smiled and returned to the courtroom with his ladies on his arms, figuring they didn't have long to wait. He was proven correct when the jury returned ten minutes later.

The judge reentered the courtroom, everyone stood again, then sat after the judge did. When he asked the jury if they'd arrived at a verdict, the jury foreman announced guilty verdicts on both counts. Judge McNeal sentenced them to hang the following Wednesday in just seconds, having already assumed the guilty verdict.

It was only 12:45 when they exited the courtroom.

"Ladies, I believe a lunch is in order. Shall we?" Sam asked as they left the courthouse.

With Grace on his right arm and Carol on his left Sam walked across the street and then two blocks west to L.M. Simmons Restaurant. It was a handsome trio that entered the restaurant.

They had a delicious and happy lunch, and when they finished, Sam paid the bill, then they exited the restaurant and were soon back in the carriage. There was enough room in the front seat for all three, as the women were both small.

So, with Sam happily flanked by two of his ladies, the grays pulled out and headed back to the ranch.

Once underway, Carol asked, "I heard you telling the prosecutor that you thought Soapy Smith wanted them to hang. Why did you think that?"

"They messed up, Carol. They made it easy for us to know that someone was in the house and I'm not sure that Soapy wanted them in that place or that they took that much firepower, so I think he may have lost all of his long-range rifles, too. He was probably spitting nails when he got the news. I think Soapy paid their defense attorney to make sure they were hanged, but it would be difficult to prove. I'm beginning to think that Soapy Smith has a lot more sources of information than I suspected, and that makes him much more dangerous."

"I was wondering about those questions, Sam. Especially about your background. I mean it wouldn't have taken much to find out, would it?" asked Grace.

"No, it wouldn't, especially after that newspaper story. He probably knew exactly who I was and asked the question to put another nail in his clients' coffins. Almost every one of his questions seemed to do that. He even was making faces that had him looking like a smarmy little weasel to the jury. The more I think about it, the more I'm convinced that Soapy Smith paid him to throw the case. It's the only reason for that farce of a trial."

Grace asked, "So, if Soapy Smith has that many sources of information, won't he know where we are and just about everything else?"

"I'm sure he does, Grace, and has probably known it even before that story hit the paper. I think the Ashleys might have decided to tell their nephew after all."

Both ladies just nodded as the carriage rolled on and Sam began to wonder just how much time they had before Soapy acted. If he had information from bribed officials, then he must know everything by now, so his revised plans could already be completed and ready to go.

They reached the ranch in mid-afternoon, and the construction crews were still working on the roof in both the bedrooms and the carriage house. Sam didn't think it would even take another full week to complete the work. Either it was easier than they expected, or Joe really pushed his crews, but was probably a combination of both.

Sam let the ladies out at the front porch steps, drove the carriage into the barn, then took care of the team and pushed the carriage back into place.

When he came out of the barn, he hunted down Joe Schmidt and found him right next door at the almost-finished new carriage house.

"Hey, Joe!" he shouted.

Joe waved and had to wait a few seconds while the men lowered a long beam into place. When they finished, he walked over.

"Lordy, Joe! You guys are flying along. It's only been four days. How are you going so fast?"

"Well, you have to realize that when we set the estimate, we figure in weather delays, sick workers, and surprises like water where it's not supposed to be. That way, the customer doesn't get bent out of shape if we aren't done on time. If we're done early, like we'll be done here, it keeps the customer and the boss happy."

'Well, you sure are keeping me happy. When do you think it'll be okay to move furniture into the bedrooms?"

"I'm guessing Tuesday at the latest. It really doesn't matter now anyway because the interiors are done. There may be some extra sawdust but that's about it. You could put some in there right now if you didn't care about the dust."

"We'll wait."

"How'd the trial go?"

Sam smiled and replied, "You should have seen it, Joe. I was so proud of Grace. I think the defense attorney thought he had some weak woman that he could attack and have her break down in tears, but she turned him into a steer. She emasculated the man. I could see the faces of the jury smiling as she crushed him. She is one hell of a woman."

"So, they gonna hang those bastards?"

"Next Wednesday."

"Good."

"Say, Joe. Could I borrow a pickaxe tonight? I have a shovel but can't find a pickaxe anywhere."

"Sure, but what you need to be dug? I can have a couple of guys handle it right away."

"I appreciate it, Joe, but this job is one that I have to do myself. On Monday, I'm going to go down to Hinkley and we're going to bring back my sister's body. We'll be back Tuesday. Then the undertaker will bring my brother-in-law's body down from Denver, and we're going have them buried in the cemetery you built. I feel like I should dig the graves."

"I understand. I'll leave one near your porch."

"Thanks, Joe."

Sam patted Joe on the shoulder and walked back to the house.

When he entered, the women were all chatting about the trial, and Sam was pleased to see them as comfortable with each other as usual; even Julia seemed chipper.

They were laughing about something when they saw him enter the room.

"Grace, are you telling them how you emasculated the poor defense attorney? I swear, his voice went up an octave every time you answered one of his questions."

Grace answered, "No, Mister Brown, I was telling them how you had that noticeable pause when you said that line about shoving something up his...nose."

"It was close, I'll tell you. I had to quickly come up with a body orifice that was acceptable for the court recorder. But the good news is that it's over and tomorrow will be a good day. Everyone should be relaxed and enjoy yourselves; and because Julia is the one who made the suggestion, she gets to ride up front."

That offer made Julia smile. It was small compensation, but it was the best he could come up with.

Eventually, the ladies all drifted toward the kitchen to cook dinner and Sam noticed Catherine looking a bit despondent, so he walked up to her and crouched onto his heels to be at her eye level.

"What's the matter, sweetie?"

"My puppies don't love me anymore."

"Where are they?"

"In the barn."

"I was just in the barn, and I didn't see them."

"I'll show you," she said.

She took his hand and led him outside toward the barn, then they passed the barn and headed for the corral and Sam could hear the puppies. As he passed the edge of the barn, he was greeted by a remarkable sight. The two puppies were trying to herd the horses in the corral, making Sam laugh at the sight before he looked down at Catherine who still had a sad face.

"Just a minute, Catherine," he said as he opened the corral gate, then walked behind the horses and scooped up the two dogs.

Sam brought the wriggling dogs to Catherine and closed the gate with his foot. As she held them, they began licking her face as usual, making her giggle again as they walked back to the house, where Sam saw the pickaxe leaning against the porch.

Catherine sat on the porch with her puppies and let them romp as her new father sat down beside her.

"Thank you, Papa. They love me again. How did you do that?"

"Catherine, these are border collies. They are herding dogs. Do you know what that is?"

"No."

"It means that they are bred from way back to find animals like sheep or goats or even horses that need to go somewhere. They run around behind the animals that want to go one direction and bark to get the animals to go where the collies want them to go.

"Now, your puppies already have that in their heads that it's their job to get those stupid animals going in another direction. Your little friends were just doing what collies have been doing for a long time. They feel it in their bones that this is what they need to do, so when they see other animals, they'll chase after them to practice getting them to behave. Now, when they're older, you can tell them when to do it."

"Oh! So, they were being told by their heads to do it."

"Exactly. It doesn't mean they don't love you anymore. It means that they have to do what their heads tell them to do, but after you give them their names, you call one and give her a treat. Then you call the other and give her a treat. Soon, they'll know their names and come to you with their tails wagging, looking for that treat. But after a while, you don't have to give them treats anymore. They'll come because you're their friend, even when they're out there trying to herd the horses"

"Thank you, Papa."

"You're welcome, sweetheart. Let's go see about dinner," he said before he and Catherine rose, then he took her hand and they entered the house.

––––––

They had finished dinner, the ladies were cleaning up, and Catherine was helping, trying to be one of the ladies.

Without saying anything, Sam walked out the front door, walked to the barn and picked up the spade that was there, then walked to the cemetery, grabbing the pickaxe on the way past the porch.

When he reached the cemetery, he removed his Colt and his Webley, and stripped down to the waist, hanging his guns, vest and shirt over the new railing. Then, using the pickaxe, drew a rectangle into the soil and repeated it four feet away. First, he broke the hard surface with the pickaxe and then began to dig.

It was hard work. The muscles he normally hadn't used were getting a workout and it took him over an hour of constant digging and use of the pickaxe to get to a depth that was at his head level. Then he climbed out and began on the second grave; the sweat flying as he dug.

––––––

Back at the ranch house, it was Julia who first noticed his absence.

"I wonder where Sam is?"

"I don't know," said Carol.

"I think I do," said Grace.

She dried her hands on her apron and went out the front door, followed by Julia and Carol. Catherine followed behind her aunts. They all stood on the porch and Grace looked north. In the fading light, they could barely make out Sam's head in the cemetery and watched as shovelful after shovelful of dirt left the hole he was digging.

"Monday, he's going down to Hinkley to get Cora. I think he wanted to get them dug when he knew he could," Grace said as they all stared at the distant cemetery.

No one said anything more, not even Catherine, before they turned and returned to the house.

———

When Sam was finished with the holes, he began to move the dirt out of the way to allow room for the men to lower the caskets into the graves, planning on filling them as well. When he finished, he picked up his shirt and vest, draped them over his left shoulder, strapped on his Colt and hung the Webley over his right shoulder. Then he took the shovel and pickaxe, strode back to the front yard, left the pickaxe and his weapons at the porch and returned the spade to the barn.

When he left the barn, he turned toward the corral and stopped at the pump near the horse trough, primed it and began pumping until the cold water flowed, then plunged his head under the water and then splashed it over his chest and back. It felt good. After a couple of minutes to dry, he pulled his shirt back on and returned to the front porch, picked up his guns and walked into the house. He was physically and emotionally drained as he stepped over the threshold.

The women were already there but weren't chatting as they all looked at him, and he hoped they weren't upset about something. He did notice that they were sitting in the chairs, with Catherine on Carol's lap, and that the only open place for him to sit was the couch.

"You look exhausted, Sam," said Carol.

"Maybe not that far, Carol, but close. I just had to get the job done and had to do this myself."

"We understand, Sam," Grace said softly.

Sam sat on the couch and started talking about how proud he was of each of them and how grateful he was to have them staying in the house, and as he spoke, it became more of a disconnected ramble as he began sliding to the couch's cushions and then just drifted off. His ladies covered him with blankets and let him sleep.

———

Sam awakened the next morning to the incredible aroma of cooking bacon, and noticed he still had his boots on, then remembered entering the room but little else afterwards.

He stood and was rewarded with aches in places he didn't know existed. He stretched and twisted, trying to release the tightness, but what he really wanted was a hot bath, hoping that there was time.

He went out to the kitchen, waved to the Grace and Carol on his way to the privy, and when he finished and returned the house, the women were all in the kitchen with Catherine.

"Good morning, all," he said as he entered.

"Glad to see you're still breathing," said Julia.

"I'm not too sure that I am. Surely, I've died and gone to heaven. Bacon, biscuits and all these lovely angels."

"Flattery will at least get you some biscuits and bacon," Grace said with a laugh as she rose to get his breakfast.

"It was worth it, then," he smiled before taking a seat.

———

They finished breakfast and were ready to go to Denver by eight-thirty. Sam didn't get his bath and had to settle for a normal wash and shave.

Julia enjoyed the ride sitting next to Sam, and didn't do anything overt, but on more than one occasion, when the carriage rocked, she had to balance herself by putting her hand on his thigh. Sam noticed and was glad there were three other females in the back seat.

They arrived at the furniture store first and everyone entered, with Catherine firmly holding her father's hand. They picked out nice beds that came with mattresses, and because they were nicer than the mattresses in the older bedrooms, Sam bought new mattresses for the other three. The ladies picked out the new rooms' furniture, and to the women's amazement, Sam purchased a sewing machine which earned him even more points. They had never seen one before, and it came with a book that showed how to use all of its features. Sam arranged for delivery on Wednesday.

Next, they visited the general store and bought fabric for new curtains for the entire house, some new pillows and sheets and some more quilts. The carriage was going to be full because the bulky pillows and quilts alone almost filled the boot.

337

When they had finished their buying spree, they stopped for a nice lunch and Sam treated them all to ice cream. Catherine remembered her mama buying some for her when she was even younger, but none of the adult women had ever had any before, so it was well received.

Tummies and carriage filled, they returned to the ranch, and it was a happy group that filed into the main room. They all noticed the new framed in hallway leading out of the room to the north, so they dropped their purchases on the chairs and all went to explore the new rooms.

Sam was very pleased with the construction and noted the wall of built-in bookshelves in his room.

"Can I assume this is your room, Mister Brown?" Grace asked as she walked next to him and smiled.

"Yes, you may assume that. You know, one of these days, we should add rugs to all of the bedrooms."

"Now, that is a good idea," remarked Carol, "It's summer now, but come fall these floors will feel mighty chilly against bare feet."

They had a light dinner and spent some pleasant time in the family room with no talk of shootings or anything else that could spoil the mood.

———

The weekend was uneventful and was spent just reorganizing the house; getting all of the new bedding and fixtures in place and preparing the new bedrooms for the new furniture that would soon arrive. With the events of the past week, the routine was appreciated by everyone, even though all of adults knew that it wouldn't last.

They knew that Soapy Smith had to act.

CHAPTER 12

Monday morning, the day of Cora's exhumation, found Sam sitting on Cump at the end of the access road. His ladies were on the porch watching from the distance as Grace held Catherine in her arms. Sam could be seen staring toward the north, and ten minutes later, he waved the driver of the hearse on and set Cump to a medium trot to get behind it.

Sam then kicked Cump to a faster trot to match the hearse's speed as they headed south to retrieve Cora's body.

The women watched him ride until he was out of sight, then returned to the main room. Sam said he expected to be back around noon the following day, so they were on their own until then. When they entered the house, Grace set Catherine down and each of the women strapped on her Colt.

It would be a long, somber day.

———

Sam rode behind and off to the left side of the hearse to avoid their dust, and they were making good time, so they should reach Hinkley before noon at this pace. He had talked briefly to the two men in the coach seat. They understood their job and assured Sam that they would take care of the grisly task of exhuming the body and placing it in the casket and had a special blanket to cover the remains being transferred. They had asked him to tell them the color of his sister's hair and approximate size to ensure it was the right one.

Knowing when she had died, about three and half months earlier helped, but after they asked, Sam worried about the possibility that another woman might be buried in the same spot. He should have asked the ladies, but it was too late now.

His mind was flowing with memories of Cora as he rode, and he grew so upset at one point he almost felt like turning around, but he knew he had to go and recover his sister. She didn't belong in such a place; she didn't belong in the place she had died, either, yet he still didn't know who had taken her to that place or had killed Richard. He knew that he would discover the identity of the guilty men and would extract a final justice.

The hearse pulled up in front of Waxman's, which was still boarded up and he was glad to see that. It wasn't as good as burning the place to the ground, but at least it wasn't back in business.

He walked Cump to the back of the establishment worried that the grave would be hard to find, but it wasn't. Even from horseback, he was able to see the grave-sized mound of earth just fifteen feet behind the rear door. He was surprised it hadn't settled yet but was happy it hadn't because it would have made it more difficult to find.

The two men followed Sam and brought the hearse's rear door close to the site, then sympathetically advised Sam to find someplace to go for about an hour and Sam told them he would be across the street at the dry goods store.

He walked Cump across the street, dismounted, then entered the store and was greeted by the welcoming face of John Arden.

"Welcome back, Sam. What brings you back to Hinkley?"

341

"A somber task, John. I've come to recover the remains of my sister, Cora, who they buried behind Waxman's. I've had a family cemetery built on their ranch and I'm having her and her husband, Richard, laid to rest together."

"It's as it should be, Sam. Is there anything I can do to help?"

"No, thank you. I'm just spending time while the undertakers remove her body and put it into the casket. This is harder than I had imagined, John."

John just nodded.

"I never asked. Is there a hotel here?" Sam asked.

"Nothing fancy, but it's clean. You just never noticed it because they don't have a big sign. It's the white building three doors down with the yellow stripe in the middle. I never could figure out the yellow stripe, though. Of course, I never asked, either."

"I'll wander down that way and get three rooms. I'll be back in a little while."

Sam waved as he left, stepped outside and walked down the old boardwalk to the white house with the yellow stripe, then entered and found what passed for a reception desk in the corner. There was no one there, which really didn't surprise him. He was surprised the place was even still open.

"Hello? Anyone here?" he asked in a loud voice.

A hidden female voice replied, "Just a minute, sir."

Fifteen seconds later, a girl of no more than fifteen stepped out from what he assumed was the kitchen, as she was wiping her hands on an apron.

"How can I help you, sir?" she asked.

"I'll need three rooms for the night."

She smiled and Sam guessed it had been a while since they had enjoyed customers.

"Is that with or without meals, sir?"

"With meals would be a good idea."

"That will be six dollars, sir."

Sam paid the young lady and she asked him to sign the register.

He signed his name and said, "I don't know the names of the other two gentlemen. You see, I hired the undertakers to come down and recover my sister's body. I'll have them sign when they arrive. Is that okay?"

"Yes, sir," she replied, then asked, "Sir, are you the lawman who shot Mister Waxman and his cousin and saved those three ladies?"

"Yes."

"Well, sir, I want to let you know that I am proud to have met you. That's all anyone talks about around here. Are the ladies still with you?"

"Oh, yes. They've all recovered from their ordeal and are happy, strong women. They're staying with my daughter right now. She's the little girl we saved from the Ashleys."

"I heard about that as well. She was your daughter?"

"No, she was my niece. Four men came to her ranch and killed her husband and took my sister to Waxman's. They hid her daughter with the Ashleys. After they killed my sister, I adopted her. She's a very pretty little girl."

"I'm happy to hear it, sir. Dinner is at six o'clock in the dining room which is just down the hallway on the left. Breakfast is at half past six. Is that alright?"

"Very good. What's your name?"

"Ella. Ella Watson."

"Well, thank you for your help, Ella. I'll be back with the two other men shortly."

"Goodbye, Mister Brown."

"Goodbye, Ella."

Sam went back outside, scanned the street, but the hearse was still out of sight. He had only been in Hinkley for forty minutes. He searched for a livery and saw what looked like a barn two buildings down from the hotel, so he walked over, stuck his head inside and found the liveryman asleep in one of the stalls. Once Sam awakened him, Sam arranged for Cump to be boarded for the night and paid the man twenty-five cents.

By the time he was heading for John's store again, the hearse had pulled around Waxman's and headed for the mercantile.

He stepped toward the hearse and the one of the two undertakers stepped down and met him in the street outside the store.

"Mister Brown, your sister is now safely and with all respect, moved to her casket."

"Thank you. I've paid for rooms at the hotel. That's the white building with the yellow stripe. They serve dinner at six and breakfast at six-thirty. Is that acceptable?"

"Very considerate of you, Mister Brown."

"Not at all. The livery is over in that barn. I didn't know if you used a livery for your horses or not."

"We do. We'll follow you over."

Sam retrieved Cump from the hitching post in front of Arden's General Store and led the hearse to the livery. The liveryman looked at the hearse and crossed himself.

Sam brought Cump into the barn and removed his tack, then grabbed his Winchester and saddlebags.

The undertakers arranged for the horses to be taken care of and advised the man that they'd be in around seven to pick up the horses. They had to ask if they could leave the hearse on the side of the building overnight. He agreed before the two men drove the hearse alongside the building, then unharnessed the team and walked them to the barn.

The three men then retired to the hotel, and even though it was early, Sam went to his room and opened his saddlebags. There was a sandwich that Grace had made for him, and he smiled as he opened the wrapping, finding a note inside.

He read her flowing hand.

Made with all my love and I hope you can return to me as soon as you can. I miss you already.

Grace

He ate the sandwich, then read the note several times before folding it carefully and slipping it into his vest pocket.

———

The next morning, he met the undertakers in the dining room, and shook their hands; each man had a strong handshake.

Sam said goodbye to Ella, having never seen an adult in the place.

They went to the livery, retrieved their well-rested horses and were on the road by eight o'clock. They had told him that the hearse with Richard would leave at noon, so they should meet at the Circle S about the same time. He hadn't told them about the graves he had already dug and wondered if they had arranged for their own diggers.

They trotted along at a slightly slower speed than the day before, and Sam guessed that the drivers were trying to coordinate their arrival more exactly. He didn't feel as depressed as he had the day before; maybe because he knew his little sister was finally coming home and leaving that sordid place behind, or maybe it was Grace's short note.

As they crested a small rise about a half mile before the access road, Sam spotted the second hearse approaching from the north and was astonished at the coordination. He could see the ranch house in the distance, gleaming like a pearl in its new coat of whitewash.

Now would come the difficult part.

The two black carriages met on opposite sides of the access road and stopped before Sam passed the hearse and trotted Cump to the access road. As he turned, he could see the women and Catherine waiting on the porch. They were wearing subtle, yet elegant dresses. They were his ladies and his daughter.

The two hearses pulled by their black teams followed Sam in a stately walk. When he arrived at the porch, he stepped down, tied off Cump, and then reached out and picked up Catherine. She hugged his neck as he started walking to the new cemetery while his ladies walked alongside, with Grace to his right and Carol and Julia to his left. As they climbed the slight rise, the hearses slowly followed. The construction crews had halted work and removed their hats in respect.

When they reached the gate to the small plot, the family entered and stepped aside.

The four undertakers unloaded Richard's casket first and somberly carried it toward the left gravesite; the right-side men holding black ropes in their off hands. When they reached the hole, they walked to the sides and slid the rope under the casket, then slowly lowered the casket into the earth.

They then slipped the rope from under the casket, returned and removed Cora's casket and repeated the final task. When both were safely in the ground, the men retrieved shovels. Sam was going to stop them but realized this was probably better. It didn't take them long to fill both gravesites, then they dug thin trenches at the tops of both graves for the memorial markers.

Then they walked to Richard's hearse; the men paired off and each two carried a gravestone to the mound of earth. They slid the stone into place and packed the removed dirt into the gap to keep it firmly upright, then repeated the stone emplacement for Cora's headstone. Satisfied that their work was done, they returned to the hearses, bowing their heads to the family as they passed.

They boarded the hearses and drove away quietly.

Sam looked at the two burial sites and said, "Welcome home, Richard and Cora"

It was all that was said, but it was enough.

The women all noticed the headstones. They had the usual names and dates and on Richard's headstone it read:

Husband of Cora
Father of Catherine
A Man Worthy of Their Love

On Cora's it read:

Wife of Richard
Mother of Catherine
Home with Her Sister Angels

Catherine was holding hands with Sam on her right and Carol on her left. Only they could hear her whisper, "I love you, Mama and Papa."

After a few more minutes of silence, Sam picked up Catherine and they walked quietly back to the house.

———

It was early afternoon, and Sam realized that they had to return to a normal life now, so after everyone had taken a seat in the main room, Sam remained standing.

"Ladies, it's been an emotional day for all of us, but now we need to do normal things like eating lunch. I don't know about any of you, but I could eat the back end of a horse."

It wasn't an original or particularly funny comment, but it changed the mood.

"Well, we don't have any horse butt in the cold storage, but I think we might find some smoked beef," said Grace.

The atmosphere had been restored to everyday concerns and tasks.

———

Just before dinner, there was a knock on the door.

Sam was closest, and involuntarily dropped his hand to his Colt, then realized it was unlikely that any assassins would knock, so he just opened it normally and he saw Joe Schmidt through the screen and he was gesturing for Sam to join him on the porch.

Sam wondered why Joe didn't want to enter the house and stepped outside.

"What's up, Joe?"

"We're done, Sam. I just wanted to show you the work. You need to sign off on the job for the boys back in the office. I didn't want to disturb the house after the somber events of the day."

"I appreciate the concern, Joe, but things are returning to normal now. Let's go."

Joe walked him to the north side of the two-bedroom addition and showed him the outside entrance door. That was Sam's idea. They entered the hallway and Sam was pleased that the hallway was almost six feet wide. He hated claustrophobic hallways. The west bedroom, his room, had the full wall of bookshelves across the south wall. He knew that with the large, roll top desk and matching chair that was being delivered tomorrow, it would look like a library, but with a bed inside. The second bedroom was a standard bedroom, but both rooms were quite large, about sixteen feet by twenty-two feet. It left a lot of room for additional furniture.

Then they left the house and went to the new carriage house. It was an impressive structure, especially considering the short construction time. But when you have that many men who know their craft, it wasn't hard to believe. The floor had been raised slightly to keep water flowing away, so the inside would stay free of water and keep the wood dry. There were four large stalls on one side and two on the other. There was enough room to accommodate two carriages. On the side with only two stalls, there was a large, heavy workbench. Next to the last stall was what looked like a giant toolbox with a hole in the side.

"What's that, Joe?"

"When I saw your doghouse out there for the puppies, I thought that having an inside doghouse would keep them warmer in the cold months. Especially with horses in here putting out all that heat."

"Now that's a nice touch, Joe. Come back to the house and I'll sign your sheet."

They made the short walk to the house and after entering, the main room, they sat down and Sam took out his pen and dipped it in ink.

"Joe, how many men did you use on the job?"

"Thirty, altogether. The two main teams of twelve men each and the roving team of eight men for fill-ins and extra jobs that always turn up."

Sam nodded and pulled out a bank draft. He made it payable to Joe Schmidt in the amount of two hundred dollars, then signed the acceptance sheet before he handed both to Joe.

"Joe, as an appreciation for job well done, I want you to give each man a five-dollar gold piece."

Joe stared at the large draft and said, "Sam, I'm no arithmetic wizard, but that's only a hundred and fifty dollars."

"The rest is so you can afford ammunition for that big gun. You're always welcome to come out and shoot with me, and don't give me any of that fake manure about how you can't take it. You can, and you will, or I'll take back my acceptance signature."

"Well, alright, I'll take it if you insist on playing hardball. You know, the men will be tickled. In all the years I've been in this business, no customer has every rewarded them for doing their job."

"That's kind of sad, really."

"Well, I'll be going now, Sam. The boys are waiting to get home, and I'll take you up on that shooting offer. The only places to shoot a gun in Denver are those fancy shooting clubs for gentlemen. Besides, I'll show you some of my guns."

They shook hands and Joe left the house. He'd been gone for two minutes when Sam heard an eruption of cheering and whistling from the crews. Sam smiled and guessed Joe had told them of the bonus.

Sam walked out to the kitchen where dinner was being served and found eight inquisitive female eyes looking at him. They must have heard the reaction.

"Oh. That. They were all cheering because I invited them to dinner tonight. What will they be having?"

For about two heartbeats the ladies took him seriously.

Then, with a perfect poker face, Grace replied, "We'll be having ham and potatoes. You'll be joining them outside for a nice dinner of hay and oats with the horses."

Sam laughed and said, "I gave each of the men a five-dollar bonus. No one had ever done that before."

"Well, Mister Brown, you do have a way of making people happy," said Carol.

"And the ones in this room are the only ones I really want to make happy. Now, can I have some dinner, too? I don't want to take anything from the poor horses."

"I think we can manage that," said Grace.

———

After dinner, the ladies were making plans about the furniture arriving tomorrow and the atmosphere was positively jovial.

Sam had his daughter on his lap, so he asked, "Catherine, have you thought of names for your two puppies?"

"Yes, Papa. I had help from Aunt Julia, though. Is that okay?"

"That's fine. So, what are the names?"

"The one with the black ear is Sophie. The one with the two white front paws is Millie. Is that okay?"

"Why, give your Aunt Julia a big kiss. Those are perfect names."

Catherine bounced over to Julia and jumped into her arms. Julia was bubbling as Catherine kissed her several times.

———

Around ten o'clock the next day, three large freight wagons made their way down the access road. They had been expected, so eager eyes watched their arrival. There were two drivers on each rig, and Sam went out to the front yard to direct them to the side door on the new addition. The drivers pulled their oxen teams around the side of the house and began unloading the furniture. It took almost an hour to get the beds, desks, chairs and other assorted accessories into the new rooms. When they left, Sam tipped each man a silver dollar, which was appreciated. The drivers waved as they made their way slowly down the access road heading home.

The rest of the day, except for mealtime, was spent setting up the rooms. Each room had two new kerosene lamps and they had bought four others to add additional lighting in the house. Sam had picked out his own quilts that weren't so frilly.

The women were ecstatic about the new sewing machine. It had come with a small table containing additional needles, bobbins and dozens of rolls of thread. The instruction book was set on its top, and Sam thought it was funny that the women could get so excited about a machine that would make more work for them, but then, it would make that work a lot easier, too. But he realized that he been just as excited about getting a new gun, so he could understand the reasoning – almost.

Sam gave them a tour of the new carriage house and when Catherine saw the new dog house, she wanted to go and get Sophie and Millie and toss them inside, but Sam had to tell her that it was for cold weather when they were outside and not in the house. Sam thought he'd squeeze one of the old mattresses into the doghouse to make them more comfortable and had also noticed that a pickaxe leaned against the workbench and hoped it wasn't an omen of further use.

While the womenfolk took turns experimenting with the sewing machine, Sam moved the carriage and the grays into the new carriage house and had to add hay to the floors and fill their feed boxes with oats. He also moved Emma and two others in as well. He left the ladies' horses and Cump in the barn but figured he might do some reordering later.

That night, Sam enjoyed his first night in a bed in quite some time, and as he lay there, there was something different about it, too and he couldn't figure it out for a little while.

After a couple of minutes, he realized that it was the quiet. He was used to hearing the subtle noises being made in the other rooms, but with the thicker walls and the distance, it was almost silent.

He had just fallen asleep when his eyes popped open. Something had caused him to awaken suddenly, and he listened closely. Then he heard it again. His door was being opened. He heard quiet footsteps and his quilts being pulled up as someone began crawling into his bed, and he was terrified. He thought it had to be Julia or maybe Carol. *How could he handle this?*

"Papa? Can I stay here for a while?" asked Catherine as she snuggled close.

Sam finally let out his breath and almost started giggling.

"What's the matter, sweetheart?" he asked.

"It has been so long the last time I had my own bed and I was lonely."

He let her cuddle and said, "You'll get used to it, sweetie. You can stay here tonight. Maybe we'll let Sophie or Millie stay with you."

"That would be wonderful, Papa."

She was already slurring her words as she drifted off.

Sam had to restrain laughing at his own vivid imagination and slipped off to sleep with Catherine buried into his arm.

———

Catherine was better the next night as she had both puppies curled up with her and Sam was grateful that they had already learned that the inside of the house was not a place to leave gifts.

CHAPTER 13

It was a glorious Friday morning, and everyone had settled into a routine again. The ladies were making new curtains for the entire house using the new machine and Sam had gone out early to check on the cattle.

There were twenty-six new calves this year, and he was undecided how many he would make into steers. Some of the steers would have to go to market soon, too. It was only five miles to the holding pens in Denver, so it wasn't like it was going to be a big cattle drive. Sam also rode out to check on the new gate Joe had built and wasn't surprised to find that it was an excellent piece of engineering. He used the new gate to head over and inspect Grace's ranch and as he rode over the top of the hill on the Slash F, he spotted the newly painted barn and ranch house. When Joe and his crew had found the time to do it was beyond him.

He turned Cump around and rode back to his ranch, and when he entered the house, he went to Catherine's new big bedroom where they had set up the sewing machine and found Grace watching Julia sew something or other.

"Grace, could I see you for a few minutes, please?"

"Of course, what do you need?"

"I have to show you something."

Julia never looked up, while Carol and Catherine were chatting in the corner. Both had looked at him, but then continued their conversation.

356

Sam led Grace out the back door where he had hitched Cump.

"What do you need to show me?" she asked.

"Nothing that is close by."

"Did you want me to saddle Coal?" she asked as he mounted.

"No, ma'am. It's a short ride," he said as he reached down. lifted her from the ground and swung her onto his lap.

She was surprised, but laughed as she wrapped her arms around his neck and asked, "Isn't this going to cause trouble?"

"Just taking the lazy way out," he replied as he smiled at her from four inches away.

He turned Cump to the east and headed into the pasture, his arm wrapped around Grace's waist as she held onto him tightly. Her softness was already having a serious impact him after just a few of Cump's strides.

When Grace saw the new gate, she said, "That is a marvelous gate, Sam. It was worth the trip. Of course, it would be worth the trip if you had shown me a grasshopper."

Sam grinned, then opened the gate, which could be done on horseback, and closed it behind him.

"You weren't just showing me the gate?"

"No, ma'am."

Soon after his answer, she saw the house and knew why she had been brought along, or at least one of the reasons.

The sight of her old home gleaming in the Colorado sun took her breath away.

"Sam! How did you do this?" she asked breathlessly.

"I asked Joe to inspect the place and give me an estimate. He said it was in good shape and he'd have his crew come over and check it out, meaning that they'd do the repairs it needed. Did you know that he was one of the workers that built this house?"

Grace replied, "You didn't tell me. That is a very nice coincidence."

They stopped at the corral and Sam slipped Grace to the ground, then uncomfortably stepped down and tied off Cump. He wrapped his arm around her waist again, and they walked to the porch, seeing that Joe and his crew had done some excellent work.

After they crossed the porch, they entered the house, and Grace's mouth dropped open as did her eyes as she surveyed the main room. It looked like a new building but with old furniture. As they slowly walked through the house, they found each room clean and the wood on the floor polished to a better shine than they had ever had while Grace had lived there.

"Sam! This is amazing. It looks better now than I can ever remember. I can't thank you often enough, Sam."

When they entered the main bedroom, they noticed that the bedding had been at least shaken out and the bed remade.

Grace swung in front of Sam and locked her arms around him.

"Sam, how much longer do we have to wait? I need you so much."

Sam lifted her and kissed her with her feet almost a foot off the ground.

"Soon, I hope. I think Julia is getting ready to move on and Carol knows how I feel about you, I believe. I don't think it will be much longer."

"I hope not, Sam. This is keeping me awake nights."

"You're not alone, Grace. I want you more than any man has ever wanted a woman. And trust me, that's saying something."

He kissed her again then set her down and said, "I love you, Grace Felton."

"And I love you, Sam Brown," she whispered.

They left the bedroom hand in hand and walked out of the kitchen door, crossed the small porch and headed for the barn. When they swung one of the big doors open, they found it had been cleaned and restored, to maybe a not new but still good condition.

They finally returned to Cump and Sam stepped up, then lifted Grace to his lap again.

"Once more before we go?" she asked, smiling.

He leaned forward and passionately kissed her. His left hand holding her so close but wanting to feel her body remembering that first almost prophetic feel at Waxman's, but he knew that would lead to an inevitable conclusion. It was a long kiss, as both knew it would be their last for a while.

At last they sighed and looked into each other's eyes, saying nothing as no words were necessary.

They returned to the back of the house, and Sam dropped her to the ground and walked Cump to the barn. He gingerly stepped down from the saddle, removed the tack and brushed him down, then added some oats to his feed box, before he returned to the house, using the front door, his discomfort having finally resolved itself.

Catherine was playing with Sophie and Millie before the porch and Carol was sitting on the top step watching her with a small smile.

"So, what did you show Grace?" Carol asked as she turned to look at him.

"I had asked Joe to give me an estimate on fixing up her ranch house and barn, and after I had checked out the new gate, I rode that way and found that he had handled all the repairs and whitewashed the house instead, and I had to show her. She was really excited to see her old home in such good condition."

"Is she going to move back in?"

Now there was a twist he hadn't expected before he replied, "I have no idea. I'll have to ask."

He stepped back to the original part of the house, then walked back to the kitchen where Grace was getting ready to make lunch, but he didn't ask because he knew her answer. He wouldn't want her away from the safety of the house anyway.

———

As the tranquil domestic scenes were taking place at the ranch house, a quarter mile north, three riders had pulled off the main road onto the ranch and tied their horses to a small group of trees fifty yards off the road and just three hundred yards from the new family cemetery.

"Why don't we split up?" asked the smallest one, Henry Olsen.

"Because, I don't want to," replied their burly leader.

"Yeah, Henry. We just do a short run and open up. We don't even have to get close with these Winchesters," added the third man.

Henry didn't like it but felt outvoted by the other two.

They each pulled their Winchester '73s from their scabbards and started trotting diagonally toward the ranch access road four hundred yards away. At this angle, they'd intersect the road only a hundred yards or so from the front of the house.

They had seen their primary target, the little kid, out front just minutes before when they had scouted the place from the road, and as they drew close, they were sure that they couldn't miss when they saw the little girl still in the dirt with a woman sitting on the porch just watching her. Neither the girl nor the woman had seen them coming and they were already within range of their cocked Winchesters.

———

Out front, Carol was watching Catherine chase one of the puppies that she thought was Sophie. Suddenly, the other puppy at her feet looked down the access road and began barking. Carol turned and saw three men running along the road about eighty yards away. They all had rifles in their hands, and she suddenly stood.

When they saw her look their way and stand, they stopped and raised their Winchesters.

Carol never hesitated; she didn't shout an alarm but quickly stepped toward Catherine and scooped her into her arms.

Catherine started to protest, but Carol didn't take time to do anything but try to save Catherine as she turned and trotted up the steps.

Finally, as she stepped onto the porch, she screamed, "Sam!" and ran for the front door, desperately trying to stay between Catherine and those men.

She had almost reached the door when she felt the hammer blow and then the searing pain of a bullet striking her lower chest and was falling as the rifle's report echoed across the front yard.

She dropped Catherine and pushed her away as she shouted, "Go! Go inside and get your papa!"

Carol fell to her knees as Catherine first glanced at her, then yanked open the door and ran inside. She dropped to the porch and felt her life flowing from her as she struggled to breath, but happy knowing Catherine was safe, and that Sam would kill those bastards who had just killed her.

Catherine was frightened, but she did as she was told and ran inside as Sam was racing to the front door after hearing the rifle shots and Carol's scream. He knew there was more than one shooter, but he wasn't sure how many, but it didn't matter. He would kill them all.

Chaos was breaking loose in the house as Julia came stumbling out of the hallway and Grace ran into the room from the kitchen, her hands covered in flour.

Sam scooped up Catherine, then turned and yelled, "Julia! Take Catherine and both of you get into the bathtub. Now!"

Julia was anxious, but not scared witless, and took Catherine from Sam then ran to the bathroom.

Sam didn't waste time to see if they were in the tub.

He turned to Grace and said, "Get on the floor, Grace. Lie flat and stay there."

Shots then rang out every few seconds and bullets were shattering glass and splintering wood.

———

"Did we get her?" shouted Henry.

"I don't think so. Let's get closer!" yelled the leader as the three men began walking toward the house, keeping up a staggered firing to minimize the use of their ammunition yet keep the bullets flying into the house to keep that big man's head down.

Sam smashed the screen door against the side of the house as he scrambled onto the porch and swept Carol into his arms as two .44s smashed into the house's wall beside him. The blood still flowed across her back and dripped onto his arm as he turned back into the house. With bullets cracking into the wood all around him but miraculously not hitting him at fifty yards, he carried her into the living room and set her on the floor between the chairs. Grace was nearby on her stomach as Sam had told her to do.

Sam laid Carol down on the carpet and held her shoulders close to his chest. She was losing blood too rapidly and being as small as she was, he knew there was no chance for her.

Her eyes opened slightly, and she looked at Sam, his face only inches from hers.

"Sam, will you kiss me? Kiss me like a man who loves a woman?" she asked in a wheezing voice.

Sam leaned over and gave her a deep kiss, knowing he was losing one of his ladies.

He pulled away a few inches, and with her voice growing even weaker, she whispered, "Thank you, Sam. I love you."

"I love you, too, Carol. Always."

"Sam? One more thing."

"Anything, my love."

"Kill those bastards."

"Count on it, sweetheart."

"And, Sam...," she began to say but her voice and her life left her.

Carol was gone and Sam wanted to break down to let his sorrow flow, but it wasn't the time. Those bastards needed to die.

He leapt to his feet and shouted, "Grace, stay with Carol. I'm going to kill every last son-of-a-bitch out there."

"Sam, I can help!" she screamed.

"Not this time, Grace! I need you to protect Catherine. Julia's unarmed. I'm going to slide one of those Winchesters to you. You shoot anyone that comes through that door that isn't me. I don't care if he looks like Abraham Lincoln."

Grace nodded as she got to her hands and knees.

Sam took three long strides toward the door and grabbed the two Winchester '76s. He hurried back to Grace and slid one of the rifles on the floor toward her. Now, it was his turn.

The three shooters, having seen Sam, had dropped to the ground expecting return fire, but continued their fusillade as the barrels of their Winchesters grew hotter.

Sam had his cocked Winchester in his hands as he stepped backward away from the door and then angled toward the window, so he could see the access road. He saw puffs of gunfire from three locations and marked them in his mind. They were in prone position, roughly ten yards apart, and only fifty yards from the porch. One on the right side of the road, one on the left side and the big guy in the center. He knew that the only direction he could take out all three would be from his current angle. He couldn't use the new side exit and his only concern was if there were more shooters somewhere else on the ranch.

Sam waited, as they just continued wasting ammunition firing at the house. The Winchester held a lot of rounds, but even it would run dry at the rate they were using them. More importantly, they seemed to be shooting at the same rate, so he waited as bullets continued to blast through the front walls. Suddenly, there was a pause by one of the shooters, and then a second. They were reloading, and it was now his turn to show them his new repeater's power.

After taking a deep breath, Sam walked quickly to the front door and paused behind the door jamb. He waited for a shot and when one smashed through the window to his left, he stepped out, saw the two on the sides of the access road fumbling with their guns as they were pulling cartridges from their gunbelts and shoving them into their Winchesters' loading gates.

Not hesitating, he aimed at the center shooter, the only one still firing. He fired two quick rounds and slid left three feet, fired two at the left side man and slid right and fired two more shots at the last shooter. He had executed a killing waltz; fire, fire, slide, fire, fire, slide, fire, fire. There were no more shots from the access road as his Winchester's barrel leaked the last of its gunsmoke.

Sam was reasonably sure that the shooters had all been hit by at least one of the big, .50 caliber bullets, so he blasted off the porch and sprinted toward the shooters keeping an eye on them for movement. One was rolling on the ground and screaming, so he ran to the wounded man, and when he reached him, kicked his rifle out of his hand then yanked the pistol from his holster.

The man then stopped screaming and began moaning. He had taken one shot in the top of his left shoulder, and the killing shot that angled into his belly. The shot must have hit the ground and ricocheted into his gut, which is why he was still alive even with the massive .50 caliber round. He'd die, but not quickly as his two partners had.

"Mister, I'm dyin'. It hurts real bad. Do me in. Please!" he begged as Sam looked down at him.

"Tell me who sent you or I'll leave you to your pain."

"Soapy. He said to kill the little girl. He said some guy in St. Louis paid big money to get her. We really didn't want to do it, mister. But we had to. Soapy said so."

"Where's Soapy holed up right now?"

"He told us to meet him at the brown house when we finished the job. Now, please mister, do me. I can't stand the pain."

"The brown house on 11th Street?"

"Yeah. Now put me down."

"I would if you hadn't killed one of my ladies. But now you're going to suffer, you, worthless piece of garbage. Some man tells you to kill a little girl and you do it just because he said so? You're too much of a coward to kill, and I couldn't care less how much pain you'll have because you caused more pain than you'll ever know."

Sam stood amid a combined flow of curses and groaning from the dying man and walked away, wondering if he'd told a lie or not by implying that he'd help him, but it didn't matter right now.

He walked slowly back to the house with a deep hate in his soul; a deep, seething hate for the man who had brought so much pain to him and those he loved; his brother-in-law, murdered, his beloved sister, kidnapped, placed into prostitution and murdered, his daughter kidnapped, his ladies kidnapped and thrown into that life and now one of his precious ladies killed. Just because two self-important, greedy bastards wanted something that wasn't theirs.

He walked across the bloody porch and entered the bullet-riddled house. Grace was kneeling over the lifeless Carol, sobbing as Sam walked over to the closed bathroom door and swung it open.

He picked up Catherine from the tub then helped Julia out.

"Julia, just go across the hall to the bedroom and sit on the bed and keep Catherine with you."

"Is everyone all right?"

"Carol was killed," he replied quietly.

Julia was stunned; her friend and fellow aunt was dead, and she felt as if she couldn't breathe.

Catherine looked at Sam and tears rolled down her face as she clutched onto Julia.

"Julia, I'm going to take her to the undertaker. I need you and Grace to be armed, but before I leave, I'm going to make a quick scan of the area to make sure there were only those three. Okay?"

Julia nodded, too shaken to speak.

Sam returned to the main room and found Grace standing and staring down at Carol's body.

"Did you kill them all?" she asked numbly.

"Almost. Two were dead and the third begged me to kill him because he was in such pain. I got the information I wanted and let him suffer."

"Good."

"Grace, I'm going to wrap Carol in a blanket and take her to the undertakers. I need you to stay here armed with Julia to watch over Catherine. I'll scan the area to make sure it's safe before I go."

"Okay," she said still staring at Carol.

Sam walked to the hallway closet, removed a blanket, then returned and laid it flat on the floor near Carol's body. He gently lifted her and laid her on the blanket, kissed her on her forehead and folded the blanket over her.

"Grace, go and get your Colt. Make sure Julia does as well, and both of you keep a Winchester with you, or close by. I'm going to hitch up the carriage."

"Okay," she said then slowly walked to her room where Julia and Catherine were still sitting on the bed crying.

Sam went outside to the new carriage house and harnessed the team then led the carriage into the front yard near the house. Before going in, Sam walked around the house, searching the area for any signs of more shooters, finding no one else out there.

Even then, Sam was thinking how stupid these men were to do what they did and how they did it and wondered if Soapy Smith just hired men that he knew would blindly follow him and not think for themselves. It was smart from his point of view, as there would be no challenges to his power, but it meant that he was vulnerable, and Sam planned on taking advantage of that vulnerability. Today. Now.

He went back into the house and saw Catherine standing between Julia and Grace beside Carol's covered body. They looked at him as he walked to Carol's inert form, then slid his hands under her lifeless body and gently carried her out to the waiting carriage. He laid her on the floor, having to bend her legs to fit.

"Can we come?" asked Grace.

"No, Grace. I need you to stay here. You and Julia take care of Catherine."

They nodded, unsure of his reason for keeping them at home, but trusting his judgment. Sam reentered the house and walked to the kitchen where he put on his back scabbard and loaded his shotgun with double aught shells. He put two more shells in his pocket and with his Colt and Webley still in place as he walked out of the kitchen and through the main room.

Grace saw the shotgun, knew what he intended to do, and knew he would die if he tried.

She pleaded, "Sam! You can't do this! Please just take Carol to Denver and come back to us."

"I'll come back, Grace." Sam said as he marched past her but didn't dare look into those dark blue eyes.

He stepped into the carriage and had the grays moving down the access road before she could make any more appeals.

"What do you think he's going to do, Grace?" Julia asked as they watched the carriage turn onto the road heading north to Denver.

"He's going to try to kill Soapy Smith," Grace answered quietly.

"Smith must have ten gunmen protecting him!' Julia exclaimed.

"I know. So, does he," she said quietly, a sense of dread filling her soul and mind.

They turned and went back into the house. Catherine was unsure of what her papa was going to do, but he knew it scared her aunts a lot, especially Aunt Grace. She knew that her Aunt Carol was with her mama in heaven now, but all of the shooting had scared her terribly and seeing her aunt lying on the floor made it worse. She wanted to talk to her mama and ask if Aunt Carol was with her and her papa but didn't know how.

————

Sam drove the grays hard, and they reached Denver in fifteen minutes. He slowed down when he was inside the city and steered the carriage to the undertaker. It was only three blocks from the brown house; his next, and maybe final destination. He was enraged, but he wasn't letting that overtake his ingrained lawman skills that he would desperately need.

He pulled the carriage into the undertaker's reserved lot, stepped down from the carriage and tied the reins to the post, then walked into the outer area, seeing the same fresh-faced young undertaker behind the desk.

"Mister Brown, how can I be of assistance?"

"Could you follow me outside, please?"

The young man stood and followed Sam to the carriage, and as they walked, Sam explained what had happened.

"An hour ago, three men tried to shoot my daughter. They shot her aunt and killed her instead as she was trying to protect the child. I need her to be embalmed, have her placed in a casket, and have her buried in the family plot at the Circle S."

"I'm so sorry, sir. Were the guilty men caught?"

"I killed all of the shooters, and they're laying out there in the sun. I'll notify the sheriff. Can you take care of removing her body?"

"Of course, Mister Brown. I'll see to everything."

"If possible, I'll be back later this afternoon, and if I'm not back, can you arrange for my burial at the cemetery as well?"

The young man was taken aback as he asked, "Sir? Are you all right?"

"Yes. We'll see who is and who isn't shortly," Sam said as he stepped away.

The undertaker watched him stride purposefully away, noting the shotgun on his back, and he knew he was going to face death or provide it.

––––––

Sam crossed three blocks ignoring the street traffic as he watched for signs of observation from any guards at the house as he stepped onto 11th Street. He could see the brown house in the distance and took notice of an eight-foot high wall surrounding the residence.

The only open area was facing 11th Street, so any guards should be there watching the single gate on this side of the house. The larger carriage gate would be facing the alley on the other side.

He walked quickly down the street on the opposite sidewalk, keeping an eye on the area behind the gate looking for guards. As he walked, his vision panned across the yard, and he soon spotted two men lounging against a small tool shed. As he passed, he kept looking and found no other guards. Everything depended on whether the gate was locked or not.

He crossed the street and approached the gate on the latch side. He expected it to be locked and was almost shocked that it wasn't. He blew out his breath, removed the shotgun from the scabbard and drew back both hammers.

He yanked the gate open and stepped through, pointing the shotgun at the two guards who must have grown bored with standing watch, but when the gate creaked sharply, they jerked their heads around to see their worst nightmare approaching.

"Good morning, boys!" he said loudly.

"Who are you?" the taller of the two goons asked as they stood.

"Someone who needs to talk to Soapy Smith. Now I want you two boys to quietly get on your knees. I have this little scattergun loaded with double aught shot. Have you ever seen someone hit with a double aught shotgun blast at this range? It isn't pretty. On your knees and hands behind your backs. Now!"

They may have been acting as guards, but no one ever said that they had to die for it, so they dropped to their knees and locked their hands behind their backs.

Sam didn't have time to fool with pigging strings. He walked behind the pair, who hoped this shotgun-wielding bastard didn't blow them in half. He raised the shotgun parallel to the ground and brought the gun down on both of their heads simultaneously. The man who got the barrel end was out and fell face first to the ground, and Sam wasn't sure if he was dead or just unconscious, but really didn't care. The man who had caught the stock end was moaning after his fall, so Sam let him have another smack with the barrel end, then unhitched the hammer loop from his Colt.

He didn't even check on the condition of the two guards, but just turned and walked up the stairs to the porch. He knew the best tactic was to just walk in like he belonged there, so he did. He opened the door loudly and stepped inside finding the parlor empty, then he heard laughing down the hall and walked toward what he assumed was the sitting room in the large house.

As he turned the corner to the sitting room, he saw eight men. Four were playing poker, two were watching behind them making a nice grouping, and two were off to the right, talking.

Sam pointed the shotgun as the two talkers and one of the watchers glanced his way. He aimed at the card players and their two kibitzers.

"Boys, I want you to drop your weapons. I'm serving a warrant on Soapy Smith for the murder of Carol Early," he said in a firm voice.

"The hell you say!" said one of the talkers to his right, thinking he was safe from the shotgun's wide blast. He went for his Colt, as did one of the watchers, which was all Sam could hope for.

Sam didn't let the revolver clear leather before he pulled the trigger. The shotgun rocketed from his hands, then he took a quick step left as his right hand shot down to his Colt, pulling his pistol, and even as the first of the two off to the side was fumbling with his hammer loop, the second had his pistol free, was cocking it and bringing it to bear.

Sam instantly judged the greater threat and fired two quick .44s into the one who was closest to firing his weapon, but the only shot the man could get off went right into the floor as the two bullets drilled through his chest and dropped him to the floor.

By then the second pistol shooter, the only man still standing in the room, had pulled his pistol, but never even had a chance to pull the hammer back before he felt the punch from two .44 caliber slugs of lead, making him stumble back two steps, hit the back wall and slide to the polished oak. The card players and watchers almost didn't exist any longer, but one of them was still groaning. Sam didn't think he'd be making any sounds at all for much longer.

Sam took a few seconds to reload his Colt from his belt before he quickly left the sitting room to find Soapy Smith, who should be alone now and very aware of his presence. Sam scanned each first-floor room quickly, not seeing anyone but was about to leave the office when he looked under the desk in the office and saw a pair of boots.

He aimed his Colt at the desk and said, "Soapy Smith, I am Deputy Sheriff Sam Brown. You are under arrest for the murder of Carol Early."

Slowly a man emerged from behind the desk and Sam was surprised to see an unarmed, smallish man with a receding hairline and wearing a suit and tie. But it didn't matter if he looked like Abe Lincoln, he was the man responsible for Cora, Richard and Carol's death and he had to die.

Soapy had his hands in the air, which he knew would keep him alive as he said, "I know who you are. You're that bastard that has been giving me grief. Well, Mister Brown, you've stepped in it now. You'll never get a conviction in this town. I have connections."

"I don't care who you know. I just want to know one thing. Who paid you to kill Richard Short?"

"You don't know?"

"Of course, I know. Ferguson Short in St. Louis. I just wanted confirmation."

"If you know, then why come in here and kill all my men when you can just go there and kill him."

"I have two very big reasons: You killed my sister, my brother-in-law and one of my ladies and I want to get him legally. To do that, I need evidence."

Soapy ran his tongue across his lips and said, "I'll tell you what. I'll give you your evidence if you'll just walk out of here and promise not to use it against me."

Sam thought about it or pretended to think about it. He knew what men like Soapy Smith were capable of and it wasn't difficult to guess what he was planning even as he made the offer.

"Okay. Just write it out and include details. If I'm satisfied, I'll walk."

"You're smarter than I thought," Soapy said as he sat at his desk.

Soapy reached across his desk, took a blank sheet of paper, pulled out a pen, dipped it into his inkwell and began to write. Two minutes later, he handed the sheet to Sam, who took it with his left hand as his right was still holding his cocked Colt.

Sam read:

On September 27, 1878, I, Soapy Smith was contacted by Ferguson Short of St. Louis Missouri and offered $1,000 to kill the Short family residing at Circle S ranch.

Soapy Smith

Sam blew on the sheet to make sure the ink was dry, and once he was satisfied that it was, he nodded.

"Alright, Mister Smith, this satisfies me. Good day."

Sam released the Colt's hammer, then slid it into its holster but didn't hook the hammer loop over the pistol, hoping that the gang leader would try and shoot him in the back and would be surprised if he didn't. He watched the outlaw chief as he folded the incriminating sheet, then slipped it into his inner vest pocket, then turned his back on Smith listening for the tell-tale click of a hammer being cocked. After taking one cautious step, heard a metallic noise, stepped quickly to his left, and drew his Colt as Smith's pistol fired. Sam unloaded three shots at close range, and Smith collapsed back into his chair.

Sam went to where he had fallen and picked up the pistol and almost threw up. It was a Webley Bulldog like the one tucked under his vest in its shoulder holster. It was a double action pistol and didn't have to have the hammer pulled back separately. Maybe Soapy didn't know it was a double-action and had cocked the hammer anyway. He didn't know what noise had initiated his response, but he knew he had been very lucky.

He dropped the pistol into his jacket pocket and was preparing to leave the office when he froze. He suddenly remembered what Soapy had said about never getting a conviction in this town and quickly recalled the defense attorney acting like a second prosecutor in the trial of the two men that had offended Soapy Smith.

Crooks like Smith invariably kept good records. To most people, it made no sense, but they did it as insurance to keep bribed officials on their side. Those important men wouldn't dare turn on him if they knew he had damning evidence against them.

He returned to the desk, then after pushing Soapy's lifeless, sitting body aside, he rifled through the drawers and didn't find anything interesting. But he'd seen desks like this before and many of them had a false bottom on one of the side drawers.

Sam pulled the top drawer and tapped the bottom. It was solid, but the middle drawer wasn't. He slid the drawer out fully and found a string on the back. He emptied the drawer and pulled the string, finding a green ledger inside. He pulled out the ledger, quickly opened it to a random page and as he read, a smile grew ever larger across his face as his eyes flew across the pages. This was a very damning book.

He lifted his jacket and vest, tucked the ledger in his back waist and let the vest and jacket back down, then went down the hallway, retrieved his shotgun, and slid it into his scabbard. His last act was to remove his deputy sheriff's badge from his shirt and pin it on the outside of his jacket. He expected company and didn't want to be shot leaving the house.

He walked out the front door and was greeted by several Denver deputy marshals with firearms drawn.

He put his hands in the air and said loudly, "I'm Deputy Sam Brown out of Sheriff Dan Grant's office. I came to issue a warrant for the arrest of Soapy Smith for murder. There was resistance. If you take those two unconscious guards into custody, I'd appreciate it."

They slowly lowered their guns.

The senior deputy then approached him and with arched eyebrows, asked, "Did you walk in alone into Soapy Smith's house to serve him with a warrant?"

"I did. He had eight gunmen inside. They were a bit unfriendly and didn't cooperate at all, and three pulled their weapons. Now, Soapy Smith, he was acting very cooperative and played like he was willing to come along because, as he said, 'I have connections', but as soon as I turned my back on him, he tried to shoot me. When you go inside, you'll find that all those men have their bullet holes in the front. I'll write up my report for Dan when I return to the office. Any questions?"

The deputies were all stunned by his statement and stood wide-eyed as Sam walked past them then through the throng of onlookers outside the gate that had heard the gunfire. He acted as if they weren't there and continued walking until he reached the undertaker's and stepped inside.

The young man saw him enter and leapt to his feet, exclaiming, "Mister Brown! I am happy to see that you returned."

"Not half as happy as I am. Is Carol being cared for?"

"Yes, sir. She was such a young and beautiful woman to have lost her life."

"Yes," Sam replied quietly.

"Did you want to write the particulars for her memorial carving?"

"Yes. I'll take care of it now as well as your bill. How much is it?"

"$53."

"Fine," Sam wrote out a draft and the wording for Carol's headstone.

"When would you prefer that we arrive at your ranch?"

"Is tomorrow afternoon alright?"

"Yes, sir. I'll get the stone carver working on the headstone right away. He should have it done in time."

"Thank you for your help. I have to make a couple of stops before I head back. Oh, and by the way, I think there's a lot of business for you over on 11th Street. Soapy Smith and eight of his men are awaiting burial."

"*Soapy Smith*?" he asked with a look of shock.

Sam nodded and left.

He untied the team's reins, stepped into the carriage and drove to the bank, where he stepped down, walked through the lobby, leaving his shotgun and scabbard in the back seat of the carriage so he didn't create panic in the bank, and headed for the desk of the nearest clerk.

When he reached the desk, he said, "I have some unusual requests. Are you senior enough to handle them?"

"I can do most banking functions."

"Okay. I need to close my account and put what remains into the account of Richard and Cora Short. Both are deceased, and my name is on that account as well. The second thing I need to know is if Soapy Smith had an account here."

"I'm not at liberty to divulge that information, sir."

"I only need to verify a signature. I just went to his home to arrest him for murder. He objected and fired at me, so I'm here and he's dead. But before he died, he signed a statement for me, and it's important in the apprehension of another murderer that his signature be confirmed by an independent agency, like your bank. If you can have someone just examine his signature and write a written confirmation on the statement that you certify that the signatures match to the standard required of your bank. That's all I need."

The clerk looked at the badge and appreciated his legal familiarity, so he asked, "Do you have the statement with you?"

"Yes, I do."

Sam reached into his pocket, removed the sheet of paper, and handed it to the clerk who read it and tried to control his astonishment.

"I think we can do that, Deputy. Now, about the accounts; you wish to transfer the money from one account to the other?"

"Yes."

"Very well, sir. This shouldn't take long."

Sam figured his old account was less than two thousand dollars by now. He didn't have any more plans, except to marry Grace and start their new life together. He was still deep in his thoughts about Grace when the clerk returned.

"Here you are, sir," he said as he handed him the statement, "The signatures matched and the document notarized. Your new balance is $10,783.22, and I've given you some drafts for the account"

"Thank you for all your help"

He shook the clerk's hand and left the bank, sliding the statement and the drafts into his jacket pocket, then drove the carriage to the sheriff's office, stepped down and walked into the office.

Zeke was at the desk and said, "The sheriff is expecting you, Sam. All hell is breaking loose."

"I figured it would be," Sam replied as he passed Zeke and winked at him, which was not what Zeke must have been expecting.

Sam walked back to Dan Grant's office, and as he turned the corner into the open door he was met by a deep, unhappy voice.

Dan shouted, "Jesus Christ, Sam! *What am I going to do with you?*"

"Good morning to you, too, Dan," Sam said with a smile as he removed the ledger from under his jacket and vest.

"Close the door, will ya?" Dan asked in a slightly calmer voice.

Sam closed the door and sat down, keeping the ledger on his lap.

"I just had a visit from the city marshal wondering what the hell one of my deputies was doing serving a warrant on Soapy Smith without notifying him. Then he launches into a tirade about excessive use of force and finding body parts all over the place and Soapy Smith dead. What the hell happened?"

Sam sighed, then replied, "Dan, remember Carol Early, one of my ladies? The one who came with Grace to the trial? You met her before that as well."

"How could I not remember her? She's a very pretty lady."

"Was, Dan. I dropped her off at the undertaker an hour ago. This morning, she was playing on the front porch with my daughter," Sam said as his voice began to shake.

He paused, then took a deep breath before continuing, "Dan, she was with my little girl and three gunmen sent by Soapy Smith to kill Catherine began peppering the house with gunfire. Carol grabbed Catherine to protect her and tried to get her into the house. She took a shot in the back of her chest, but still managed to push Catherine inside. I was in the kitchen when I heard her scream my name. I was already running as the shots began, and I grabbed my daughter, gave her to Julia and told her to hide herself and Catherine in the bathtub. I ran out onto the porch and grabbed Carol and brought her back in. She died in my arms, Dan."

Sam took another deep breath and continued, his voice under control now.

"I grabbed a Winchester and after looking for the locations of the shooters, I stepped out and fired two rounds at each location as I moved around. I killed all three of the shooters and put Carol in the carriage and took her to the undertakers. I brought my shotgun with me. One of the shooters who was still alive was begging me to end his misery, so I had him tell me who had sent him. He said that Soapy had told them to kill Catherine and then he told me where he was."

"Did you do what the last shooter asked?"

"No. I let the bastard suffer."

Dan just nodded his approval before Sam said, "Those three bodies are still there. Can you send someone to pick them up?

"I'll send Zeke right away. He'll get them out of there for you."

"Thanks. Anyway, I walked down to 11th Street where the wounded gunman said I would find Soapy. I found two guards outside, but they were bored. The gate was even unlocked, if you can believe that. I walked in and held them under the shotgun. I didn't have time to tie them and gag them, so I coldcocked them with my shotgun.

"Then I walked into the house and found eight of them in the sitting room. By the way, four of them were on those descriptions given to me by Grace. Anyway, you would think with a shotgun pointed at them from twenty feet, these morons would just toss down their guns like I asked, but they didn't. Three of them drew and I let loose. Six of them were so close together that the shotgun did them in, but I had to use the Colt on the two that were still standing and pulling their pistols. Then I went next door and found Soapy hiding behind his desk. He offered me a deal to walk away, so I acted like I accepted and as I turned, he tried to back shoot me. I was expecting it, so I took him out. You'll find all of the gunshot wounds are in the front Dan."

"I know, Sam. So, what was the deal he offered you?"

"This," Sam replied as he handed Dan the notarized note.

Dan read it and noticed that Sam had already taken it to the bank and had the signature verified.

"Sam, this is solid evidence against that bastard."

"Yes, and I plan on going to St. Louis and see him arrested and hanged."

"I'd like to see you do that, Sam, but that may be a problem."

"Why?"

"The city marshal is going to have Judge McNeal issue an arrest warrant for you."

"I don't think so, Dan."

"Sam, he's serious."

"Dan, I've only known you for a few months, but I trust you, and now I'm going to trust you with my life."

"And I trust you, Sam, but it doesn't amount to a hill of beans in this."

"No, Dan, in this case that trust is critical. What I am saying is that I'm about to prove just how much I trust you. After my meeting with Soapy and with his body sitting right there, I rifled his desk. I know how much these big-time crooks like to keep records. Well, I found a ledger hidden in a false-bottomed drawer. After he had told me that he had connections and would never be convicted in this town, I knew he had to keep records of the bribes so he could use it on them if he needed to keep those whom he bribed from turning on him. I just scanned the first couple of pages, and guess whose name shows up more than any other?"

Sam then handed Dan the ledger.

The sheriff took the book, flipped it open and leaned back as he scanned the entries.

"Sam! This is dangerous stuff! Look at these names!"

"I'll bet you won't find Judge McLean's name in there, and I hope you don't find the county or state prosecutor's either. If we go to the county courthouse right now, I think the judge can understand your city marshal's anxiety."

"Let's go. Fast," Dan said as he stood, grabbed his hat and followed Sam out of the office.

Before they left, Dan told Zeke to head down to Sam's place and pick up the three bodies, then they trotted out of the office, and quickly crossed the street to the courthouse.

As they entered, Dan saw the city marshal leaving the judge's chambers with a sheet of paper.

The marshal saw Sam walking rapidly toward him with Dan beside him, and stepped forward pompously and announced, "Sam Brown, I am arresting you for nine counts of murder and assault."

"Stick it up your ass, Harold," growled Dan.

Sam snickered as they passed the befuddled marshal and entered the judge's outer offices.

———

Thirty minutes later, Judge McNeal leaned back in his chair.

"Mister Brown, I'm thoroughly astounded. We've been trying to stop Soapy Smith for years, but no one could get close, and now we know why. In one day, you've rid the city of that menace and will allow us to bring to justice many who pretend to stand for the public welfare. I noted that the county prosecutor is not listed, either. The sheriff and I will meet with him shortly. You're welcome to sit in, if you wish."

"Normally, I'd love to your honor, but I have three anxious ladies back at my ranch that probably believe me to be dead. I also need to dig another grave for Carol, so I'll come back tomorrow or the day after to write a report, Dan."

Both men shook Sam's hand and wished him well, and the judge took a minute to write an order rescinding Sam's arrest warrant. Sam pocketed it along with the all-important note from Soapy.

Ten minutes later, he was on the road home moving the greys along rapidly, and about a mile before the access road, he ran into Zeke trailing three bodies on their horses.

Sam pulled the team to a halt and waited for Zeke to arrive.

When he did, Sam asked, "Where'd you find their horses, Zeke?"

"They were in some trees about a quarter mile from your place. Sam, I gotta ask you. These fellers were all hit straight on. Why didn't you come around the other side of your house?"

"I had marked them from the back of the room, and I knew exactly where they were. From straight on, I could get all three. If I went around, the best I could do was get two because one would be on the other side of the raised access road. I wanted all the bastards. So, as soon as two of them had to reload, I stepped out and began a little dance. I'd pump two rounds at one, move and then two more and move again. Aiming at a moving target is bad enough, but one that's shooting at you makes it worse."

"I never would have thought of that. It was pretty good shooting, too. Each one had two holes in him."

"Well, I gotta go, Zeke. Thanks for your help."

When he made the turn onto the access road just minutes later, he could see familiar female shapes on the porch. When they spied the carriage raising clouds of dust as it headed toward them, they didn't wait for him to reach the front yard but began running toward the carriage.

Catherine was being held by two different aunt's hands, her feet barely touching the ground.

Sam, not wanting to run them down, brought the team to a halt short of the house.

Sam stepped down and was bowled over by a female avalanche. Catherine had him by the knees, Grace had his left side and Julia his right. His face was being pummeled by female lips while he had his arms around both women.

"Ladies, I'm fine. I need to breathe."

It went from a rapturous greeting to a furious attack in an instant.

Grace fumed as she stepped back and exclaimed, "Sam Brown, what the hell do you mean going off like that! You had us scared to death! The thought of you going in there to try to get close to that notorious gangster was just plain stupid! Luckily, it appears someone with brains talked you out of it."

"*What were you thinking!* You would have been killed before you got close!" shouted Julia.

"I was scared, Papa," Catherine said quietly.

"Can I get some lunch, please?" Sam asked politely.

"We'll feed you, but you had better come up with answers. Fast!" snapped Grace.

"Want a ride?" he asked guiltily.

"No. We'll walk. It'll burn off some steam," Julia said sharply before they turned and walked away.

"Yikes!" thought Sam.

He walked the carriage back to its new location and unhitched and stabled the grays, then he went in to face the music.

He entered the house through the back door, finding them seated at the kitchen table. On the table's flat surface was a sandwich and some water. He wouldn't be surprised if the bread was already stale and there were just a few potato peels between the slices.

He sat down as the two angry females glared at him, but the smallest one was just looking at him sadly.

"Okay. Let me say one thing. If anything had happened to either one of you or Catherine, I would have done the same thing. How could I let the man who tried to have my daughter killed and instead killed a woman I loved simply sit in his

389

house in Denver and let some more of his minions try again? I love each of you so much that I would do anything, I repeat, anything, to keep you safe."

Grace replied, "But Sam, it didn't change anything. Going into Denver hasn't changed anything, and it scared us to death. We thought you might have been killed. We had to sit here for hours worrying that you might be lying in the street bleeding to death like Carol did. Sam, you can't do this to us anymore. Tell me you won't be going after Soapy Smith ever again. Promise me."

"Fine. I promise that for the rest of my life I will never even think about going after Soapy Smith."

Grace thought that came too easy and was suspicious as she asked, "Why did you agree so quickly, Sam?"

"Because, my love, Soapy Smith and his entire organization, including the men that took you and Julia and Carol as well as those who murdered my brother-in-law and kidnapped Cora and Catherine no longer exist. They are all dead."

The two women almost went catatonic. *Sam didn't have a scratch on him, and all of those hoodlums were dead?*

Grace asked, "Sam, tell me that you're not just saying that. What happened? Did you have a hand in it?"

"Actually, I kind of did it myself. I was mad, Grace, but I wasn't stupid. They were just too complacent in their operation. They thought they were untouchable. Their guard was down and after I got into the house, they were all massed in the sitting room playing cards. They tried to shoot it out and I had my shotgun. It wasn't that hard, really. Then I found Soapy hiding and he wanted to make a deal, so I let him think

I made one and then when I turned my back, he tried to shoot me, so I shot him."

"Just like that?" asked a stunned Julia.

"Pretty much. Like I said before, I wasn't going to let that bastard hurt any more of my ladies or my precious daughter. Do you know what the ironic part of this is?"

"I hate to ask," said Grace.

"The city marshal was so mad that I took out the whole crowd, he had the judge issue a warrant for my arrest for murder. They've been trying to get rid of this guy for years, and now that it's done, and I had a legal warrant for his arrest, by the way, they want to charge me with murder. Can you believe it?"

Julia asked wide-eyed, "*You're being charged with murder and you think it's not important?*"

"Not at all. After the judge signed the arrest warrant, Dan Grant and I walked over to the courthouse and after showing him some evidence, he issued an order rescinding the warrant. I'm going back tomorrow or the day after to meet with him and Dan."

Now they were both totally confused as Grace asked, "What evidence?"

"When I was chatting with Soapy, he bragged about how nothing could happen to him because he had connections. So, after he was dead, I went through his desk and found a ledger listing the dates, the amounts of the bribes and who got them. I gave it to Dan, and we ran it over to the judge. Judge McNeal was almost jumping up and down in his robes he was so happy."

Sam looked at Grace and Julia's astonished faces and continued.

"So, after all is said and done, the immediate local threat is gone. Those who hurt you both and caused you so much trouble are dead, and the evidence Soapy gave me means that the source of all the trouble for Catherine will be gone as well."

"You never did show us that," mentioned Julia.

"Oh. Sorry."

Sam took out the note and they both read it.

Grace stared wide-eyed at the sheet and said, "Oh, my God! Sam this will get him hanged. You even had the signature authenticated. That was a brilliant thing to do."

"Before I forget, the undertaker will be bringing Carol back to us tomorrow afternoon. I'll dig a new grave later, but I'm just going to eat first."

Before he could pick up the sandwich, Grace snatched it from the table.

"This was a punishment lunch. I think you've earned a better meal," she said and kissed him on the forehead as she passed.

———

After a much better lunch, Sam walked out to the barn. He wasn't wearing any weapons at all and felt almost naked. He picked up the spade from the barn and the pickaxe from the carriage house and walked out to the cemetery.

He took off his shirt and began digging. He didn't feel as sore this time and had the grave dug in thirty minutes. When he was done, he moved the dirt out of the way as he had the last time. It was ready for Carol, but he wished he hadn't had to dig it at all. She would be next to Cora and he was sure that Richard would understand. Sam never wanted to do this again.

Sam walked back to the barn and set both tools together before returning to the outside pump and began soaking himself off. The cool water was what he needed for his body and his soul. Just as he finished, a towel appeared on the right side of his vision and he knew it was Grace again.

"Thank you, Grace."

"You're welcome, Sam. May I ask you something, Sam?"

"Of course, you can. You always can."

"Were you afraid today, Sam?"

"I know the standard answer is that only a fool isn't afraid when facing death, but no, I wasn't afraid. I was resigned, Grace. When I left Carol at the undertaker, I made arrangements to have me brought here for burial if I failed."

Grace shuddered and said, "Sam, what about me? Don't you care enough about me to think what your dying would do to me?"

He hung the towel around his neck, then looked at her as he replied, "Yes, Grace, I thought very much about you. It was all I did think about aside from how I was going to do it. But, you see, I had no choice. I felt that sooner or later, he'd try again and there was a very real chance that he would kill you

393

the next time. So, what I did was to choose you over me. That's how important you are to me."

Grace stood frozen for almost a minute before she said softly, "Sam, I'd kiss you right now, but Julia is on the porch with Catherine."

"Soon, sweetheart. Now, let's go inside and talk about what we need to do about that bastard in St. Louis."

Sam slid the towel from his neck, handed it to Grace, then pulled on his shirt and walked with Grace to the front yard.

When they reached the porch, he said, "Julia, could you and Catherine join us in the main room?"

Sam had noticed that there were no blood stains on the porch, and when they got to the room, Sam noticed that the rug had been removed and no blood was visible on floor either. Grace and Julia had been busy, probably working off their worries while he was in Denver.

They all sat down with Catherine perched on her papa's lap, glad that her aunts weren't mad at him anymore. Why they had been angry in the first place still confused her.

"Carol, I just told Grace that we need to talk about St. Louis. In a few days, I'll be heading that way to finally end this thing. I don't want Catherine to stay here while I'm gone. Cousin Ferguson may have found out by now that she's still alive."

"Why don't we move her over to Grace's place?" Julia asked.

"Because they know about it already. I must be certain that Ferguson hadn't been getting information from Soapy about the progress of the assassinations. I think I know a place that no one will think of looking. Julia, I'll need you to stay there for a week or so. Grace will either be coming with me or staying at her place. I'm still working on that end. I think Catherine is more comfortable around you, probably because you're so much fun, but the confrontation with Ferguson could get ugly, and I may want to go alone, although I see an advantage of having Grace there. It has to do with Catherine's inheritance. Catherine, do you understand what's going on?"

"No."

"Okay. Do you know what inheritance is?"

"No."

"Inheritance means that when someone dies, all that they leave here that they can't take with them to heaven, has to be given to someone here on earth. Now, there are laws that say if someone dies, what they have left goes to their wife first. But if the wife already died, then it goes to their children. If the children have died, then it goes to the grandchildren."

"Okay."

"Now, your papa's papa, your grandfather, owned a lot of ships. They were worth a lot of money. When he died, it should have gone to your papa. But a bad man, a nephew to your grandfather, paid a bad man in Denver to kill your papa so he couldn't inherit your grandfather's ships. They were supposed to kill your mama and you, too. With both your mama and papa dead, the evil man in St. Louis tried to have you killed so he could get the ships.

"He hired that bad man in Denver that I killed today, along with all the bad men that stole your mama, you, and your aunts. I am going to go to St. Louis and stop the evil man and have him arrested. I don't want him hurting you while I'm away, so I'm going to have you and Aunt Julia stay at a different ranch. Do you understand all that?"

"Yes, Papa, but I don't want any ships."

"I know that, sweetheart. When I get to St. Louis, I'm going to show them the papers that made me your papa. Then I'll have them sell the ships for you and send the money to a Denver bank. That will be your money to do with as you wish when you get older. You'll be able to go to any school you want to or travel the world or anything else you wish to do. I think it's better than having ships that need to be managed and I'm sure the company that runs the ships is upset because right now they have no boss. If you sell your ships to them, they can be boss again."

"Okay, Papa. I can do it."

"Good girl. Now you need to understand something. This will be your money. I am going to the bank and set up what they call a trust fund for you. That way all the money, plus whatever it earns, will be waiting for you when you're a grownup."

"You can have my money, Papa."

Sam smiled at her, knowing she would have said just that, and replied, "No, sweetie. Thank you for the thought, but it is yours. Now, if it's okay with you ladies, I need to avail myself of the bathtub."

They all agreed that it was a wise thing to do and let Sam have his time in the tub with his plain white soap.

CHAPTER 14

After breakfast, Sam wandered out to the barn and saddled Cump, then mounted and rode east toward the Slash F. After transiting the new gate, he crossed the pasture to the ranch house. There was no smoke coming from the chimneys, nor were there any horses in the corral, but Sam hadn't expected any now that Soapy was no longer around to send assassins.

He looped Cump's reins around the repaired hitching rail and walked inside. *What would Grace do with the ranch after they were married?* He didn't really care about the whole cattle business. If he had, it would have been great to have two spreads adjoining each other.

As he walked through the house, his mind was really on St. Louis. *What if he got there and Ferguson was already in control?* It would be a little stickier, but he could still be arrested. The money that was due Catherine didn't really concern him. He could provide for her and Grace without any problem. He just hated seeing anyone deprived of what was rightfully theirs.

And what about Julia? He believed that Julia was more of a free soul than either Grace or Carol. Show her a handsome young man and she'd forget about him. But he still loved the woman and needed to make sure she'd be happy. He didn't want to see her hurt again. Maybe he'd have to give her beau the same scrutiny that he gave Richard, and hopefully with the same results.

Richard. Poor Richard. All he wanted to do was to make his own way. He and Cora were so happy together in the ranch house. They had everything a young couple could want. They loved each other and had a beautiful daughter, then that bastard Ferguson had to want what wasn't his. Sam would make sure he got what he didn't want; a date with the hangman.

He walked into the kitchen and pumped some water into a glass and sat down, trying to devise the best way to confront Ferguson. He could go to the local law in St. Louis, but he couldn't be sure that they weren't as corrupt as those in Denver. Even if he used them, he was sure that any confrontation had to be in the view of the other company officers.

He was deep in thought and didn't notice the footsteps behind him. He was losing his touch. When a hand touched his shoulder, he nearly pulled his Colt from his holster despite the hammer loop.

"Sam, what's bothering you?" Grace asked as he twitched and then looked up at her.

"Just a couple of things," he answered as she sat down beside him in the next chair, "Ferguson, mostly."

"And what else?"

"This place."

"Why is this a problem?"

"Not so much a problem, but I was wondering what you were going to do with it after we're married."

"I thought we'd just run cattle on both ranches."

"That would be fine if you were marrying a cattle rancher, Grace. But I never worked cattle, and I never really wanted to."

"Did you think I should sell it?"

"No, never that. This is your home, Grace. I'm sure some solution will present itself."

"I think all of those horrible events yesterday are pulling you down, Sam."

Sam nodded, then sighed and said, "So many people dead or having their lives ruined because of the greed of two men. Good people. Wonderful people. Why did it take me having to kill twelve men just to stop it? No one should have to take another man's life, Grace, even when it's justified. Even those bad men had mothers and fathers. Did they turn wrong or were they just bad?"

Sam took in a deep breath and let it out before saying, "I'll be all right, Grace. I just needed to think."

Grace smiled at him and said, "Sam, do you realize that in two consecutive statements you said we were going to be married as if it was already done."

He looked at her and smiled back, saying, "I'm sorry, Grace. I never take you for granted. It's just that I wanted it for so long, that in my mind, it has already happened. I've thought of you as my wife from almost from the day I met you, Grace, and it wasn't because I was able to give you a husbandly caress. Things just always seem to be getting in the way all the time."

Grace remembered that moment, and at the time, it was a defensive more than provocative move, but it didn't matter now. Now, she wished she could pull his hand to her bare breast again for a totally different reason.

She sighed, then asked, "So, Sam. Am I going to St. Louis with you?"

"Of course, you are. I said what I did so Julia didn't couldn't raise any objections. Like that fib about Catherine liking her the best. You know she always tells me how much she loves you, don't you?"

"No. I really believed that she liked Julia the most."

"Remember when I told you that Julia was younger than you were? Well, Catherine sees that, too. She sees Julia as more of a playmate than an adult. She sees you as a mother."

"Do you think I'll ever be able to be her real mama?"

"You already are, Grace. She's asked me when I was going to marry you. I believe she wants you to be her mama almost as much as I want you to be my wife."

"I need to ask you a difficult question. One that's difficult for me to ask."

"If you can ask, I'll answer."

"I know how much you loved your sister and I know that we look alike. Do I remind you of her?"

"What you're asking is, do I expect you to be a replacement for Cora. My answer is an unequivocal, no. Cora was an extraordinary person, as you are, but you are totally different too. Yes, you do resemble her in hair and eye color, but not as much as you seem to think. It is in your characters and personalities that you are so very different.

"She was all sparkle and light, a bit like Julia. She was effervescent. When I was growing up with her, she was always able to use that vitality to perk me up when I was down; you know, like after my one liaison.

"But you, on the other hand are more thoughtful. Now, don't take that to mean I don't enjoy having you around. I think of you as much more than just a beautiful woman with a shape that can drive me crazy. I think of you as my best friend, my confidant, and someone who can share my deepest thoughts. I could never do that with Cora. So, no, my love, you are anything but a fill-in for my sister. But I'll tell you something that stunned me a few days ago."

"What did?" Grace asked quietly.

"It was morning and you were holding Catherine and were standing on the kitchen doorstep watching me do something that I can't even remember because of what I saw when I looked your way. Your face and Catherine's were almost even as I looked at you both and couldn't breathe, Grace. It was that amazing. In that morning sun, you both looked at me and I saw the same dark blue eyes, the same reddish golden hair, the same round, pretty face. Grace, she looked like your daughter."

"I never noticed, Sam. No one ever said anything before."

"I was too amazed to say a word. I just kept that image in my mind. But know one thing, Grace Felton, I love you as you. You are the perfect woman for me, and I'll love you till the end of my days."

Grace stood, walked over and sat on his lap and kissed him. Not the passionate kiss as the one that they enjoyed the day before, but a soft, loving kiss that two people share when they know that they are ordained to be together.

———

Later that afternoon, Grace and Julia put on dresses and Sam dressed in his suit as they waited for the arrival of the hearse for the second time in a week and didn't have to wait long. Just after one, the hearse arrived, and they walked outside as the black carriage approached the front yard, then made the slow walk to the cemetery as they had the week before.

The four men removed the casket and lowered it into the ground, shoveled the dirt back into the hole and placed the headstone. Again, they nodded to the family and climbed aboard their hearse and left the property. It was a sad repetition to watch so soon after the last one.

Sam couldn't help himself this time. Looking down at that mound of earth that held a dear young woman who only yesterday had saved his daughter, he wept. The tears just wouldn't stop. He couldn't say a word as he clung to Grace and Julia, his last two ladies, who were also leaving puddles of their grief on the ground.

After the three adults finally controlled their grief, they could read her memorial. Beneath her name and dates, it read:

Sister of Cora
Sister of Grace
Sister of Julia
Aunt to Catherine
A True Lady

Sam picked up Catherine and they slowly returned to the house.

———

This death hit them harder than the burial of Cora and Richard. They had shared a home with Carol for almost three months and were together almost every day. Grace and Julia had been with Carol through the torture of Waxman's, then had their lives returned to them, only to have hers taken away again.

Sam knew that they were as heartbroken as was he. There was nothing he could do or say to change that. They would have to let it subside, as it always did, but he needed to make Ferguson pay for the grief he had caused them.

As they sat somberly in the main room, Sam decided the only remedy was to continue with the most important topic facing them now.

"Grace and Julia, let me tell you where I planned on hiding Catherine while I'm in St. Louis. When I was looking for the notorious puncher of women, I went to where he worked, the Bar C. The owner of the ranch, Orville Crandall is about sixty years old. He was horrified that such a man worked for him, and after the fight, Crandall told me to get him and his horse out of there and he never wanted to see either again. He was very upset. The foreman even spit on him as he lay on the ground. I'm going to ask Mister Crandall to hide you for a week or so. Can you do that, Julia? It should be pleasant enough. Crandall has enough young men to protect the place against any intruders."

"I can do it, Sam."

"Good. Right now, I'm leaning toward having Grace come along. Grace, I'd need you to make sure you bring your derringer. Neither you nor I can pack our Colts. We'll be going to the biggest city west of the Mississippi, plus we may be going into more refined areas, like the boardroom of the Short Shipping Company. You can bring the derringer and another

403

six rounds of ammunition should do it. I'll be packing the Webley."

"Alright," Grace replied.

Sam thought he'd try something a bit different to try to return everyone to a normal mood.

"You know, we're about to head off to St. Louis to stop this guy, and I have no idea what he looks like. Any guesses?"

Grace picked up on his desire to improve everyone's spirit.

"I'm guessing he has a face like a rat and has greased back hair. He has a thin mustache that he twirls all the time with his finger. Like this," Grace said then scrunched up her lips and began rolling her finger above her upper lip.

Catherine began laughing, so Julia took up the challenge.

"No, Grace, you're wrong. I think he'll be a big fat man. He'll have fuzzy black hair that looks like a porcupine. He has a flat nose and a pink face that makes him look like a pig. He doesn't walk; he waddles, and he squeals when he doesn't get his way."

Grace joined Catherine in laughter as Sam shook his head.

"No, you're both completely wrong. He'll be a distinguished gentleman about fifty years old. He'll have gray-streaked brown hair and a gentle smile. His face will be distinguished, and everyone will admire him and hope to count him as a friend."

Grace and Julia stared at him and wondered where he was going with this and didn't have long to wait.

"Oh, I'm sorry. I was describing myself in twenty years."

He paused for the effect, and as they smiled, he continued.

"I think he'll have black hair with a wide white stripe running down the middle and a tail in back. He'll have small beady eyes and instead of a mustache, he'll have long whiskers. His nose will be thin and pointy. When he gets mad, and that tail starts sticking in the air, run for your lives!"

His skunky description had them all laughing and even Sam was pleased with his effort.

"Now, tomorrow I'm going to have to go to Denver to meet with Dan Grant and Judge McNeal. Do you all want to come along?"

His question was met with instant agreement as each of them seemed anxious to get away from the ranch for a day.

———

They were on the road to Denver by nine o'clock having taken a leisurely morning to prepare for the drive. The back seat was empty as Sam sat between the two women who alternated having Catherine sit on their laps and everyone seemed in a much better mood.

As they approached Denver, Sam said to his daughter who was on Grace's lap at the moment, "Catherine, the sheriff can't wait to meet you. He said he'd throw me in jail if I didn't bring you to see him."

"Really?"

"No, sweetie," Sam replied as he laughed, "I'm just kidding about the jail part, but he really does want to meet you."

Then he turned to his left and asked, "You've never met Dan, have you Julia?"

"Not yet."

"He's a good man. He saved my hide already."

———

He parked the carriage near the sheriff's office and Sam escorted the women and carried Catherine into the office, spotting Zeke at the desk.

"Good morning, Zeke. This is Grace Felton, whom you have already met, and Julia Crook who's staying with us. This is my daughter, Catherine."

Zeke never heard a word as he stared at Julia, and she was staring back. His mouth wasn't open, but it may as well have been.

"Zeke!" Sam almost shouted to get his attention, "We'll be heading back to see Dan, if that's alright."

Zeke snapped out of it enough to say, "Go right ahead. He's been expecting you."

Sam started walking back to see Dan and he noticed that Julia wasn't with them.

When they reached the sheriff's private office, Dan was already standing and smiling.

"Morning, Sam. See you brought your ladies with you."

"Dan, this is Catherine," Sam said as Catherine looked with big eyes at the giant lawman.

Dan held out his hand and Catherine shook it, her tiny hand disappearing completely into his giant palm.

"Nice to meet you, Catherine. Hello again, Miss Felton."

"Dan, will you please call me Grace?"

"Thank you for that, Grace," he said, then looked at Sam and said, "I heard you introduce someone else to Zeke outside."

Sam said, "I think you couldn't pry him away from talking to Julia with a crowbar, Dan."

"That's interesting. Zeke has always been shy around women."

"Julia can have that effect on the male gender even if they aren't shy," Sam replied.

"Anyway, Sam, I have some news for you. Did you want to stay, Grace? You're more than welcome."

"No, that's okay Dan. You two go ahead and talk. I think there's more of a show out front."

She smiled at Sam and led Catherine off to the front office.

"So, where is everything, Dan?" Sam asked as he took a seat.

"Good stuff, Sam. The county prosecutor has the state prosecutor on board. They were both very pleased with your discovery. They were even more impressed that you had the brains to go looking for it and not to show it to the city marshal; or should I say, ex-city marshal. He's been removed from office and is under investigation. Those two guards you

407

popped on the noggin have been blabbing their mouths off, too. They figured that with no Soapy, it's every man for himself.

"By the way, one of the things they mentioned was that Soapy did want to see those other two hang. He told them to stay away from that place, and when you caught them, he went crazy because it wasn't their first screwup. So, all I need from you is your report on the incident.

"Oh, and there's one more thing I need to tell you about. I sent a letter yesterday to a friend in St. Louis who used to be my deputy about ten years ago; a real sharp kid. Anyway, the U.S. Marshal's Office recruited him away from me and now he's the head of their St. Louis office. His name is Thomas Charles, and don't call him 'Tom', either. He doesn't cotton too it much. I explained all of the particulars in my letter, so you might want to stop at his office first."

"Thanks, Dan. I'll start getting that report done before the ladies get bored; except for Julia, maybe."

Sam took the paper and pencil that Dan slid across his desk, then stood and walked to the next office.

Out front, Grace was enjoying the show as she watched while Julia flirted. It made her happy for more than one reason. Her friend was happy and returning to her normal self, and it meant that Sam was right. Put a handsome young man in front of her and she would leave Sam alone; alone for Grace. Grace wondered if Julia was toying with Zeke or really interested, but only time would tell.

Sam dropped off the two-page report with Dan and told Dan that he'd look up Thomas Charles when he got to St. Louis.

When Sam reappeared in the front office, Julia looked over and Sam could see the disappointment on her face.

"Now this is surprising but good news," he thought.

Sam asked, "Ladies, are we going to head out?"

Grace and Catherine stood and were anxious to leave, but Julia slowly rose and said to Zeke, "Well, don't be a stranger, Zeke. Of course, I won't be at the ranch while Sam and Grace are gone to St. Louis, but they should be back in a week or so."

She turned to Sam and asked, "When will you both be going to St. Louis?"

"Talk about a change," thought Sam, "Now she wants to get rid of us and let us go together."

He answered, "Probably in three days. I need to stop by the construction company and see about having them stop by and fix the holes in the ranch house."

Zeke ignored everything but Julia's invitation to visit and said, "Well, maybe I can stop by tomorrow. I get off at four o'clock."

Julia turned to Sam and asked, "Is that okay, Sam?"

"Sure, Zeke. Why don't you stop over for dinner?"

"Thanks, Sam," replied a floating-on-air Zeke, "I'll be there."

Sam waved and guided Grace to the door, and said to her softly, "I'll bet he's there by four-thirty with a lathered horse."

Grace smiled, reached over and patted his arm, then he threw another morsel Julia's way.

He turned to look back at her and said, "Julia, if you'd rather stay while we go to the construction company, we can pick you up on the way back in half an hour or so."

"Thanks, Sam. I didn't want to go there anyway."

"Fine, Julia. We'll see you later."

Julia waved merrily as Grace and Sam left the jail, then helped Catherine into the carriage.

As it pulled away, Sam looked over at Catherine and said to her, "Did you see how happy Aunt Julia was when she was talking to Zeke?"

"Yes, Papa. I think she wants to marry him. She looked at him the way you look at Aunt Grace."

"Well, Catherine, in a little while, I don't think you can call her Aunt Grace anymore."

"Why not, Papa," she asked with a hurt look.

"Because I think you'll be calling her mama."

Catherine squealed, *"Really? You're going to marry her, and she'll be my new mama?"*

"Yes, sweetie. Will that make you happy?"

"That would make me the happiest girl in the world. I love my Aunt Grace, but I think I would love her more as my mama."

Grace couldn't handle it much more as she grabbed Catherine in her arms and hugged her tightly, her tears running down her face and onto Catherine's hair.

"You've made me so happy, Catherine. I never thought I could have such a wonderful daughter."

Then Grace looked across at Sam's face and mouthed, "Thank you," as he just smiled back at her.

"It can't get any better than this," he thought.

Sam rode past the construction company and circled around an extra block to give Grace time to recover. When they finally stopped, Sam looked over at Grace, whose blue eyes were more red than blue and said, "Grace, why don't you and Catherine stay here and talk while I go inside to take care of this. It shouldn't take that long."

Grace nodded with a huge smile spread across her face and Catherine smiled at him as well as she waved goodbye.

He stepped down from the carriage and bounded across the boardwalk before walking inside expecting to talk to an engineer but was pleasantly surprised to find Joe Schmidt.

"Sam! I hear you've been causing more trouble with that nasty little shooter of yours again."

"Only to those who cause me grief, so don't press your luck."

Joe was chuckling as he walked up and shook his hand, then said, "I was truly sorry to hear that one of your ladies was killed by those bastards. I'm glad you shot all of them. The whole city is talking about it; how one man on his own took down the whole operation, walked right in and blasted them all to hell. Anyway, what can I do for you?"

"Those bastards shot up my place pretty good, Joe. About forty .44 caliber rounds hit the front of the house. Took out the

411

windows and made a mess. Can you send somebody down and get me an estimate? It shouldn't be a bad job."

"Nah. We'll take care of it. The boss is already pleased we worked on your place. When I tell him that you want us to fix all those bullet holes, he'll be popping buttons."

"I'll be heading off to St. Louis in three days and should be gone for about a week. No one will be there while we're away."

"What's going on in St. Louis?"

"The greedy cousin who wanted my brother-in-law's shipping firm in St. Louis paid Soapy to kill his entire family. When I saw Soapy, he tried to make a deal by giving me a confession that the guy paid him to do it. I have it at home. It's been certified as authentic and I'll be going there to have him arrested."

"Well, good luck to you, Sam. When you come home your house will be as good as new. Maybe better."

"Thanks, Joe. When I get back, we have to do some shooting."

"Sound like fun."

He shook Joe's hand and left the office.

As he climbed back aboard the carriage, Grace asked, "So is it taken care of, Sam?"

"You can't believe how that went. I walked in and met Joe Schmidt. He told me that the bosses were so happy to be able to claim me as a client that they'd do the work while we were gone for free."

"Really? You've become that famous?"

"At least in Denver. I'd rather it not be that way, though," he said before he turned to Catherine.

"Catherine, now, until we get married, you keep calling your new mama Aunt Grace. Okay? It's a secret just between the three of us three for now."

"Okay, Papa. But can I call her mama when it's only us? I like to call her mama."

"Yes, you can, sweetie."

Catherine swiveled to Grace and said, "Did you hear that, Mama?"

"Yes, sweetheart. It won't be long now, will it, Sam?"

"No, Grace. I'm guessing three days before we can get married."

That surprised her and Grace asked, "Three days?"

"Sure. Is that too soon? Do you want to delay the date a few months for a big wedding?"

Grace shook her golden locks as she replied, "You know I don't want a big wedding, but why do you think that we'll be able to get married so quickly?"

"If I know Julia, and I do, I think in the next day or two, she's going to find some way to tell me to stop thinking about her as a potential mate and that I should marry you instead."

"You're kidding!"

"Nope. You watch. And, as there is no Julia here now," he said, he then leaned across and kissed her.

Catherine giggled. It was like her mama and papa used to do.

After the kiss, Grace asked, "But doesn't she know? I mean even early on, she and Carol said that I was your favorite."

"I think that Carol believed that, but I think Julia was just saying it to go along. If you'd seen the suggestive looks that she gives me when you're not around, then you'd know. When our daughter first came to my bed that first night, I was terrified thinking that she might be Julia. Then, there was the request to take her to Denver alone, too. But after that demonstration in the sheriff's office, I'm sure that I'm no longer her top priority. She just needed to find a good, handsome young man. Besides, I think Zeke is a good five to seven years younger than I am."

Grace grinned, then took his hand and said, "You're not too old for me and I'm two years younger than she is."

Catherine was listening but wasn't sure why her new papa and mama were so happy that her Aunt Julia wanted to be with someone else. Maybe she'd ask Aunt Julia later.

———

They arrived at the sheriff's office, Sam stepped out of the carriage leaving Grace and Catherine sitting on the leather cushioned seats, then walked to the office and entered.

Julia and Zeke were still engaged in one of those useless conversations that has no other purpose than hearing the sound of the other person's voice.

"Julia, are you ready to go back?" Sam asked.

Julia took a few seconds before she turned, then stood and said, "Sure, Sam. See you tomorrow, Zeke," then smiled and waved at the lovesick deputy.

Zeke smiled back and replied, "See you tomorrow, Julia."

When Sam let Julia climb into the carriage, he noticed that she sat on the back seat, so he glanced at Grace and winked.

Grace stifled a giggle as she turned to look straight ahead.

On the way back, Julia asked what Sam knew about Zeke and whether he had any girlfriends, if Sam liked him, etc., as Grace kept smiling.

When he turned the carriage onto the entrance road twenty-five minutes later, Sam stopped at the front porch and dropped the ladies off, then drove the carriage into its parking spot in the new carriage house, which no longer required that he push it anywhere.

————

In the house, Julia walked into her bedroom and was troubled. *How could she break the news to Sam?* She knew he loved her, and she loved him, but suddenly, it was as if he had been transformed into an older brother. Zeke was a different story altogether, but she didn't want to break Sam's heart. Maybe she could convince him to fall for Grace. Carol always said she was his favorite, although she knew better. She had agreed with Carol to hide her own embarrassment that Sam favored her. *What to do?* Maybe the best thing was to tell him privately and make a clean breast of it. She'd have to let him down gently.

———

After dinner, when Sam was alone in his room, Julia slipped out of her room while Catherine and Grace were in the kitchen.

Sam's door was open, so she stuck her head in and asked, "Sam, could I talk to you for a minute?"

"Sure, Julia. Come on in. What's on your mind?"

Sam could hardly believe it was coming this early. He had to tread carefully, because he didn't want to wound her pride.

Julia sighed, knowing that this was going to be hard as she carefully chose her words, saying, "Sam, since I've met you, you've been nothing but kind and generous to me. I love you dearly. You know that."

"Of course, I do, Julia. And you know how much I love you, as well."

"Yes, I do. Well, that's what I need to talk to you about. When I met Zeke today, I realized that sometimes I may have misled you to believe that I wanted you to marry me. I know that you desire me, and I can understand that, yet you've been nothing but a perfect gentleman since we've been here. But how do I say this? I suppose I have to just tell you straight out how I feel because it's probably the best way. I only love you as an older brother, Sam. I know this is hard to understand, and I hope that you'll try."

As she paused, Sam said, "I understand, Julia."

Julia then quickly said, "Carol always thought Grace was your favorite. I knew better, but I think Grace believed that she was, too. It would make me very happy, Sam, if you could

416

focus your attentions on Grace now. I know that she loves you in the way a woman loves a man. So, could you do that? For me?"

Sam made a thoughtful face as he chose his own words just as carefully and said, "This must have been very difficult for you, Julia. I'm proud of you for showing such strength of character to tell me. Of course, I'm a bit upset, but I'll go and talk to Grace in a few minutes alone and see how that goes. Just for you, Julia. I'm happy that you and Zeke get along so well, and I'll still always love you, Julia, but as a big brother."

Julia sighed and smiled, then leaned over and kissed Sam on the lips softly before she said, "That's to show my appreciation, and it will be the only time I will ever kiss your lips. Thank you, Sam. Once again you've given me something special."

Sam was beginning to think he might be going too far, so he quickly said, "Now, go ahead and mind Catherine and I'll follow you then talk to Grace and see what she says."

"Thank you again, for being so understanding, Sam," she replied, then turned to walk back down the hallway.

Sam stood and followed Julia to Grace's room. After Julia continued on to the kitchen, he rapped on the door, and seconds later, Grace walked out with a curious look on her face, made worse by the apparent hurt on Sam's. He didn't want to lose the façade in case Julia reappeared.

Sam spread it on a bit thick when he said, "Um, Grace, could I talk with you for a few minutes. You know, if you're not too busy?"

"Of course, Sam. Where would you like to talk?"

417

"Um, can we walk outside, do you think?"

"Sure."

Even Sam was embarrassed by his overacting as he and Grace crossed the main room and stepped onto the porch.

When they were on the ground, Sam led her to the other side of the carriage house as Sophie and Millie chased after them.

Once hidden from view, Sam lifted her from the earth, clamped her in his arms and gave her a deep, passionate kiss.

"Does this mean what I think it means?" she asked while taking deep breaths to recover the oxygen she'd missed.

"Yes, my love, it means that Julia just asked me to pursue you as my second choice."

"You're kidding!"

"No, sweetheart, it was amazing. Let me put you down. I can hold your hand now. It's perfectly acceptable."

As they walked from the carriage house heading to the east pasture, Julia watched them through the window. She noticed that they were holding hands and was impressed and pleased. She was one hell of a matchmaker.

She then made the innocent mistake of mentioning to Catherine that she thought Grace might marry Sam, which rekindled Catherine's own questions about why her papa and mama wanted Aunt Julia to be with someone else.

———

Sam and Grace walked for quarter of a mile as Sam told her every bit of the conversation while Grace laughed until she couldn't walk any longer.

"Sam, you're scary sometimes. You read us too well."

"Sometimes. I..." Sam said, then stopped in mid-sentence, suddenly saying the one word that could yank Grace from her humor.

"Catherine!"

They turned and scurried back to the house hoping to get there before Catherine mentioned anything to Julia, but it was too late. They hopped onto the small back porch and entered the kitchen door and found a fierce-looking Julia standing before them beside a confused Catherine.

"So, Mister Brown, you've been toying with me!" she exclaimed, "All this time, you and Grace were planning on getting married and here I was being considerate of your feelings."

Sam knew this was going to be tough situation to correct, but had to try and thought that honesty was the best solution.

"Julia, come on into the main room with Grace and I'll explain."

A steaming Julia followed Sam and Grace into the family room with Catherine trotting behind, knowing that somehow, she had caused the argument. After Aunt Julia had told her that she hoped that her papa and Aunt Grace would get married, Catherine had said that she already knew that Grace was going to marry her papa. When Aunt Julia got mad, she didn't know why.

They all took a seat, with a contrite Catherine sitting on the floor with Sophie and Millie.

Sam looked into her stormy eyes and said, "Julia, I want you to remember back to those first days we were all together. Remember how you and Carol and Grace thought of yourselves? Well, I had to dispel those feelings. I had to remind each of you that you were still young and beautiful women and that your lives were your own. You were all fragile in that respect because you thought you were nothing.

"As I got to know each of you better, I could see different strengths and personality traits in each of you. I'll be perfectly honest, Julia. I've always loved you, but just as you just explained to me, it was as a brother loves a sister. I felt the same way about Carol, but it was always Grace, Julia.

"What I couldn't do was to let you know that. I needed you each to feel that you were all still women men wanted to marry and have their children. I felt that if I started treating Grace as a wife and you and Carol as sisters, you'd think there was still something wrong with you. I believed that each of you was a highly desirable woman, but with much more to offer than simply that. The difference is that love is made up of so much more than physical attraction. I had to let you discover that on your own, Julia.

"Now, I've known for some time that if you found a young, attractive young man that connected to you because you are an intelligent, compassionate woman, you'd finally understand that what I told you was true. You don't want a man who just wants to bed you. You want a man who loves you for who you are; and also wants to bed you, by the way. When you were in Waxman's did you enjoy being with those men?"

"No," she answered softly.

"Of course, you didn't. There was no love there, Julia; just some man having his way with you. You were unimportant to him. All he cared about was your body, but that's not enough. When you make love with someone you love, Julia, it's the biggest difference in the world."

"Have you made love to Grace?"

"No, but if I had, you'd have known it. You can tell. When two people who are in love; true, deep love, their passions ignite that love into a flame that leaves a lasting glow. Grace thought I was wrong when I told her, but I think she believes me now. It doesn't mean that I have to make love to her, either. I was worried that you or Carol would see the impact of the love we shared."

Grace looked at Julia and said, "I believe him, Julia. I can't wait to get that feeling, and I know you'll feel the same way."

Julia sighed, then said, "I'm sorry, Sam and Grace. I just didn't understand."

"Well, now we can tell you that we're going to get married in three days."

"Three days?" she asked with wide eyes.

"We were just waiting for you to bloom, Julia. When I saw you talking to Zeke, I knew you were ready. I even told Grace that you and I would soon have the conversation we just did. It was that obvious to us, Julia. You were beginning to glow."

Julia looked down, smiled and said, "I did feel warm."

Julia then stood, gave Grace a congratulatory hug and kiss and gave one to Sam as well, only on the cheek.

Catherine was just happy that the grownups were happy again.

———

Later that night, when they had all turned in, Sam lay under his quilts. It was beginning to get colder, and soon, it would be autumn and he'd have to lay in more wood for the fireplace and stove. Luckily, they had services for that in Denver. When he was living alone, Sam usually slept without any clothes, but had to give that up while he slept on the couch, but now he could return to that habit. Besides, maybe if he was lucky…

He didn't have to wait long for his good luck to arrive, when he heard his door open and the sound of bare feet. He knew this wasn't Catherine or Julia and could make out her form in the moonlight. After she silently closed the door, he watched as she slid her nightdress over her head and was treated to a glimpse of her small, yet very well-proportioned body.

She pulled up his covers and slipped underneath without saying a word. Their next reaction was not one that either expected. When Grace slid under his quilts, she was expecting to find the ubiquitous union suit, instead she found naked muscle and skin. She glanced at Sam's smiling face and they both began fighting the laughter that wanted to escape from their mouths. Here were two young, healthy adults that were deeply in love; who had been yearning for this moment, yet when were finally naked together, they were laughing at themselves.

Grace whispered, "I guess we both had the same idea."

"I was going to give you about another forty-one seconds to arrive before I snuck down to your room. I thought my room would be better because it was further away from Julia's. I didn't want to give her the satisfaction."

422

They began stifling their laughter again. It was the best possible way to begin a new life together, but it didn't last much longer.

After the laughter subsided, Sam looked at the small, perfect face just inches from his, put his hand behind her head and kissed her as her hand found the back of his neck.

"Grace, for months now, I've been tortured by seeing you and not being able to touch you in those places that I wanted to feel, that I only caressed that one brief moment," he said as his hands slid across her soft curves and Grace sighed.

"Sam, I've felt the same way. Now, I can really explore you as you are discovering me," Grace said before did just that, running her small hands over Sam's hard body.

Sam didn't sigh, but he was ready to begin making other noises as he began kissing her all over.

She wanted him so badly it ached. and Sam felt the same, but as much as Sam wanted Grace, he wanted even more for her to feel his love and passion, so he took longer to make her experience nothing less than magical, knowing that her only experiences in this realm were short, often disgusting or violent episodes.

Grace had been slightly worried that she wouldn't feel the glow that Sam had promised, but that worry evaporated when he first kissed her, and she felt his skin against hers. It was as if he was on fire and the heat just flowed through her. This wasn't making love. This was just love.

When they were laying molded together forty minutes later, it was Grace who spoke, in a low, husky voice.

"Sam, you undersold this. I've never come close to anything like that before," she said as she leaned across and kissed him, "Love does make all the difference. I wanted so hard to please you, I felt almost guilty with all the pleasure I was feeling, but it was so wonderful."

"I wish I could tell you from experience that it was going to be like this, Grace, but I explained it to each of you from what I thought it should be. I have never felt this way, either. It was incredible. It feels perfect having you so close to me and I never want to let you go, Grace."

Grace wedged in even closer and they remained that way for a while, but not for very long before they resumed their exploration.

———

The sky was getting lighter when Grace gave Sam one last kiss and slipped from the blankets. Sam watched appreciatively as she stood and slid her nightdress over her naked body before she smiled at him as she opened the door and padded away.

Sam finally sighed and got out of bed, dressed and went out to the kitchen to make coffee and visit the little house. A few minutes later, Grace joined him after her own quick visit to the privy.

As she stepped within range, Sam plucked her from the ground and kissed her, then whispered, "I see that you are dressed, Grace. That's too bad. I wouldn't mind having my way with you."

Grace whispered back, "If it wasn't for the presence of another adult in the house, I would have already yanked you into the nearest bedroom and ravaged you."

424

"I wouldn't let you leave the kitchen," he answered as he let his hand wander to one of her perfect breasts.

She had her head back with her eyes closed and sighed before he knew that they had to stop and set her gently to the floor.

Grace opened her eyes, then took a deep breath before she walked to the shelf and retrieved the skillet and the coffee pot.

Julia arrived a few minutes later, took one look at them and knew instantly where they had spent the night and what they had been doing to pass the dark hours.

Then she began laughing and asked, "Couldn't wait two more days, could you?"

Sam and Grace looked at Julia and then at each other before they joined in the laughter.

After breakfast. Sam wanted to inspect the damage to the ranch house more closely, and after he had gone, Julia sidled up next to Grace.

"Well, Grace? Did Sam exaggerate? I mean, let's face it, we've done this quite a few times. It can't be that much different."

Grace closed her eyes, recalling the night, then sighed and opened them again.

"Julia, if anything, Sam understated the experience. It was nothing short of miraculous. It was amazing. When I was with him, it was like nothing else in the world mattered. I couldn't get close enough. Even when we were together, I wanted him even closer. We cared so much about each other that all we

425

could do was to try to make each other happy. Julia, it was as close to heaven as I could imagine."

Grace had her eyes closed again by the time she finished and shivered at the memory.

Julia watched her friend and was awed by her emotional experience. She saw Grace's glowing face as she relived the night in her mind. *Sam hadn't been making it up at all!*

Grace opened her eyes again and said, "Julia, do you know how much Sam loves me? After we were mad at him for going after Soapy, I asked him later if he was afraid. He told me that he wasn't afraid at all. His word was that he was 'resigned' to death. He had even told the undertaker when he dropped off Carol that if he didn't return that afternoon to bury him in the family cemetery.

"I was furious with him and asked him if he cared for me so little that he didn't realize that his dying would destroy me. He said, so very quietly, that he had to stop Soapy from sending someone else here to try to kill Catherine and risk having me die as well. It wasn't any kind of false bravado or loose words to try to impress me, Julia. My man would rather die than to risk having someone hurt me. How can anyone love someone else that much?"

Julia stared at Grace for ten quiet seconds before she replied, "I didn't know, Grace. I knew he sacrificed a lot to protect us all, but that is beyond belief."

"I know. It just confirmed what I already knew. I had to do anything I could to protect him. When we go to St. Louis, I know that he'll be in danger, but I'll be ready to do what I need to do to keep him safe."

"I am really happy for you, Grace. That's not just some pleasantry. It pleased me immensely to see you and Sam so happy when you were together. I want that kind of happiness, too. Maybe it'll be with Zeke. I don't know. But now I know it's out there waiting for me. Sam has done so much for us, Grace. How can we let him know?"

"He knows. I think what makes him happiest is how much we've changed. That's why Carol's death hit him harder than it even affected us. He knew that she had just had her life returned to her when some greedy bastard took it away. Sam was crushed by her loss and wants no more losses. Luckily for us, he's very good at what he does."

"I'll say. Zeke was telling me that the whole city was talking about him like he was some mythical hero."

"He is one. Look how much he has done to avenge and protect those close to him. Now there is only one of them left. If he wasn't such a miserable son-of-a-bitch, I'd almost pity Ferguson Short."

———

Eight hundred miles away in St. Louis, Ferguson Short sat at his desk at Short Shipping. He was furious. Ever since that botched assassination that had only claimed Richard, he had someone bring him a copy of *The Rocky Mountain News* every day. It may have been three days old, but it told him a lot. He had been following events closely, watching for anything that could scuttle his plans. His long-delayed plans because that idiot in Denver hadn't produced the bodies of the wife or the kid.

He may have been on the board of directors now, pending resolution of the company's status regarding his cousin's will, but he wasn't even getting paid for it, as the position was just honorary until the wife and daughter were legally declared dead. He was so close, too; just a few more weeks, but then this happened, he thought as he shook the newspaper.

He had intently read about Soapy Smith's demise at the hands of Richard's brother-in-law, according to the newspaper. It was all there in black and white.

He didn't care in the least about that idiot Soapy Smith's death and the destruction of his whole gang. It was that other piece of news that had enraged him. The one that had thrown his plans into such disarray. The one line that he cared very much about that said that before Brown had killed them all, he had rescued his niece, Catherine Short, heir to the Short fortune. *How the hell could she be alive*?

He had to do something before any of the directors got wind of the story, too. Luckily, few paid any attention to the news out West.

They were making this Brown character to be some sort of hero too. They even had his picture right there on the front page, and, to make matters worse, he had the kid. The kid that was supposed to be dead, and like a five-year-old Lazarus, that damned brat shows up still alive. *And he had to discover that little tidbit of information when he read the Denver newspaper!*

Ferguson hurled the newspaper across his room, only to have it explode into separate sheets and float gently to his carpeted floor.

Ferguson was still fuming about the Denver tough guy's bumbling. That money he had sent to Soapy Smith had drastically cut into his personal resources, and the idiot had told him that every one of them had been killed shortly after he'd gotten the money, but they had only produced Richard's body and claimed that wild animals had walked off with the wife and kid. So much for that lie.

He had to think. He knew that Brown would have to bring the kid to St. Louis now to meet with his cousin's attorney to claim her inheritance, and he'd have to stop that from happening.

There were only two trains a day that arrived from Denver, the express and the normal run. He couldn't see him taking the long ride with the little girl, so he'd take the express. He'd have his man board it in Kansas City, check the passengers and if they weren't there, he'd get off at the next stop and board it the next day and check those passengers. He may not find them until he boarded the train in Columbia, but he'd find them.

He realized that the newspaper might help, so he stood, walked to the scattered *Rocky Mountain News* and picked up the front page, folding it until only the picture of that cowboy showed.

This wasn't going to be as clean as the first one should have been, but it could be done.

No more games this time; the only thing left to do would be to stop Brown and the child from walking into that lawyer's office.

CHAPTER 15

Sam had ridden Cump south to talk to the Bar C owner, and Mister Crandall was more than pleased to offer his home as a refuge for Julia and Sam's daughter. It had been a long time since there had been a woman in the house, and he felt that caring for Catherine would help ease his guilt for harboring her mother's murderer.

Meanwhile, as Sam was setting up Julia and Catherine's sanctuary, Zeke was driving Dan Grant crazy. He kept offering to go and check on Sam, to make sure that none of Soapy's associates were stalking him, or he'd offer to head south for some other reason. Dan thought very highly of Zeke, and was happy with his performance as a lawman, but this love-struck Zeke was something different. Finally, around two o'clock, Dan gave in and kicked Zeke out of the office. He needed the peace.

Zeke only needed to be told once before he thanked Dan, even shook his hand, and was gone in a cloud of dust. Dan smiled as he left, remembering when he was young and met Irene. Those were heady times.

Zeke didn't kill his horse on the seven-mile trip, but the beast wasn't too pleased with the man on her back when he arrived. He made the trip in thirty-two minutes. Finally, he walked the labored animal down the access road to the Circle S.

Sam was on the porch, making minor repairs where he could when he heard the hooves and turned, not surprised to see Zeke a few hours early. Sam smiled and shook his head, but he understood his eagerness, and hoped it worked out for both of them.

"Afternoon, Zeke. A little early for dinner, isn't it?" he asked when Zeke was close enough to hear him.

"Well, things were slow in the office now that you're behaving yourself, Sam," Zeke replied as he stepped down from his exhausted horse.

"Zeke, I think you'd better take care of your horse. I think she's about to collapse."

"She needed a good run."

"Well, you go and take care of that girl before you go taking care of the human one."

Zeke nodded, and with his face a light shade of crimson, led his horse into the barn.

Sam watched him go, then turned and walked into the house, knowing that Julia was in Catherine's room with his daughter. She was sewing when Sam stepped into the room and Catherine smiled at him. He returned her smile before looking down at Julia.

"Julia, someone just rode up on a horse that was ready to fall over. He's in the barn seeing if he can get the poor animal revived."

"Zeke's here already?" she asked with enthusiasm.

"I can't imagine why."

Julia smiled, popped to her feet, then winked at Sam and left the room, leaving her hem half-done.

"Where's Aunt Julia going?" Catherine asked.

"To the barn, unless I'm missing something."

"Why? Is she going to see Suede?"

"No. Remember that deputy sheriff she was talking to yesterday? Well, he came to visit."

"Oh. This is one of those things."

"Exactly," Sam said, laughing at her perfect description of the situation.

"Let's go visit your mama."

"Okay."

Sam took her hand and led her to the kitchen where Grace was baking some biscuits. She never seemed to have enough around for some inexplicable reason.

"Grace, Julia just went out to the barn," he said as he released Catherine's hand.

"Is that significant?"

"Zeke showed up early and his horse was in sad shape because he'd been in a bit of a rush to come to dinner. He's taking care of the horse now. He must really be hungry."

Grace laughed and answered, "Hungry, maybe, but not for food."

"Catherine described it perfectly. She said, 'it's one of those things.'."

Grace laughed again and said, "That's about as right as I've ever heard it defined."

"We could get a little payback and walk over to the barn."

"We could, but it's too early. We'll have to strike when the timing is perfect."

Catherine just sat in her chair smiling at her new parents while her little dogs slept in the warmest room in the house.

Julia stayed in the barn for a long time after the horse was brushed and fed. They spent most of the time talking and getting to know each other better now that the initial giddiness of their first meeting was past.

Grace did the cooking for dinner, knowing better than ask help from Sam and not expecting any assistance from Julia.

When they finally entered the house and took a seat at the table, Zeke and Julia were lively during dinner and tried to avoid ignoring Sam and Grace, but Sam and Grace didn't mind if they did.

————

After Zeke had gone and Sam was spending time with Catherine and her puppies in he bedroom, Grace asked Julia how it was going.

"Grace, Zeke knows my history and told me it didn't matter at all. We talked for a while about his past, too. He's had an interesting life. Did you know that he grew up in an orphanage just like me? When he left, he didn't know what he was going to do, but found a job at the sheriff's office as a jailer, then he became a deputy when another deputy was shot, and he's been there with Sheriff Grant now for six years. We are both the same age, too, but I'm a bit older. He's a very sweet man, Grace."

"Well, Julia, the decision is yours about where it goes from here. We'll be here for you no matter what you decide."

"Thank you, Grace. So, are you going to sneak off again tonight?"

"I can foresee that happening. I'm just so comfortable with Sam," Grace said followed by a soft sigh.

Sam and his daughter, followed by the fast-growing Sophie and Millie, could be heard entering the main room and Catherine was laughing as the puppies ran loops around the room, chasing each other.

Sam assumed that Grace and Julia were talking about Zeke, and that he'd be able to ask her about it later.

———

After they were all in bed, Grace did as Julia had expected and quickly and silently made her way to Sam's room as he lay under his quilts, anxiously awaiting her arrival. He smiled at her as she repeated the previous night's disrobing and entry to his bed. She immediately snuggled in tight, taking advantage of his heat.

Sam pulled her close and before he could say or do anything, she said, "Sam, there's something that has been bothering me for a while."

"What is it, Grace? Maybe I can help."

"Well, it's difficult, but I need to talk to you about it. In all the time I was in that place, the one thing that had me most worried was if I got pregnant. I never did, and part of it was because of the ways that we learned quickly to avoid it, but it didn't work that well. Now, more than anything, I want to have a baby, but I'm afraid that I can't conceive anymore. I don't know if there's something wrong with me or I've been damaged. Sam, I want to have a baby with you so much and I'd feel like I failed somehow if I couldn't."

Sam could feel her shaking as she spoke and knew how much it meant to her.

"Grace, let me ask you something. Did any of the girls at Waxman's get pregnant?"

Grace had to think back for a few seconds before replying, "No. Now that you mention it, none of us did."

"There's a plant that the Indians use to prevent their women from getting pregnant. From what I hear, it has a bitter, sour taste. Did Freddie give you anything that tasted like that?"

"Is that what it was? Freddie told us it was a vitamin."

"So, my love, now that you are now in my bed and haven't been drugged for months, I would think that it will be a short time before your tummy starts growing."

Grace's mood picked up immensely as she asked, "Do you think so, Sam? Really? You're not just telling me that to make me feel better."

"Grace, I'm telling you what I truly believe. We have Catherine to raise, and I believe she'll have a little sister to play with before long."

"Not a son?" she asked as she smiled.

435

"Nope. I seem to have this tendency to collect females."

She buried her face in his chest to keep the sound of her laughter inside the room.

After she calmed down, she looked at Sam and whispered, "Then, let's not waste time, Sam."

They didn't waste time for much of the night and the early morning.

————

The next day Sam had Julia and Catherine pack for a week. Mister Crandall assured Sam that there would be enough room and food for them, so they only needed to bring their clothing. He also vowed that he would make sure his cow hands behaved themselves, but Sam wasn't worried. They had all seen what he did to the biggest of them.

At nine o'clock, Sam and Grace took the front seats of the carriage with Julia and Catherine in the back. Catherine had been worried about her puppies, but Sam assured her that they would be cared for in her absence. Zeke had promised to stop by and bring them food, so she was mollified, but would still miss Sophie and Millie.

After the hour and a half drive, Orville Crandall met them at the house wearing a grandfatherly smile. When he saw Catherine being helped out of the carriage he stepped forward and greeted the little girl with a gentle handshake.

They all went inside and made introductions, then Orville explained the ranch layout and showed them their bedrooms. Sam had already explained the threat against Catherine on the last visit, and Orville had been outraged that any man would threaten a child. He said he'd ensure his hands were briefed on the situation and put on alert for any possible intruders.

After everything was settled, Sam and Grace said their goodbyes to Julia and Catherine. Julia's parting words were, "Stay safe."

Sam and Grace boarded the carriage, waving at Orville, Julia and Catherine as they rolled away.

———

It was just after noon when Sam turned the carriage north to go to Denver.

Sam pulled Grace close to him and said, "Our final test, Grace. One more bad apple and then we can live our lives as we want to."

"I hope so, Sam."

They rode past the Circle S as they needed to go to Denver to buy some things before the trip.

After arriving in Denver, they found a leather goods store and purchased two travel bags and a medium-sized trunk, and Sam also bought a money belt.

Then Sam drove to the bank but didn't take her inside. Instead, he took Grace to the shop next door, where he had bought the turquoise necklaces.

"We'll be needing some rings, my love," he said as he smiled at her.

"I'd totally forgotten," she replied, embarrassed to admit it.

"I hadn't. Let's go inside."

When they had entered the jewelry store, they were immediately greeted by a clerk; the same man who had sold Sam the three necklaces, one of which he spied around the lady's neck.

"Back again, sir?"

"Yes, we'll be needing a wedding band set."

"Congratulations, sir and miss. Please follow me."

He took them to a large glass case with rows of rings of all types. Sam and Grace picked out a simple yet elegant set. They had their fingers measured and the clerk picked out the correct size.

"Will that be all?" he asked.

Grace answered 'yes' while Sam answered 'no', and she looked at him curiously.

"Do you have one of the sapphire rings in my fiancée's size?"

The salesman's face lit up. It was going to be a good day.

"Yes, sir," he replied as reached below the counter and produced a small blue box.

When he opened it, Grace gasped. It was exquisite in its elegance and simplicity, and the band was the same color as the wedding set that they had picked out.

"That is perfect," Sam said, "If you'll package the rings, I'll settle the bill."

"The total is $95.45."

Sam wrote out a bank draft and handed it to the clerk who passed the small leather bag to Sam.

"Thank you for your business, sir. It's been a pleasure."

"Thank you for your help," Sam replied.

They left the store and climbed into the carriage. Grace was still speechless.

After they had left the city behind, Sam brought the team to a stop, opened the small leather bag and removed the smaller box.

"Grace, when I saw this ring. I saw your eyes and I knew it belonged to you."

He opened the box and took her hand, slipping it onto her finger where he would place the wedding band tomorrow.

"Sam, I don't know what to say. This is beautiful, and I love it, but it was so much money."

"Well, you're beautiful and I love you, so the money in unimportant. My whole life is about you now, Grace."

She hugged him and kissed him, but not for the ring.

They finished the ride to the ranch, and when they arrived, they were greeted by its only occupants, Sophie and Millie, who seemed more interested in chasing the horses than the humans.

Grace decided she'd go to the carriage house with him, so they took the carriage and horses to their home. After the horses were put away, Grace took the two travel bags and Sam took the trunk to their silent home.

"The house seems so empty," Grace said once they were inside and had set down their new luggage.

"It does seem naked, doesn't it?"

"Let's get our things packed so we won't be in a rush tomorrow. When did Judge McLean expect us?"

"We're going to be in his chambers at ten o'clock. After the ceremony, and you are my bride, Grace, we'll take Dan and Zeke to lunch and then we'll ride over to the train depot. There's a livery next door so we can leave the carriage and they'll take the trunk straight to the station. We board our train at 3:35. It's going to be a long ride, sweetheart. We'll arrive in St. Louis around seven o'clock the following day, and that's only because it's the express train and only stops at major cities for water and coal. Then we'll go to our hotel and recover, and we'll go to see the U.S. Marshal the next morning to see what develops after that."

"It sounds like a busy day."

"Except it will be boring most of the time until we get there. Let's start packing our clothes."

Sam took his travel bag and put in two pairs of pants, three shirts, socks and underwear, and his shaving kit. He was done, so he wandered to Grace's room.

He found her staring at the open travel bag.

"What should I take with me?" she asked.

"Well, take three changes of clothes and put those in the trunk. I have nothing for the trunk anyway. All I need is in my travel bag. You'll be wearing a dress tomorrow and carrying a purse, so that gives you four different dresses. You won't need any pants or riding skirts. If I were you, I'd put all your toiletry items in your travel bag. I'll be carrying those on the train, so we'll have them with us. Before I forget, I need to show you something."

He led Grace into the kitchen and slid the rug away. Then he took his knife and popped open the security board and removed the leather bag. She watched as he placed the contents on the table, which is why he bought the money belt.

"When I first arrived on the ranch, I thought it had been a robbery attempt. Richard had shown me the safe location he had made. This is what I found inside. I knew it hadn't been a robbery because it was here. I'd rather not leave that much money under the floor anyway. But here's what's interesting."

He handed her the senior Short's letter to his son. After reading it, she handed it back.

"He loved Richard dearly. He seemed like a good man," she said.

"I thought so, too. He let Richard be his own man without animosity. Not too many fathers do that. I'm taking that letter to St. Louis, along with Catherine's birth certificate, the adoption papers and the note from Soapy Smith. I'll put them in this money belt along with most of the money. I don't want to have to write bank drafts in St. Louis on a Denver bank. I want you to take fifty dollars and keep it in your purse. I'll have a hundred dollars in cash for expenses and another two hundred in emergency funds in the money belt."

"Do we need that much money?"

"I have no idea, but it's better than running out."

"Okay."

"I need to go to Carol's room and get her derringer. I want you to keep yours in your purse. I'll keep Carol's in my pocket. I'll have the Webley as well, but that'll be all our protection. Unless you carry your knife around your thigh."

"I don't. Do you want me to?"

"Only if I get to strap it on and off," he replied with a grin.

Grace smiled and said, "That sounds like an exciting offer, sir. Sam, do you think, well, you know, being alone in an empty house and it's the middle of the day and, well, we never…"

"Say no more, my love. And this should be even better."

"Why?"

"Because we get to undress each other and see what we're getting into before the wedding."

"What, you weren't inspecting enough before?"

"Not like I will now in the bright light of day."

He lifted Grace off her feet and carried her willingly to her bedroom.

CHAPTER 16

Early the next morning, Grace made a quick breakfast, still wearing her night dress. Sam had been boiling water for her bath for twenty minutes knowing it would make the trip a bit easier for her.

Their bags were packed, and Sam had found Carol's derringer and made sure it was loaded. He checked Grace's derringer as well and pocketed four spare rounds of the .41 caliber ammunition. They decided to forgo the knife.

While Grace was bathing, Sam dressed in his suit. Once he was satisfied with his appearance, he walked to the carriage house and harnessed the grays.

He rolled the carriage to the front of the house, hitched them to the rail and went inside. Grace was finishing dressing in her room with the door open, letting Sam watch as he leaned against the doorjamb, appreciating the show.

When he returned after loading the carriage, Grace was ready, so Sam picked up her travel bag and carried it to the carriage, Grace closed the front door behind her and stepped to the carriage and climbed in. She was serene on the outside but bubbling with emotion inside. In just a few hours she'd be married to a man she loved completely and was still in a state of disbelief and wondered if it would ever end.

Sam unhitched the team, climbed into the seat and the carriage rolled out of the ranch toward Denver. Sam was somewhat negligent in his handling of the team as he had one arm around his bride. For the entire ride, they said nothing, but would just steal smiles and an occasional quick kiss as the team carried them to the start of their lives together as husband and wife.

———

Forty-five minutes later, Sam pulled the carriage up to the sheriff's office, climbed down from the carriage and, although she hardly needed it, held Grace's hand as she stepped down.

"Thank you, Mister Brown," Grace said with a demure smile.

"Your servant, ma'am," Sam replied, smiling at Miss Felton who shortly would be Mrs. Brown.

Grace hooked her arm in his as they entered the office.

Zeke popped up from the front desk and said, "Good morning, Sam, Grace."

"Good morning, Zeke," answered Sam, "You and the boss ready to go over to the courthouse?"

"Last chance to get out of this," Dan commented as he came around the corner.

"I'd rather get out of having to see your ugly mug again," Sam retorted.

Dan smiled and stepped up to Grace and kissed her on the cheek before he said, "You're getting a good man, Grace."

"The best," she replied, her eyes sparkling as she looked at Sam.

Zeke was hoping he could make the same walk to the courthouse or church with Julia sometime in the future.

Sam kept Grace on his arm as they set out for the courthouse, trailed by the two lawmen. Sam was recognized by several strangers because his face had been on the front page of *The Rocky Mountain News* the day after the big shooting. The artist who had drawn the picture relied on the memory of the schoolmarm reporter he had met. She had a good memory, so it was quite accurate.

They entered the courthouse and Dan led the way to Judge McLean's offices. The judge was already waiting for the couple, but Sam and Grace had to stop at his clerk's desk and fill out a form, which only took a few minutes, then they and their witnesses were ushered into the judge's chambers.

It was a very un-ceremonial ceremony. The judge would drop an occasional comment about the events that had led to this day but to Grace, it didn't matter. She had known many young women who had demanded large, fancy weddings, and doubted if any of their marriages were as successful as she knew hers would be. She just looked at Sam's face and saw the glow that she knew would be there. No big wedding or fancy clothes could replace what she felt as she and Sam shared much more than words.

Sam hadn't listened to the judge at all, as he stared at his bride. She was smiling and there was something more. Grace was glowing with the reflection of his love for her. This is what he had been trying to explain to his ladies so often.

When Judge McLean pronounced them man and wife, Sam kissed his new wife softly. He and Grace then took another ten seconds taking a journey into each other's eyes and souls before returning to reality.

They finally turned and smiled at everyone in the small party.

The judge exercised his option as senior man and kissed the bride. Dan and Zeke stood in line, and then there were handshakes all around before the newlyweds went off to a restaurant with Dan and Zeke.

It was too early for lunch, so they decided to have some coffee and ice cream to pass the time until they could eat and ordered lunch forty minutes later. By the time they had had their coffee and paid the bill, it was time to head for the depot.

They boarded the train on time and because Sam had splurged for first-class tickets, the seating was comfortable; at least for the first hundred miles. The train surged through the night. It had a full coal load but needed to stop for water every hundred miles or so, but the express had priority, so it saved more than sixteen hours on what was already an exhaustive journey.

———

As the sun rose the next morning, Grace was sore from sleeping in the seat and sitting so long and found relief by walking the aisle every hour or so. At ten o'clock in the morning, they stopped in Kansas City.

Sam had been observing the other passengers as they boarded, as he had at the other stops along the way. He hadn't seen anyone that looked suspicious until the last passenger came on board.

It wasn't as if he had a BAD MAN sign on his forehead that made Sam suspicious. It was that he seemed to be examining the passengers, especially the men, until he saw Sam, then he stopped scanning, locked his eyes on Sam for a moment and then hurriedly looked away. He tried to appear casual as he walked past, and Sam marked his attire.

Sam stabbed Grace's thigh with his fingers, and she looked at him smiling, until she caught his eye and saw that he wasn't being playful. Sam indicated with his eyes to look at the man who just passed. Trying not to be conspicuous, Grace stood and walked to the front of the car, acted as if she was reading the posted instructions, then returned, taking a quick look at him. Then she sat down but said nothing to Sam. Sam was proud of how she had managed to get a look at the man without appearing to be doing just that.

The train restarted fifteen minutes later and was soon rolling across the Missouri farmland.

"Sam, what do you think?" she said in a normal tone as she pointed out the window.

Sam looked outside but didn't care what he saw.

In a low voice, he said, "I'm certain he's a Ferguson hire. He recognized me, probably from that *Rocky Mountain News* story. He won't try anything here. There are too many people and it's broad daylight. He'll wait until we get to St. Louis where it'll be dark, and he knows that we'll be getting off the train."

"What will we do then?"

"It depends on what he does. Keep your purse close, though."

"Okay."

The train rolled on. The next main stop was Columbia, Missouri, and Grace continued her hourly walks. Most of the customers were used to her taking them, and some of the others did as well. Grace took a good look at the man as she passed. On one of her walks, Sam took the opportunity to move the Webley from its shoulder holster to his right jacket pocket. Since they had departed from Kansas City, he was thinking of different ways to prevent the violence that the man was planning.

———

Jim Watson was thoroughly confused as he sat on his seat. His orders said there would be a man matching Sam's picture that he had in his pocket and a little girl. The man most assuredly matched the drawing, but if the woman with him was a little girl, he'd better go back to the third grade.

He was still wondering after the train made its last stop before St. Louis. He really hadn't wanted the job, but he was in desperate shape and needed the money. His orders were to kill them both, which bothered him when he was told what to do, and he'd come up with the idea of just taking the little girl to an orphanage rather than shooting her. But now, the man was with a pretty woman and not the girl. *Did that mean that without the little girl, he was supposed to shoot the woman? Damn!*

Grace sat down after her last jaunt, then in a low voice said, "He's troubled about something. You can see it in his face. His mouth is tight, and his eyes are staring off into nowhere."

"I think I know what it is, too. I'll bet Ferguson thought I'd be bringing Catherine with me. He doesn't know about the adoption because it wasn't in any of the stories in the paper. The only ones who knew were the judge, Dan, Zeke and the family. He doesn't know what to do about you. That gives us an advantage. I think he'll wait until we're separated somehow."

"Sam, what can we do?"

448

"I think I'll go say hello."

"What? Sam, you can't shoot him!" she exclaimed in a whisper.

"I don't intend to. I'll be right back."

Sam stood, stepped past Grace and walked down the aisle. The man was studiously looking out the window as Sam swung down and sat next to him, then he jerked his head around, looking at Sam.

"Good afternoon!" Sam said cheerily.

"Afternoon," he replied.

"Say, how is Ferguson these days?"

The question stunned Watson and he began to believe that Ferguson might have been setting him up for some reason.

He replied, "I don't know anyone by that name."

"Sure, you do. Ferguson Short. He's the man that hired you to kill me."

Things were getting worse for Watson now as sweat began to form on his forehead. *It was bad enough that he didn't like the job in the first place, and then there was the added confusion of the woman, but now this?*

"Are you a nut case or something? Leave me alone!"

"Did Ferguson tell you who I was before he sent you on the errand? Or did he just give you that picture from *The Rocky Mountain News*?"

"I got no idea what you're talking about, mister."

"Well, Ferguson must not care if you live or die. You see, the reason that they put that picture in the newspaper was because a little while back, I was mighty angry with a thug leader named Soapy Smith. He was a big gang leader in Denver. So, I walked in there and killed eight of his gunmen and then Soapy himself.

"Now Soapy had been hired by Ferguson to kill my family. He killed my brother-in-law and kidnapped my beautiful sister and her four-year-old daughter. My sister died because of him, but I rescued their little girl. You know, the one you were sent to kill along with me? Now, how happy am I going to be with you if you try to kill me or my wife?"

Watson was beyond nervous. He had heard snippets about the shootout. *This guy took out a whole crew by himself? Why hadn't Ferguson told him that little piece of information?*

"By this time tomorrow, United States Marshal Thomas Charles is going to be arresting Ferguson, and he will hang for what he did. The question is; do you want to join him?"

Watson began reaching for straws.

"You ain't even armed."

"Now, there you go making errors in judgment. I have two guns on me right now. Even my wife is armed. And now, I know you, and I'll be looking for you. And do you know something else? I was a lawman for over nine years and took down dozens of gunmen and general bad men. I've never even gotten a scratch. Even if you didn't include those nine at Soapy's, I've taken out six miscreants in the past four months. So, don't think you're messing with some newbie who's afraid to fill you full of lead. If I get angry enough, somebody dies. If you have half a brain, you'll light out when we get to St. Louis. You can live a long and happy life; all you have to do is leave."

Watson didn't say anything. He was too busy balancing facts.

Sam could see him thinking, so he said, "Well, I'm going back to see my wife. We just got married, and I love my wife dearly. Anyone who threatens to hurt her would make me angrier than I've ever been before. Have a nice day."

Sam stood and walked back to Grace.

Sam had intentionally spoken in a little higher than normal speaking voice so that some of the other passengers could hear it over the train noise, and quite a few did.

Watson knew they had as well, so it was no use to continue. They had all seen his face. Even if he could do the job, he'd be wanted for murder. Then, there was the wife. *She was armed? To hell with Ferguson!* He had only paid him fifty dollars for the job anyway. Besides, if Ferguson was going to jail, it didn't matter anyway. As soon as he made his decision, he felt an enormous sense of relief.

Grace watched Sam slide in next to her after she had moved to the window side of the seat. She had heard most of what he had said, and was just going to ask him about it when she saw someone appear next to Sam. It was that man, and every eye in the place was on him as he drew his pistol.

"Brown," Watson said, "I got no quarrel with you. Ferguson only paid me fifty dollars for the job. I was broke and needed the money. I didn't want to kill no kid anyway, but I'm leaving. Here's my Colt to show you I'm serious."

He handed the gun butt first to Sam.

Sam looked at the weapon, reached into his pocket, took out two twenty-dollar gold pieces and handed them to him.

"I appreciate you coming clean. This will help you get away from St. Louis. You can keep your gun."

Watson slipped his Colt back in his holster and stuck out his hand. Sam shook it and Watson left the car to cross over to the next one.

As soon as the back door closed, the other passengers broke into applause.

Grace looked at him and marveled that he could have pulled this off without bloodshed.

Then she said, "I am ever so grateful to be your wife."

"Grace, people think I'm a violent man because of all the things that have happened, but I hate doing it. If I can avoid violence, it's always better."

Then he returned his Webley back to his shoulder holster where it belonged and took Grace's hand.

———

The train arrived in Denver a little early at 6:45. The first passenger off the train was Jim Watson, who stepped off the still-moving passenger car and disappeared into the streets of St. Louis.

Sam and Grace disembarked and stood on the platform waiting for their trunk. Sam had watched Watson leave and trusted his instincts that he would never see the man again. Passengers came by and shook his hand and tipped their hats to Grace on their way to their homes and families to tell them about the amazing experience they had witnessed on the train.

When their trunk was brought to the platform, Sam had the porter take it to a line of carriages for hire. The trunk was loaded on back, and Sam told the driver to take them to the Metropolitan Hotel. It was an upscale hotel, and close to the U.S. Marshal's Office. At least, it looked that way on the city map he had in his pocket.

They took a room and paid for five nights. Sam was tempted to ask for the bridal suite, but he knew Grace would find the décor a bit too ostentatious for them, as would he. Even the normal room was a bit showy, but Grace was pleasantly surprised with the fully equipped bathroom with hot and cold running water and a flush toilet.

"Sam, we need to get one of these put in our house. It would save us those cold runs to the privy."

"Then we'll do that when we return, so why don't you relax while I go take a nice, long bath."

"Mister Brown! I don't think you understand a woman's need for a bath after a long trip."

"Mrs. Brown, haven't you learned yet that I love to tweak your cute nose?"

Grace walked up to Sam, wrapped her arms around his neck and smiled as she said, "Could you call me that again, Mister Brown."

"Mrs. Brown, I love you. Now go ahead and take your bath while I unpack."

Grace kissed him, then hurriedly ran to the bathroom and closed the door. Sam heard the toilet flush and then the sound of running water and smiled. He hoped she wasn't going to ask for hot and cold running water next, but if she did, he knew he'd have it installed regardless of the cost.

He began unpacking. There was a closet with coat hangers, so he hung her dresses and his pants, and moved their other clothes into drawers.

He was relaxing when the door opened, and Grace came out with her blonde hair still wet and wearing a thick hotel bathrobe.

"Sam, they have bottles of shampoo in there. I feel so much better."

"Well, I'll get cleaned up and we can go down to get something to eat."

"Good food would be a step up from what we had on the train or even at some of the stops."

Sam walked up to her and hugged her. When he kissed her, he untied the robe and slid his hands underneath.

An hour later, they emerged from their room and went downstairs to the restaurant.

Grace was right. The good food and a hot bath did wonders for relaxing after the long train ride, as did the break between the bath and the food.

They returned to the room immediately after leaving the hotel restaurant, undressed, crawled into bed and promptly fell asleep; newlyweds or not.

———

The next morning, Sam and Grace dressed, Grace took another bath, and was wise enough to bring her clothing into the bathroom and dress there rather than spending another hour in bed. They had things to do.

Sam knew it as well, and as much as he enjoyed the robe event, he wanted to go and meet with Marshal Charles.

After a very big breakfast, Sam and Grace left the hotel. There was a light drizzle, but both were wearing jackets and it was a short walk, so they stepped off and crossed the two blocks to the office of the United States Marshal.

It was a surprisingly small and utilitarian building, and once there, Sam opened the door for Grace before he entered.

There was a deputy marshal at the desk who asked, "May I help you?"

"I'm Sam Brown from Denver. Sheriff Dan Grant told me to see Marshall Charles when I arrived."

"Yes, sir. I'll let him know you are here. And, may I add, we were all very impressed with your actions in Denver in taking out Soapy Smith."

"Thank you, Deputy. I appreciate it."

The deputy stepped around a second desk and walked back into a hallway. Thirty seconds later he trailed a much larger man. Sam assumed it was the marshal, and he was. Sam guessed he was a little taller than he was, maybe six feet and three inches and outweighed him by twenty pounds.

"Mister Brown, mind if I call you Sam?" he asked, before saying, "Dan wrote quite a lot about you, so I feel I know you already. I'm Thomas Charles," then offered Sam his hand, which he shook.

"Sam is fine, Marshal."

"Call me Thomas. And you must be Grace," he said as he shook Grace's hand as well, "Come back to my office and you can give me more details."

He led them down a long corridor until he reached the last office that looked like it had been made from taking out a wall between two smaller offices. He sat behind his desk and offered the two chairs for his visitors. Sam held the chair for Grace as she sat.

"Sam, Dan gave me the basics. I'm really sad for your losses. When greedy men want something, they don't care who they hurt to get it. Dan said you were here to have Ferguson Short of Short Shipping arrested for ordering the murders and kidnapping."

"That's right. He's still active, too. Yesterday, on the train, I spotted a man who was obviously planning on killing me before we could make it to the Short Shipping Company. He admitted that Ferguson paid him fifty dollars to kill me and my daughter, who Ferguson thought was coming with us."

The marshal's eyebrows went up as he asked, "*Did you kill him*?"

"No, sir. I went back to where he was sitting and exposed him for an assassin and suggested he move on. He offered me his pistol and told me the story. I let him keep his gun and he left."

Charles leaned back in his chair and exclaimed, "You're kidding!"

Grace answered, "Thomas, he's not. After what he said to the man in a loud voice, he knew he couldn't do it because everyone in that car knew he had been hired to assassinate Sam. When Sam told him to keep his gun and gave him forty to buy a ticket out of St. Louis the whole car of passengers began clapping."

"So, would I, if I had I witnessed something like that."

Sam continued, saying, "The point is, Thomas, that Ferguson's getting desperate. He knows that he's out of time and options. I have no idea what he'll do next. My plan was to go to the boardroom and present the evidence against him. If you could send a deputy along to make the arrest it would be great. The murders occurred in Colorado, so only your office has the jurisdiction."

"Could I see the evidence you have against him?"

"Sure," Sam replied as he opened his shirt and took out the papers from the money belt.

He found the note and handed it to Charles, who read it, then sat back again and whistled.

"How did you get him to write this? Having the signature authenticated was a brilliant idea, by the way."

"When I entered his house and after his gunmen were gone, he tried to hide. But after I found him, he told me he wanted to make a deal. I pretended to agree, knowing he'd plug me in the back as soon as I tried to leave. He wrote that note, I turned to leave and heard what I thought was the hammer being pulled back. I rolled and shot him as his shot hit the wall where I had been."

457

"Thought you heard a hammer being pulled back?" the marshal asked with raised eyebrows.

"I have no idea what the sound was, whether it was his chair creaking, or a drawer being opened, but it set me into motion. I only found out later that he was trying to shoot me with a double-action revolver."

The marshal grinned and said, "You must be one lucky man. When you get back, you're going to have to tell me the whole story. Dan said your report read like a dime novel. I tell you what I'm going to do. I'll send a deputy with you, but I'd like to swear you in as a temporary U.S. Deputy Marshal. That way, anything you have to do to put him under arrest will be covered."

"That's good. Believe it or not, Thomas, I always prefer to let the law handle these miscreants. Even when I went into Soapy's, I offered them all a chance to surrender. You would think that staring down two barrels of double aught shot would be incentive to do that. I have no idea what they were thinking when they drew those hoglegs."

"As a rule, they aren't the brightest. Now let me swear you in."

Charles administered the oath and gave Sam his temporary badge, then gave him a John Doe warrant.

Sam turned to Grace and said, "Did you want to wait at the hotel?"

"No. I want to be there. I have my purse."

Sam nodded and said, "Okay."

Charles hadn't seen this one coming, and gave a glance to Sam, who said, "Thomas, my wife can use a Colt and a Winchester better than most men I know. She has a .41 caliber derringer in her purse, so I'm not worried about her in this situation. It's those damned drygulchers that Ferguson keeps hiring that worry me."

Charles understood and said, "Okay. This is your call. I'll send Deputy Marshal Dave Miller with you. He's a good man."

"Thanks, Thomas. We'll take a cab over to Short Shipping and see what it leads to."

They shook hands and Charles left his office to notify Deputy Miller.

Sam looked at Grace and said, "Let's end this."

Grace nodded, then stood and took Sam's hand.

A few minutes later, Charles brought an average-sized man with a ready smile and deep black hair with him.

"Sam, this is United States Deputy Marshall Dave Miller. I've given him the basics."

Sam shook Dave's hand and introduced him to Grace. Dave didn't seem to be taken aback by having a pert blonde woman along. Marshal Charles must have included that in the short briefing.

They went out front and hailed a cab. One stopped quickly and drove them to the offices of the Short Shipping Company, and after stopping, the driver asked if he wanted him to wait and Sam told him this may take some time and paid the fare.

The two men with badges on their chests escorted the pretty lady into the main office building, and Sam was impressed with the size. This was a big operation, and Sam recalled reading that their New Orleans offices were bigger.

They approached a reception desk that was staffed by a young woman slightly older than Grace, but not nearly as pretty.

"May I help you, gentlemen?"

Sam replied, "Yes, miss, we're here to serve an arrest warrant for Mister Ferguson Short. Is he in the building?"

"They are in a board meeting at the moment. You'll have to wait until it's over, I'm afraid. It'll be another thirty minutes or so."

"That's perfect. Now, miss, I want you to tell me where the board meeting is being held. Under no circumstances are you to notify anyone in that boardroom that we are here. Doing so would make you liable for charges of obstruction of justice. Do you understand?"

The young girl was shaken. This was well beyond her instructions as receptionist.

"The boardroom is on the second floor, the first door on your left," she squeaked.

"Thank you."

The girl was upset before but thoroughly mystified by Grace's presence.

The three climbed the stairs with Sam in the lead and Grace trailing Deputy Miller.

When they arrived outside the boardroom, they paused, then Sam looked at Deputy Marshal Miller, who nodded.

Sam opened the door and walked in with Dave Miller and Grace right behind.

One man stood and shouted righteously, *"What's the meaning of this?"*

Ferguson, who was in total shock at the sight of a man who should be in the river floating down to New Orleans by now, knew the meaning of this, but said nothing.

"I'm temporary United States Deputy Marshal Sam Brown and this is United States Deputy Marshal Dave Miller. We have a warrant for the arrest of Ferguson Short on multiple charges of soliciting murder and kidnapping."

Sam wasn't sure which one was Ferguson until he finished his declaration. Then all heads swiveled to the man in the first chair on the right. Sam was amazed when he set eyes on him because Grace's supposedly cartoon-like guess of his appearance was uncannily accurate. He didn't twirl his mustache, though, but he did pull on it.

The standing man looked at him and asked loudly, "Ferguson, what is this charge?"

Ferguson finally spoke, saying, "There must be some mistake. I had nothing to do with any murders. This is preposterous. I demand that you show just cause for intruding in this manner."

Ferguson firmly believed that they had no evidence that would stand up in court because he had been fastidious in keeping all correspondence between him and Soapy Smith unsigned. They might have hearsay, but nothing substantial.

The standing man, who Sam assumed was the president of the firm, turned to look at Sam and said, "I agree. I've known Mister Short for years. After the founder of the firm, Amos Short passed away last fall, and with the death of his son and wife and the loss of the only blood relative, his granddaughter, he will become the owner of the firm within two months. Without any evidence, you must leave this office."

Sam could see Ferguson thinking. He knew his bluff would be called if they knew about Catherine, so he quickly reached behind his jacket and pulled out his Webley, causing a loud gasp from the collective board members.

"Deputy Miller, could you please cuff Mister Short?"

"With pleasure, Deputy Brown."

With that, Dave Miller walked behind the right-hand row of executives and unceremoniously dumped Ferguson Short on the ground and placed his knee on the small of Ferguson's back. He snapped on a pair of handcuffs, then lifted the still unbelieving Ferguson Short to his feet.

Sam returned the Webley to the holster, walked up to Deputy Miller and said, "Dave, I have some more business with these gentlemen. Can you escort Mister Short to his new place of residence?"

"I was going to offer to do that very thing. I'll tell the marshal that you'll stop by as soon as you're done here."

"It may be a while, but I should be back by early afternoon."

Dave nodded and gripped Ferguson's arm and led him from the boardroom.

After Ferguson was gone, Sam looked at the staring eyes of the well-dressed businessmen and said, "Now, gentlemen, let me tell you what just happened. But first, I must make sure my beloved wife is comfortable."

He led her to Ferguson's seat, pulled it out for her, and Grace took the seat holding back her smile.

Sam began, saying, "After Amos Short died last year, Ferguson Short hired a gang leader in Denver named Soapy Short to murder his son Richard's entire family, including my sister and their daughter, Catherine, who was my niece."

One of the men spoke up, asking, "You said *was*. Does that mean that she has passed on?"

"No, sir. She's alive and well and staying at my ranch south of Denver. What I was saying is that she is no longer my niece, and that she is now legally my daughter. After her mother died, as her closest relative, I adopted her. She is a happy and vital little girl. I have her staying with a fellow rancher for her safety until Ferguson was arrested."

Sam let that piece of information sink in for a few seconds before continuing.

"I had been a sheriff in Boulder, Colorado for eight years and when I went down to Denver, I found the entire family gone. I checked their safe and found this letter."

He handed the letter to the president. After reading it, he passed it along.

As each of them read the short letter, Sam continued, saying, "I discovered that Soapy Smith had been behind the killings and kidnappings. By the way, my sister and her daughter were only alive because two of the gunmen sent to

463

kill Richard balked at killing a woman and a child. I subsequently found my sister had been murdered by a different man and found my niece.

"After another attempt at killing Catherine at our ranch failed, but resulted in the death of a dear friend, I entered the house of Soapy Smith and after I had eliminated his henchmen and had him under my pistol, he tried to bargain his way out by giving me this."

He reached into his pouch and drew out the signed confession and handed it to the president.

"If you notice, his signature has been authenticated by the bank where he did business. Gentlemen, that is the evidence that will hang Ferguson Short."

Sam didn't say anything more until the short note had been read by each of them. When the last executive handed the papers back to Sam, he returned them to his money pouch.

"Do any of you have any doubt as to his guilt?" Sam asked as he scanned their shocked faces.

They all shook their heads.

"Any questions?"

The president asked, "As Miss Short's legal father and her guardian..."

"Her name is now Catherine Brown, sir," Sam said, interrupting whatever he was going to say.

"Yes, of course. As her legal guardian, you have control over her finances?"

"Yes."

"We have a problem with having a young child as the owner of the firm. Unless you plan on staying here in St. Louis, there would be many difficulties going forward."

"Yes, I can understand that," Sam said, knowing what was coming.

They needed to buy out Catherine's interest, which is what he wanted anyway, but hoped that they didn't know that.

"I believe it would be in the best interest of all involved if we were to purchase Miss Short's, I mean Miss Brown's shares and return them to the company."

"How many shares are owned by the family?"

The president turned to another man, who had some papers with him. It took a few seconds of rifling to find the right one.

He said, "The family owns controlling interest in the firm with 74.3% of the stock, or 123,375 shares. At today's market price of $2.73 per share, her net interest in the firm is," he paused to calculate on the back of another sheet of paper, before saying, "$336,813.75."

Sam wasn't surprised judging by the size of the operation.

"Your proposal, gentlemen?"

"Naturally, such a large disbursement from our operating funds would put the firm on shaky financial footing. We could offer her $1.55 per share."

"Gentlemen, you are not dealing with a country bumpkin. I'll make you a counteroffer. You'll pay the full value of the shares to be paid in five annual installments. The first payment due on contract signing. I'll set up a trust fund in Denver for Catherine. Each year on the anniversary of the signing, you will wire an installment to the account. If you default, the agreement is null and void, and you lose all prior payments."

"Could you and your wife step out into the hall for a few minutes while we discuss your offer?"

"Surely."

Sam walked over to Grace who rose and took his arm. They left the boardroom and closed the door.

Once closed, Grace whispered to Sam, "*$300,000?* Sam, I didn't know there was so much money!"

"That's pretty close to what I estimated. I did some checking with the newspaper and found that their New Orleans office was larger than this one. Now there's a lot of money to be made shipping on the river, but a lot more to be made on the open ocean trade. I bet they'll take the offer, too."

Sam was right. They called them back in just three minutes later, accepted his terms and said they would have their attorney draw up the paperwork which would be ready the following day around noon. They shook hands around the boardroom.

Before they left, Sam asked, "I'll need to meet with the attorney handling the probate of Amos Brown's will. Can you direct me to his office?"

"I'll have a staff carriage take you there. He's the senior partner of the Jameson & Cutler law firm."

"Thank you. We'll wait in the lobby."

Sam took Grace's arm again and they left the boardroom then walked down the stairs to the lobby.

"Now, where do we go?" asked Grace.

"We're off to meet the attorney handling the Short estate. This was only the business end. Catherine also inherits whatever Amos left behind, and I imagine it's a house and a substantial bank account, at least. We'll find out shortly."

———

The carriage arrived shortly and took them to the center of the city. The buildings were all tall and made of brick and reeked of wealth. Grace was still in a state of continuous disbelief since hearing that first amount. The carriage stopped, and Sam and Grace exited and walked into an office building. There was another young woman at a reception desk. She was older than Grace and almost as pretty.

"May I help you?"

"We need to see Mister Jameson of Jameson & Cutler."

"Do you have an appointment?"

"No, we just arrived from Denver, Colorado. I'm sure he'd like to see us, though. He has a probate case that I'm sure he'd like to have off his desk."

"Let me ask his clerk."

She stood and walked to an office on her left. A few minutes later, she returned followed by a young man, a bit on the skinny side with thinning hair to match.

"Miss Jenkins tells me that you wish to see Mister Jameson. May I ask, what is the nature of your visit?"

"I am the legal guardian of Miss Catherine Short, who is now my adopted daughter. I was her closest living relative after her mother, my sister, died. I know that her grandfather Amos died almost a year ago, and the will must still be in probate because his son Richard, my brother-in-law was murdered two months after his father's death and his wife and daughter have been missing since we rescued Catherine. I would imagine that Mister Jameson would like to clear the file."

The young attorney's eyebrows shot up when Sam uttered the word 'murdered'.

"I believe we can get you in to see Mister Jameson. Just follow me."

He led them to a much larger office with a front office and secretary. The secretary saw the young lawyer and nodded, so they all walked past, and the attorney rapped on the door. He waited for three seconds before he opened it.

He leaned inside and said, "Sir, this lady and gentlemen are here from Colorado to settle the Short probate."

Sam was right. They were anxious to close it out.

He waved them inside, then followed them into the ornate office and closed the door behind them. Mister Jameson rose, then shook both their hands and asked them to have a seat.

"I'm Elias Jameson. I represented Amos Short for thirty years. And you are?"

"My name is Sam Brown, and this is my wife, Grace Brown. We just arrived from Denver, Colorado.

Jameson noticed the U.S. Deputy Marshal's badge that was still on his jacket.

"And you are a United States Deputy Marshal, Mister Brown?"

"Just temporary, Mister Jameson. I met with the United States Marshal, Thomas Charles and showed him evidence showing that Mister Ferguson Short had paid money to a Denver gang leader to murder Richard Short and his family. He succeeded in killing Richard, but my sister, Cora and their daughter were kidnapped.

"My sister was murdered three months ago under totally different circumstances. We rescued Catherine from her captors just recently. The marshal made me a temporary deputy to serve a warrant for the arrest of Mister Ferguson, which we just executed. He is now in custody. After he was taken, I arranged for the sale of Catherine's shares of Short Shipping stock to be deposited in a trust fund account. The president of the firm advised me that you were the firm handling the probate, so here I am."

"You are Miss Short's legal guardian?"

Sam was impressed that he hadn't even flinched at the news about Ferguson.

"I am her adoptive father."

Sam reached into his money belt and produced Catherine's birth certificate and adoption papers, then gave them to Mister Jameson, who looked them over.

"How is Miss Brown?"

"She is an incredible little girl, Mister Jameson. I had both of her parents' bodies moved to a family cemetery on the family ranch. She understands what happened and misses her parents, as do I. Her mother, my sister, and I were extremely close. She was my only sibling and was a beautiful person. Richard was the only man I thought worthy of her."

"I'm sorry for your loss. As you noticed that I didn't appear to be shocked by Ferguson's behavior. It's because I wasn't. He was a ruthless man, and I was hoping against hope that his daughter-in-law or granddaughter would be found before they could legally be declared dead. Where is she now?"

"I have her at a ranch that I know Ferguson never knew about. She's guarded by our good friend Julia Crook and an entire ranch of cowboys."

"Wonderful. I'd like to meet the young lady one of these days."

"If you look at my wife, Mister Jameson, and imagine her as a five-year-old, that's what she looks like. When I first saw them together, I was stunned. The resemblance is uncanny."

"Then she must be a pretty little girl, then."

"She's very pretty, and just as sweet as her mother."

"I'm glad to hear it. Now, I had my clerk retrieve the will, so I'll give you the particulars."

He pulled out a multi-page document.

"Amos had most of his money in the shipping firm, and it was wise of you to get them to sell her shares and put the money into a trust fund. I'm surprised they didn't try to give you less than the full value of the stock."

"They did. They offered a little more than half, claiming that a full buyout would ruin the firm. So, I told them to make five equal payment, the first due with the signing of the contract. And if they fail to make a payment, the agreement is null and void, and they lose any payments already made. They agreed to the terms."

"Those are very good terms, Mister Brown. Do you have any legal or business background?"

"No, sir, but I do read a lot."

"I wish some of my clerks read as much. Anyway, speaking of reading, here are the particulars of the will."

Mister Jameson read off the assets that belonged to Catherine. The most notable were a large furnished house, 157 State Street, a bank account with $37,232.86, two carriages and eight horses, and a yacht that he kept anchored in New Orleans.

Sam said, "I'm sure that Catherine won't want to leave the ranch. What I'd like to do is go through the house and remove anything that I believe she might like in the future. I'd especially like to find a photograph of her parents. I could arrange for a shipping firm to have them sent to Denver. Then, we would sell the house with the carriages and horses and the yacht. Can we arrange to have the bank account funds transferred to her trust fund?"

"Mister Brown, as her legal guardian and father, I can give you a draft for the amount tomorrow along with the deed to the house and keys. I can arrange for the sale of the yacht and house after you've gone. We'll subtract the fees from the sales amount. If you'll give me your address, we'll send you the proceeds. Also, if you'd like, and I'd recommend it, I'd like to send one of my young attorneys with you to the meeting with the board tomorrow to make sure they don't try to pull a fast one."

"I thank you for that, Mister Jameson. We'll stop by around eleven o'clock, if that's all right."

"That will be fine. I'll have everything ready for you."

After handshakes all around, Sam and Grace left the law offices, then caught another carriage and rode to the marshal's office.

Sam turned in his badge and spent some time explaining the whole Soapy Smith episode to a room full of marshals as Grace sat by his side and occasionally answered questions.

Ferguson Short was already arraigned and charged with conspiracy to commit murder and was being held in the city jail awaiting trial. The murders may have taken place in Colorado, but Mister Ferguson's hiring of Soapy Smith took place in St. Louis. Charles told him they would advise him of the trial date.

They would have to stay for the trial, which he guessed would be held in four or five days, so Sam told Thomas where they were staying for any messages and left the damning note with the marshal to give to the prosecuting attorney.

After they left the office, Sam and Grace decided to have lunch at the hotel restaurant rather than hunt for another location.

As they were eating, Grace said, "I can't believe how much money is involved. No wonder Ferguson wanted it."

"It wasn't his, Grace. The amount is irrelevant."

"I know. How is it going to affect Catherine?"

"It'll have no effect for a few years. She won't even care about it. The problem comes when she approaches her eighteenth birthday. By then, she should have close to a half-million dollars in her trust fund, maybe a lot more. She'll have every male within a thousand miles after her. Let's face it, a beautiful young woman who also happens to be the wealthiest woman west of the Mississippi is a big problem. We're going to have our hands full raising our daughter, Mrs. Brown."

"I never thought that far ahead. I never thought of money as a curse, but for Catherine, it might be."

"All we can do is trust that she'll have a good foundation in common sense. She'll need you more than me as she gets older, Grace. You'll be her counselor and confidant."

Grace was suddenly overwhelmed with the thought.

Sam noticed the impact instantly, and quickly said, "But don't let it bother you. She's five, and she loves her puppies."

Grace laughed and asked, "So, what do we do about the house?"

"The day after tomorrow, we arrange to meet a moving firm representative at the house and go through the house, marking what we want moved and what stays for the new owners. If you like something, mark it. Furniture, pictures, and, for you especially, the kitchenware, towels and other household items. Realize that when most people buy a house, they bring those things with them. So, just mark whatever you want."

"It'll be like Christmas, Sam."

They returned to their hotel room and enjoyed a delightful newlywed afternoon and evening that made full use of the large bed, the bathtub and even the thick carpets.

———

The next morning, the sky had cleared, and it was brisk. Sam and Grace exited the hotel at ten-thirty and hired a carriage to take them to the law offices of Jameson & Cutler. When they approached the desk, the receptionist told them that Mister Jameson was expecting them and to go right in.

Jameson's door was open, and he saw them enter his outer office, so he just waved them inside, and his secretary followed.

"Welcome back, Mister & Mrs. Brown. Please have a seat. Miss Lavoisier will notarize the documents after we have signed them. I had the marshal verify your identity to satisfy my ethical requirements. I hear that Ferguson has been arraigned for murder. With that evidence and your story, I have no doubt he will hang for his crimes, and deservedly so. Here is the necessary paperwork."

Sam signed thirteen legal documents. He gave power of attorney to sell the house, its contents, and the yacht, then was given the key to the house, the name of a recommended moving firm, and a bank draft for the full amount of Amos Short's bank account. After signing the final forms closing out the probate, they all shook hands and as they were preparing to leave, the same young attorney that they had met yesterday entered.

Jameson introduced him to Sam and Grace, saying, "Mister Brown, this is one of my rising stars, attorney John M. Reynolds. He'll accompany you to Short Shipping and verify the accuracy of the agreement."

"Glad to be of assistance, Mister Brown," said Mister Reynolds.

Sam shook his hand and they left the offices.

They used the law firm's carriage to take them to the shipping offices. Once there, they were shown to the private office of the president, and the heavy man greeted them.

With him was a much thinner man, looking almost like a scarecrow. He was almost six feet tall and couldn't have weighed more than one hundred and twenty pounds.

Sam noticed he wasn't pleased to see John Reynolds, and Sam guessed that they were going to try to slip something past him on the contract.

They were, and it was easily spotted, even by a non-attorney. As he was reviewing the contract himself, he found a clause that effectively said that if Miss Catherine Brown were to expire prior to the terms of the contract being fulfilled, the firm was under no obligation to make further payments. Sam stopped reading at that point and handed the contract to John Reynolds.

Reynolds read the contract and Sam noticed when he reached the offending clause as his eyebrows suddenly dropped and he looked at the skinny Short Shipping attorney.

"I believe, gentlemen, that you have altered the agreement reached between the company and Mister Brown. If this clause is not stricken, then the contract will not be signed, and I would advise Mister Brown to sell his shares at the exchange later this morning."

Sam knew that selling that many shares would drive the stock into the ground and ruin the company.

They crossed out and initialed the offending clause of both copies. John Reynolds approved the rest of the contract. A bank draft made out to Sam Brown in the amount of $67,362.75 was given to Sam and hands were shaken.

Sam left the offices and placed both documents in his money belt.

John Reynolds said to Sam as they were leaving, "I checked the stock prices today before we left. Rumors of Ferguson Short being arrested actually had a positive impact on the value of the firm, and the price of stock went up two cents a share. I knew that we could have argued for more money, but I had the impression that it wasn't important to you. Was I right?"

"Absolutely. Catherine is five years old. By the time she comes of age, she will be enormously wealthy. I have no idea how it will impact her life. The added cash would only make it worse. I just wanted to make sure she received what was rightfully hers."

"That's what I thought. Did you want me to drop you off at your hotel?"

"No. Could you drop us off at the house on State Street? I'd like to give it a preliminary review. I'd really like to see if there was a photograph of Catherine's parents because I know that she'd treasure that more than all of the money."

"Of course, I'll instruct the driver."

———

Twenty minutes later, Sam and Grace stepped out of the carriage and saw a large house, bordering on being a mansion. As the carriage drove off, Grace said, "Sam, this place is like a museum."

"More like a mausoleum. Let's go inside."

Sam opened the door with the key. Grace entered, and Sam followed and soon found he was right. It looked like it had been designed by an undertaker.

"Sam, I doubt if anything here would work in our ranch house."

"Let's see."

The large parlor and sitting room contained nothing worthwhile except the sumptuous Persian rugs, which he knew would find their way west. The sitting room's chairs were richly upholstered but would look wildly out of place in a Western home. The paintings on the walls were all subdued and dark.

But when Grace entered the dining room her eyes lit up.

"Sam, look at the dining table and buffet!"

The dining table was large and made of a lighter maple than the rest of the house's dark oaks and mahoganies. The matching buffet and china cabinet, filled with beautiful china, had Grace mesmerized.

"Sam, this is a beautiful set. We don't have a dining room, though."

Sam walked next to her and hugged her closely as he said, "Then we'll build you one, my love."

She smiled and kissed him, saying "Thank you, Sam. I just couldn't walk away and leave this here."

"I know."

All the kitchenware would also be on the train with the rugs and the dining room.

The final room did to Sam what the dining room did to Grace. It was the library.

Sam looked at the hundreds of volumes gracing the built-in shelves then said, "I guess our little library will have some new visitors."

Next, Sam went to the desk and opened each drawer. There were all business papers in the main drawer and the top drawer, but the middle drawer revealed what he was looking for. He found a box containing personal letters between Richard and his father and set the box on the desk. He began flipping the letters and found a small key on the bottom of the letter box. He picked up the key, then looked around the library and noticed that a painting on the far wall was askew.

As Grace watched, he walked to the painting and lifted it and looked underneath finding was a small wall safe. He took the painting down and used the key to open the safe.

Inside was a small stack of bills, a small sheaf of papers, and most valuable of all, two photographs. Sam handed the money and papers to Grace and looked at the first picture. It was of a young Richard and his new bride, Cora.

Sam's chest tightened, and his eyes misted as he looked at their faces. They were so happy. Unlike so many photographs of the day, there was no somber staring at the camera. Long shutter times didn't matter if you could keep those smiles on your face. He handed the picture to Grace as he wiped his eyes. The second picture was of the bride and groom standing on either side of an older man. They were less animated in this one, and Sam was sure the new face was that of Amos Short. It was a good face.

Grace recognized Cora but had never seen Richard's face until now. She noted that it was a gentle face. A happy face. She put her hand on Sam's shoulder.

"This will be Catherine's greatest treasure."

Sam just nodded, then showed her the second one, but she made no additional comment.

There had been almost four thousand dollars in cash in the safe. The papers were shares in other companies, most notably Union Pacific and First National Bank.

Sam put the cash and stock certificates in his bulging money belt. He'd have to either buy a second one or put the valuables somewhere else. He suddenly realized that he had over a hundred thousand dollars on his person, and, depending on the value of the stock certificates, it could be well over that. The thought made him a bit uneasy, despite the presence of his Bulldog.

But the photographs he kept close, along with the box of letters.

There was nothing else in the house that Grace would consider moving.

Sam said, "Let's go outside. I was wondering about the carriages."

Grace followed Sam out the back door to the carriage house. It was quite large, but still elegant. Before he got there, he heard a horse nicker. *Surely the horses hadn't been left neglected in the carriage house for almost a year!*

When they entered the carriage house, the two carriages dominated the interior, but along the side, were eight stalls. Each was housing a magnificent black horse. They had obviously not been neglected. There was hay on the floor and oats in feed boxes next to individual almost full troughs.

"Grace, look at them! They're magnificent!"

"Sam, who's been taking care of them?" she asked as she walked beside him to the handsome animals.

"I imagine that Amos has a contract with a livery to care for them. They'd probably take them out and walk them daily. I noticed the torn-up grass in the area just outside."

He walked close to the horses and talked to them and stroked their necks. They were very disciplined and accustomed to human touch. There was almost no disparity in height, either.

"Grace, we've got to bring them to the ranch. They need to be able to run."

"You're right, Sam. It's almost inhumane to leave horses like this standing for so long."

"We'll see what we can do."

They left the carriage house and Sam thought it was ironic that they left those carriages and horses, that technically he could take, as they hailed a carriage and returned to the hotel.

When they passed the desk, the clerk handed him a message.

Sam opened it and read:

Ferguson killed in jail. Beaten to death by other inmates. I guess trying to have a four-year-old girl killed was over the edge for even hardened criminals. I hear he was bragging about it to make himself sound like tough guy.

Thomas

Sam handed the note to Grace.

"It still doesn't make it better. Does it?"

"No. Not at all. That's twice that we've had to avoid a trial, Grace. I don't ever want to even worry about one in the future."

"Amen to that, my husband," Grace agreed.

Now, all that remained was arranging for the shipment of the household items they had chosen and the horses.

———

They arranged to meet with a large shipping firm the next morning, and Sam told them what they needed done and drove to the house with one of their clerks. Sam and Grace walked around the house and pointed out the items to be shipped, and the man told them they'd pack everything in the morning and have it delivered to the ranch within a week.

The last item was the horses. They found the name of the livery that had been tending the horses and talked to them about shipping them on the westbound train to Denver the day after tomorrow. The train would leave at 9:15. As they were leaving, Sam asked if Amos had kept any other horses besides the eight in the carriage house, and it turned out that he had four more adults and three foals; three mares and a stallion that he had kept for breeding more carriage horses. The foals were the first three. Sam walked out to the corral and identified them immediately. They were in a separate, large pen. Sam paid the shipping fees for all twelve horses and the three youngsters. The liveryman assured him they would be on the train.

The only purchase they made that day was a small steel lockbox. When they returned to the hotel that afternoon, Sam moved the pictures, letters, almost all the money, the bank drafts, the stock certificates and the legal paperwork into the box. He locked it and put the key in his money belt.

"So, Grace, what do you think of the little bank?"

"The little bank with more money than most banks in Colorado."

"That's about the size of it."

———

On the way to breakfast the next morning, Sam took the steel box down to the hotel desk and ask that it be stored in their safe until their departure the following morning. They gave him a receipt and Sam watched as they opened the safe and placed the box inside.

After they had eaten, they took another carriage to the Short mansion, as they had been calling it.

They had only been at the house for twenty minutes when four large freight wagons arrived. There were two crews of four men each and had large crates on one of the wagons and large squares of excelsior. Sam opened the door and showed them the major pieces in the dining room, the books, the kitchenware, and the rugs. They wasted no time, and by noon, everything was packed.

While they were packing, he went out to the carriage house and noticed that the horses were gone. After the men had finished packing, Sam gave the foreman two double eagle gold pieces to divide among the men, then shook their hands before they drove off with their heavily laden wagons. Once they were alone again, Sam locked the house and, as it was a beautiful day, they decided to walk to the hotel, only six blocks away.

They were ready to leave after all the excitement and were anxious to return to their ranch.

———

That evening, Grace enjoyed one last bath while Sam went down to the lobby, retrieved the metal box, and returned to the room. Most of the packing had been done the night before, so Sam opened the trunk, slid the box along the side of the trunk, slipped it beneath some of Grace's clothes, then closed and locked the trunk, putting the key in the money belt with the other key.

Three hours later, they were on the train heading west.

Grace watched St. Louis disappearing and said, "Sam, when we get back, I think I'll sleep for a week."

"I'll join you, Mrs. Brown, but don't think all that time in bed will be spent sleeping. We are still newlyweds, you know," he said as he smiled at his wife.

"I would expect no less," she replied as she took his hand.

"Which room are we going to use?" she asked.

"I thought we'd move into your room. It has the biggest bed, and the bathroom is right across the hall," Sam replied.

"Maybe we could share the tub," Grace said with a smile.

"Only if you don't use the lilac soap until after I leave."

Grace laughed, laid her head on his shoulder and quietly said, "I can't wait to get home."

———

It was early afternoon two days later when the train rolled into the Denver station. Sam and Grace were beyond tired. It had been an emotional, stressful week, and the long train rides didn't help.

They stepped off the train and walked with stiff legs next door to the livery and notified the liveryman of their arrival and placed their travel bags in the back floor of their carriage. After the grays were harnessed and Sam had paid the bill, he walked the grays to where the porter had their trunk.

He placed it in the boot, Sam gave him a tip, and then rolled the wagon to the corral where the dozen horses and three foals were already in the corral. The horses all were wearing bridles, so Sam worked with the corral keeper and tied lead ropes to the dozen horses, and then the two lead horses had their ropes lashed to the carriage. The three foals weren't tied to anything as they would stay with their mothers, but it would be a slow drive back to the ranch.

Soon afterward, the unusual caravan proceeded through the streets of Denver. If the horses weren't so impressive, there would have been laughter, instead, there were nods of approval.

They turned south and walked the grays in deference to the foals. Sam would lean outside the carriage occasionally to ensure they were all safe. It may have taken longer, but they turned into the long entrance road toward the ranch house before four o'clock.

"We're home, sweetheart," Sam said as he hugged Grace's shoulder.

Grace simply sighed; the shining white ranch house looked much more enticing than the Short mansion.

Sam pulled the carriage to the front yard, and something looked different, but he couldn't put his finger on it. The repair work was easy to see and appreciate, but there was something different.

He and Grace stepped down and were immediately set upon by two bouncing puppies that must have missed the human companionship. Sam didn't doubt that they missed Catherine much more.

He let Grace carry the travel bags while he lugged the trunk into the main room. Once they were inside, he carefully put the trunk down, then he went into their bedroom where Grace had dropped the two travel bags, then picked her up and kissed her.

"This is where we belong, Grace."

She smiled and replied, "And, Mister Brown, after you've put the horses away, maybe I could talk you into letting me have a bath."

"I'll think about it."

He set her down, gently slapped her cute behind, getting a smile in return, then left the house, went out to the carriage, unleashed one line of lines of blacks and led them to the corral with Sophie and Millie trailing.

This group had the stallion, and he was not pleased with the puppies. Once in the corral Sam untied the trail lines and ropes and let them loose. There was a fresh pile of hay nearby and a full trough, so Sam was sure that Zeke had stopped by recently, probably hoping that Julia was home.

He did the same with the second line of mares and foals, and soon they were all trotting and getting adjusted to their home. Sam moved the carriage to its house and unhitched the grays. After everything was back to normal, Sam returned to the house.

Grace was already making dinner. It was early, but they were both hungry, having passed up the train fare at lunch.

"Grace, tomorrow, we'll head over to the Bar C and pick up Julia and Catherine. We'll spend the day getting reacquainted, but the day after that, you and I need to go to the bank. I want to add you to the account, and we'll deposit the cash we have into that account and set up the trust fund for Catherine with the two bank drafts. We'll have the bank give us the account info to send to the Short Shipping Company, then we'll go over to the land office and get you added to the Circle S."

"What about the Slash F?"

"What about it?"

"Can't we just join the two ranches?"

"That's up to you, Grace. It's your ranch."

"Sam Brown, sometimes you can go too far with this Mister Nice Guy behavior. You're my husband. What's mine is yours. You have been mighty generous with what you've given me. Now, let's stop doing this right now."

Sam laughed and said, "I have been a bit much, haven't I?"

"That, Mister Brown, is an understatement."

Sam took two steps until he was inches away from Grace, then wrapped his arms around her.

"Well, forgive me, ma'am, but if it's all right with you, we'll just join the two ranches. Why don't we call them the S-F connected, because, ma'am, you and I are most decidedly connected."

She laughed and forgave him.

Sam rewarded her forgiveness by filling her bath with warm, bordering on hot water and letting her enjoy her extended bathing in peace.

She rewarded him shortly after.

CHAPTER 17

It was nine o'clock the next morning and the Brown carriage was moving at a good clip toward the Bar C, another twelve miles distant. Even though it hadn't taken a week, both Sam and Grace missed having Catherine and Julia around. They had brought a picnic lunch with them, complete with fried chicken, biscuits, potato salad, and even an entire apple pie. They had packed all the other essentials as well, including plates, utensils and a large blanket.

Two hours later, they turned into the ranch access road, spotted the house and noticed a beehive of activity. Something was wrong, and Sam's stomach turned as he kicked the grays into a faster trot.

"Sam, what's happening?" Grace asked as she saw the commotion.

"I don't know yet, but we'll find out soon."

He could see Orville and, thankfully, Catherine on the porch looking at them, but he couldn't spot Julia. He brought the carriage to a halt and leapt onto the dusty surface.

"Orville, what's happened?"

Orville stepped down from the porch with Catherine and looked as if he'd been shot. He was sheet white as he looked at him and said, "Sam! I'm so glad you're back. We got up a little while ago and found Julia missing. I just called the hands in and was one short. The man's name is Oscar Rooney. I don't know if she ran off with him or he just took her. We were just getting ready to hunt for them."

Sam put up his hand and said, "Orville, hold up for just a second. Let me borrow a horse. Catherine, come here, sweetie."

Catherine bounced closer to her father and said, "Papa, Aunt Julia's gone."

"I know, sweetie. Did she say anything to you?"

"No, Papa. But she had been talking to that other man and was mad. I didn't like him either."

"When did you see Aunt Julia last?"

"She got out of bed after it was sunny. I heard some funny noises and then I got up and couldn't find her."

"Okay, Catherine. You did a good job. You stay with your mama, now."

"Okay, Papa," she said as she reached out to Grace, who picked her up.

"She hasn't been gone that long. I think I have an idea where to find her. Keep your guys here."

"Okay, Sam. Go ahead and borrow Slick here. He's got great lungs and can run for hours."

"Thanks, Orville. I should be back with Julia in a little while."

Grace gave her usual 'be careful' warning as Sam mounted Slick, turned the big gelding, then after riding down the access road, turned south and raced toward Hinkley.

He made the eight miles to Hinkley in a little over forty minutes then slowed the winded horse to let him breathe easier and pulled up in front of Waxman's. The doors were still boarded, so he tied Slick to the rail and loosed the hammer loop on his Colt. Sam then stepped around to the back of the saloon, and found a saddled horse hitched to a post. The back door was still open, and he could hear arguing in the background and recognized Julia's voice as he entered.

As Sam crossed the empty barroom, he heard her shouting from upstairs, "I don't do that anymore! I'm not like that!"

Julia's protest was followed by a man's angry voice, yelling, "Then you shouldn't have come on to me, you little bitch! Now you can protest all you want, but it ain't gonna matter."

Sam let them argue, as it covered his quiet, but rapid climb up the stairs. He was within ten feet of the open door when Julia screamed.

Two long, fast steps and he was at the door with his Colt drawn.

As Sam turned the corner, a semi-naked Julia was clutching at her dress while the Bar C hand was taking down his pants. Sam didn't hide his arrival as he banged into the open door and the man whipped his head to the left and thought about going for his gun that was already on the floor with his pants but knew he didn't have a chance.

He threw up his hands and said, "Hold on, Sam. I didn't do nothin'. She wanted me and told me herself. Now she's acting all high and mighty."

Sam slammed his Colt into his holster and grabbed the back of the cowboy's shirt and yanked him away from Julia.

He walked steadily backwards, pulling a flailing Oscar out of the room, then turned and kept going down the hallway.

The cowboy was fighting to get his footing or grab something, but Sam was pulling too fast and his feet were restricted by his britches around his ankles. When they reached the stairs, Sam dragged down the long flight of steps with Oscar's naked butt bouncing off each one. When he reached the bottom, Sam stood him up and began to beat him.

This was no fair fight, and Sam didn't care. He was just tired of his ladies being hurt. He wasn't going to put up with this any longer. Sam was bigger and stronger, but Oscar was bigger and stronger than Julia, too, so that balanced the scales.

Sam didn't want to kill him, he wanted to make him sorry he had ever been born. Finally, after Oscar collapsed in a heap, Sam ripped Oscar's Colt from his holster, snapping the hammer loop in the process, then emptied the chambers before he broke off the hammer by cocking it and slamming the side over the stair rail. He tossed it across the room and left Oscar whimpering in a ball on the floor.

He quickly climbed the stairs and soon found Julia in the corner of Grace's old room, sobbing with her hand grasping the torn portion of her dress. Sam sat down next to her and hugged her close.

"Julia? This is Sam? Are you all right?"

She looked up at him as if he was a stranger.

"Sam?" she asked weakly.

"Yes, sweetheart, it's Sam."

491

He stood, took off his shirt, then sat down and put her arm through a sleeve, sat her forward, ignoring her nakedness, and pulled her other arm through the sleeve. He fastened all the buttons and lifted her into a full hug as she continued sobbing.

Finally, she whispered, "Sam, I'm sorry. I was trying to be nice. He knew about what I had done before because he had been a customer. I'm so ashamed."

Sam was worried how badly she had been wounded, not physically, but in her recently repaired heart, mind and soul.

"Julia, you have nothing to be ashamed about. That bastard took advantage of you. This was no more your fault than being kidnapped was. Do you understand?"

She didn't answer, so Sam decided to shift to the mundane.

"Julia, you won't believe what happened in St. Louis."

Julia's curiosity overcame her despondent thoughts, so she asked, "What happened?"

"I'll tell you on the way home."

"I don't have a horse."

"Yes, you do. Oscar gave you his. It's in back."

She looked at him and said, "Sam, you don't have a shirt."

"I know. It'll give me a chance to work on my tan."

She smiled, and Sam hoped it was the start of the return of his Julia.

He stood, then took her hand and led her out the door.

As they stepped down the stairs, she saw the bloody mess that had been Oscar.

"Did you kill him?" she asked quietly.

"No. I just beat him to within an inch of wishing I had. He'll wake up sore with no job and no horse. It was the ranch's horse, anyway. Speaking of horses, wait till you see what I brought back from St. Louis. It's the start of a new method of ranching for us, Julia."

They walked past Oscar's moaning form and out the back door where he helped Julia onto the horse and helped her fiddle with her skirts, so they acted more like a riding skirt. The stirrups were way too low, but it would be a short ride.

She walked the horse out front where Sam mounted Slick, and they began the slower ride back to the ranch. As they slowly walked the horses, Sam told Julia about the events in St. Louis. She was so astounded by the amount of money that Catherine would be getting that she almost forgot what had happened to her. Sam told her about the furniture that was coming and the plans to build a new dining room. He told her about the twelve horses and the three foals, and she was very interested with that. Sam kept talking about them because she showed so much interest.

Finally, she said what she had been thinking from the moment she had been taken away for the second time.

"Sam, what will Zeke say? Will he think I was going back to my other life? I'm worried. I think I love him, Sam."

"If I know Zeke, he'll want to do two things. He'll want to hunt down Oscar and administer a worse beating than I gave him, and before that, he'll want to hold you close and kiss you and tell you how much he loves you."

"Really?"

"Have I been wrong before?"

She laughed lightly, and said, "No."

"Now, I want to make a proposition to you. I don't think Grace will object. We're going to combine the two ranches. I'm planning on selling all the cattle and turning it into a horse ranch. Now, if you and Zeke, or anyone else you choose would agree, Grace and I would let you live in the other ranch house. It would be your home, Julia. Yours to raise your children to play with ours. Does that sound agreeable, Julia?"

"Sam, if I wasn't on this horse, I'd lean over and kiss you."

Sam angled Slick to the right, leaned as far over as he could and kissed Julia on the lips.

"Now that, Julia, was some fancy riding."

She laughed fully this time making Sam happy and relieved and hoped that it was permanent.

———

They turned up the road to the Bar C in mid-afternoon, and Grace saw them coming first. Her bare-chested husband for just days and Julia, wearing his shirt, and she knew that it would be an interesting story. They both waved at her, so she didn't think it was too bad, but probably just slightly less bad than what it could have been.

Sam stepped down and helped Julia to the ground.

Then, he leaned over and whispered in her ear, "Julia, if you could go and put on a new dress, I'd appreciate getting

494

my shirt back. As it is, I need to do some fast talking to my new wife."

Julia giggled and told him she would do just that.

Catherine had been hugged by Julia and they both went into the ranch house, passing Orville and Grace who stepped down to talk to Sam.

When they arrived, Sam said, "I found Oscar's horse tied up behind Waxman's, and could hear an argument upstairs. I snuck in and found Oscar telling Julia that she still worked there and had ripped her dress apart. He had his pants down when I grabbed him by the scruff of the neck and dragged him down the stairs to the floor."

"Did you kill him?" asked Orville.

"No. I just beat him pretty good."

"Good."

"I was worried about Julia, Grace. She didn't even recognize me, even after I put my shirt on her. When she finally came around, she said that she was trying to be nice to Oscar, but he had been a customer of hers and thought she was still available. It took me a while to bring her back to our Julia."

"What did you do with Oscar?" asked Grace.

"I left him on the floor. He was moaning, and unlike Steve Rawls, who deserved what he got, I didn't hit him anywhere that would cause permanent damage. What he does now, I have no real concern."

Grace nodded, and they went inside. Orville was mumbling about getting out of the whole ranching business if he had to put up with hands like him and Rawls.

Just a minute after sitting down, a cleaned-up Julia walked in and handed Sam his shirt. She noticed that his shoulders and back were already a deep red and knew it was going to hurt.

"Thanks, Julia. Now we need to be getting back. Are you ladies packed?"

"Yes, Sam. We're ready to go."

He turned to the elderly rancher and said, "Orville, don't get down on yourself. You're a good man. What happened wasn't your fault, just like Rawls wasn't your fault. A man gets an idea in his head sometimes and it squeezes all the good behavior out."

Orville nodded and shook Sam's hand as he said, "You take care, Sam."

"You should come up and visit sometime, Orville. You won't believe the horses that I picked up in St. Louis. Twelve incredible tall blacks. There are three foals, too. It'd be worth the trip."

Once again, the talk of the horses changed the mood as Orville brightened and replied, "I think I'll do that, Sam."

Sam shook his hand once more and after gingerly putting his shirt back on, which didn't seem to help once the wool was pressed against his damaged skin, they headed for the carriage.

———

As they drove, Sam and Grace talked about their adventures in St. Louis, as much to keep Julia's mind off what had just happened to her. About six miles north of the Bar C, Sam pulled the carriage off to the right, but didn't even bother unhitching the grays. He just drove the carriage to the creek and let them drink, then he drove to a grassy area to let them graze.

Grace and Julia left the carriage with Catherine, spread out the blanket, and unloaded the plates and accessories. There were four glasses that Grace filled with some lemonade she had made earlier. They began taking out the food and utensils and setting them on the blanket.

After they were enjoying their picnic, Sam thought it was time to talk to Catherine about what affect the St. Louis would have on her.

He rose, walked to the carriage and opened the steel box. It was empty now except for one item. He took out the picture and walked toward the blanket. Grace looked over and smiled in anticipation. Sam hadn't told Julia and wanted her to be surprised.

He sat down with the picture lying face down on the blanket.

"What's that, Papa?" asked Catherine, who had spent most of the ride back listening and asking about Sophie and Millie.

"Catherine, when your mama and I went to St. Louis we found a lot of things in your grandpapa's house. There was furniture and rugs and kitchen things that will be here soon, but the most precious thing we found is right here on the blanket."

"That is worth more than big things? Is it money? Mama said you found lots of money."

"No, sweetie, it's not money. It's much better."

She crawled over and sat leaning against him, and when she was close, he turned the photograph upside down and showed it to her.

Her eyes widened, and her mouth dropped open, then she closed it again and looked back at Sam before returned to look at the photograph.

"It's mama and papa!"

She reached her small hands for the picture and Sam smiled as she pulled it close to her. She looked at it for almost a minute, then she slowly brought it to her face, and she kissed it twice. Then she pulled it to her chest and said quietly, "It's mama and papa."

She turned, and her face was bright with a quiet smile as she asked, "Is this for me, Papa?"

"Of course, it is, Catherine. That picture was made when your mama and papa were married."

"They look very happy."

"They were very happy. You're always happy when you're with someone you love."

She gently laid the picture down and wrapped her arms around Sam's neck.

"Thank you, Papa."

Then she turned and stepped up to Grace and hugged her as well, saying, "Thank you, Mama."

Not wanting to leave Julia out, she hugged Julia and said, "Thank you, Aunt Julia."

She walked back to her picture, picked it up from the blanket and offered it to Sam.

"Can you keep it safe, Papa?"

He nodded, then stood and took the photograph to return it to its safe.

When he returned, he said, "You know, Catherine, I have another picture at home of your mama and papa that has your grandpapa in it, too."

"Really? Is it mine, too?"

"Yes, of course, it is."

"I'm the luckiest girl in the world!"

Sam smiled and said, "I hope you can still say that in thirteen years, Catherine."

Grace smiled because she knew what Sam meant, but Julia had no idea.

———

They returned to the house by five o'clock and Sam still couldn't figure out what was different about the house until he went to his room to begin moving his clothes into Grace's room. When he entered, he saw a heat stove near east wall. A shield had been placed behind it to keep the stove from damaging the wood. What he had seen was the chimney in the roof and knew it was Joe's idea.

After he had finished his intra-house move from the new bedroom to his and Grace's, he went into the kitchen while Catherine and Julia were out with the puppies admiring the new horses.

Sam used the opportunity to broach the subject of the Slash F with Grace, who was busy preparing dinner.

"Grace, remember how you weren't pleased with me yesterday because I was being too noble?"

"Of course, I remember everything."

"Well, I took your criticism to heart."

Grace stopped, looked at him warily, then asked, "And how did you do that?"

"When I was riding home with Julia, I was concerned with her sliding into depression about what happened. She had told me that she was worried about how Zeke would take the news of what had happened. By the way, she also mentioned that she thinks she loves him."

He paused to continue his confession.

"Anyway, after I had told her about the new horses, I kind of made a leap and told her that I was thinking of turning the ranch from a cattle ranch to a horse ranch."

"Sam! That's a wonderful idea. What's so bad about that?"

"Well, then I told her that if she and Zeke got together, or if she found someone else, that she and her husband could live in the Slash F ranch house and raise their children there, so they could play with ours."

Grace put down the rolling pin she was using, much to Sam's relief. Then she wiped her hands on her apron and took one long step and then hopped onto his lap.

"Mister Brown, you offered her to spend her life and raise her children in the house where I was raised?"

"Um, yes. I did tell her that I'd ask you about it, but knowing what a compassionate woman you are, I was sure you would agree."

"You know, Sam, you don't have to resort to flattery to get my permission. First, I believe it's a marvelous idea, and now that it's in good condition, it would be perfect. Second, it's the right thing to do. And lastly, it shows that you are still the incredible man I fell in love with in Hinkley."

She held his face and kissed him, leaving some missed flour from her hands on his cheeks, but he didn't notice.

"And tonight, good husband, you'd better start on giving me those babies you promised me."

"I've already done that. I'll bet you already have our daughter growing inside you."

Sam placed his palm on her stomach and Grace put hers on top of his.

"I hope so, Sam. I truly hope so," she whispered, as she hugged him tightly, before he winced.

Grace quickly released him.

"I forgot about that burn. How bad is it?"

"Not enough to keep me from performing my husbandly duties."

Grace laughed and said, "I can't think of anything that could keep you from that."

––––––

After dinner, Sam and Grace sat with Julia and Catherine in the main room.

"Ladies, I'll tell you what will be happening in the next few days. Now, tomorrow, Grace and I are going to Denver. Our first stop is to go to the bank."

He had removed the money, drafts, and stock certificates from the small safe area.

"We'll deposit the cash in the main account, then create a trust fund for you, Catherine. A trust fund is a way of keeping money that belongs to a child until they are old enough to spend it wisely. So, sweetie, we are going to be putting a lot of money away for you. When you are eighteen, it will be yours to do with as you please."

"Can I buy more puppies?"

"If you want, but that would be a lot of puppies. Then, we're going over to the land office and join the two ranches together. Finally, we're going to go to the construction firm and arrange for them to build a dining room addition for the new furniture. The furniture and other things should be coming next week. The good news is that there are a few large, thick rugs, so the floor won't feel so cold in the morning."

"That's good," said Catherine, "I don't like getting out of bed, but I have to go pee sometimes."

"Don't we all," said Julia.

About that time, there was a knock on the door and Sam had no doubt who it was.

"Come on in, Zeke."

As Zeke stepped into the room, Julia raced to him and jumped at him, then as they were wrapped together she kissed him. Zeke made no objections, but was a trifle embarrassed to have Sam and Grace watching.

"What brought that on?" asked Zeke.

"Sam can tell you. I'm just so happy to see you," she replied as she dropped to the floor.

Sam understood why she wanted him to explain.

Julia turned to Grace and said, "Let's get some coffee going now that Zeke's here."

They held Catherine's hands as they led her to the kitchen.

Zeke stepped closer to Sam with a puzzled look on his face.

Sam stood and motioned for Zeke to follow him outside. It was chilly, bordering on cold, and it was time to get a fire going in the fireplace.

Once away from the house, Sam said, "Zeke, when we arrived to pick up Catherine and Julia from the Bar C, we found Julia missing along with one of the hands. I asked

Catherine what happened, and she gave me the impression that Julia hadn't gone willingly."

Sam could see Zeke's hands clenched into fists and his eyes clouding.

"I took a horse and rode to Hinkley because I had a good idea what had happened. Julia was trying to be friendly, as she usually is, and this one hand had recognized her from Waxman's. He had been a customer. I rode down to Waxman's pretty hard. I knew he couldn't ride very fast with Julia on the horse and they had only left an hour or two before we arrived.

"When I got to Waxman's, I found his horse in back and the door open. I heard an argument and as I got to the second floor, I heard Julia scream. This bastard was telling her how she was going to be what she was before, and she kept telling him she didn't do that anymore."

Zeke looked like a man ready to explode.

"I came around the corner and found Julia crouching in the corner, her dress front had been ripped off and she was trying to cover herself. The son-of-a-bitch was pulling down his britches when he saw me. I guess he remembered what I had done to Steve Rawls, because he began whining about how she had asked him to do it. So, I hooked him and dragged him down the hall and down the stairs. And then I beat him until he was unconscious."

Zeke snarled, "Why didn't you kill him like you did Rawls? Is it because she wasn't your sister?"

"Zeke stop thinking like a wounded man and start thinking like a lawman. If I had killed him, I'd be rightfully charged with murder. He didn't physically hurt Julia, unlike Rawls, who not only killed my sister, but beat Grace, Carol and Julia. Rawls deserved to die, but even then, my intention was to deliver a crushing blow to him for each of my ladies that he had punched. But it would be the law that delivered justice for my sister by hanging him. It was just bad luck for him that I hit him harder than I thought I could.

"When I left him, he was moaning like a wounded heifer. I left him, went upstairs to Julia, who needed help. Zeke, she was so upset she didn't even recognize me. I gave her my shirt, so she could come back. It wasn't until we were on the road back that she began to talk. And do you know what he first concern was?"

"No," replied Zeke, his temper moderating.

"She was worried about what you would think about her. She was afraid that you would think she had gone back to those bad days after she was kidnapped. Zeke, she was concerned that you wouldn't want to see her anymore."

"Sam, that's crazy. I love Julia."

"Have you told her that yet?"

"No. I was afraid it was too early. I've only really known her for two weeks."

"Don't worry. Tell her. You stay on the porch and I'll send her out to talk to you. Okay?"

Zeke's mood improved immeasurably as he said, "Thanks, Sam. And sorry about that snotty comment about your sister."

"I understand, Zeke. Wait here."

C.J. PETIT

Sam reentered the house and headed for the kitchen where he motioned for Julia over, and she looked at him with trepidation.

He put his arm around her shoulders and leaned closer.

Talking softly, he said to her, "Julia, I told Zeke about what happened. He was outraged. He was even mad at me for not killing Oscar."

"He was?" asked Julia with a slight smile.

"Yes. He was very angry. He changed to being very distressed when I told him how I found you and how disoriented you were. When I told him what you said how worried you were about his reaction to what happened, do you know what he said?"

"No."

"He said, 'that's crazy. I love Julia.'"

Her face glowed as she stood staring at Sam and asked, "He said that?"

"Absolutely. And then I asked him if he had told you yet, and he said he hadn't because it's only been two weeks."

"That's silly, but understandable."

"So, Julia, I told Zeke to wait out on the porch and I'd send you out to talk to him. Is that okay?"

She gave Sam a quick kiss and stepped quickly across the main room to the porch.

Sam walked to the kitchen and told a curious Grace, who was relieved by what Sam told her.

506

Dinner became a time for discussing the future of the two ranches and not the past.

CHAPTER 18

As Sam and Grace walked into the ban, Sam had his traveling bag with him and found the clerk who had helped him with Soapy's signature. He had seemed a competent man, so they headed for his desk.

He had seen them approaching, so he smiled and said, "Good morning, Mister Brown."

"Good morning, Mister Frampton. I need assistance in multiple areas, including setting up a trust."

"I can handle that."

"Good. The first thing I need is to add my wife, Grace, to my account."

"Very simple, sir. Let me pull your account records."

When he returned, he had Grace sign a form, then he made some additional changes and that was done.

"Now, I'll need to make a deposit to the account."

Sam put the cash on the desk. After the Soapy Smith incident, nothing Sam could do would surprise Mister Frampton; or so he believed.

"Very good, sir."

He counted out the cash, added it to his balance and slid a piece of paper across to him indicating their new balance of $16,211.64. He also gave him a receipt.

"Finally, the trust fund. I need it established in the name of Catherine Brown. Who will manage the trust fund?"

"I can do that if you'd allow me, Mister Brown. I have a degree in finance."

"Do a good job, Mister Frampton, and the fees you earn could make you the highest paid employee of the bank."

Now he had Frampton's interest as he took out more forms and began writing then needed both Sam and Grace's signature. Finally, Sam opened the travel bag and removed the two drafts and the stock certificates.

"These will be the initial deposit."

Frampton looked at the two bank drafts, and even his calm demeanor was rattled when he quickly arrived at a total just under a hundred thousand dollars.

He looked back at Sam and said, relatively calmly, "I'll need your signature on both these drafts, Mister Brown."

Sam signed and as he did, he said, "For each of the next four years, you will receive a deposit in the exact amount as the larger draft from St. Louis. If it doesn't arrive, I'll need to know."

More than three hundred thousand dollars? Frampton understood Sam's earlier comment, realizing that if he managed the account well, it could add three thousand dollars to his income annually.

"Is there anything else we can do for you today?"

"I have four stock certificates that are part of the trust fund. I need you to tell me if they should be kept or sold and the cash deposited," he said as he handed him the certificates.

Frampton looked at the names of the companies and the number of shares, ran some quick numbers in his head, then said, "I'd keep the certificates, Mister Brown. These are all solid, well-financed firms. Just a quick perusal of the number of shares, I'd estimate their overall value in excess of twenty-five thousand dollars."

"It's up to you from here on out, Mister Frampton."

"Mister Brown, in light of the trust you've placed in me, I think it would be quite appropriate if you were to call me John."

Sam and Grace stood, Sam shook his hand and said, "Thank you for your assistance John. Call me Sam, by the way. I'm sure we'll see each other often."

"I hope so, Sam. It has been a genuine pleasure."

Sam knew it had been, too.

———

Their next stop was the land office where they completed the merger of the two ranches and had their names listed as the owners.

Sam and Grace spent over an hour at the construction company. They had to bring a second engineer to help with the new, revised and more extensive plan. This was not going to be an eight-day job.

They eventually decided to expand the entire south side of the house for symmetry. The east side near the kitchen would house the new dining room with a second fireplace. There would be a new, coal-burning heat stove in the southwest corner. The bathroom that Grace wanted would be created out of what used to be Carol's room. As it would have to have running water, they would build a small water tower east of the house and a windmill pump to fill it.

As long as they were adding running water, they would run pipes to the bathtub and the kitchen as well as to the new wash sink in the bathroom. And, with the new boiler, it was fairly simple to add hot water pipes to the new bathroom. It also meant they would have to dig and install a septic tank. They even had new entrance signs to both ranches created. It was a lot of work and wound up costing the Browns over eighteen hundred dollars.

––––––––

Three days later a train of freight wagons plodded down the access road. The dining room furniture would have to wait, so Sam had them store it in the barn and then cover it with tarps. The rest of the items were either stored or rolled onto their appropriate places on the bare floor in the case of the rugs.

The freighters received a generous tip from Sam then took all the empty crates and packing excelsior, despite Sophie and Millie disappointment watching the excelsior leave. They had enjoyed chasing the flying wood shavings floating through the air. Although they were getting larger, they were still puppies at heart.

––––––––

Four weeks later, the family moved back into the old Circle S ranch house, now the main F-B ranch house. Grace had insisted on the B rather than the S, and BF sounded too close to another well-used set of initials, so it had become the F-B connected. They had moved out of the main house for the past two weeks as walls were removed. They didn't have to move far though, as the old Slash F ranch house was more than adequate.

The new additions were a welcome change. Grace loved the bathroom and the new fireplace. Replacing the pump with a simple faucet was a blessing as well. Having heat and hot water and a flush toilet seemed, well, civilized. Their home was complete.

———

Sam had arranged for the sale of the entire herd of cattle to the Diamond J ranch, about six miles west. The ranch's hands moved all three hundred and sixty head of cattle to their new home, and all Sam had to do was to deposit the hefty seven-thousand dollar plus check into their account. Now they could begin their horse raising business in earnest, although Sam and Grace really didn't envision making much money.

Zeke and Julia had become engaged and had set the wedding date for early June the following year.

It was getting cold; seriously cold, and they were all grateful for the second fireplace and the new heat stove. The rugs were a bonus, as well.

———

One particularly cold night, Sam and Grace were snuggled under the warm layers of blankets and comforters.

"Grace, it has been a momentous six months since I first left Boulder. I could have never, in my most remote dreams, imagined that I could be here like this. I can't imagine ever being happier than I am right now. And it is all because of you, my love. Nothing would have mattered if you weren't here. Thank you, Grace, for everything."

Grace looked at his face in the moonlight and whispered, "I think you're wrong about something, Sam. I think you can still be happier."

She took his hand in hers and pressed it on the smooth skin of her flat belly.

Sam started and whispered back, "You're pregnant?"

"Mm-mm. Probably from the time you first told me I was carrying our daughter. I can't tell you the joy that I felt when I missed a month. I never had before. Ever. I didn't say anything until I was sure. Now, I'm sure."

Sam didn't say another word, but just kissed her and pulled her even closer. Grace was as content as she could imagine. Her relief upon the discovery of her pregnancy had been overwhelming. Ever since falling in love with Sam, her deepest fear had been that she could never have children. Sam had given back her life and so much more, but even he couldn't give her back the ability to have babies if that had been taken from her at that hideous place. But that concern was now gone, and she was going to be a real mama.

———

Four months later, her pregnancy was going well. She hadn't even experienced morning sickness. Sam had insisted that she see the obstetrician in Denver rather than use a midwife. If they could afford a water closet, he told her, they could make sure that she received the best possible care for her and their new daughter.

Grace wondered if he would be disappointed if they had a son, then laughed at the thought. Except for her husband, every man she had ever listened to had hoped for a son. Sam wanted a blonde-haired, blue-eyed daughter like his wife and Catherine.

But the doctor had told Sam he was concerned about Grace's weight. She was a small woman and hadn't gained enough weight to suit him. He told him to make her eat more, and did as much as he could, but the doctor was never satisfied.

So much so, that the doctor had her admitted to the hospital two weeks before she was due. Sam spent hours on the road between the ranch and the hospital and had help from Zeke and Joe Schmidt who had become a close friend. Dan Grant was liberal with Zeke's time to allow him to help as much as he could.

———

Grace went into labor on the morning of April 23rd, and Sam, like many expectant fathers before and after, paced the hallways and waiting room. Unlike other fathers, he had room for concern as it was a difficult time for Grace. She had been in labor for almost twelve hours and Sam wanted to be with her to try to take away some of the pain but felt helpless.

It was an agonizing night for Sam as he had to hear his beloved Grace cry out in pain, knowing there was nothing he could do for her.

At long last, she gave birth to beautiful twin daughters. After the newborns were wrapped in blankets, the doctor and his staff had to use all their skills to help Grace. She was bleeding, and she was bleeding badly.

The nurse told Sam that she was very weak from the extended labor and loss of blood and asked him if he wanted to have a priest or minister come to her room. Sam shook his head; he didn't want an intermediary. This was between him and God.

After she left, Sam dropped to his knees and closed his eyes. Tears flooded from his eyes as he implored God not to take his beloved wife. He already had his sister, Richard and Carol. *Why did He want his Grace?*

Grace was in a nether world. She could hear the doctor and nurses working on her. She knew that they were worried. *Why?* She had heard the doctor say that there were two baby girls and had smiled inside. She was the mother to two little girls. *Why were they so upset?* Sam would be happy. She was happy. *What else mattered?*

She looked to her right and was surprised to see that Carol had come to tell her how happy she was to see her again. Grace didn't even wonder why she was there but was just glad to see her. Then she saw Cora and her husband Richard next to Carol, and all of them were smiling at her.

She was happy to meet him for the first time and they seemed so happy to see her. He and Cora were glowing and so was Carol. They were all filled with such joy to see Grace, *but where was Sam?* Sam should be here with them, and he'd be so happy to see Carol and Cora again. We are all his ladies; his angels.

Then Carol, Richard and Cora all faded away, and she slid into darkness.

EPILOGUE 1

June 11, 1885

It was a beautiful late spring day as Sam sat in a rocking chair on the back porch of the main house. In the pastures, he could see the young foals prancing as their mothers stood nearby. The herd was much bigger now, and there were now three distinct herds. He could see Sophie and Millie working to keep the herds separated.

Sam could hear Cora and Carol's laughter as they played hide-and-seek with their big sister. Catherine was almost eleven now, and her birthday was just a week away. Her twin sisters, while not identical twins, were about the same age that Catherine had been when he had found her in that shabby ranch house. They both had the golden hair and dark blue eyes of his beloved Grace.

Sam thought how much life changes. Before Grace had entered his life, he had nothing to show for his thirty-one years. Now, just six years later, he had all of this; and all of it was because of Grace.

He stood and slowly returned to the kitchen, thinking of that extraordinary woman who had filled his life with love.

He walked to the stove and waited.

When he thought it was safe, he reached out, picked up Grace, lifted her into his arms and kissed her like it would be the last. After that horrible night more than five years ago when he was afraid that he had lost her, he never failed to let her know how precious she was to him. The cost of her having their two priceless daughters was that she could never have any more children. At first, she had been devastated, and it took days to convince her that she should be happy that they had two healthy, perfect little girls and to be thankful.

Naming them had been simple. It was as if God had told them that here were two ladies to love to replace those that they had lost.

Zeke and Julia were coming over for dinner with their two boys. Sam and Daniel. Julia was pregnant again, and Grace was genuinely happy for her and not the least bit resentful that she could have no more babies. There was one advantage, although neither Grace nor Julia spoke of it. Grace had retained her small, slim, yet well-rounded shape, while Julia had added a few pounds after each pregnancy. She still retained her youthful spirit, though, and Zeke seemed to admire the added Julia.

Julia and her family arrived a little early, so Julia could help with the food preparation. They always enjoyed meals in the well-appointed dining room.

Before eating, they all bowed their heads while Sam said grace. Since that night, when Sam had fallen to his knees and begged God to return his Grace to him, the family had been regular churchgoers.

Grace had returned to him and Sam would be eternally grateful to a merciful God. She had not only returned to him, but brought two precious gifts into the world who made their lives and love complete.

EPILOGUE 2

June 13, 1892

Grace and Sam were a bit nervous. They were at the train station awaiting Catherine's return from her first year at college. She had decided on becoming a veterinarian and was attending school at Kansas State University in Manhattan. She had enrolled as Catherine Short in hope of seeking some measure of anonymity.

In Denver, she was well known for the immensity of her wealth that would soon be hers. The last accounting by John Frampton had placed her net worth at a little over $1.3 million. It was a staggering amount.

But the release of the trust wasn't what made them nervous; it was Catherine's arrival on the train with her steady boyfriend for the past six months. She had met him in one of her classes. He was two years older than she was, but still a freshman. He was working his way through school and was totally unaware of her wealth, even as he boarded the train with her. It was her personality and compassion that had won his heart. Her red gold hair and dark blue eyes hadn't hurt, either.

She enjoyed talking with young George Peterson, and each was passionate in their views of the world. And now, she was returning to Denver, so George could meet her parents. She had cautioned him that her father might be a bit ornery at their initial meeting.

They stepped out onto the platform and Catherine was swept up by her papa, who missed her immensely. When he put her down, she embraced her mama as Sam gave a quick examination of George and immediately liked the honest eyes that didn't back down.

Catherine was busy hugging and kissing her sisters as he approached the young man.

"George? I'm Sam Brown. Nice to meet you," Sam said as he shook his hand.

"Nice to meet you too, sir."

"Call me Sam. The only ones who don't, call me papa, and they're all female."

George laughed and said, "I can do that, Sam."

"Let's go home."

After the carriage ride, Sam and George carried the luggage into the extensive ranch house. George had no idea that she came from such wealthy parents and was a bit ashamed of his own background. He was awed by the size of the ranch and the beauty of the herds of beautiful horses.

He had grown up in Manhattan, Kansas with his father, who worked at a mill. George himself had worked at the mill for two years to save enough to pay for his first year's tuition and was still unsure of what to do for the upcoming year's costs, especially now that he had met and fallen in love with Catherine. She had never acted like she came from a well-to-do family and had always been pleased when she would verbally abuse those who made fun of George's less than high-quality clothing.

519

Julia had wanted to see Catherine on her first day back, but Grace had asked her to wait until tomorrow so they could get acquainted with the young man who may be their future son-in-law.

After their clothes were put away, Sam took George outside and showed him the ranch. This served a two-fold purpose; first, it gave him a chance to get a read on George and his intentions and second, it gave Grace some time to be alone with Catherine to determine how she felt about George.

The more time he spent with George, the more he liked him. Sam found him to be an honest and bright young man and seemed to care deeply for Catherine despite not knowing about her immense wealth.

In the kitchen Grace and Catherine were preparing dinner so mother could talk to daughter. Grace had asked Carol and Cora to spend some time in their rooms doing their homework.

Catherine explained to Grace how much she loved George and that she knew he wanted to propose to her but didn't see himself as financially ready to support a wife, and that put her into a genuine quandary. *What should she do?*

George would never accept any money, even if it meant having to drop out of college. He was at the top of their class already and seemed to have no limit to his potential. Grace told her not to worry and told Catherine that she had a feeling her papa was going to fix that before they returned to the house.

Catherine had always been astounded by the stories that everyone told her about her father and had seen him do amazing things herself, *but how could he handle this?*

———

Sam could tell that George was uncomfortable with his clothing despite them being the best that he owned, and they still seemed threadbare. He'd have to do something about that, but he was also very well aware of his sense of pride, which he found admirable.

"George, Catherine wrote to us and said that you had the best grades in your year. That's pretty impressive."

"Thanks, Sam."

"So, are you studying veterinary science?" Sam asked, already knowing the answer from Catherine's letters.

"No, I'm studying animal husbandry."

"Really? Now that is a useful thing in Colorado. I'm sure you've noticed the horses."

"It's hard not to. They're magnificent animals."

"I've kind of reached my limit on what I can do myself, and I need an expert. How far are you from graduating?"

"Three years, but that may be extended."

"Why? If anything, with your grades, I would think it could be shortened."

George shifted uneasily and said, "Well, to be honest, I need to return to work for a while."

Sam pretended to be thinking then said, "I'll tell you what, George. I think I can make you an offer that works out to both of our advantages."

George's hopes skyrocketed as he replied, "I'll be glad to hear it, Sam."

"I told you that I really need someone to manage my herds. I'll give you the job and pay for your schooling. You can come here in the summer to help and when you graduate, you can open an office in Denver, and I'll be your first client. You can pay off the loan for your schooling from the fees you make. But they won't be that much, because each summer's work will just about offset the tuition costs. You get your degree, and I get those herds in better shape. How does that sound?"

George was elated and shook Sam's hand, saying, "It's perfect. When do I start?"

"You started when you stepped down from the train, George. There are a few other things that we need to discuss. We need to get you some better clothes. I want you to look as good as you perform, George. And one more thing," he said before he paused, then asked, "Do you love my daughter?"

The last question smacked George in the head, and he took a few seconds to answer.

"Yes, Sam. I do. She's a remarkable woman. She's smart and doesn't beat you over the head to show it. When we met in school, I was so impressed with her compassion and kindness, but at the same time, I could see how strong she was. Yes, Sam, I most assuredly do love Catherine."

"Good. I'm glad to hear it. Have you told her?"

"Yes."

"Have you asked her to marry you?"

"No. I have to wait. We both graduate in three years."

"Those are three wasted years, George. At least propose to her. Let her know that her future is with you."

"Do you think I should?"

"Absolutely."

George was astonished. Far from being ornery, Catherine's father had not only given them his blessing, but told him to propose.

"Let's go back in George, dinner should be ready in a little while."

———

Inside, Catherine was anxiously awaiting George's return. *What could her papa possibly do?*

When she saw them both walking into the kitchen laughing, she was somewhat startled. Mama had warned her that papa was going to give George a thorough examination, and she wondered what had just transpired. She glanced at George's smiling face, then he raised his eyebrows at her and winked. *Now what?*

During dinner, the conversation was about school in Kansas and the twins talked about school in Denver. Grace had warned her daughters not to say a word about money.

After they had eaten, George and Sam sat in the main room with a large fire burning; more for mood setting than the heat. It was time to spring the news about Catherine on George.

"We have plenty of room, George. We can set you up in the spare room next to the kitchen. That way I can prevent any sneaking around at night. Besides, we have two twelve-year-old spies in the house who prevent the adults from having too much fun."

George laughed and said, "I wouldn't worry on that score, Sam. Catherine operates on very strict guidelines that I think she learned from her mother."

Sam noticed Grace and Catherine approaching, and knew that they had heard George's comment.

Sam glanced at Grace and said, "She did, but my wife has always been a bit of a prude."

Both women burst into laughter and George was unsure of the reason but judging the way Sam and his wife behaved together, he had a good idea.

They all sat down, as Grace had charged the younger girls with the final cleanup, then sat next to her husband and curled her legs under her.

"Catherine, just to let you know, I've offered George a position here to help with the horse breeding. As you know, it has been a major concern of mine for a while now. The arrangement is that I'll pay for his tuition, books, room and board and give him an allowance for incidentals, and he'll spend his summers here to help me with the horses.

"Once he has graduated, he can set up an office or work out of his home, depending on which he chooses. Most of his school debt will be paid off by his expertise in the summers. What's left he can pay back in continuing to work with the herds. This is not charity, nor is it anything less than a business arrangement. But there is a side benefit, isn't there George?"

"Yes, there definitely is."

"Why don't you and Catherine take a short break out on the porch. I need to talk to her mother for a few minutes."

George smiled as he rose and offered Catherine his hand. She smiled back, took his hand, then stood and they walked out to the porch.

After they left, Grace grinned at Sam and said, "You pulled it off very well, husband. You shall be rewarded later."

"I thought I was going to reward you in the same manner just because you had enough faith in me to let me handle it."

"Well, either way, it's rewarding in itself."

They heard Catherine's voice echo from the porch, as she almost shouted, "Yes! Oh, yes, George!" which was followed by an extended silence.

"Can I guess that he just proposed?" asked Grace, suppressing a laugh.

"Could be."

A minute later, the couple returned to the room with linked arms. Both were flushed but wore enormous smiles.

"Mama, George has proposed, and I've accepted. We must wait because married couples can't attend college. We'll marry soon after we graduate."

George and Sam shook hands and Grace and Catherine hugged. Their daughters had waited for the moment at their mother's direction and joined the celebration.

When it was over, they all sat down, and the ladies all waited for Sam to deliver the rest of the news.

"George, there was a good reason for us being so happy for you and Catherine. Her mother and I had to be sure that you were who she said you were. She loved you, George, and we never doubt her judgment, but in this case, we had to be sure. We need to tell you her story, and she agreed that I would be best to tell you because I have the most first-hand experience."

George was more than just a trifle curious about what this could possibly be. He had no idea just how much he would learn over the next few minutes.

"First, you need to understand that my wife and I are not Catherine's birth parents. I was her uncle, her mother's brother. When she was five, her father was murdered, and she and her mother were kidnapped. Her mother was killed a month before I found out about the crime.

"Grace and I found and rescued Catherine. As her closest relative, I adopted her, then after I married Grace, we became her parents. We love her no less than Carol and Cora. Cora is named after her mother. Both her parents are buried in the family cemetery, along with our good friend Carol, who died protecting her when hired gunmen tried to kill her."

George sat stunned but listened intently as Sam continued.

"Her birth name was Catherine Short. The name she uses in college now to is to maintain some level of anonymity. The man who arranged to have her and her parents killed was a cousin named Ferguson Short. He was trying to gain control of the Short Shipping Company, which was owned by her grandfather.

"I arrested Ferguson Short and he died in jail. Catherine was the surviving heiress to the Short fortune. We sold her shares in the shipping company and placed them in a trust fund for her when she came of age, which will happen next week. Her net worth is now over $1.3 million, but she doesn't care about the money at all. She's a wonderful and complete person, as you have discovered and fallen in love with.

"That's why we had to make sure that you truly loved her as she was, because that is who she is. We're extremely proud of her. We knew that as soon as she turned eighteen, the supplicants for her hand and her wealth would be extensive. By falling in love with you, George, all that annoying cloying will not happen. Treasure her for who she is, George."

George was now stunned beyond belief. *The girl he loved was a millionaire?* Before he could say a word, Catherine spoke.

"Papa, I want you to know that I've already decided what to do with the money, or at least most of it.

"I want to establish a scholarship foundation to allow academically qualified people with no other way of attending college to be able to achieve that dream. I'll keep fifty thousand dollars in my account. I'll buy a ranch and we can live there where I can run my veterinary clinic and George can do his husbandry work. Does that sound alright, Papa?"

"Catherine, you have made me prouder than you could imagine. It's perfect. George, what do you think about all this?"

George had been digesting what he heard and was still mentally behind the times.

"I'm still trying to absorb all this. I can understand why you would need to keep that hidden, but it still does cause a bit of disruption. It has no impact on how I feel about you, Catherine. I still want to marry you, but I don't want to have to depend on your money. I'm very happy that you're giving most of it away but give me some time to think. Sam, could I spend some time with you to try to work this out in my head? When I'm with Catherine, I can't think straight in normal times."

Sam laughed and said, "I understand that. I was the same way with Grace. Whenever you want to talk, let me know. Now, Catherine, there's something else you may want to know. Three months ago, when you began to write about George expressing how you felt, we bought the neighboring ranch to the north, the Bar P. It's the same size as the Circle S was. It has good water and a nice ranch house and barn. Any improvements or expansion, you can pay for. Consider it an early wedding gift. You won't even have to change the brand."

Catherine smiled at her parents and said, "Thank you, Papa and Mama. I'm just happy that we'll be so close to you."

Sam smiled back at her, then looked down into Grace's deep blue eyes and saw the glow in her face that never seemed to fade.

———

Over the next few days, George talked with Sam extensively. He became more comfortable with the entire family and realized that there wasn't a dishonest bone in the group. He had met Julia, Zeke and their family as well, and felt as if he belonged.

Sam convinced him that money in itself had no value, it's what you choose to do with it that is important, so George decided he could live with having a wealthy wife, as long as she wasn't enormously wealthy.

———

A few days later, Catherine celebrated her eighteenth birthday. The same day, Sam and Grace took her to see John

528

Frampton, now the bank president. He still managed the trust fund and was sorry to think of its imminent loss.

He was delighted to hear that she was going to turn it all over to him to manage as a scholarship fund. They would set up a small board, chaired by Grace, who would review the applicants. They would issue one hundred scholarships annually, which shouldn't affect the core of the fund. Each student would receive full scholarships including books and tuition, room and board, and a small stipend for living expenses.

His first act was to give an interview with *The Rocky Mountain News*. They loved the story of a beautiful heiress giving away her entire fortune (Frampton did not divulge the fifty-thousand-dollar deposit) to help educate deserving poor young people. The story was picked up nationwide and included the fact that Miss Brown was now engaged, and Sam hoped it had its desired outcome and kept the suitors at bay. It did, but it helped when the story included the fact that her father was the famous Shotgun Sheriff who had single-handedly taken down the entire Soapy Smith gang in one day.

———

Three years later, Sam stood at the back of the church in a nice, but not overly fancy suit. He looked down toward the front of the church and caught the eye of his own ever-beautiful bride. Grace smiled at him, and he nervously returned her smile.

He saw George waiting at the altar with Zeke, his best man. Julia, Cora and Carol were on the other side of the aisle and all eyes were on the back of the church.

The organist began playing that familiar, yet always heart-wrenching melody. First came Julia's young daughter, Grace, spreading flower petals as she walked behind her older brother, Daniel.

Sam stepped over and took Catherine's arm. Even behind the veil he could see her face clearly as she smiled at him.

He saw in that beautiful face, his sweet sister Cora and the deep blue eyes of his most perfect love, his wife. And as they briefly held that one look between father and daughter, he saw something else. She glowed.

1	Rock Creek	12/26/2016
2	North of Denton	01/02/2017
3	Fort Selden	01/07/2017
4	Scotts Bluff	01/14/2017
5	South of Denver	01/22/2017
6	Miles City	01/28/2017
7	Hopewell	02/04/2017
8	Nueva Luz	02/12/2017
9	The Witch of Dakota	02/19/2017
10	Baker City	03/13/2017
11	The Gun Smith	03/21/2017
12	Gus	03/24/2017
13	Wilmore	04/06/2017
14	Mister Thor	04/20/2017
15	Nora	04/26/2017
16	Max	05/09/2017
17	Hunting Pearl	05/14/2017
18	Bessie	05/25/2017
19	The Last Four	05/29/2017
20	Zack	06/12/2017
21	Finding Bucky	06/21/2017
22	The Debt	06/30/2017
23	The Scalawags	07/11/2017
24	The Stampede	07/20/2017
25	The Wake of the Bertrand	07/31/2017
26	Cole	08/09/2017
27	Luke	09/05/2017
28	The Eclipse	09/21/2017
29	A.J. Smith	10/03/2017
30	Slow John	11/05/2017
31	The Second Star	11/15/2017
32	Tate	12/03/2017
33	Virgil's Herd	12/14/2017
34	Marsh's Valley	01/01/2018
35	Alex Paine	01/18/2018
36	Ben Gray	02/05/2018

37	War Adams	03/05/2018
38	Mac's Cabin	03/21/2018
39	Will Scott	04/13/2018
40	Sheriff Joe	04/22/2018
41	Chance	05/17/2018
42	Doc Holt	06/17/2018
43	Ted Shepard	07/13/2018
44	Haven	07/30/2018
45	Sam's County	08/15/2018
46	Matt Dunne	09/10/2018
47	Conn Jackson	10/05/2018
48	Gabe Owens	10/27/2018
49	Abandoned	11/19/2018
50	Retribution	12/21/2018
51	Inevitable	02/04/2019
52	Scandal in Topeka	03/18/2019
53	Return to Hardeman County	04/10/2019
54	Deception	06/02/2019
55	The Silver Widows	06/27/2019
56	Hitch	08/21/2019
57	Dylan's Journey	09/10/2019
58	Bryn's War	11/06/2019
59	Huw's Legacy	11/30/2019
60	Lynn's Search	12/22/2019

Made in the USA
Columbia, SC
10 May 2020